Regency RAKES

2 Glittering Regency Romances

FRANCESCA
by Sylvia Andrew

AN INDEPENDENT LADY
by Julia Byrne

THE Regency RAKES

THE
Regency
RAKES

by
Sylvia Andrew & Julia Byrne

MILLS & BOON

*MILLS & BOON and MILLS & BOON with the Rose Device
are registered trademarks of the publisher.*

*First published in Great Britain 2003 by
Harlequin Mills & Boon Limited,
Eton House, 18-24 Paradise Road,
Richmond, Surrey TW9 1SR*

THE REGENCY RAKES © Harlequin Books S.A. 2003

The publisher acknowledges the copyright holders of the
individual works as follows:

Francesca © Sylvia Andrew 1997
An Independent Lady © Julia Byrne 1999

ISBN 0 263 83667 3

138-0303

*Printed and bound in Spain
by Litografía Rosés S.A., Barcelona*

FRANCESCA
by
Sylvia Andrew

Sylvia Andrew taught modern languages for a number of years, ultimately becoming Vice-Principal of a sixth-form college. She lives in Somerset with two cats, a dog, and a husband who has a very necessary sense of humour, and a stern approach to punctuation. Sylvia has one daughter living in London, and they share a lively interest in the theatre. She describes herself as an 'unrepentant romantic'.

Also by Sylvia Andrew
in Mills & Boon® Historical Romance™

LORD CALTHORPE'S PROMISE
AN UNREASONABLE MATCH ★
AN INESCAPABLE MATCH ★
LORD TRENCHARD'S CHOICE

★ **The Steepwood Scandal** mini-series

Chapter One

Lightning was flickering over the hills ahead, and every now and then came a distant roll of thunder—another storm was on its way. The field workers had given up for the day and were hurrying home before the storm broke, the children clinging to their mothers' skirts, fathers carrying the littlest ones on their shoulders. But they smiled at the shabbily dressed young woman who passed them on the outskirts of the village, and greeted her with respect.

Miss Fanny was on her own way home to the Manor, where she lived with her aunt, Miss Cassandra Shelwood. Though she was wearing an old dress and a tattered sun-bonnet, though all the world knew that her mother had run off with a well-known rake and had never been seen again, all the same, Miss Fanny was the late Sir John Shelwood's granddaughter. She and her aunt were the last of a long line of Shelwoods who had owned most of the land round about for as long as anyone could remember.

Miss Shelwood had a heart of stone—everyone was afraid of her—but Miss Fanny was usually very friendly. Today she seemed preoccupied. Perhaps what they were saying about her aunt's health was true after all. There were long faces at the possibility, for what would happen to the estate if—when—Miss Shelwood died? It was well known that Miss Shelwood wouldn't give her niece the time of day if she could help it. So what was going to happen to the Shelwood estate?

Francesca Shelwood had been so deep in thought that she had barely noticed the lightning and was only faintly aware of the thunder rumbling ominously round the valley. The villagers were upon her before she had noticed them. But she smiled at them as they bobbed and nodded their heads, and turned to watch them as they hurried on, anxious to reach shelter before the rain came. They would have been astonished to learn how much she envied them.

Few would claim they were fortunate. Their days were hard and long, they were under constant threat of disaster—sudden accident or illness, the failure of the harvest, the whims of a landowner, or the caprices of the weather. But they laughed and joked as they went back to their modest dwellings, and the ties of affection, of love and family, were obvious.

She would never know such ties. Nearly twenty-five years old, plain, without any prospect of fortune, and with a shadow over her birth—who would ever think of marrying her?

Now the problem of her future was becoming more urgent with every day that passed. That her aunt was seriously ill could no longer be in doubt, though this was never admitted openly at Shelwood. Miss Shelwood refused to discuss the state of her health with anyone, least of all with her niece. But her attacks had been getting worse and more frequent for months, and yesterday's had been the worst yet, though no one dared dispute Miss Shelwood's assertion that it was simply a result of the excessive heat.

Francesca sighed. Years ago, when she had first come to Shelwood as a bewildered child, snatched away from everything she loved, she had looked to her aunt

Cassandra, her mother's sister, for consolation. What a mistake that had been! How often she had been snubbed, chastised, ignored, before she finally realised the harsh truth. Her aunt disliked her, and wanted as little as possible to do with her. Why this was so she had never been able to fathom. As a child she had asked her grandfather, but he had merely said that she was too young to understand. She had even screwed up her courage one day and had asked her aunt directly.

But Miss Shelwood had given Francesca one of her cold stares and replied, 'A stupid question, Fanny! How could anyone like such a plain, naughty, impertinent child?'

One of the older servants, who was now dead, had once said cryptically, 'It's because you're your mother's daughter, Miss Fanny. Miss Cassandra never wanted you here. It was the master who insisted. You can understand it, though.' And she had then maddeningly refused to say anything more.

It had not been so bad while Grandfather was alive. He had loved her in his fashion, had tried to make up for the lack of affection in his elder daughter. But he had been an old man, and since his death Aunt Cassandra's animosity had seemed to increase—or at least become more obvious. Francesca knew that only her aunt's strong sense of duty persuaded her to give her niece a home, for she had been told so soon after her grandfather's funeral. She had been eleven years old at the time, and had been very surprised to receive a summons to her aunt's room. The scene was still bitterly vivid, even after all these years. . .

'I have something to say to you.'

Francesca was frightened of her aunt. She looked like a great crow, perched behind the desk, hair scraped back under a black lace cap, hooded dark eyes, black dress, black shawl. . . And, though her aunt was motionless, the child could sense a seething anger behind the still façade. There was a chair in front of the desk, but Francesca knew better than to sit down without an invitation, so she remained standing.

'Mr Barton has been acquainting me with the terms of your grandfather's will.'

Francesca shifted uneasily and wondered what was coming. Mr Barton was the Shelwood family lawyer, and Aunt Cassandra had been closeted with him all day after the funeral, and most of the day after. What was her aunt going to do about her? Was she going to send her away— to school, perhaps? She rather hoped so—it could hardly be worse than staying alone at Shelwood with her aunt. Her hopes were soon dashed, however.

'Your grandfather has left you a sum of money, the interest on which will provide you with a small allowance—enough to pay for clothes and so on. It is not intended for school fees, since he wished you to remain at Shelwood for the time being. I have been asked to give you a roof over your head during my lifetime, and will obey my father's wish. You have, after all, nowhere else to go.' Her tone made it clear how much she regretted the fact.

'Perhaps I could go back to St Marthe?'

'That is out of the question. There is no place for you there. You will remain here.'

The young Francesca had looked with despair on the prospect of the future stretching out in front of her, alone at Shelwood with Aunt Cassandra. She offered another solution. 'I might marry someone, Aunt—as soon as I am old enough.'

'You might, though that is rather unlikely. . .'

*   *   *

Francesca's lips twisted in a bitter little smile at the memory of what had followed. Her aunt had gone on to make it clear just why marriage for Francesca was practically out of the question.

'Very unlikely, I should say, in view of your history.'

'My history?' Francesca cast her mind over her various small misdemeanors and found nothing in them to discourage a suitor. 'What have I done, Aunt Cassandra?'

'It is not what *you* have done.' She paused, and there was a significant silence. Francesca felt something was required of her, but what?

'Is there something I should have done and haven't?' she asked. She knew that this, too, was frequently a source of dissatisfaction.

Miss Shelwood's expression did not change, but Francesca shivered as she waited for her aunt to speak. Finally, she said, 'It has nothing to do with your activities. The damage was done before you were even born. Did your grandfather not tell you about it in all those cosy little chats you had with him? When he talked to you about your mother?'

'I. . .I don't think so. He was often sad when he talked about her. He said he was sorry he never saw her again before she died.'

'He was always very fond of her.'

'He said she was beautiful—'

'She was quite pretty, it is true.'

'Everyone who met her loved her—'

'She knew how to please, certainly.'

'He used to tell me stories about when she was a little girl. She used to laugh a lot, he said. And she did.' Francesca was so nervous that the words came tumbling out. Normally she would have been silent in her aunt's presence. 'I remember her laughing, too. She used to laugh

a lot when we all lived together on St Marthe. She and
Maddy used to laugh all the time.'

'Maddy?'

'My. . .my nurse. The one who brought me here. The
one you sent away.'

'The native woman.'

'Maddy was a Creole, Aunt Cassandra. She and Mama
were friends. I loved them both. Very much.'

'A most unsuitable woman to have charge of you. Your
grandfather was right to get rid of her. So your mama
laughed on St Marthe, did she? I am surprised. But then
she always found something to amuse her. I daresay it
amused her to run off with your father. Whether she was
quite so amused when you were born, I do not know.
You see, Fanny. . .' Miss Shelwood paused here as if she
was wondering whether to go on. Then her lips tightened
and she said slowly, 'Tell me your name.'

Francesca wondered why her aunt should make such a
strange request, but she took a deep breath and answered
quietly, 'Francesca Shelwood.'

This time the pause was even longer. 'Fanny
Shelwood,' said Miss Shelwood in a voice which boded
no good for Francesca. 'Fanny. Not. . .Francesca.
Francesca is a ridiculously pretentious name. An absurd
name for such a plain child.'

Francesca remained silent. This was an old battle, but,
though everyone else now called her Fanny, she would
remain Francesca in her own mind. Her mother—the
mother she only dimly remembered—had called her
Francesca, and she would never give it up. Her aunt
waited, then went on, 'Where did the name, Fanny
Shelwood, come from?'

'You said I had to be called Fanny, Aunt Cassandra.'

'Are you being deliberately obstructive, Fanny, or
simply very stupid? I refer to your surname.'

'Grandfather said I was to be a Shelwood. After I came here.'

'Quite so. Have you never wondered why?' The little girl had been pleased that her grandfather wanted to give her his name. It made her feel more wanted, more as if she belonged. She had accepted it, as she had accepted everything else. She had never questioned his reasons. She shook her head.

'It was because, Fanny, as far as we could tell, you had no other name to call yourself.'

'I. . .I don't know what you mean, Aunt Cassandra. I was called Francesca Beaudon at home on St Marthe.'

'Francesca. . .Beaudon.' Her aunt's lip curled as she pronounced the name. 'What right had you to such a name, pray?'

Francesca was completely puzzled. What did her aunt mean? She shook her head. 'I. . .I don't know. Because Papa's name was Beaudon?'

Miss Shelwood leaned forward. 'You had no right whatsoever to the name of Beaudon, Fanny Shelwood! None at all! Your father's name is not for such as you. Richard Beaudon never married your mother!'

'Of course Papa and Mama were married!' cried Francesca in instant and scornful repudiation. What did this woman know about life on St Marthe? 'Of course they were married,' she repeated more loudly. 'Everyone called Mama Lady Beaudon.'

'Do not raise your voice to me, Fanny. I will not have it!'

There was a silence while Francesca wrestled with her sense of anger and outrage. Finally she muttered, 'They were married. It's not true what you say!'

'Are you daring to doubt my word?' A slight pause, then, 'You must accept it, I'm afraid. And, unless you learn to control your feelings better, I shall wash my hands

of you, and then where would you be? You might well go
the way your unfortunate mother went—with disastrous
consequences to herself and you.'

'It isn't true,' said Francesca doggedly. She sounded
brave, but deep down she felt a growing sense of panic.
She was not sure of the exact significance of what her
aunt was saying, but there was nothing good about it.
There was a girl in the village who had a baby though
she wasn't married. Everyone was very unkind to her and
called her names. They called the baby names, too. It was
impossible that her darling mama had been like Tilly
Sefton! 'It's not! It's not!' she said, her voice rising again.

Miss Shelwood said sharply, 'Do stop contradicting me
in that ridiculous way! What does a little girl like you
know about such things? People called your mother
"Lady"—' Aunt Cassandra's voice dripped contempt
'—"Lady Beaudon", because they did not wish to offend.
It was merely a courtesy title!'

When Francesca remained silent she went on, 'Deceive
yourself if you wish—but tell me this if you can, Fanny.
What happened after your mother died? Did your father
keep you by him, as any real father would? He did not.
He packed you off to England as soon as he could and
we, your mother's family, were more or less forced to
give you a home and a name! And what have you heard
from your father since you left the West Indies? Nothing!
No visits, no letters, no money, no gifts—not even on
your birthday. Why is that, Fanny?'

Once again Francesca was silent. She had nothing to
say in defence of herself and her father. She had been
hurt that she never heard anything from him, had tried to
find out why, but her grandfather had always refused to
mention the Beaudon name.

Satisfied that she had made her point, Miss Shelwood
went on, 'So you see, Fanny, a marriage is most unlikely

for you, do you not agree? What have you to offer a respectable man? A girl without fortune, without name and—you have to admit that you are hardly a beauty. But you may stay here with me as long as I am alive.'

Even fourteen years later, Francesca still resented the cruel manner in which her aunt had told her of her situation. It had been like crushing a butterfly. For months afterwards she had cried herself to sleep or lain awake, thinking of her life with Maddy and her mother in the West Indies, trying to remember anything at all which might contradict what her aunt had said. But she had found nothing.

Her father had always been a dim figure in the background, especially after Mama had fallen ill and most of her time had been spent in the pretty, airy bedroom with fluttering white curtains and draperies. It was Maddy who had been the child's companion then, Maddy who had sworn never to leave her young charge.

But, of course, Maddy had been forced to go when Aunt Cassandra dismissed her. Aunt Cassandra, not Grandfather. Francesca's heart still ached at the memory of their parting. She had clung to Maddy's skirts, as if she could keep her nurse at Shelwood by physical force, had pleaded with her grandfather, even with her aunt. But Maddy had had to go.

As Francesca grew older, she came to accept the hard truth about her birth, if only because she could not see why her aunt should otherwise invent a tale which reflected so badly on the Shelwood name. The rest of it—that she was poor and plain—was more easily accepted. It wasn't just what her aunt said—everyone seemed to think that she was very like Miss Shelwood, who was tall, thin and pale, with strong features.

Francesca, too, was tall, thin and pale, and though she didn't have the Shelwood eyes—the Shelwood eyes were dark brown, and hers were a greyish-green—her hair was very much the same colour as her aunt's, an indeterminate, mousy sort of blonde. How Francesca wished she had taken after her small, vivacious mother, with her rich golden curls and large pansy-brown eyes, who had always been laughing!

A sudden rumble of thunder quite close brought Francesca back with a start to the present. She glanced up at the sky. The clouds were gathering fast—which direction where they travelling? Then a horn blared behind her and she nearly leapt out of her skin. She turned and was horrified to see a chaise and four bearing down on her at speed. She leapt for her life to the side of the road, but lost her balance, skidded into the ditch, and ended up in nettles, goose grass and the muddy water left over from the previous night's rain.

The chaise thundered past, accompanied by shouts from its driver as he fought to bring his team to a halt. At first she made no attempt to move, but lay there in the ditch, content to recover her breath and listen to crisp orders being issued some way down the road. It had taken a while to stop the chaise. Footsteps approached the ditch where she lay and came to a halt beside her.

'Are you hurt?' Betsy's old sunbonnet had tipped forward and covered her eyes, so that all she could see when she looked up was a pair of long legs encased in buckskins and beautifully polished boots.

'You were well clear of the coach, so don't try to pretend. Come, girl, there's sixpence for you if you get out of that ditch and show me that your fall hasn't done any harm. Take hold of my cane.'

That voice! It was cooler and more authoritative than she remembered. And the undercurrent of mockery was new. But the rich timbre and deep tones were still familiar. Oh, it couldn't be, it *couldn't*! Fate would not be so unkind. Francesca shut her eyes and fervently hoped that memory was playing her false. Then the end of an ebony cane tapped her hand, and she grasped it reluctantly. One heave and she was out of the ditch and standing on the road. A exquisitely fitted green coat and elegant waistcoat were added to her vision of the gentleman.

'You see? You're perfectly unharmed.'

Francesca was not reassured by these words. She listened with growing apprehension as he went on, 'There's the sixpence—and there's another penny if you'll tell us if this lane leads to Witham Court. We appear to have taken a wrong turning.'

Francesca swallowed, tried to speak and uttered instead a strangled croak. Fate was being every bit as unkind as she had feared! He had not yet recognised her, but if he did. . .

'What's the matter? Cat got your tongue?' The gentleman pulled her towards him and, before she could stop him, was running his hands over her arms and legs. 'Yes, you're quite sound,' he said, drawing a large handkerchief from his pocket and wiping his fingers fastidiously on it. 'So stop shamming—there are no more sixpences, Mary, or whatever your name is. Nothing more to be got out of me, until you tell me where Witham Court is.' His movements had been impersonal—rather as if he were feeling the legs of a horse—but Francesca's face flamed and she was seized with a sudden access of rage.

'You can keep your money,' she said, pushing her hat back from her face, and glaring at him. 'An abject apology would be more in line, though I doubt it will be forthcoming. The last thing any of us expect is decent behaviour from the owner of Witham Court, or his guests.'

His eyes narrowed, then he said slowly, 'I appear to have made a mistake. I took you for one of the village girls.' He eyed her shabby dress and bonnet. 'Understand-

ably, perhaps. But. . .' he eyed her uncertainly again
'. . .it can't be. Yet now I look. . .we've met before,
haven't we?'

'Yes,' said Francesca stonily, wishing she could lie.

'Of course! You were wet then, too. . .we both were.
Why, yes! How could I have forgotten that glorious
figure. . .?'

He laughed when Francesca gave an involuntary gasp
of indignation and then pulled himself together and looked
rueful. 'I'm deeply sorry—that slipped out. I do beg your
pardon, ma'am. Abjectly.'

Francesca was unreconciled. He didn't sound abject.
'The details of our previous acquaintance are best forgotten, sir. All of them. And if you offer me an apology, it
surely ought to be for knocking me into the ditch.'

'We did not knock you into the ditch. You jumped and
fell. No, I was apologising for not recognising you.' He
regarded the wet and bedraggled creature before him. 'Not
even for a gentlewoman. As for our previous meeting—
it shall be erased from my mind, as requested. A pity,
though. Some details have been a most pleasant memory.'
He raised a quizzical eyebrow.

How dared he remind her of such an unfortunate and
embarrassing interlude! Had he no shame? Of course he
hadn't! He was a rake and a villain, and she was a fool
to be affected by him.

'You surprise me,' she said acidly. 'But are you suggesting you would not have practically run me down if
you had realised I wasn't one of the villagers? What a
very strange notion of chivalry you have to be sure! As
if it mattered who or what I was!'

'Forgive me, but I did not practically run you down.
My nephew, who is a trifle high-spirited, gave us all an
uncomfortable time, including my horses, in his efforts
to prove himself a notable whip. I shall deal with him

presently. But allow me to say that you were standing like a moonling on that road. You must have heard us coming?'

'I thought it was thunder—You're doing it again! How rude you are to call me a moonling!'

'It wasn't your good sense that attracted me all those years ago, Francesca! And standing in the middle of a highway is hardly the action of a rational being. Nor is it rational now to stand arguing about a trifle when you should be hastening to change out of your wet clothes.'

The justice of this remark did not endear the gentleman to Francesca. She was about to make a scathing reply when they were interrupted.

'Marcus, darling! Have you taken *root*, or something? We shall be caught in the storm if you don't hurry.'

The speaker was picking her way delicately along the road, holding up the skirts of an exquisite gown in green taffeta, her face shaded by a black hat with a huge brim. As a travelling costume it was hardly suitable, the hat a trifle too large, the dress a touch too low cut, but Francesca had never seen anything so stylish in her life. Under the hat were wisps of black hair, dark eyes, red lips, a magnolia skin with a delicate rose in the cheeks—an arrestingly vivid face. But at the moment an expression of dissatisfaction marred its perfection, and the voice was petulant.

'I'm not coming any further—the road is quite *dread-ful*—but do make haste. What is the delay?' The dark eyes turned to Francesca. 'Good Lord! What a *filthy* mess! What on *earth* is it?' She stared for a moment, then turned to the man. 'Really, Marcus, why are you wasting time on such a wretch? Pay her off and come back to the coach. And *do* hurry. I shall wait with Nick. No, don't say another *word*—I refuse to listen. Don't forget to get her to tell

you the way—if she knows it,' she added, looking at
Francesca again with disdain.

'You mistake the matter, Charmian. Miss Shelwood's
accident has misled you into thinking she is one of the
country folk. In fact, her family own much of the land in
the district.'

'Really?' The dark eyes looked again at the shabby
dress. 'How very odd! Don't be long, Marcus.' Then
the vision turned round and picked her way back to the
carriage.

Francesca felt her face burn under its streaks of mud.
She was well used to snubs from her aunt, but this was
different—and from such a woman!

The gentleman tightened his lips, then said gently, 'You
must forgive Lady Forrest. She is hot and tired—Nick's
driving is not a comfortable experience.'

'So I have observed,' said Francesca. 'I am *sure* the
lady has had a quite *dreadful* time of it. *Pray* convey my
sympathy to her—my *abject* sympathy.'

He acknowledged this sally with a nod, but said
nothing. Then he appeared to come to a decision. 'You
must allow us to take you home. Shelwood Manor, is
it not?'

'Are you mad?'

'I fail to see why Lady Forrest's manners, or the condition of your clothes, should prevent me from doing my
clear duty. No, I am not mad.'

'My concern is neither for Lady Forrest nor for the
state of your carriage! I can perfectly well walk home—
indeed, I insist on doing so. To be frank, sir, I would not
go with you in your carriage to Shelwood, nor to Witham,
nor anywhere else, not even to the end of the lane! I am
surprised you should suggest it. Have you forgotten the
circumstances of our previous acquaintance?'

'Why, yes, of course!'

Francesca, the wind taken somewhat out of her sails, stared at him.

'I thought that would please you. You said you wished me to forget the lot,' he said earnestly.

Francesca pressed her lips together firmly. He would not make her laugh, she would not let him—that was how it had all started last time. She said coldly, 'I suggest you rejoin your friends—they will not wish to miss any of the. . .pleasures Witham Court has to offer.'

'Of course—you know about those, don't you?' he asked with a mocking smile.

'Only by hearsay, sir. And a brief and unwelcome acquaintance with one of its visiting rakes some years ago.'

'You didn't seem to find the acquaintance so unwelcome then, my dear.'

Francesca's face flamed again. She said curtly, 'I was very young and very foolish. I knew no better.' She started to walk along the road. 'I suggest you turn the carriage in the large drive about a hundred yards ahead and go back to the village. The road you should have taken is the first on the left. This one does lead to Witham Court, but it is narrow and uneven and would need expert driving.'

'You don't think I can do it,' he asked, falling into step beside her.

'Nothing I have seen so far would lead me to think so. Good day, sir.'

'Very well. I shall take your advice—my horses have suffered enough today, and this road surface is appalling.' He took a step, halted and turned to her. 'You are sure there's nothing I can do for you?'

'I think you've done enough! Now, for heaven's sake, leave me in peace!'

The gentleman looked astonished at the violence in

Francesca's voice. And in truth she had surprised herself. Such outbursts were rare. The child's impulsively passionate nature had over the years been subdued under her aunt's repressive influence. Nowadays, she exercised a great deal of self-discipline, and Miss Fanny's air of calm dignity, of lack of emotion—a defence against the constant slights she was subjected to at the Manor—was no longer totally assumed.

But this man had a talent, it seemed, for reaching that other Francesca of long ago. She must regain control of her emotions—she must! The little interlude years before had meant very little to him, that was obvious, or he would not now be able to refer to it in such a light-hearted manner. She must not let him even suspect the profound effect it had had on her. She would apologise for her outburst in a civilised manner, then bid him farewell.

But he forestalled her. The teasing look had quite vanished from his eyes as he said, 'Forgive me. I did not mean to offend you.'

Then, without another word, he turned on his heel and strode back to the chaise. Francesca found herself hoping he would trip on one of the stones that had been washed loose by the previous night's storm. She would enjoy seeing that confident dignity measure its length in the dust. But, of course, it didn't happen. Instead, he got into the chaise and exchanged some words with the young man who had remained with the horses.

There was a slight altercation which ended when the young man—his nephew, she supposed—got down and strode on up the lane. A few minutes later, the chaise passed on its way back to the village, the driver giving her exaggerated clearance and an ironical salute of the whip as he went.

Chapter Two

Lady Forrest saw the incident and felt a little spurt of irritation. Marcus was impossible—acknowledging a wretch like the girl on the road! Of course, he was just doing it to annoy her. He hadn't wanted to come to Charlie Witham's—it was not the sort of gathering he enjoyed and all her wiles had at first failed to persuade him to accept the invitation. But she had won in the end! And now he was showing his displeasure by teasing her.

'Are you so very displeased, Marcus?' she asked, looking at him sideways as the carriage turned into the village street.

He negotiated the tight left turn before replying. 'About Nick's driving? Not any more. Nor do you need to suffer any disquiet about him, either. By the time he's found his way to the Court, he'll have got over his fit of temper.'

Lady Forrest had forgotten Nick. 'That's not what I meant. You didn't want to come to Charlie's, when I first mentioned it. Are you regretting having changed your mind?'

'Not at all. You produced a master card and played it.' When she raised her eyebrows, and feigned surprise, he went on, 'Come, Charmian. You don't usually underestimate my intelligence so badly. You are quite ruthless in pursuing your wishes. When it became obvious I had no intention of escorting you to Witham Court, you beguiled Nick into performing the office. You counted on the fact that, although my nephew's capacity for getting into trouble seems to be infinite, I am fond of him. You knew that I was most unlikely to abandon him to the mercies of Charlie Witham's rapacious cronies.'

He looked at her with the quizzical smile she always found irresistible. 'But tell me, what would you have done if I had called your bluff? It would hardly have enhanced your reputation to arrive at Witham Court in the company of a lad half your age.'

The smile, then the rapier. He could be a cruel devil when he chose! Lady Forrest coloured angrily. 'You exaggerate, Marcus. In any case, the question did not arise. You have come—as I knew you would.' She changed her tone. 'Now, be kind. You have had your fun pretending to be concerned over that creature on the road, and attempting to introduce her—'

'You were quite ruthless there, too. Did you have to give the girl such a snub?'

'Why are you so concerned? If she were pretty I could understand it, but she is quite remarkably plain!'

'Plain? How can you say so?'

'Stop making fun of me, Marcus. Of course she is plain. Too tall, too bony, too sallow, a hard mouth—Really!'

'Her mouth is not hard, it is disciplined. And I suppose the streaks of dirt on her face disguised from you the loveliest line of cheekbone and jaw I think I have ever seen.' When Lady Forrest regarded him with astonishment, he added, 'Oh, she is not your conventional Society beauty, I agree. She lacks the rosebud mouth, the empty blue eyes, the dimpled cheeks. Her conversation is less vapid, too. But plain she will never be—not even when she is old. The exquisite bone structure will still be there.'

'Good Lord! This is news, indeed! What a sly fellow you are after all, my dear! When are we to congratulate you?' He gave her an ironic look, but refused to rise to her bait. She went on, 'Perhaps you will allow me to lend the girl a dress for the wedding? I can hardly think she owns anything suitable—nor, from the look of her, any dowry, either. Still, you hardly need that, now.'

There was a short silence and she wondered whether she had gone too far. Then he said calmly, 'Don't talk nonsense, my dear. I can admire beauty wherever I find it—I don't necessarily wish to possess it! Thank God—here are the gates. I suppose it is too much to hope that Charlie Witham has learned moderation since I was last here. So I warn you, you will have me to reckon with if you lead Nick into trouble, or make him miserable. My nephew is the apple of my sister's eye, God knows why!'

They were received warmly by their host, who could hardly believe his good fortune in snaring one of London's most elusive bachelors as a guest. Marcus Carne tended to move in circles of Society that Lord Witham and his friends, who would never have been admitted to them, apostrophised as devilish dull, riddled as they were with clever johnnies—academics, politicians, reformers and the like! But they found Carne himself perfectly sound. In fact, they termed him a Nonpareil.

He belonged to all the right clubs, was a first-class, if rather ruthless, cardplayer, and could hold his wine with the best of them. His skill with horses was legendary, and his life as an officer under Wellington had provided him with a fund of good stories, though he never bored his company with talk of the battles.

And, though he was what was generally called 'a proper man's man', he was equally popular with the ladies—not only with the frail beauties such as Charmian Forrest, who lived on the fringes of society, but with perfectly

respectable dowagers and debutantes, too. His good looks
and lazy smile, his air of knowing what he was about—
such things appealed to the ladies, of course.

And he had another virtue that even outclassed his
looks, his charm, his manliness, his straight dealing and
all the rest. Marcus Carne was quite disgustingly rich.
Once his cousin Jack fell at Waterloo, it was inevitable
that Marcus would inherit the Carne title—his uncle had,
after all, been in his seventies when his only remaining
son was killed. But who would have thought that old Lord
Carne would have amassed such a fortune to leave to his
nephew—especially as Jack and his brothers had, in the
short time allotted to them, done their best to disperse it!

However, Marcus was a different kettle of fish
altogether from his wayward cousins. Though frequently
invited, he was seldom seen at the sort of gathering Lord
Witham enjoyed. And though he was not afraid to wager
large sums at the gambling table, he had a regrettable
tendency to win. In spite of this, however, his reputation
was such that he was welcomed wherever he went.

So Lord Witham paid Marcus the compliment of conducting him personally to one of the best bedchambers,
indicating with a wink that Charmian was lodged close
by. Marcus waited patiently till his host had finished list-
ing the delights in store and had gone to see to his other
guests, then he summoned his valet, who had arrived with
the valises some time before, and changed.

Suter busied himself discreetly about the room, obviously expecting his master to go down to join the
company. But Marcus was in no hurry to meet the ram-
shackle bunch Charlie Witham had undoubtedly
assembled for several days of cards and drinking. Instead,
he went over to the window, which overlooked the park
behind the Court.

It was nine years since he had last been at Witham. At

that time there had still been three cousins available to inherit their father's title. He himself had been an impecunious junior officer on leave, with no expectations except through promotion on the battlefield. His room then had been much less imposing—what else would he have expected? The view from its window had been the same, though. And the signs of neglect and decay, which even then had been evident, were now greater than ever. He wondered if that bridge had ever been repaired. . . Probably not. Nine years. . .

Nine years ago Francesca Shelwood had, for a brief while, filled his thoughts to the exclusion of everything else. Curious how one could forget something which had been so important at the time. Seeing the girl again had brought the memories back, memories which had been swamped under the horrors of the campaigns he had fought, and the turmoil and sea-change in his fortunes which had followed.

He had never expected to succeed his uncle. But first Maurice and Ralph, Lord Carne's twin elder sons, had both been killed in a coaching accident, then Jack had fallen at Waterloo. Lord Carne himself had followed them soon afterwards, and Marcus had, against all the odds, succeeded to the title.

Francesca had changed surprisingly little. How well he now remembered that intriguing surface air of discipline, the tight control of her mouth and face, which might lead the uninitiated to believe her dull—hard, even. He knew better. The real Francesca's feelings could suddenly blow up in rage, or melt in passion. . . His blood quickened even now at the memory of her total response to his kisses.

How absurd! Nine years of living in the world, three of them as a very rich man, had provided many more sophisticated affairs. None had been permanent, but few had lasted for as short a time as one day—yet he remembered none of them with half as much pleasure. How could he have forgotten?

From the first moment, he and Francesca had felt no constraint in one other's company. Their initial encounter had effectively done away with the barrier she customarily put up to protect herself from the rest of the world. It was difficult to retain an air of cool reserve when you have just sent a perfect stranger flying into the river! But he rather thought that, even without that sensational beginning, he would have found the real Francesca. From the first he had had a strange feeling of kinship with her that he was sure she had felt, too.

He pulled a chair up to the window and sat down, his eyes fixed on the untended lawns of Witham Court without seeing them. The years faded away and what he saw was the sun, glinting through the leafy branches of the trees down on to the stream which formed the boundary between the Witham and Shelwood lands. He had come with his cousin Jack—he would never in those days have been invited for himself. Jack's father had begged Marcus to go with his son, for the play there was deep, and Jack a compulsive gambler. It hadn't worked.

Heedless of Marcus's attempts to restrain him, Jack had wagered vast sums, more than he possessed, and had lost to everyone, even including his cousin. After a disastrous night of yet more hard drinking and gambling Jack, quite unable to honour his debts, and mindful of his father's words the last time he had asked for more money, had attempted to shoot himself—a dramatic gesture, which his cousin and friends had fortunately frustrated.

Marcus smiled wryly. Jack had survived the attempt to take his own life, but it hadn't done him much good. Just a few years later he had fallen at Waterloo along with so many other, better men. Marcus blanked out the thought of Waterloo—the memory of that carnage was best forgotten. He got up and went to the door.

'There you are, Marcus! I was just about to send someone to look for you. Charlie's waiting for us.'

Marcus suppressed a sigh, then smiled. 'How charmingly you look, Charmian. That dress is particularly becoming. Do you know where Nick is?'

Later that night, when the company was relaxing over an excellent supper, he was reminded again of Francesca. Charmian brought up the incident on the road that afternoon.

'And then we met this *scarecrow* of a girl! Nick pushed her into the ditch, and I swear it seemed the best place for her!'

She looked magnificent in a wine-red silk dress, her black hair piled high and caught with a diamond aigrette given to her by Marcus in the heyday of their relationship. An impressive array of other jewels—trophies from her many admirers—flashed about her person, but they glittered no more brightly than her dark eyes. She was in her element, flirting with Marcus, making the others laugh with her wicked comments on London life, and teasing a besotted Nick about his driving, laughing at him over her fan.

Nick flushed and muttered, 'The horses were scared of the thunder. And she just stood there. I didn't know what to do.'

'Oh, but, Nick darling, you were *marvellous*, I swear! Then Marcus got down and went to see what had happened—the wretched girl had vanished. Just the odd boot waving in the air, *covered* in mud. Pure rustic farce. Marcus insisted on going to see if she was all right, and of course she was, once he'd pulled her out. But what a *sight*! There she stood, draped in mud and weeds, a quiz of a sunbonnet stuck on her head. But Marcus seemed

quite taken with her. I began to think he had fallen in
love at first sight with this farmyard beauty.' She paused
dramatically. 'I was almost jealous!'

There were shouts of disbelief and laughter and
Charmian smiled like a satisfied cat. 'But I haven't
finished yet—you must hear this—it beats all the rest.
She wasn't a village girl at all, it seems. Marcus said she
owned most of the land round about. A positive *heiress*
in disguise, looking for a prince. So which of you is going
to rescue her, muddy boots and all?'

Marcus walked over to the side and helped himself to
more wine. He said nothing.

'I wager it was Fanny Shelwood,' said Lord Witham.

'Shelwood?' said one of the others. 'Of
Shelwood Manor?'

'Yes—her mother was Verity Shelwood. Now, ask me
who her father was. . . No? I'll tell you. Richard Beaudon.'
There was a significant pause. 'D'you see? The girl was
sired by Richard Beaudon, but her name is Shelwood. Not
Beaudon. Adopted by her grandfather. You follow me?'

Having ensured by sundry nods and winks that his
guests had indeed followed, Lord Witham went on in
malicious enjoyment, 'I don't suppose many of you know
about the Shelwoods. They keep quieter now than they
used. But when the old fellow was alive, he was always
boring on about the company I invited down here. As if
it was any of his business! A bunch of killjoys, the
Shelwoods. I told him more than once—a chap can have
a few friends in his own house if he wants, can't he?
Have a bit of fun?

'But Sir John never liked me—a real holier-than-thou
johnny, he was. And then—' he started to grin '—and
then old Sir Piety's daughter kicks over the traces with
Rake Beaudon, and runs off to the West Indies with him.
All without benefit of clergy.'

'You mean that girl is a. . .a love-child?' breathed Charmian. 'The poor thing! So very plain, too. It hardly seems fair. But who was Rake Beaudon?'

'You never met him? A great gun, he was. Played hard, rode hard, had more mistresses than any other man in London. Didn't give a damn for anyone.'

'I don't think I'd have liked him,' said Charmian.

Lord Witham smiled cynically. 'Oh yes, you would, my dear. The ladies found him irresistible. That's how he managed to seduce the daughter of old Straight-lace Shelwood himself. Didn't profit from it, though. Sir John disinherited her. Refused to see her again. That's probably why Beaudon never married her.'

'Then why is this Fanny girl here now?'

'Father packed her off when her mother died. Didn't want to be saddled with a bastard, did he? Cramped his style a bit.'

'If she's coming in to the Shelwood estate, I wouldn't object to making an offer and giving her a name myself. Tidy bit of land there,' someone said. 'I could do with it, I don't mind telling you. Shockin' load of debts to clear.'

'Don't think of it, Rufus, old dear. Waste of time. Charmian's wrong to say the girl owns the land. She don't own anything, and, what's more, she never will. The estate belongs to her aunt, and she wouldn't leave her niece her last year's bonnet. Hates little Fanny.'

'I find this all quite remarkably tedious,' said Marcus, yawning. 'I don't mind gossip—Lady Forrest's latest Society *on-dits* are always worth hearing—but. . .what one's neighbours in the country get up to. . .really! The last word in boredom.'

'Don't stop him, Marcus! I've finished my fund of stories, and I find this quite fascinating!' said Charmian. 'Come, Charlie. Tell us the rest. It's just the thing for a good after-supper story. What did this Fanny do?'

'Oh, it wasn't Fanny who dished Cassandra Shelwood. It was her mother. Verity Shelwood stole her sister's beau—the only one the poor woman ever had.'

'*Rake Beaudon* was going to marry Cassandra Shelwood? I don't believe it,' said the man called Rufus.

'It hadn't got as far as that. But he was making a push to fix his interest with her. He wanted the Shelwood money, y'see, and Cassandra was the elder sister. But when he saw Verity, he lost his head, and ended up running off with her. Not surprised. The elder Miss Shelwood was always a hag, and Verity was a little beauty. Tiny, she was, with golden curls, brown eyes—a real little stunner.'

He paused. 'Y'know, it's damned odd—she was a beauty, Rake Beaudon was a devilishly good-looking fellow, but Fanny, their daughter, is as plain as they come. And when Auntie kicks the bucket, which, from what I've heard, could happen any minute, the poor girl will be looking for a roof over her head. Shame she don't take after her ma—a pretty face might have helped to find one, eh, Rufus? But she must be well into her twenties; she don't even know how to begin to please. Never been taught, d'y'see?'

'I thought we were here to play cards,' said Marcus coldly. 'Or is it your intention to gossip all night?'

'Don't be such a spoilsport, Marcus,' said Charmian. She turned to Witham. 'Marcus doesn't think she's plain.'

'You may ignore her, Witham. I made the mistake of saying something complimentary about one woman to another. It is always fatal, even to someone as beautiful as Lady Forrest. Are we to play?'

Marcus was angry, but taking care to conceal it. His first impulse had been to rush to Francesca's defence, to tell them to stop their lewd, offensive gossip about a girl who had never done any of them any harm. But second thoughts had prevailed. To enter the lists on her behalf would do more harm than good—it would merely give them more food for speculation. Better to keep calm and distract their tawdry minds. They would soon lose interest now they had got to the bottom of Francesca's story, as they thought. Cards would soon occupy their thoughts, once they were back at the tables.

But he himself found concentration difficult that evening. From all accounts, Francesca's life was no happier now than it had been nine years before—and there was every reason to fear that it might get worse. He had been angry at her rudeness on the road, and with some justice, but looking back, surely there had been desperation in her tone? She had looked. . .ridiculous, standing there covered in mud as he drove past. Ridiculous, but gallant. Endearingly so.

Francesca had refused to gaze after the chaise as it disappeared in the direction of the village. Instead, she had turned to walk briskly back to the Manor, for as the mud dried her clothes were becoming stiff and uncomfortable. She had no wish to compound her discomfort by getting caught in the storm. But she was in a state of quite uncharacteristic agitation.

She was normally a philosophical girl. She had learned over the years to endure what she could not change, to find pleasure in small things instead of pining for what she could not have. She had gradually taught herself to be content with her friendship with Madame Elisabeth, her old governess, who lived in the village, to find pleasure in her drawing and sketching, and to abandon childish dreams of encountering love and affection from anyone else and of having a home and family of her own.

But just this once, she found herself wishing passionately that she was powerful, rich and beautiful enough to give this oaf the set-down he deserved! The awareness that she still felt a strange attraction to the oaf was impatiently dismissed. Her conduct during their earlier acquaintance was a dreadful warning to any girl—especially one in her precarious situation. Twenty-four hours only, but from beginning to end she had behaved like a lunatic, like a. . .like a lightskirt! She pressed her hands to her cheeks in an effort to cool them. If only she could treat it as casually as he had! If only she could forget it as easily as he seemed to!

She reminded herself angrily that she had been not yet sixteen at the time, still hoping vaguely that one day someone would rescue her from life with Aunt Cassandra. There had been some excuse for her. But for him? It was true that she had lied to him about her age. . . Nevertheless! He had been old enough to know the effect his kisses would have on her. And all to relieve a morning's boredom—or perhaps to revenge himself for the loss of dignity she had caused him? Though he hadn't seemed angry after the first few minutes.

It all started because of that stupid conversation. It hadn't been meant for her ears, and now she wished passionately that she had never listened to it. But what else could she have done? She had been so engrossed in her sketching that the gentlemen had been within earshot before she noticed them. And then, aware that she was trespassing on Witham land, she had deliberately concealed herself. . . Francesca walked on towards the Manor, but she was no longer aware of her dirty clothes, nor of the threatening storm. She saw herself as she had been nine years before—half child, half woman—peering nervously through the bushes. . .

Francesca peeped through the bushes at the two figures walking along the banks of the stream that ran down between the two estates—they were both in shirt sleeves, but were quite clearly gentlemen. However, they were decidedly the worse for wear—cravats loose, hair all over the place, and the older, shorter one had half his shirt hanging out. The other. . . She caught her breath. The other was the most beautiful man she had ever seen in all her life. He even eclipsed her dimly remembered father. Tall, dark-haired, with a powerful, athletic build, he moved with natural grace, though he was carrying himself a trifle carefully, as if his head hurt. They came to the bridge just below her and stopped.

She knew instantly that they were from Witham Court. Lord Witham must be holding another of his wild parties. The parties had been notorious for years, even as far back as her grandfather's time. He had fulminated about them, but had never been able to stop them. It was universally known that they were attended by rakes and gamblers, a scandal and danger to every decent, God-fearing neighbour! The village girls would never accept a position at the Court if they valued their virtue, for these lecherous villains found innocence a challenge, not a barrier.

So, in spite of the fascination the young man had for her, she withdrew a little further into the bushes to avoid being seen. But she was unable to avoid overhearing their conversation.

'Freddie,' the tall, handsome one solemnly said. He sounded as if he was experiencing difficulty in speaking clearly, but the timbre of his voice was very attractive— rich and warm and deep. 'I'm in despair! What th' devil am I goin' to say to m' uncle? He trusted me, y' see, and I've failed him.' He paused, gave a deep sigh, then added, 'Failed him c'mpletely. Absolutely. Devil's own luck with th' cards last night. Never known an'thing like it! Ruined, both 'f us.'

'Course you're not, Marcus! Rich as Croesus, your uncle.'

'He trusted me, I tell you! And he's sworn not to pay 'nother penny for any more gambling debts! Said he'd die first. Ruined. I'd be much better dead myself, I swear.'

'Don't talk like that, Marcus. It will be all right, you'll see. Look, hate to interrupt—don't want to sound unsympathetic—but we ought to turn back, old fellow. Been out long enough—ought to get back to poor old Jack. Coming?'

'No,' Marcus said moodily. 'I'll stay here. Think things out before I see'm again. How 'm I goin' to tell m' uncle?'

From her bushes, she saw Freddie walking uncertainly away up the hill on the other side, and then her curiosity got the better of her. She crept forward to see what 'Marcus' was doing.

He was standing on the bridge, leaning on the thin plank of wood that served as a balustrade and gazing moodily down into the waters. He banged his hand down on the plank and, with a groan, repeated his words of a minute before. 'I'd be better dead myself! Drowned! Oh, my head!'

Francesca gazed in horror as he put one leg over the plank. Convinced that this beautiful young man was about to drown himself even while she watched, she jumped to her feet and launched herself down the hill. A second later, unable to stop, she crashed into the unsuspecting young man on the bridge and sent him flying into the water. She only just managed to stop herself from following him.

Francesca gazed, horrified, while he picked himself up, shook himself like a dog and pushed his hair out of his eyes. The shock of the water seemed to have sobered him up.

There was an ominous silence. Then, 'What the devil did you do that for?' he roared. 'Are you mad?'

'I. . . I. . .' Francesca had a cowardly impulse to run away, but she suppressed it. 'I wanted to save you.'

'Wanted to save me? From what?'

'From drowning.'

'I don't think much of your methods—' He stopped suddenly and looked down. The stream was unusually low—the water barely came up to his knees. 'In this?' he asked. The irony in his voice was gall to Francesca. She blushed and hung her head.

'I. . .I didn't think,' she confessed. 'I just ran down the hill without pausing to consider—then I couldn't stop, so I. . .I. . .er. . .I pushed you in. I'm sorry.'

'Sorry? I should think you might be, indeed!' He took a step towards the bridge, then said irritably, 'Damn it, my boots are full of water, I can hardly move. Help me out, will you? I need a pull up.'

'But I'll get wet myself!'

'So you will. Now give me your hand—just to give me a start, so I can get a hold on the post there. It won't take much once I'm moving.' He looked up and said impatiently, 'Come on, girl—stir yourself! What are you waiting for?'

She extended a reluctant hand. It wasn't just that she was afraid of getting wet. To get too close to a perfect stranger—especially one who was staying at Witham Court—was a touch foolhardy. And anyone so handsome was almost certainly a rake!

'For God's sake, girl, give me your hand properly! What are you? The village idiot?'

Francesca was noted in the neighbourhood for her withdrawn manner, and most people found her almost unnaturally reserved. But at these words, she forgot years of self-restraint, and flamed into anger. Handsome or not, this oaf's rudeness had gone too far! He needed a lesson. So, without a thought for the consequences, she let go of his hand and shoved him back into the water. 'I don't think I want to help you after all,' she said coolly, and walked away across the bridge.

Chapter Three

With a roar of fury, Marcus struggled to his feet, waded clumsily to the side, scrambled up the bank and caught up with her halfway up the hill.

Francesca gave a cry of fright as he grabbed her by the arm and swung her round. 'Now, you little wretch, you'd better explain yourself before I give you what you deserve.'

'Let go of me!'

'Not till I have an explanation. And you'd better make it a good one. Or are you the sort of Bedlamite who does this as a regular sport?'

'I'm not the lunatic!' Francesca cried. 'I tell you, I was trying to stop you from drowning—you said you wanted to.'

'But I didn't mean it, you. . .ninny!' he said, giving her a shake.

Francesca lost her temper yet again. She pulled herself free, but though she took a step back, she made no attempt to escape. 'How was I to know that?' she blazed at him. 'You stood on that bridge, draped over the water like a. . .like a weeping willow, and said you were going to drown yourself! How was I to know you were playacting?'

'A weepi—a weeping willow!' he said, outraged. 'You

don't know what you're talking about! I wasn't feeling quite the thing—I had a headache! A hangover, if you must know. But I wouldn't be such a clunch as to do away with myself. Why on earth should I?' He had glared at her. 'And if I did, I'd find a better way than to try to drown myself in two feet of water! What rubbish!'

'Then why did you say you would?'

'I didn't, I tell you.' She opened her mouth to contradict him, but he held up a hand and said slowly and distinctly, in the tones of one talking to an idiot, 'I was expressing unhappiness. I was just unhappy.'

'Well, you deserve to be! People who are rakes and who gamble all their money away deserve to be unhappy!'

'Gamble all my money aw—You are a lunatic! An impertinent, lunatic child! What on earth do you mean? I'm not rich enough to gamble any money away! Anyway, I won last night, damn it!'

'A fine story! If that's the case, why are you so worried about facing your uncle?'

The young man's eyes narrowed and he said slowly, 'You little sneak! You were eavesdropping—that conversation was private!'

Francesca was instantly abashed. 'Yes, I'm sorry. I couldn't help hearing it—I certainly didn't do it intentionally. I really am very sorry. Please, please forgive me. I meant well, really I did.' She looked up at him beseechingly. 'I promise I shall forget all about that conversation, now that I know you don't really mean to. . .to— you know.'

He was staring down into her eyes, seemingly fascinated. Francesca's heart thumped, but she didn't— couldn't move. He muttered, 'A lunatic child, with witch's eyes. . . I've seen you in paintings. . .' and he slowly drew his finger over her cheekbone and down her jaw. He held her chin and lowered his head towards her. . . Then he jerked back, and said in astonishment, 'I'm going mad. It must be the hangover.'

Francesca was not sure what he meant, but said nervously, 'And. . .and now I shall go home.'

'No, don't!' He took her by the arm once again and marched her into a patch of sunshine. 'I still want my explanation. . . You're shivering!'

Francesca thought it wiser not to explain that this was due to nerves and reaction to his hand on her arm, rather than to feeling cold. She said nothing.

'Sit in the sun here—you'll soon be warmer. Now, where were we?'

'I was telling you I'd heard you say you wanted to drown yourself because you'd gambled away all your money. And I was trying to stop you. But I forgot how steep the bank was, and I got carried down the slope and. . .and I pushed you in.' Francesca was gabbling, as she often did when nervous.

'I suppose it makes some sort of inverted sense,' he said doubtfully. 'I suppose I ought to be grateful that you meant well—though I still think I'd have been better off without your help.' He looked down thoughtfully at his sodden clothes. . .

Francesca tried, and failed, to suppress a giggle. 'I think you're right,' she said. 'Much better off. You squelch when you walk, too!' and, after another vain struggle with herself, she went off into a gale of laughter.

For a moment he looked affronted, but as she laughed again at his face he smiled, then he, too, was laughing. The atmosphere lightened considerably.

'Look, let's sit down here for a moment, and you can help me with my boots while you tell me the story of your life.'

'Well, that's a "blank, my lord",' she said, as he sat down on a fallen tree trunk and had stuck his foot out.

'Where do you live?'

'Down there, at Shelwood. With my aunt.' Francesca tugged hard and the boot came off, releasing a gush of water over her dress. She gave a cry. 'Oh, no!'

'It will dry. Now, the other one.' She cast him a reproachful look, but gingerly took hold of the second boot. She took more care with this one but, when it came away with unexpected ease, she lost her balance, tripped over a root and fell flat on her back. The second boot poured its contents over her. She got to her feet hastily. 'Just look at that!' she cried.

'I am,' he said. Francesca was puzzled at the sudden constraint in his voice. 'I. . .I seem to have made a mistake. I thought you a child.' He swallowed. 'But it's clear you're not. You may be a lunatic, but you're all woman— and a lovely one, too!'

She looked down. The water had drenched the thin lawn of her dress and petticoat, and they were clinging to her like a second skin. The lines of her figure were clearly visible.

'Oh, no!' Desperately she shook out her dress, holding it away from her body. 'I must go!'

'No! Please don't. Your dress will dry very soon, and I won't stare any more. Look, if you sit down beside me on this log I won't be able to. We could. . .we could have a peaceful little chat till your dress dries. I'd like to explain what I meant when I was speaking to Freddie.'

She looked at him uncertainly. He was really very handsome—and he seemed to be sincere. Perhaps not everyone at Witham Court was a rake. But. . .'Why did you call me lovely,' she asked suspiciously, 'when everyone else says I'm plain?'

'Plain? They must be blind. Sit down and I'll tell you why I think you lovely.' This sounded like a very dangerous idea to Francesca. So she was at something of a loss to understand when she found herself doing as he asked. She kept her distance, however—she was not quite mad.

'Is Freddie the man you were with?'

'Yes—we were talking about my c—about someone we both know. He lost a great deal of money last night. He. . .he wasn't feeling well this morning, and we're worried about him. But you don't really want to talk about this, do you? It's a miserable subject for a lovely morning. Tell me about yourself. What were you doing when you saw us? On your way to a tryst?'

'Oh, no! I. . .I don't know anyone. I was drawing— oh, I must fetch my book and satchel! I dropped them when I ran down the hill. Excuse me.'

She jumped up, glad to escape from the spell the deep voice and dark blue eyes were weaving round her.

'I'll come with you.'

'But you haven't anything on your feet!'

'So? I've suffered worse things than that in the army. And I want to make sure you don't disappear. You're my hostage, you know, until we are both dry.' She looked at him nervously, but he was laughing, as he got up and took firm hold of her hand. 'Where is this book?'

They soon found the orchid plant she had been drawing, and her sketch pad and satchel were not far away. He picked the pad up, still holding her with one hand, and studied it. 'This is good,' he said. 'Who is your teacher?'

'Madame Elisabeth.' She blushed in confusion. 'I mean Madame de Romain. My governess.'

'Let's get back into the sun. My feet are cold.' They collected the satchel, then went back to their tree trunk and sat down. This time it seemed quite natural to sit next to him, especially as he still held her hand in his. 'Will you show me some more of your work?'

Francesca coloured with pleasure. 'Of course!' she said shyly.

From then on, he directed his considerable charm towards drawing her out, and Francesca found herself talking to him more freely than she had with anyone for years. Sometimes, she would falter as she found his eyes intent on her, looking at her with such warmth and understanding. But then he would ask a question about some detail in one of the pictures and she would talk on, reassured.

There came a moment when she stopped. 'I. . .I haven't anything more to show you—not here,' she said. When he didn't immediately answer, she looked up, a question in her eyes.

'Why did you say you were plain?' he said slowly.

'Because I am! Everyone says so.'

'No, you're not, Francesca. You're like your sketches—drawn with a fine, delicate grace.'

'It's kind of you to say so,' she said, nervous once again.

'I'm not flattering you!'

'No, I'm sure you mean to be kind. But it isn't necessary. I'm really quite used to my looks. Please—if you carry on talking like this, I shall have to go. My dress is dry now. Your things are dry, too.'

'How old are you?' he asked abruptly.

She hesitated. Then, 'Seventeen,' she lied. When he looked sceptical, she had added, still lying, 'Almost.'

'It's young. But not too young. Have you ever been in love?'

'Me?' she asked, astounded.

He laughed at her then, and let go of her, but only to put both of his hands on her shoulders. 'Yes, you,' he said.

'Certainly not!'

'There's always a first time,' he murmured. He drew her closer. 'What about kisses? Have you ever been kissed?'

'Not. . .not often,' she whispered, hypnotised by the

blue eyes gazing into hers. 'My grandfather, sometimes.' She swallowed. 'I suppose my father did. I. . .I can't remember.'

'That's not quite what I meant. I meant. . .this.' He lowered his head and kissed her gently. Francesca felt as if she had just had been hit by lightning. The strangest feeling overcame her, a feeling compounded of fear and pleasure, chills and warmth, a feeling that she ought not to be doing this—and an urgent wish for more.

'That was nice,' she breathed, bemused and hardly knowing what she said.

They were now standing up, face to face. 'Put your arms round my neck,' he said softly. She took a step forward and slowly lifted her arms. 'That's right. Then I can put mine round you—like this.' He pulled her closer and kissed her again, not gently this time. Francesca gave a little cry and he relaxed his grip immediately. 'Did I hurt you?'

'No. I. . .I didn't expect. . .I didn't know. . .' She tightened her arms and pulled his face down to hers. 'Kiss me again,' she said.

A world of unimaginable delight opened now for Francesca. Absurd though it was, she felt safer than ever before in this man's arms, and more alive than ever before. He was in turn gentle, then passionate, charming, then demanding. He called her his idiot, his love, his witch, but she didn't hear the names—only the warmth and feeling in the deep voice. He laughed at her lack of guile, but tenderly, as if her vulnerability had disarmed him.

And, just occasionally, he sounded uncertain, as if he, too, was unable to understand what was happening to them. They were both lost in a world of brilliant sunshine and glinting shadows, of whirling green and gold and blue. . .

Perhaps it was as well that they were recalled to their

senses before the situation went beyond recall. Shouts in the distance proved to be those of Freddie, looking for Marcus. Marcus swore, then whispered, 'Tomorrow? In the morning? Here?' Then he kissed her once more, got up and turned down the hill. 'Here I am,' he had shouted. 'What do you want?'

Once again, Francesca listened to their conversation from her hiding place.

'It's Jack. He's asking for you. And your uncle's coming down to Witham. Thought you'd like to know. What the devil have you been doin' all this time, Marcus old fellow?'

'Er. . .nothing much,' Marcus said. . .

Francesca was startled out of her memories and brought back to the present day by a brilliant flash, followed almost immediately by a crash of thunder. The storm was now imminent. She quickened her pace. But her thoughts were still on the girl she had been nine years before.

'Nothing much'—she ought to have taken warning. But at the time she had been totally dazzled, bewitched. It had been so easy, she thought, for a man of his experience and charm. And she had been so gullible. She had met him the next day, of course, pleading to Madame Elisabeth that she was ill, so that she was excused her morning lessons. And this had not been so far from the truth—she had been ill, gripped by a fever, a delirium which suppressed all her critical faculties, all thought of self-preservation. She winced now as she remembered how eagerly she had run up the hill to meet him again all those years ago.

She had to wait some time before Marcus appeared; when he arrived, he seemed preoccupied. She felt a chill round her heart—did he despise her for being so open about her feelings the day before? They walked in silence for some time, she waiting for him to say something—anything to break the constraint between them.

'You're very quiet, Francesca,' he said finally.

Francesca was astonished. He was the one who had not spoken! And now he was accusing her, in such a serious voice. . .he *did* despise her! 'I. . .I'm not sure I should have come,' she said.

'Why?'

Francesca hesitated. She didn't know the rules of this game, and accustomed though she was to rejection, she was afraid to invite rejection from this man. It would hurt too much.

'I didn't behave well yesterday.'

'When you pushed me into the stream? I've forgiven you for that.'

'No—afterwards.'

He stopped, turned and took her hands. 'You were. . .wonderful. But I was wrong to kiss you.' He fell silent again.

After a while, she asked timidly, 'Why?'

'Because you're far too young. Because you're innocent. Because Jack's father arrived this morning to take him home, and. . .and, Francesca, I have to leave with them. I was only here in the first place to look after my cousin. And I failed.'

For the life of her, Francesca could not hold back a small cry. He swore under his breath, and said, 'I ought to be whipped. I failed him and I've hurt you, and that was the last thing I wanted. Believe me.'

Francesca pressed her lips tightly together. She would not plead, she would not beg. This was the very worst rejection she had ever suffered, but she had hidden her distress before, and she would not show it now. But it was taking all the resolution she had.

'You needn't feel too badly,' she said finally. 'I knew you were staying at Witham Court, after all, but I still let you kiss me. That's only what rakes are expected to do, isn't it?'

'Rakes!'

Francesca hardly heard the interruption. She continued, 'You needn't feel sorry for me——I enjoyed it. And they were only kisses. I daresay I shall have many more before I am too old to enjoy them. When. . .when I make my come-out and go to London.' She had even managed a brilliant smile. 'My father will fetch me quite soon, I expect. He said so just the other day in one of his letters.'

'Francesca.' He said her name with such tenderness that she was almost undone.

'So you can kiss me again, if you like. Just to show that it doesn't mean very much.'

'Oh, Francesca, my lovely, courageous girl! I know just how much it meant to you. God help me, but how could I not know? Come here!'

He kissed her, at first gently, as he had the first time. But then he held her so tightly that she could hardly breathe, kissing her again and again, murmuring her name over and over again. But gradually the fit of passion died and he thrust her away from him.

'It's no use,' he said, and there was finality in his voice. 'My uncle is right——I have nothing to offer you. And even if I had, you are too young. We both have our way to make. It's no use!'

Then he kissed her hand. 'Goodbye, Francesca. Think of me sometimes.' He strode off down the hill, but Francesca could not see him. Her eyes were burning with tears she would not allow to fall.

But that was not the end. Hard though it was, she could have borne that much, could have cherished the memory of his care and concern for her, the thought that someone had once found her beautiful enough to love. But this consolation had not been for her.

Some days later she was standing on the bridge, looking down at the stream, when Freddie's voice interrupted her unhappy thoughts. 'You must be the little goddess Marcus spent the morning with the other day,' he said. 'He was very taken with you, give you my word! Wished I'd seen you first. Missing him, are you?'

Something inside Francesca curled up. She hated the thought of being a subject of conversation at Witham Court. Surely Marcus couldn't have done such a thing?

'I don't know what you mean, sir,' she said coldly, not looking at him.

'Don't you? Marcus seemed to know what he was talking about. Never seen him so much on the go, and he's known a few girls in his time, I can tell you. Very good-looking fellow. But he did seem taken with you. We were all no end intrigued, but he wouldn't tell us who you were. It was Charlie who said you must be the Shelwood girl. Are you? Marcus was right about the figure, though I can't see your face. Why don't you turn round, sweetheart?'

Francesca shut her eyes, bowed her head and prayed he would go away.

'Don't be sad, my dear! Ain't worth it! It wouldn't have lasted long, you know, even if he hadn't had to leave with Jack and his father. It never does with these army chaps. Off and away before you can wink your eye. And if you cast an eye around you, there's plenty more where he came from.'

She would have left the bridge, but he was blocking the way.

'Cheer up, sweetheart! It's always the same with the army. Rave about one woman, make you green with envy, and then before you know it they're over the hill and far

away, making love to another! Seen it m'self time and
again. Mind you, I'm surprised at Marcus—leaving Jack
lying there in misery while he pursues his own little game.
And a very nice little bit of game, too, from what I can
see. Come on, sweetheart, let's see your face.'

When Francesca shook her head and turned to run back
to the Manor, he ran after her, caught her hand and pulled
her to him. 'You shan't escape without giving me a kiss.
You were free enough with them the other day, from all
accounts. One kiss, that's all, then I'll let you go, give
you my word. Give me a kiss, there's a good girl.'

'Fanny!' For the first time in her life, Francesca was
glad to hear her aunt's voice. Miss Shelwood was standing
a few yards away, with Silas, her groom, close behind.
Her face was a mask of fury. Francesca's tormentor let
her go with a start, and took a step back.

'Come here this instant, you. . .trollop!' With relief,
Francesca complied. Her aunt turned to Freddie. 'I assume
you are from Witham Court, sir. How dare you trespass
on my land! Silas!' The groom came forward, fingering
his whip.

Freddie grew pale and stammered, 'There's no need
for any violence, ma'am. No need at all. I was just passing
the time of day with the little lady. No harm done.' And,
within a trice, he disappeared in the direction of
Witham Court.

'Take my niece's arm, Silas, and bring her to the
Manor.' Miss Shelwood strode off without looking in
Francesca's direction. Silas looked uncomfortable but
obeyed.

Francesca hardly noticed or cared what was happening
to her. All her energies were concentrated in a desperate
effort to endure her feelings of anguish and betrayal. She
had believed Marcus! She had been taken in by his air of
sincere regret, had thought he had been truly distressed

to be leaving her! And while she had lain awake, holding the thought of his love and concern close to her like some precious jewel in a dark world, a talisman against a bleak future, he had been joking and laughing at Witham Court, boasting about her, making her an object of interest to men like Freddie. It was clear what they all thought of her.

Oh, what a fool she had been! What an unsuspecting dupe! She had fallen into his hands like a. . .like a ripe plum! Her aunt could not despise her more than she already despised herself. She had been ready to give Marcus everything of herself; holding nothing back. Only Freddie's timely interruption had prevented it. She had indeed behaved like the trollop her aunt had called her. Occupied with these and other bitter thoughts Francesca hardly noticed that they were back at the Manor.

Miss Shelwood swept into the library, then turned and said coldly, 'How often have you met that man before?'

Never. Francesca said the word, but no sound came.

'Answer me at once, you wicked girl!'

'I. . .' Francesca swallowed to clear the constriction in her throat. 'I have never seen him before.'

'A liar as well as a wanton. Truly your mother's daughter!'

'That's not true! You must not say such things of my mother!'

'Like mother, like daughter!' Miss Shelwood continued implacably, ignoring Francesca's impassioned cry. 'Richard Beaudon was at Witham Court when he first met your mother. Now her daughter goes looking for her entertainment there. Where is the difference? No, I will hear no more! Go to your room, and do not leave it until I give you permission.'

Exhausted with her effort to control her feelings, Francesca ran to her room and threw herself on her bed.

She did not cry. The bitter tears were locked up inside, choking her, but she could not release them.

In the weeks that followed, she castigated herself time and again for her weakness and stupidity. She, who had taught herself over the years not to let slights and injuries affect her, to keep up her guard against the hurt that others could inflict, had allowed the first personable man she met to make a fool of her, to destroy her peace of mind for many weary months. It would not happen again. It would never happen again.

Her aunt remained convinced that Francesca had been conducting an affair with Freddie. Francesca was punished severely for her sins. She was confined to her room on starvation rations for days, then kept within the limits of the house and garden for some weeks. It was months before she was allowed outside the gates of the garden, unaccompanied by her governess or a groom. She was made to sit for long periods while Mr Chizzle, her aunt's chaplain, expatiated on the dreadful fate awaiting those who indulged in the sins of the flesh.

This last Francesca endured by developing the art of remaining apparently attentive while her mind ranged freely over other matters. Since she felt in her own mind that she deserved punishment, though not for her escapade with Freddie, she found patience to endure most of the rest.

But the worst of the affair was that Miss Shelwood took every opportunity it offered to remind Francesca of her mother's sins. That was very hard to endure. And, in her mind, the distress this caused her was added to the mountain of distress caused by one man. Not Freddie— she forgot him almost immediately. No, Marcus What-ever-his-name-was was to blame. She would *never* forgive him.

* * *

The first few drops of rain were falling as Francesca found, to her surprise, that she had reached the Manor. She slipped in through the servants' door—it would never do for Aunt Cassandra or Agnes Cotter, her maid, to see her in her present state. Betsy was in the kitchen.

'Miss Fanny! Oh, miss! Whatever have you been doing?'

Francesca looked down. The mud from the ditch had now dried and the dress was no longer plastered to her body. But she was a sorry sight all the same.

'I fell,' she said briefly. 'Help me to change before my aunt sees me, Betsy. I'll need some water.'

'The kettle's just about to boil again. But you needn't fret—your aunt won't bother with you at the moment, Miss Fanny. She's had another of her attacks. It's a bad one.'

Suddenly apprehensive, Francesca stopped what she was doing and stared at Betsy. 'When?'

'Just after you went out. And. . .' Betsy grew big with the news '. . .Doctor Woodruff has been. Didn't you see him on your way to the village?'

'I went through the fields. Did my aunt finally send for him, then? What did he say?'

'They wouldn't tell me, Miss Fanny. You'd better ask that maid of hers. Miss Cotter, that is,' said Betsy with a sniff.

Worried as she was, Francesca failed to respond to this challenge. Agnes Cotter had been Miss Shelwood's maid for more than twenty years and jealously guarded her position as her mistress's chief confidante, but Francesca knew better than to quiz her. If Miss Shelwood did not wish her niece to know what was wrong, then Agnes Cotter would not tell her, however desperate it was. So, after washing, changing her clothes and brushing her hair back into its rigid knot, she presented herself outside her aunt's bedroom.

'Miss Shelwood is resting, Miss Fanny.'

'Is she asleep?'

'Not exactly—'

'Then pray tell my aunt that I am here, if you please.'

With a dour look Agnes disappeared into the bedroom; there was a sound of muted voices, which could hardly be heard for the drumming of the rain on the windows. The storm had broken. The maid reappeared at the door and held it open. 'Miss Shelwood is very tired, miss. But she will see you.'

Ignoring Agnes, Francesca stepped into the room. The curtains were half-drawn and the room was dim and airless. Her aunt lay on the huge bed, her face the colour of the pillows that were heaped up behind her. But her eyes were as sharply disapproving as usual, and her voice was the same.

'I expected you to come as soon as you got in. What have you been doing?'

'I had to change my dress, Aunt,' said Francesca calmly.

'You were here before the rain started, so your dress was not wet. There's no need to lie, Fanny.'

'My dress was muddy. How are you, Aunt Cassandra?'

'Well enough. Agnes has a list of visits for you to make tomorrow. I've postponed what I can, but these are urgent. See that you do them properly, and don't listen to any excuses. I've made a note where you must pay particular attention.'

Miss Shelwood believed in visiting her employees and tenants regularly once a month, and woe betide any of them who were not ready for her questions on their activities. During the past few weeks, Francesca, much to her surprise, had been required to act as an occasional stand-in, so she knew what to do. Since both she and her aunt knew that she would perform adequately, if not as ruthlessly as Miss Shelwood, she wasted no time in questions or comments. Instead she asked, 'What did Dr Woodruff say? Does he know what is wrong?'

'How did you know he'd been? Betsy, I suppose.'

'She told me, yes. I am sorry you were so unwell.'

'I'm not unwell! Dr Woodruff is an old woman, and I shan't let him come again. I don't need him to tell me what I am to do or not do. Don't waste any time before seeing those people, Fanny. I shall want an account when I am up. You may go.'

Against her better judgement Francesca said, 'Can I get you anything? Some books?'

'Don't be absurd! Agnes will get me anything I need. But you'd better see the housekeeper about meals for the rest of you. Agnes will let her know what I want. Agnes?'

Francesca was given her aunt's list, then she was escorted out and the door shut firmly behind her. She made a face, then walked wearily down the dark oak staircase. It was not easy to feel sympathy or concern for her aunt—not after all these years. But she was worried. Whether her aunt lived or died, her own future looked bleak indeed. If no post as a governess was forthcoming, where could she look for help? In spite of her brave words to Marcus, her claim on her father was non-existent. She had not heard a word from him since she had left the West Indies nearly twenty years ago, and had no idea where he might now be.

The world would say that her aunt ought to do something for her, there was no doubt about that. But Francesca had every doubt that she would. Shelwood was not an entailed estate—Miss Shelwood could dispose of it as she wished—and whatever happened to Aunt Cassandra's money, her sister's child would see none of it—nothing was more certain. Her duty, such as it was, would end at her death.

Francesca came to a halt, thinking of the cheerless years since her grandfather had died. She had always been required to sit with her aunt at mealtimes, though the meals were consumed in silence. She was adequately clothed, though most of that came out of her allowance. She had a bedroom to herself, though it was the tiny room allotted to her when she had first arrived as a child of six. She had been taken to church twice every Sunday, and forced to join in her aunt's weekly session of private prayers and readings with the Reverend Mr Chizzle. But there was nothing more.

Was it that Miss Shelwood could not tolerate the evidence of the shame that her sister had brought on the family? But Sir John Shelwood had never shown any sense of shame. Regret at not seeing his daughter again before she died, at not telling her that she had been forgiven, perhaps, but there had been no sense of shame. There had never been anything in his attitude towards his granddaughter that even hinted at the shocking truth. Strange. . .

The next morning Francesca rose early; by midday, she had completed her round of visits. She had made notes of complaints and requests, and, in order to satisfy her aunt, had written down one or two criticisms—nothing of any consequence—together with some recommendations. She attempted to see her aunt, but was denied access, her civil enquiries about Miss Shelwood's health being met with a brusquely indifferent reply from Agnes Cotter. Resolving to see Doctor Woodruff for herself when he called that evening, she left the papers and escaped from the house.

At the end of an hour, she found she had walked off

her frustration and anger and was enjoying the woods and open ground above Shelwood. The air was still heavy, however, and swallows and martins were swooping low over the swollen expanse of water left by the storm, catching the insects in the humid air. Francesca watched them for a while, marvelling at the speed and skill with which they skimmed the surface.

But even as she watched, one bird's judgement failed disastrously. It dipped too low and, as it wheeled round, its wing was caught below the water line. Francesca drew in her breath as it dropped, then rose, then dropped again. By now both wings were heavy with water, and the bird's struggles to fly were only exhausting it further. It would soon drown.

Without a second thought, Francesca hitched up her skirts, took off her shoes and waded in. The water was very shallow—it shouldn't be difficult to scoop the bird out.

'I never knew such a girl for water! You must have been a naiad in your previous existence.'

She recognised the voice, of course. But she said nothing until she had captured the bird and released it on dry ground. Then she said calmly, 'And you seem to be my nemesis. I lead a very dull, dry life in the normal course of events. Excuse me.' She bent down and put on her shoes. 'Let me wish you a pleasant walk.' She wanted to take polite leave of him, but realised that she had no idea what to call him other than 'Marcus'. That she would never do again. She started off down the hill without saying any more.

'Wait!'

She pretended not to have heard, but he came striding after her.

'I was hoping to learn how you fared.'

'Thank you—very comfortably. But my aunt is not

well—I must get back to her. I know you will understand and forgive my haste. Goodbye.'

'Not so fast! I want to talk to you.'

The pain in her heart was getting worse. He was still as handsome—more so! The years had added one or two lines to his face, one or two silver strands to the dark hair, but this only increased his dignity and authority, and the blue eyes were as alert, as warm and understanding as ever. The villain! The scheming, double-dealing villain! Where was the lady from the carriage?—if 'lady' was the right word! He should be using his charm on her, she might reward his efforts—probably had done so long before now. But she, at least, was old enough to see through him. She was well past the age of innocence!

But none of these uncharitable thoughts showed in her expression as she said coolly, 'That is a pity. I have no wish to talk to you. I doubt that we now have very much in common. You must find someone else to amuse you.'

'Is your aunt as ill as everyone says?'

He blurted this out with none of the polish she expected of him. What was he thinking of? Had he heard the rumours and was daring to be sorry for her? Francesca fought down a sudden rise in temper, then said in measured tones, 'I am surprised that Lord Witham's guests indulge in village gossip. I would have thought they had other, more interesting, pursuits.'

'Don't be such a awkward cat, Francesca—tell me how your aunt is.'

He had no right to sound so anxious. It weakened her, made her vulnerable once again to his charm.

'I don't know why such a thing should concern you,' she said, maintaining her usual air of colourless reserve as she lied to him once again. 'But if you insist on knowing, my aunt is suffering from the heat. I am sure she will be quite well again in a few days.'

'That isn't what I have heard.'

They must have been discussing the situation at Witham Court. Once again she had been made the subject of gossip there. It was intolerable! 'You must think what you choose, sir. However, I am sure my aunt would not welcome speculation by strangers. And nor do I.'

'Strangers, Francesca?'

Francesca had been avoiding his eye, but now she looked directly at him. She did not pretend to misunderstand. 'Whatever happened nine years ago, sir, we were, and are, strangers. Of that I am certain. Now please let me go!' In spite of herself, her voice trembled on these last words.

He took a step forward, hesitated, then bowed gracefully. 'Very well. Good day to you, my dear.'

She felt his eyes on her as she set off again down the hill. She hoped he could not see how her hands were trembling, or hear how her heart was pounding.

Chapter Four

Marcus was astonished to discover that, even after nine years, the strange line of communication between Francesca and himself was still there. The horrors of war, the problems and anxieties of peace, the totally absorbing task of learning to run a huge and prosperous estate had caused him to put her out of his mind, but no sooner had they met again than he was once more caught in a strange web—a curious feeling of kinship with her. It was as infuriating as it was inexplicable.

He stood watching her as she went down the hill, and knew, though he didn't know how, that, in spite of her gallant attempt to deceive him, she was lying about her aunt, just as she had lied to him all those years ago about her future with her father. Francesca was desperately worried about the future. And if the gossip last night had any foundation, she was right to be worried. The impulse to run after her, to shake her till she admitted the truth, then to reassure her, swear to protect her from harm, was almost irresistible.

It was absurd! It had been absurd nine years ago, when he had been a penniless and inexperienced officer in Wellington's army. At that time, he had been convinced that Francesca was the love of his life, and only the intervention of his uncle had stopped him from making what would have been a disastrous mistake. His uncle had been right—he had indeed forgotten the girl once he was back with the army!

But to find, now, that he had the same impulse to protect Francesca nine years later was ridiculous. A man of thirty, rich, sophisticated and, not to put too fine a point on it, extremely eligible. . .how London would laugh! He must take a grip on himself, before he did something he would later regret. Shrugging impatiently, he strode off down the other side of the hill.

When Francesca got back to Shelwood Manor she found Agnes Cotter waiting for her. The woman was clearly distressed.

'Miss Shelwood has suddenly got much worse. But she won't hear of sending for Dr Woodruff. I don't know what to do, Miss Fanny.' The situation must be grave indeed—this was the first time ever that Agnes had appealed to anyone for help.

'We must send Silas for him straight away,' Francesca said calmly.

'But Miss Shelwood will—'

'I will take the blame, Agnes. Go back to my aunt but say nothing to her—it would only cause her unnecessary agitation. Stay with her till the doctor comes, then I shall take over.'

Dr Woodruff came with a speed that showed how grave he thought the situation was. 'I knew this would happen. It is always the same in cases like these.'

'Cases like what, Dr Woodruff?'

'You mean you don't know that your aunt is dying, Miss Fanny? No, I can see she hasn't told you.'

'You mean she knows?'

'Of course. I warned her some months ago, but she

refused to believe me. A very determined woman, your aunt, Miss Fanny. I'm afraid that very little can be done for her, except to ease the pain. I prescribed laudanum yesterday—perhaps she will accept it now. Take me to her, if you please.'

Francesca went up the stairs with a heavy heart; when she entered her aunt's room, she was shocked at the change she saw in her. Miss Shelwood was a ghastly colour, and gasping for breath. Agnes was bathing her mistress's forehead, but when the doctor came in she glided away.

'What are you doing here?'

Francesca was not sure whether her aunt was speaking to the doctor or to her. She went up to the bed and said gently, 'It's time you had some medicine, Aunt Cassandra. Dr Woodruff has something to make you feel better.'

'I don't want his morphine! If I'm going to die, I want to die in my right senses! But you can stay. I have something to say to you. A-ah!'

'Drink some of this, Miss Shelwood. You won't feel less alert, but it will take away the worst of the pain. And if you wish to be able to talk to your niece, you will need it.'

'Very well.' The voice was but a faint thread of sound.

Dr Woodruff held a small vial to the sick woman's lips, and then stood back. He said quietly, 'That should make her feel better for a while. I'll be in the next room.'

After a moment, Francesca said tentatively, 'You wished to tell me something, Aunt Cassandra?'

'Yes. Box on the desk. Fetch it.' Francesca did as her aunt asked, then on request opened the box. 'Letter. . .underneath.'

The letter was dry and yellow. It began, 'My dear Cassie'. . .and was signed 'Richard Beaudon'.

'Do you wish me to read it?'

'Later. No time now. It's from your father. Richard Bcaudon. To tell me my sister had stolen him.' The dark eyes opened, and they were glittering with malice. 'Why I hated you. Still do.'

'Aunt Cassandra, don't! I have never done you any harm, you know that.'

'Never should have existed. He'd have married me if she hadn't told him. . .told him. . .' The voice died away again.

'Shall I fetch Dr Woodruff?'

'No! Not finished. It's the money. Chizzle's got to look after the money. Told him.'

'Mr Chizzle? The chaplain?'

'Don't be stupid. Who else? Do as he tells you. M'father had no right. . . A pauper—that's what you ought to be!' Miss Shelwood raised herself and stared malevolently at her niece. This time she spoke clearly and with intense feeling. 'You'd better do what Chizzle tells you—you needn't think anyone will marry you for love! A plain, dull child, you were. Plain, like *me*! Not like. . .' She sank back against the pillows, and her words were faint. 'Not like Verity. You'll never be the honeytrap she was.' The lips worked, then she added, 'Seen your father in you, though. The eyes.' A dry sob escaped her. 'God damn him!'

Francesca was appalled. 'Please, don't—I'll send for Mr Chizzle. He ought to be here—he'll help you.'

A grim smile appeared on her aunt's pale lips. 'I won't be here myself. Remember what I said, Fanny. Plain and dull, that's you. She called you Francesca—what a stupid name for such a plain child. . . Rake Beaudon's child. . .'

The voice faded away and Miss Shelwood closed her eyes.

Francesca ran to the door. 'Dr Woodruff!'

But when the doctor saw his patient, he shook his

head. 'It won't be long now,' he said. 'I doubt she'll be conscious again.'

'But. . .' Francesca gazed at the figure on the bed. 'She didn't have time to think! She didn't have time to make her peace with the world, to forgive those who had hurt her! And those who hadn't,' she added forlornly.

'Miss Shelwood is dying as she lived. A very unhappy woman,' said Dr Woodruff, adding drily, 'But God will forgive her. It's his job, after all.'

These were the most sympathetic words Francesca was to hear about her aunt. Words of respect, of conventional regret, of admiration for her energy and devotion to duty—all these were paid to her memory. Madame Elisabeth came, but her sympathy was for Francesca. Only Agnes Cotter truly mourned Cassandra Shelwood.

Following her aunt's death, Francesca underwent a time of confusion and shock. Mr Chizzle was much in evidence, though she wished he wasn't—his attempts to provide consolation were misplaced, to say the least. The funeral was well attended, and though Francesca was surprised at first, on reflection she decided it was to be expected. Although Miss Shelwood had been something of a recluse, she had, after all, been one of the great landowners of the district. But the biggest shock of all came after the funeral, after her aunt's will had been read.

The will was very much on traditional lines. Various small sums had been left to the servants, in proportion to their length of service. Mr Chizzle, as the local curate and Miss Shelwood's chaplain, received a modest sum, Agnes Cotter quite a large one. The rest of Miss Shelwood's estate was left to a fund for building and maintaining almshouses in a neighbouring town. Francesca's name was not mentioned in the document.

Gasps of astonishment came from the servants—Betsy

even voiced her disapproval out loud. But Francesca herself was not at all surprised. It was a blow, but one for which she had been prepared. The question of a post as a governess had now become urgent, and she decided to consult the family lawyer, Mr Barton, on the best way to set about doing this.

The others finally went. Mr Chizzle took his leave so warmly that Francesca began to wonder whether she had been mistaken in him all these years. He was most pressing that he should come again to see her the next day and, though she was reluctant, she eventually gave in, largely because it was the only way she could be rid of him.

But when she mentioned her intention of seeking a post as governess, Mr Barton was astounded. 'My dear Miss Shelwood! What on earth for? You now have control of the money left by your grandfather.'

'It is hardly enough to keep me, sir!'

'Well, that is a matter of opinion. I should have thought that seventy thousand pounds was enough for anyone! Together with what the Shelwood estate brings in, it is a considerable fortune.'

Francesca sat down rather suddenly on a convenient chair. 'Seventy. . .? Do you. . .do you mean to tell me that my grandfather left his *whole estate* to me?'

'Most of it. He left a sum of money outright to the late Miss Shelwood, and the rest was put into trust for you until you reached the age of twenty-five, in November of this year. The arrangement was that, during her lifetime, your aunt would run the estate and receive half of the income from it. The other half was put back into the Shelwood trust, which is why it has now grown to such a handsome fortune.'

'How much did you say it was?' asked Francesca faintly.

'About seventy thousand pounds. The trust was set up for the benefit of you and your children, and has certain safeguards which are in the discretion of the trustees. But you will have more than enough to live on, nevertheless. Shelwood is a thriving concern, and should provide you with an income of about ten thousand pounds per annum. Do you mean to say that Miss Shelwood never told you of this?'

'No. I had no idea. . .'

Mr Barton looked uneasy. 'I have been remiss. I agreed with your aunt that you were too young to be burdened with it at the time of your grandfather's death, but I ought to have made sure you knew later. But I have to say in my own defence that it simply never occurred to me that she would keep it from you. Why should she?'

'My aunt. . .my aunt was a secretive woman, Mr Barton,' was all Francesca said, however. Aunt Cassandra was dead. No good would be done by raking over the past.

'Hmm. I knew of course that she was dissatisfied with the arrangement, but still. . .' He cleared his throat. 'I can see that you have had a shock and need time to assimilate the news, Miss Shelwood, so I will not weary you. I should perhaps just add that one, somewhat curious, condition of the trust is that no one else—neither your father, Lord Beaudon, as your legal guardian, nor a future husband could benefit from it. Only you or your children may have use of it.'

'Since my father has never acknowledged me, he could hardly claim legal guardianship!'

'You are now of age, of course. But until you were twenty-one, he could always have claimed it, had he wished.'

'Even though I am illegitimate?'

The lawyer was astounded. 'Whatever gave you that impression, Miss Shelwood?'

'I. . .I was told. . .that is to say, I. . .was led to believe that there is no record of my parents' marriage.'

'What nonsense! Of course there is! I have all the relevant documents in my safe. Your grandfather gave them into my care just before he died.'

'But Aunt Cassandra said. . . Did my aunt know of these documents, Mr Barton?'

'Why, yes. We discussed them after Sir John's death.'

So Aunt Cassandra had lied to her, had lied to an eleven-year-old child about her parentage. For so many years Francesca had carried a burden of shame around with her, had worried over her future, had made no effort to be received into society or make friends with the surrounding families, sure that she would be rebuffed. Aunt Cassandra had done her best to ruin her niece's life in the way that her own had been ruined. How could she?

Perhaps, in her twisted unhappiness, she had convinced herself that her lover had really not married her sister, in spite of incontrovertible evidence to the contrary. Or had she been exacting a terrible revenge on the child of those she felt had wronged her?

'Miss Shelwood?'

'Forgive me, I. . .it has been a shock.'

'A shock? But why should you think. . .?' His face changed. He said sternly, 'Are you telling me that Miss Cassandra Shelwood, your own aunt, gave you to understand that you were not. . .not legitimate? I find that very hard to believe, Miss Shelwood. Your aunt was not an easy person to know, but she was generally respected throughout the neighbourhood as a just and upright woman.'

'I am not *telling* you anything, Mr Barton,' said Francesca, forcing herself to speak calmly.

'But you have obviously been under a misapprehension—for many years. Why did you not consult me?'

'It never occurred to me to do so. I never thought I had any sort of claim on the Shelwoods, except one of charity.'

'But this is disgraceful!'

With an effort, Francesca put aside her own feelings of outrage. Her aunt was dead—it would do no one any good to reveal how badly she had treated her niece. 'Mr Barton, whatever. . .misunderstandings there may have been in the past, the truth is now clear and we will, if you please, leave it at that. The future is now our concern.'

Mr Barton nodded. 'You are very wise, Miss Shelwood.'

'Do you. . .do you know why my father has remained silent all these years, Mr Barton? Unless. . .unless he is. . .dead?'

'I have no reason to believe he is.'

'Then. . .why?'

'When your parents eloped, Miss Shelwood, Sir John Shelwood refused to have any further contact with his daughter Verity. But when she died, he asked me to write to your father, offering to bring you up in England, and make you his heir. This would be on condition that Lord Beaudon should have no further communication whatsoever with you, once you had arrived at Shelwood Manor.

'I have to say that I disapproved of the arrangement, and was surprised that Lord Beaudon eventually agreed. Of course, the inducement was a strong one. You were motherless; as the Shelwood heiress your future would be assured, and—I have to say—your father's previous manner of life was not one in which a young child could flourish.'

Francesca said slowly, 'I suppose so, but. . .'

'However, your grandfather and aunt are now both dead, you are of age, and, in my opinion, it would not be improper for you to meet Lord Beaudon, if you wished.'

'I. . .I'm not sure. . . Mr Barton, you must excuse me. I am. . .overwhelmed by what you have told me. This change in my circumstances has come as a complete surprise, as you see. But tell me, how many others knew of my grandfather's will? Why did no one ever indicate something of the matter to me, even if my aunt did not?'

'You said your aunt was a woman who kept her secrets, Miss Shelwood. She always said she was very anxious that your position as a considerable heiress should not lead others to court and flatter you. She required my silence, and led me to believe it was out of a desire to protect you. As you know, you both led a somewhat reclusive life here at Shelwood. I doubt anyone else knows.'

With this Francesca had to be satisfied. She felt she had had enough for the moment, so asked Mr Barton to come again after she had had some time to reflect on the change in her fortunes. They fixed on the morning of the next day but one.

'You have been so discreet in the past, I know that you will continue to be so, Mr Barton. I need time to think things out for myself. To decide what I am going to do about Shelwood and my own life.'

The lawyer agreed, then took his leave with a deference that demonstrated, more than any words could have done, Francesca's new importance as owner of Shelwood and all that went with it.

The fact that Miss Fanny had not even been mentioned in her aunt's will scandalised the countryside. The news soon reached Witham Court, where there was a certain amount of speculation over her fate, now that she had been left penniless, together with some ribald suggestions. But after a while the company grew bored with this and forgot her in other pursuits. Everyone, that is, except

Marcus. Once again he had the urge to seek Francesca out and offer what help he could, but the gossip and lewd suggestions about Francesca's likely future gave him pause.

What could he possibly offer that would not compromise her further? A girl without money, without friends and without respectable background would have to be more than ordinarily circumspect. She could not afford the risk of scandal. After some thought, he decided that Francesca would be safe at Shelwood for a short while until the lawyers sorted things out. Meanwhile, he would consult his sister about her when he returned to London. Sarah might be able to find something suitable for Francesca—a post as a companion, or governess, perhaps?

When they got to London, Marcus delivered Lady Forrest to her house in Chiswick, and went on without further ceremony to see his sister, depositing Nick on the way. But Lady Chelford was not at home, and Marcus found to his annoyance that she would not be able to see him till the next morning. He spent the night haunted once again by Francesca's image, and was relieved when morning came and he could go round to Duke Street.

But here he was doomed to disappointment. Lady Chelford, somewhat put out at having to receive her brother at a ridiculously early hour, was unhelpful.

'Marcus, when will you direct your considerable talent for helping others into more suitable channels? I am sure your family could do with your counsel, and. . .and help.'

'My dearest Sarah, you need neither! Your husband may be a touch stuffy, but he is perfectly sound financially, and has a great deal of common sense. Too much so!'

'But he does not understand the children as you do! He is talking of sending Charlotte to a seminary! He says she needs the discipline of school life.'

'Since the child has had four governesses in as many months, I am not sure I disagree with him there, Sally.'

'Then there's Nick. . . He is so often at odds with his father.'

'There's nothing wrong with Nick that can't be cured by a little experience. He'll soon grow up. Indeed, he showed surprisingly good sense at Charlie Witham's.'

When his sister looked doubtful, he added impatiently, 'Sally, he's no gambler, I promise you. In any case, I'll keep an eye on him. Now, what can you do for Francesca Shelwood?'

'Why are you so anxious about this girl? She's nothing to you, is she? *Is* she, Marcus? It would never do!'

'My God, women are all the same! Your imaginations leap from a slight comment, a simple desire to help someone who badly needs it, to wedding bells and the rest. No, I have no personal interest in Francesca Shelwood. I simply wish to preserve her from a fate she does not deserve! Now, can you help or not?'

'It's all very well, but you cannot reasonably expect me to come up with instant ideas for a girl who has no experience and no. . .background! What would my friends say if I foisted Rake Beaudon's love-child on them as a governess or whatever? This is yet another of your quixotic impulses and I have suffered from these before! Ever since you were a child, you have leapt in to help those you regarded, often mistakenly, as less fortunate than yourself. Your reformed pickpocket, whom I placed as a groom with Lady Castle, ran off with a selection of her best silver, and she hasn't forgiven me yet.

'Then there was the widow of a serviceman, a certain Mrs Harbottle, whom I took on myself as an assistant housekeeper. She created havoc in the servants' quarters before I managed to get rid of her. I have no doubt there have been others, if I chose to remember them. No, I will not help you.'

'This is different, Sarah! Miss Shelwood is a lady!'

'She cannot be a lady if, as you tell me, she is Rake Beaudon's illegitimate daughter. I'm sorry for the girl— it sounds as if life has treated her most unfairly—but I cannot help you. And if you wish the girl no harm, you will stay away from her. Tongues will soon wag if you are seen to be taking an interest, however platonic it is.'

'Dammit, of course I mean her no harm!'

'Then leave her alone.' There was a short silence, then she said irritably, 'I suppose I'll have to find something— if I don't, I can see you marrying the girl out of a more than usually stupid attack of conscience. And I owe you something for looking after Nick. If you wish, I will keep an ear open for anyone who seems to be looking for a companion, and is not likely to ask too many questions about the girl's breeding. But I warn you, such a one is most unlikely to be an agreeable employer.'

Marcus left Duke Street in an even gloomier frame of mind. It was clear that Francesca was doomed either to penury, or to life as a drudge, unless something intervened. His sister's words haunted him throughout the night; by the morning, he had come to a desperate decision. He set off for Shelwood later that day.

Francesca was not given much opportunity to consider her situation in peace. First, Agnes Cotter left Shelwood after a final, mercifully brief, interview, then Madame Elisabeth called to sympathise and to renew her offer of help, though she did not stay long, either. Francesca was glad of this—her old friend would be the first to know of the change in her circumstances, but not yet.

But the other servants and people on the estate trailed in one after the other, anxious to express their concern, both for Miss Fanny and for their livelihood. It took all her ingenuity to deal with them tactfully and reassuringly, without telling them anything of the changes in store.

The morning after the funeral, Mr Chizzle arrived to keep his appointment. Francesca was still reluctant to receive him. She had never liked him. He had been unctuously ingratiating with Miss Shelwood, but had followed his patron's example in dealing with her niece. His manner to Francesca had always been either indifferent or suffocatingly condescending. And she found it difficult to forgive those hour-long sermons on the question of her moral welfare after her escapade with Freddie. But she made herself welcome him. He was probably fulfilling some duty to Aunt Cassandra, who had mentioned him that last afternoon. Was it to do with the money she had left him?

'Miss Fanny—'

'Mr Chizzle, you have known me since I was a child, so I suppose it is difficult for you to think of me as Miss Shelwood—as I now am. But if you insist on using my Christian name, I should like you to use the correct one, which is Francesca, *not* Fanny.'

Mr Chizzle was full of confusion and fulsome apologies. Then he took up a position in front of the fireplace and began sonorously, 'I hope you will not condemn me, or think me presumptuous, if I claim a certain interest in your happiness, Miss Francesca. I like to think we have always understood one another very well, and that my efforts towards providing you with spiritual guidance and comfort over the years have not been unappreciated.'

'Of course,' Francesca said, somewhat confused. This was a different Mr Chizzle from the one she had been used to. What could account for it? She was quite certain that no word of yesterday's revelations had reached any other ears. What was this about?

After some small talk, in the course of which he expatiated on the virtues of her aunt—a subject which was hardly likely to make him popular with his audience—he said gravely, 'Your dear aunt, your late and sadly mourned aunt, was much exercised in her mind about what would become of you after she had passed on to higher things— an inexperienced girl, lacking any protector, and, dare I say, with certain unfortunate propensities—' Francesca straightened up at this, and he said with a kindly smile '—though these seem to have been somewhat subdued of late. But your aunt did me the honour of confiding her anxieties to me, and I have to say that I shared her fears.'

'Your concern does you credit. But I assure you, sir, it is misplaced. I am in no need of protection or guidance.'

Mr Chizzle smiled, and he shook his head in tolerant understanding. 'My dear Miss Francesca, that is precisely the problem! You are too young, too. . .headstrong to see it. You need someone—someone with maturer wisdom— to save you from the many pitfalls that life presents. Someone such as my humble self, perhaps.'

'Well, if I should ever feel the need for a friend—' Francesca began doubtfully.

'Ah, I shall not allow your modesty to cause you to misunderstand. Nor should you let the thought of your shameful birth—or any incident in the past—give you pause, either. Let him who is without sin. . . I do not regard it, I assure you. I am here, Miss Fanny, to tell you that my dearest wish—and that of your aunt as expressed to me on her deathbed—is to share your life, to give you companionship where there is loneliness, guidance where there is confusion, wisdom where there—'

'I am not sure what you mean, sir. Can you be more plain? Are you. . .*can* you be asking me to marry you?'

Mr Chizzle, put somewhat off his stride with this blunt question, mopped his brow and said that he was.

'I see.' Francesca turned away to hide her expression. Then she turned back and asked calmly, 'Did my aunt discuss with you the terms of my grandfather's will before she died, Mr Chizzle?'

'As it happens, she did mention it, yes. We both saw the inheritance as a source of danger to you and a temptation to unscrupulous men, attracted by your riches, rather than your. . .lovely self.'

'I see,' said Francesca flatly. 'So you knew about the money.'

'But I flatter myself that you would not dream of ascribing a mercenary motive to my efforts to secure your hand and heart, Miss Fanny—'

'*Francesca*, if you please.'

Mr Chizzle got somewhat awkwardly on to one knee. The effort made his face red, and he mopped it once again before saying, 'My heart is all yours, believe me, dearest Francesca, without any taint of venality. Even had it not been your aunt's dying wish that we two should carry the burden of the great Shelwood inheritance together, had you been the merest pauper, as bereft of fortune as you are bereft of name—I should still have offered you all I have—my admiration, my heart and my life.'

'I. . .I am flattered, of course. That you should be prepared to overlook the stain on my birth means a great deal to me. And what it pleases you to call my. . .propensities. But I cannot permit you to compromise your own good name, dear sir. Why, what would less worthy people say? That you are prepared to marry a bas—love-child as long as she is rich enough? That sin can be washed out in a stream of investments? That the Shelwood gold can persuade you to overlook the Shelwood shame? It is unthinkable! No, much as I am touched by your. . .disinterested offer, I'm afraid I must decline it.'

'But your aunt assured me—she said you would be fortunate to find a man willing to marry you—'

'My aunt is dead, Mr Chizzle. My fortune was never hers to give away. And though I am sure that you have a noble indifference to the personal possession of wealth, I should tell you that any future husband of mine will have no control of the Shelwood inheritance. Under the terms of the trust set up by my grandfather, the income remains mine and later that of my children, even after I marry.' Her suitor's jaw dropped. He looked rather like a stranded fish, thought Francesca, somewhat unkindly. She said, 'Do please get up.'

Mr Chizzle recovered himself and rose with commendable dignity. 'Your aunt warned me,' he said sadly. 'You do not have that nobility of character a man should seek in his wife. I had hoped that with precept and discipline we should succeed in subduing the baser aspects of your nature. But it is not to be. To impute mercenary motives to a man who wishes merely to protect you, to save you from the dangers that surround a young girl left alone. . .' He gave a great sigh, then turned to go.

'Mr Chizzle!'

'Yes?'

'My aunt, as patron of the living of Shelwood, had full confidence in your discretion. I trust that I may repose equal confidence?'

The chaplain drew himself up, then said coldly, 'Your threats are unnecessary, Miss Shelwood. I wish to forget an episode which has been painful in the extreme. I will not mention this matter—or you—to anyone. Anyone at all. Goodbye.'

Francesca could hardly wait for him to leave. She struggled with a wild desire to laugh at the ridiculous picture Mr Chizzle had presented, bending his spindly, black legs in a travesty of a suitor's supplication, his face scarlet with his exertions. But then she was overcome with a feeling of sadness. So much for romance! Was Mr Chizzle merely the first in a succession of such suitors?

It was clear that the Shelwood estate and seventy thousand pounds were attractions which would more than compensate for any shortcomings in herself. Well, let the suitors come! And in her own time and at her own choosing, she would take a husband—but she doubted very much that she would be in love with him, whoever he was.

The sound of a carriage coming up the drive sent her to the window. Another visitor come to commiserate! She was in no mood for yet more verbal fencing. What she needed was time to herself—time in which she could come to terms with her new situation. It looked as if she was soon going to have to learn to deal with fortune seekers, if the last half hour was anything to go by. She would escape through the kitchen, while the visitor was waiting at the front of the house.

But here she miscalculated. The visitor had taken his carriage round to the stables; as Francesca came out through the gate to the kitchen garden, she was confronted with a tall, handsome, self-assured figure. She stopped dead.

'Good afternoon, Miss Shelwood.'

'What are you doing here, sir?' she asked, ungraciously.

'I heard of your aunt's death. I want to talk to you, Francesca.'

There was a silence. 'Well?' said Francesca. 'I'm listening.'

Marcus hesitated, then said, 'It. . .it is a somewhat private matter. May we go inside?'

Chapter Five

Francesca led the way in silence to the small parlour, where the ridiculous scene with Mr Chizzle had so recently taken place. But the tall, elegant figure that followed her in presented a very different picture from that gentleman. She was puzzled. What was Marcus doing here? What did he want of her? She stole a glance at him. He looked calm enough, but there was an air of reluctance about him—as if he was being driven down a road he was not quite sure he wanted to travel.

'And now?'

'Francesca, I want you to marry me.'

Francesca sat down suddenly. Whatever she had been expecting, it had not been another proposal. A feeling of apprehension chilled her bones. Perhaps Mr Chizzle and Marcus were not so very different after all?

He went on. 'Forgive me if I express myself a little abruptly—I know this must come as a surprise to you. Though our acquaintance is longstanding—'

'Nine years,' she said expressionlessly.

'Nine years—it has been short in terms of hours and minutes we have spent with one another.'

'Very short.'

'But I have always felt a. . .a communion of spirit with

you, and believe we could make as good a marriage as any other I have seen.'

'Always?'

'Always what?'

'Always felt this communion of spirit, as you call it?'

'Damn it, you know we share it!'

'I thought we did, certainly. Nine years ago. But you said that you were poor, that you had nothing to offer me, that we each had our own way to make. I remember what you said, you see. I was. . .quite distressed at the time.'

'I know. I behaved badly, Francesca. I never intended to hurt you, but I know I did. Please forgive me.'

Francesca carried on as if he had not spoken. 'Then you disappeared for nine years. We met by chance in the lane the other day—you hadn't come to seek me out. Indeed, at first you didn't even recognise me.'

'You will allow that that was unsurprising. Your dearest friends might not have recognised you in all that mud.'

'You are right, of course. In spite of the "communion of spirit", as you called it. Er. . .I still don't quite understand this proposal of marriage, however. Are you now trying to say that you have loved me all this time—unknown even to yourself?'

'Of course not! Look, nine years ago you were very young, without a penny to your name, and I was an ill-paid soldier. Marriage was out of the question.'

'And now?' asked Francesca. Try as she might, she could not keep the cynicism out of her voice.

Marcus was too intent on what he was saying to notice. 'But things are different now! And I feel I could give you the protection, the support that you lack in your present circumstances. You need a man to take care of you, give you the things you never had—'

A sudden vision of Mr Chizzle saying very much the

same thing, not an hour before, flashed through Francesca's mind. 'Thank you, but I really don't need anyone,' she said. 'I have plenty of money—enough for everything I need. I see you've heard the news.'

'Yes.'

'I wonder how? Did you know that I have seventy thousand pounds, too?'

He smiled, the old quizzical, deceitfully tender smile. 'That much?' Then he came over to her, took her hand and kissed it. 'My dearest girl! Still the same, gallant spirit!'

She waited in stony silence.

He eyed her closely, then said with an air of admiration, 'Well, I admit, that puts icing on the cake. It does indeed. Seventy thousand pounds, ay? A great deal of money.'

When she still said nothing, he put his arm round her and drew her to him. 'But you know in your heart that I'd want to marry you, whatever your dowry, Francesca. I'd marry you even if you had nothing, if you were a pauper. Come, stop prevaricating. Say you'll let me look after you for the rest of your life. I swear you won't regret it.' His manner was tender, but somewhat complacent. There was no suggestion that he was uncertain of the outcome.

Francesca badly wanted to stay calm, to deal with him as she had dealt with Mr Chizzle, but, as always seemed to be the case with this man, her emotions were getting the better of her. It was obvious that he expected her to fall into his arms as easily as she had done all those years ago. That she would be so dazzled by his blue-eyed charm, so blinded by the powerful attraction he knew he could exercise, that she wouldn't see the greedy self-interest behind it, the desire to better himself at her expense. She must have given him a pretty poor opinion of her wits during their brief affair, indeed she must!

Her efforts to hide her rage and humiliation were

choking her. Mr Chizzle had been bad enough, but this was ten—twenty times worse. She suddenly lost the battle with herself, and gave vent to her feelings. 'I won't pretend to feel grateful or flattered,' she said, thrusting him violently away. 'I don't need looking after; to be honest, I think you'd marry me if I had a squint and a wooden leg, as long as I had the rest.'

'What the devil are you talking about? I'm offering you the protection of my name and all that is mine.'

'Really? Well, I wouldn't marry you if you had five hundred thousand pounds and half of England for your heritage! My father was a charmer and a scoundrel, a rake and a fortune hunter, who didn't give a damn for the hurt he caused. The last thing I want is a husband just like him!'

'Now, listen to me, young lady—'

'No, I will not listen to you!' Years of distress and resentment rose up inside Francesca as she stormed on. 'I listened nine years ago, when you charmed me off my feet and then told me you had nothing to offer me. At the time I was fool enough to believe you sincere. I soon learned differently, and it's a lesson I am very unlikely to forget.

'So, allow me to tell you, sir, that *nothing* is now what I have to offer you! Take yourself and your professions of concern, your offers of protection, back to Witham Court, or wherever your other ladies are hiding. They might listen to you, but I never will—my only wish is never to see you again!'

He stood, staring at her as if she had gone mad.

'Have I not made myself plain, sir?' she said passionately. 'Why do you not go?'

'You have made your opinion of me perfectly plain,' he said, rigid with rage. 'If you really think of me in such terms—though God knows why you do—then I understand your refusal to marry me. But I question the need to express yourself quite so offensively, with such remarkable lack of moderation. A simple refusal would have sufficed. We have obviously each been mistaken in each other. Good day, ma'am. I wish you well in your future life, and will do my best to comply with your wish that we should not meet again.' He bowed and left the room.

Francesca sat down and buried her face in her hands. She sat there a long time, listening to the sounds of his carriage dying away down the drive. . . It was strange how painful the final disillusionment was. They had been so close, and so far apart. They had fought, and made love, all in the space of one day. They had met after years of separation, and now they had quarrelled for the last time. And the strange thing was that, during all of this, she had only ever known half his name.

'Marcus!' she whispered, 'Oh, *Marcus*!' and then at last the bitter tears fell.

Marcus drove back to London in a worse temper than he had ever known before. He was furious with himself and with Francesca Shelwood. After all these years, after all the women he could have asked to marry him and who would have been more than eager to receive his proposal with delight, he had exposed himself to a refusal from a penniless nobody! He must have been mad! His sister had already told him he was too quixotic—she would think he was out of his mind, if she learned that he had actually offered to marry Francesca Shelwood to save her from life as a drudge—or even worse!

His sense of injustice grew. His motives had been of the purest. Many would say he had acted nobly in asking Francesca to be his wife—to choose a nameless pauper when he might have chosen from any number of London's most eligible debutantes. Whatever she said, he didn't for one minute believe her claim to have seventy thousand pounds. She was merely putting on a front, as she had done at least twice before. Seventy thousand pounds, indeed! What a story! She might have seventy guineas, but not much more. The depth of her ingratitude was immeasurable. . .immeasurable!

But why had she refused him so angrily? Her father's neglect had done much to sour her view of life—that was obvious. And his own behaviour in the past had not been the sort to reassure her. But to be so excessively vituperative. . . The woman was a neurotic, and did not deserve his sympathy or his regard. From this day on he would forget her. She could find her own way through life, without any further help or interest from *him*!

Unaware of her catastrophic misunderstanding of Marcus's motives, Francesca did her best during the next few weeks to conquer her personal unhappiness and concentrate on a seemingly unending series of tasks and duties. She accomplished these with grim determination, for she had formulated a plan and was now working to it.

Thanks to her aunt's behaviour, she had very little experience of estate business, but Mr Barton was an invaluable ally. He found a very well-qualified agent to look after Shelwood and, by accompanying him round the estate, Francesca made sure that it would be looked after with understanding as well as efficiency. Shelwood Manor was partially shut down for the time being, and again with Mr Barton's help she found new places for one or two servants who were no longer needed. Betsy was put in charge of the rest.

Francesca intended to visit the Manor occasionally, if only to keep an eye on its welfare, but she would soon be busy elsewhere. One piece of business she was glad to perform. A deed of gift was drawn up, and Madame

Elisabeth was presented with the cottage she had tenanted for so many years, and given an increased annuity.

Mr Barton had performed one other service for Francesca. She had told him that she would like to meet her father, if it could be arranged.

'Miss Shelwood, I shall do my utmost to find him. He has been abroad for many years, of course. It may take some time. Leave it to me.'

But only a week or two later, he came back to Shelwood. 'I cannot believe our good fortune, Miss Shelwood! As you know, I have been trying to trace your father for you for some weeks without success. I had sent a letter to him at Packards, the family home in Hertfordshire, telling him that your aunt had died, and that I was anxious to get in touch with him. Not with a great deal of hope—the house has been unoccupied these many years.

'But see! I have here a letter from your father. It arrived this morning; I have come post haste to tell you of its contents. Lord Beaudon arrived in England only a few days ago, called at Packards, saw the letter and replied immediately. He writes that he no longer feels bound by the promise he made to your grandfather, and would like to see you again. He wonders if you would care to visit him in Hertfordshire. Is that not strange?'

Francesca agreed that it was strange, and asked him to make suitable arrangements. She would do as her father had asked. Mr Barton left happily prepared to do everything necessary to re-unite father and daughter, and Francesca was left with a curious feeling of apprehension and excitement. She decided to ask Madame Elisabeth to go with her to give her support.

So it was that, in the middle of October, Francesca found herself gazing curiously around her as her carriage bore her up the long, winding drive to Packards, the Beaudon family seat. Madame Elisabeth and Carter, her new maid, sat opposite her, two grooms were outside, and her new carriage was both comfortable and stylish. Her aunt's death was still very recent, so Francesca was dressed modishly, but quietly, in black. She was aware that it did not suit her.

'You are very quiet, Francesca,' said Madame Elisabeth. 'Are you weary from the journey?'

'It hasn't been such a long one, madame. But I have not been sleeping very well.' She gave her companion a little smile. 'Meeting my father after all these years is. . .a little nerve-racking.'

'You will have so much to say to one another.'

'You think so? We shall see.'

Francesca drew a deep breath as she stepped out of the carriage in front of a wide, shallow flight of steps. She was ridiculously nervous. The steps led to a handsome doorway and in front of the doorway stood a tall figure. Her heart gave a thump, and for a moment she thought she was seeing things. But then the figure moved towards them; she saw that this man was white-haired and used a stick. He was older than she had expected—he must have been well into his forties when she was born. And, though he had once been as handsome as that other, his face was pale and lined, and he was very thin.

'Francesca! My dear child!' He descended the steps, took her hand in his and surveyed her. 'I cannot begin to tell you how happy I am to see you again.'

For years, Francesca had resented the way in which her father had abandoned her, but the chill round her heart was melted a little by the sincerity of his voice and by the warmth of the expression in his eyes. She swallowed and said politely, 'And I am glad to see you, Papa. May

I present Madame de Romain to you? My friend and companion.'

Lord Beaudon took Madame Elisabeth's hand and held it to his lips. In perfect French he said, 'Madame de Romain, what can I say? It enchants me to meet you.'

Madame Elisabeth smiled and assured Lord Beaudon that he was too kind, and the little procession moved up the steps into the house. This took some time, for Lord Beaudon moved slowly, and the steps themselves were uneven.

'Packards is not what it once was, I am afraid, Francesca. I have lived so long abroad that it has fallen into some disrepair. But I have managed to engage some people from the village, and hope to have it put back into a better state before long.'

'You've been in the West Indies? I often wondered.'

'No—I've lived in Paris for the last few years. Ever since the monarchy was restored, in fact.'

Francesca wondered what her father's establishment in Paris might be—was he married? Did he have a family? It was not the sort of thing she felt she could ask. So she smiled and asked if she and Madame Elisabeth might refresh themselves after the journey. They were given into the care of a housekeeper who took them upstairs to two very handsome bedrooms.

A short while later, refreshed and tidy once again, Francesca collected Madame Elisabeth and went downstairs to seek out her father. She found him in the library, sitting in front of the fire, but he put down his book as soon as he saw them. There was a small silence, a silence which Francesca found difficult to break. At last she said, 'You must have been working your servants hard, Papa. Our rooms look beautiful.'

'I'm glad you like them,' he said simply. Then, as he

saw that Madame Elisabeth was standing by the door, he added, 'Come, Madame de Romain—you must join us.'

'You are very kind, Lord Beaudon but, if you don't mind, I should like to have some fresh air before it gets dark. And I am sure that you and your daughter have much to say to one another. Will you excuse me?'

Francesca did not want to be left alone so abruptly with a father she had not seen for nearly twenty years, but Madame Elisabeth smiled reassuringly and disappeared.

Lord Beaudon seemed to find the situation just as difficult. He started by making the usual kind enquiries about her journey, such as any host might of any guest. But his mind seemed to be elsewhere during these exchanges, and he seemed to be observing his daughter's movements and gestures rather than listening to her replies. His eyes seldom left her face.

After a while, however, they both felt easier in one another's company and he began to talk of old Sir John and the Shelwoods, about the district and people he had known there. He even made her smile at his description of Sir John's battles with the owners of Witham Court.

'And now they're all dead,' he said suddenly. 'You are all that is left of the Shelwoods. Sir John, Cassie and Verity—they were the last of the line. It was tragic that Verity should have been the first to go. She was younger than Cassie by a good ten years.'

'So much?'

'Cassie was the eldest child, then there were two boys who died in infancy, then lastly your mother. Everyone wanted me to marry Cassandra Shelwood, you know— and I very nearly did. It seemed a fair exchange.'

'A fair exchange?'

He smiled kindly at her. 'I expect your head is full of romantic notions about marrying for love—but in the world I was brought up in, we married for advantage, and sought pleasure elsewhere. And that is what I fully intended to do. You wouldn't have liked me in those days, Francesca—I was even more cynical than most of my contemporaries.

'I met Cassandra Shelwood just at the point when my fortunes were at their lowest, and I was beginning to feel that I ought to settle down, but was without the resources to do so. In my youth I had indulged in every folly known to man, and my reputation was such that no parents in their right mind would entrust a young girl to my care.'

'They told me you were a rake. Rake Beaudon, they called you.'

'I deserved the name. But then someone introduced me to Sir John Shelwood. Sir John didn't approve of me, but he was quite content to see me marry his elder daughter. Cassie was past thirty when I first got to know her, and he wanted to see her married. They both thought she was perfectly capable of keeping me in line.'

'You. . .you didn't ever pretend you loved her?'

'Oh, no. There was never any question of love between us. An establishment was what she wanted, and preferably a title. But then I met your mother. . . Against all the odds, I fell in love. I could never have married anyone else after that.'

Francesca kept very still. This was a very different tale from that of the heartless rake who seduced his fiancée's sister! She felt she was hearing the real story for the first time.

'Cassie was very bitter. Although I had not actually committed myself, she expected me to marry her. Nothing I said could pacify her. Sir John stormed and ranted. He was prepared to accept me as a husband for Cassie, but would not contemplate entrusting his precious little girl, his lovely Verity, to a rake and adventurer! But Verity. . .'

he gave a laugh '. . .Verity said we should have to run away.

'Up to that point I hadn't even realised that she was in love with me! I told her it was impossible, that I had nothing, and that her family would almost certainly cut her off without a penny if we eloped. She didn't care. I was twice her age and twice her weight—but she out-classed me and everyone else I knew for courage. Gaiety, too. She was always laughing.'

'I don't remember her very well, but I remember her laughter. And her bedroom—it was pretty.'

'Yes, she liked pretty things. I had a rundown estate in the West Indies. We ran off to Gretna, were married and went out to St Marthe. Then, soon after you were born, she became ill. . .and eventually she died. . .'

There was a pause while Francesca composed herself to ask the question that had tormented her for so many years. She carefully suppressed any feeling of resentment and her voice was neutral as she said, 'Why did you send me away, Papa?'

'I was no fit company for a child after I had lost your mother. What else could I have done? Your grandfather sent word to say he was prepared to give you a home—'

'But I already had a home with you on St Marthe!'

'It wasn't a home without your mother. I couldn't bear to stay there, but I didn't know where to go or what I wanted to do. I certainly didn't want to return to England. I thought I was doing the right thing for you by sending you to your grandfather. But it was a pity that they wouldn't keep Maddy.'

'Papa, what happened to Maddy? Did she go back to St Marthe?'

Lord Beaudon hesitated, then said, 'Yes. . .'

'I missed her so much. I'd like to think she is well and happy. Is she, do you know?'

'I think so, yes.' The was a touch of restraint in Lord Beaudon's voice, but before Francesca could pursue the question of Maddy he went on, 'My dear, I hope you will believe me when I say it simply didn't occur to me that Cassie would be so vindictive.'

'I. . .I think you were mistaken about her feelings for you, Papa. I think she really loved you. She kept your last letter to her, even. . .even showed it to me when she was dying.' Francesca's voice trembled as she remembered that dreadful scene. 'It's possible that you ruined her life, Papa.'

'Oh, no! I shan't allow you to say that. Cassandra Shelwood's life was spoiled before I ever met her and, if we had married, it would have been hell for both of us. I have no regrets on that score. The thing I do regret most bitterly was that I let Sir John impose the ban on writing to you. I should never have agreed to that.'

Francesca remained silent. What a great deal of misery could have been avoided if she had been able to communicate with him!

'And now, my dear? What are you going to do? And how can I help you? Do you wish to make your home with me—in Paris?'

'Thank you, but I would rather stay in England for the moment. I. . .I should like to marry. Like my aunt Cassandra, I should like to have an establishment of my own. But I recognise that this will not be easy, for, like her, I suffer from certain disadvantages.'

Her father looked sceptical, but asked, 'And they are?'

'I am plain, and I am past the age of your average debutante.'

'My dear girl, forgive me, but you are talking rubbish! How old are you? Twenty-one, twenty-two? And you are far from plain.'

'Please, Papa! You are trying to be kind, and I am

touched. But you really need not pretend. I am five-and-twenty and perfectly accustomed to the notion of being plain. But my newfound wealth—'

'No, no, no! I must stop you. You are so wrong, Francesca! I will allow that you have not learned to dress to advantage. Nor have you acquired the arts women customarily employ to make the most of their looks. But these are superficialities—easily changed. A well-trained maidservant would soon deal with them. You must not believe otherwise.'

'You are very kind,' Francesca said politely, but in a tone which dismissed the possibility. 'But to return to our original topic—the time-honoured way to find a husband is to become part of polite society—London society. And that is what I would like to do. Can you help me?'

'Of course I will help you all I can, but. . .I have been away from London for too long to help you directly. You would need a chaperon—'

'I thought Madame de Romain could act as my chaperon?'

'Very well. But in that case you would need a sponsor—someone who is familiar with London ways,' he said thoughtfully. 'She would need to be part of the great world, of course. A dowd won't do. And it would need to be someone who would teach you how to make the most of your appearance. Give you a little town polish. . . Let me sleep on it, Francesca. I'm sure I can find someone.'

Lord Beaudon slept on it to good effect. The next morning he suggested that his daughter might like to make the acquaintance of a lady who would make an ideal sponsor.

'I think she would do it. Her father-in-law was a good friend of mine. The Canfields are related to half of the top families in England, one way and another, but they are no longer as wealthy as they once were. Maria Canfield's husband was killed at Waterloo, leaving her with three children to bring up, and a limited income with which to do it. Her two sons are at Eton still, but she has a daughter she would like to bring out this next season. She might be pleased to share the expenses of a London season with me.'

'You, Papa? You are kind, but I have no intention of being a burden on you,' Francesca said firmly. 'I have more than enough to meet any expenses.'

'My dear—'

'No, Papa. I would be grateful for any help you can give me in finding my way through London society. But the expense must be mine.'

Lord Beaudon regarded her with a frown. He seemed prepared to argue, but she stared back at him with cool determination. Finally, his expression of displeasure gave way to one of great sadness, and he shrugged his shoulders, merely saying, 'Shall I arrange a meeting with Mrs Canfield?'

'Please do.'

Francesca liked the Canfields immediately. Lydia Canfield was a small, dark, lively girl with a great deal of self-confidence, and a wicked sense of humour. Her mother was still a beautiful woman, but she dressed quietly, and her manner was reserved. Lydia was her only daughter, and it was obvious that Mrs Canfield's dearest wish was to see her safely established. For this reason she was prepared to take on the task of introducing Francesca to Society in return for assistance with costs.

But she was taking no risks. Though her manners were exquisite, Mrs Canfield subjected Francesca to careful inspection, and some close questioning. Far from being offended by this, Francesca understood perfectly, and answered all enquiries as frankly as she could.

'I am somewhat older than most young ladies who seek to enter London Society, I know, and I am not looking for a debutante's "come-out", such as Miss Canfield will have. I will be open with you—my aim is to find a respectable man of moderate birth and fortune who is prepared to marry me. I do not seek a brilliant match, but it is important that the person I marry is honourable and considerate.'

'That may be more difficult than you think, Miss Beaudon! London is full nowadays of men who are rich, powerful, dashing, elegant—what you will. Honour and consideration for others do not play an important role in their ambitions.'

Francesca was slightly taken aback at hearing herself addressed as Miss Beaudon, but said nothing. It was her name, though only a month ago she would have denied it. She would soon have to make up her mind how she wished to be known in London.

'Mama, do you not think that Lord Carne would be the very man for Miss Beaudon?'

'Lydia—I had forgotten you were there. You should not be listening to this.' Mrs Canfield shook her head at her daughter, then turned to Francesca. 'I am sorry, Miss Beaudon. Lydia has been such a comfort to me since her father died, that I have perhaps indulged her too much. She is a dear girl, but. . .over-enthusiastic, shall we say? I am hoping she will acquire some discretion before next year.'

Francesca smiled and said she was quite certain of Miss Canfield's discretion.

'I wish I were half so confident,' said Mrs Canfield. 'She should not have interrupted us, however.'

'But, Mama—I had to! Lord Carne is a very kind man—you have said so a hundred times. And you have said more than once that he should think of finding a wife.'

'Lydia is right to reproach me, Miss Beaudon. Lord Carne was in my late husband's regiment, and we owe him a great deal. After Peter was killed, he helped us in all sorts of ways, and he still continues to take an interest in Lydia and my sons, even though he is a very busy man.'

'We haven't seen him in an age, Mama. Will he be in London for my début?'

'I hope so. He said he would see to it that he was.' Mrs Canfield turned to Francesca with an apologetic smile. 'You must forgive my importunate daughter, Miss Beaudon. Lord Carne is a great favourite of hers. But recently he has been away in Paris a great deal of the time.'

'I wonder if my father knows him.'

'He will know *of* him, of that I'm sure. But unless Lord Beaudon mixes in diplomatic circles, he might not know him personally. Lord Carne's work in Paris is chiefly concerned with the envoys of other nations.'

'He is a diplomat?'

'Not quite. The ambassador uses his skills occasionally, shall we say?'

The irrepressible Lydia broke in. 'He's a very important man, Miss Beaudon. But you would never guess it from his manner. Oh, he would be a perfect match for you! And he's quite old, too.'

A vision of a distinguished, grey-haired diplomat, a couple of years younger than her father, floated before Francesca's eyes. 'Well. . .' she said hesitantly.

Mrs Canfield shook her head at her daughter again. 'Please, do not listen to Lydia's nonsense, Miss Beaudon. Lord Carne is in the prime of life and a very rich man. He must be considered one of the most eligible *partis* in London.'

'In that case, he is quite beyond my touch,' said Francesca, smiling. 'I must restrain my ambition.'

'No! Oh, forgive me. I do not mean to be rude. It's just that he has been a target for matchmakers for so long, and no one has yet succeeded in engaging his attention.'

'And I am not attempting to be one of the season's sensations—I must leave that to Miss Canfield. But there's something I have to confess. . .'

Mrs Canfield looked anxious, and Francesca hastened to reassure her.

'It is not very serious, and I hope can be easily remedied. You see, Mrs Canfield, my life till now has been very restricted. I'm afraid to say that I have managed to reach the age of twenty-five without having had the smallest instruction on behaviour in polite society, and lessons in deportment and dancing. Your daughter probably has no need of such things, but I must find someone to help me.'

'My daughter has every need of lessons in behaviour, Miss Beaudon.'

'Mama!'

'And she is in dire need of a few accomplishments. I am sorry to say that Lydia has never had instruction in painting, nor any foreign language. A fact I much regret.'

'There I may be able to help you! I can soon find someone to teach your daughter. In fact, I was hoping you would accept my own dear former governess as a member of our household, and Madame de Romain would, I am sure, love to instruct Miss Canfield. We shall both have time to improve ourselves, I hope, before next May.'

'Excellent! I think we may deal with each other very well, Miss Beaudon. And Lydia will have the sort of come-out I have always wanted for her.'

'Is it settled, Mama?'

'Miss Beaudon?' asked Mrs Canfield with a smile.

Francesca nodded.

'Then, if you agree, we should put the business of finding a suitable house and servants in hand. These things take longer than one thinks. Your aunt's death is of such recent date that it would not be suitable for you to mix widely in Society. But perhaps we could plan one or two modest social events before Christmas? It would give both of you an opportunity to experience London before the Season starts. We shall be able to visit dressmakers and modistes, too.'

'A delightful prospect—I can hardly wait!'

Francesca reported this conversation to her father, not without some humour at Lydia's enthusiasm, and thanked him for arranging it.

'I might pay a visit to town myself, my dear. To see you in all your glory.'

'I leave glory to others, Papa. Talking of which—have you heard of a man called Carne? Lord Carne? Do you know him at all?'

'Carne? I haven't met him, but of course I've heard of him. Everyone talks of Carne. You'd sometimes think he was the only Englishman the French regime can bring themselves to trust. His role in the Allies' campaign against Bonaparte may be small, but it's vital.'

'Napoleon? But surely that campaign was won long since! At Waterloo!'

'This is the postwar campaign. The Bourbons are not at all popular in France. There are a good few perfectly honest Frenchmen who would be glad to see the back of King Louis and his hangers-on. Some of them would fetch Napoleon back from St Helena, if they could. It's mess, Francesca!'

'I had no idea. . . But what does Lord Carne do?'

'It's not so much what he does. . .the career diplomats do the real negotiating. But Carne seems to have the

confidence of the French as well as the Prussians and the
rest—and the English, of course. You might call him a
link. They *all* trust him, you see. Why are you so curious
about Carne?'

'Mrs Canfield was singing his praises. And Lydia said
he was the sort of man I was looking for.'

'Carne! My dear girl. . .my dear Francesca—he's a
Nonpareil! The present top of the tree—you'd have a
better chance of marrying the man in the moon! Every
female in London would give her eye teeth just to be
noticed by him! Dowagers, debutantes, heiresses—
beauties all of them. And he ignores them all. It would
be a triumph, of course. . . But, no. You must lower your
sights a little. I'm afraid Carne would never think of
asking you to marry him.'

Chapter Six

Francesca's life now changed radically. Her days were still as busy as ever, but she spent them, mostly in the company of the Canfields, in an orgy of shopping for silks, muslins and other delightful fripperies, looking at a selection of elegant houses in the best part of town with her father's man of business, and approving the staff which he had engaged for her.

Then she returned to Hertfordshire and spent hours learning from Mrs Canfield, or her father, the social skills that had been so lacking in her life. It was not easy. She had to learn in a few short weeks what most girls had time to absorb over years of normal family life and training, but the self-control she had learned in her earlier life now stood her in good stead. The results were astonishing. Fanny Shelwood, no one's child—shabby, dull, stiff and awkward in society—was replaced by Francesca, the accomplished daughter of Lord Beaudon.

This transformation did not happen overnight, nor was it without some difficulties. Francesca quickly found the company of the Canfields easy to enjoy—Lydia's vivacity and humour, her loving relationship with her mother and her willingness to regard the world, including Francesca, as her friend, warmed Francesca's lonely heart, and after a while she slowly began to join in the laughter and conversation which resounded through the rooms in Mrs Canfield's house.

But the relationship between father and daughter was a different matter. She still found it difficult to absolve him from all blame for her unhappy years at Shelwood. And, for his part, Lord Beaudon found it hard not to be disappointed in his newly discovered daughter. He looked in vain for a trace of his impulsive, laughing, loving wife in her. He was grieved by the formidable wall of reserve with which Francesca surrounded herself, and he regarded with some disapproval her lack of romance, her coolly cynical assessment of how to set about finding a husband.

But then he began to see that years of rejection lay behind Francesca's refusal to depend on others. He had not suspected, not for one moment, that Cassandra Shelwood would hate her sister's child, that Francesca would be the innocent victim of her desire for revenge, and was shocked to hear, chiefly through conversations with Madame Elisabeth, of Francesca's unhappiness and deprivation at Shelwood Manor after her grandfather's death. Though it helped him to understand her better, he blamed himself too bitterly to try to force her confidence, sadly accepting that the only contribution required of him before he returned to Paris was to find her a sponsor.

This he had done with great success. Maria Canfield proved to be the perfect choice. As well as learning to take her part in Society, Francesca was able to enjoy a loving, uncomplicated family life such as she had never known. And, as time went on, Lord Beaudon's patience was rewarded. He was delighted to hear her laughter with Lydia Canfield, to see her pleasure in mastering the intricacies of the dance steps he taught her, her enthusiasm for improving her skills in riding and driving.

Through these minor activities he began to see behind

his child's defences, to catch glimpses of the real Francesca. He saw that her self-possession was only surface deep, that Francesca was, in fact, deeply uncertain of herself. Time and time again he cursed the Shelwoods for their part in destroying Francesca's self-esteem, for his sister-in-law's efforts to break the child's spirit. Madame Elisabeth answered his questions about Francesca's life at Shelwood as discreetly as she could, but it was clear that her own sense of loyalty to her employers had been sadly stretched.

'Was there no one else for her to talk to, Madame Elisabeth? No friend of her own age?' he asked one day.

'No, *milord*. Miss Shelwood paid no visits herself in the neighbourhood, and received no one except her chaplain. Besides. . .'

'Well?'

Madame Elisabeth looked uncomfortable. 'The neighbours were as deceived about your daughter's birth as she was herself. It was unfortunate, I think, that Sir John, no doubt with the best of intentions, changed the child's name to Shelwood. It gave rise to rumours after he was dead, which the late Miss Shelwood did nothing to dispel.'

'From what I hear, she probably fostered them. Damn the Shelwoods! He was an arrogant old man and she was a cold-hearted witch. How on earth Verity came to be a member of such a family, I shall never know. And to think I abandoned her daughter to their untender mercies. . .'

'Sir John was very fond of Francesca, Lord Beaudon, but he was old. He died five years after you left her with him. It was a pity, perhaps, that he did not see fit to trust me with all the facts when he engaged me. Though I am not sure what I could have done. . .'

'He wouldn't have imagined it necessary. No one, no one at all, could have suspected the depths to which Cassie would descend. Not even I, who thought I knew her. It is a miracle that Francesca survived her treatment. With the exception of yourself, no friends at all, you say?'

'There was once talk of a man. . . He was not a desirable acquaintance, but I always thought Miss Shelwood treated Francesca with undue severity in the matter.'

'A man? From the village?'

'No,' said Madame Elisabeth reluctantly. 'He was staying at Witham Court.'

'Oh, my God! That, too?'

'Francesca always swore that he was harmless, that she had only met him once. I believe her. She was always a truthful child. But. . .'

'But what?'

'Something had made her deeply unhappy at that time. If it was not this "Freddie", then something else had caused her great distress. It took her a long time to recover her spirits. I do not know who or what it was.'

'That might explain her cool approach to marriage— I thought there must be something! Madame Elisabeth, Francesca owes you a great deal, and I too would like to tell you how grateful I am for the friendship you have shown her. I hope you will stay with her during this coming season. She needs a friend to support her.'

'Of course I will stay! But. . .may I say something?'

He nodded.

'It is you she needs, Lord Beaudon. It is your approval she seeks.'

Lord Beaudon shook his head. 'I wish I could believe that. But I fear she still blames me for what she sees as my neglect of her.'

'Perhaps a little at first,' said Madame Elisabeth, ever the diplomat. 'But no longer, I think. Her view of you has been changing, and now, for the first time in years, Francesca has someone of her own to love. Someone who belongs to her. I assure you, *milor'*, your presence at her début would give her all the assurance she needed.'

Lord Beaudon thought long and hard about this conversation. Madame Elisabeth seemed to think that he had some influence with Francesca, after all. And if it was indeed important to his daughter that he should be present during her Season in London, then he would be there, at whatever cost! He began to look at her with new eyes, to listen to her laughter with new pleasure and pride. And as he looked, he began to catch reminders of his beloved Verity in his daughter, though there was no physical resemblance.

Francesca was tall, but she moved with her mother's grace, and the timbre of her voice, which had tended to be stiff and cold, now had her mother's warmth and flexibility. Her laughter was slow to come in his presence, but when it came it was an exact echo of Verity's expression of delight with the world. Some of Francesca's former reserve was still there, but this merely gave her an air of distinction which entranced him.

'My dear child, you will be a sensation! You may have my looks, but you have all your mother's spirit! And when I hear your laughter, I can imagine she is in the room with me again.'

'*Your* looks, Papa? People always said I was like my aunt.'

'Like Cassie? Don't be absurd! They must have been blind. Look at yourself, Francesca!' He led her to the large mirror at the side of the fireplace. 'Look!'

They stood side by side in front of the mirror, a tall, distinguished man, dressed for the evening in sombre colours, and a slender girl in a dress of palest green *peau de soie*. As she stared at their reflection, Francesca could see that she was, in truth, the feminine counterpart of her father, that any resemblance to her aunt Cassandra had been pure chance. Aunt and niece had both been tall, but any possible likeness ended there.

Lord Beaudon was tall, too, and his daughter's bone structure and features, though more delicate, were those of her father. Her hair, no longer scraped back as her aunt had required, had proved to be thick and lustrous, and, dressed by an expert maid, it was coiled on top of her head in a loose knot. A few curls had been allowed to escape to frame her face, softening, but not disguising, the pure line of cheek and jaw. Her hair was still not the honey-blond she had so longed for, but its pale gilt brought out the sparkle in her gray-green eyes, and flattered the delicate colour in her cheeks.

'Papa!' Francesca turned in astonishment to her father. 'I hadn't realised. . . They all said. . .I thought. . . But I'm not an antidote, after all!'

Her father burst out laughing. 'No, you're not an antidote, my dear. Far from it.'

'And all because of a few fine feathers! How absurd! Aunt Cassandra should have tried them!'

Her father sobered instantly. 'Clothes and the attentions of a good maid enhance the picture—it would be stupid to say otherwise. But you are a delight to look at, Francesca, because something now shows in your face that your aunt never had, and never wanted. I'm not sure I can put a name to it. . .a generosity of spirit? A love of life? That's your mother's gift to you, and it's more valuable than anything the world can do for you. People call it charm.'

Francesca looked uncertainly in the mirror again. She was not sure what her father meant. 'I think you're being over-partial, Papa. But thank you.'

'Well, we'll see what your effect on Society will be. You and Lydia Canfield together will take the *ton* by storm, mark my words.'

'Now I know you're being absurd, Papa! Lydia, per-haps, but not I.'

Her father paused, then went on, 'And though I ought to be back in Paris, I have decided to spend the Season in London after all. I. . .I wish to be with you.'

'With me?' Francesca turned to look at him. What she saw in his face moved her as she had not been moved for a long time. Her own face lit up and she said joyfully, 'Oh Papa! Oh, thank you! I didn't dare to hope you would be there. Oh, this makes all the difference!' She threw her arms round her father and hugged him. It was the first spontaneous gesture she had ever made towards him.

Lord Beaudon cleared his throat and said, 'I must be there to see your triumph, Francesca. And so. . .this seems to be the moment to ask you how you intend to be known in London. You have had the name of Shelwood for so many years—and I expect you still think of yourself as one. But you *are* my daughter, my only child. . .' He stopped.

Francesca, faced with a decision she had been postpon-ing for too long, realised that it was in fact very simple. She smiled at her father and swept him a magnificent curtsey. 'The Honorable Francesca Beaudon presents her-self to you, my lord. She can't promise you a triumph. . .but she will do her best not to let the Beaudon name down.' She looked up at him, her expression, had she but known it, exactly like one of her mother's—an enchanting mixture of mischief and anxiety.

'My dearest girl!' Lord Beaudon took her hand and then pulled her to him and held her close.

The wall of reserve which lay between father and daughter had at last been breached by this decision of Lord Beaudon's to stay in London. It had only needed Madame Elisabeth's encouragement for him to do so, for he was already beginning to feel protective of this girl, this precious inheritance Verity had left him. But from the moment Francesca had spontaneously embraced her father, there was nothing and no one who could have prevented him from doing all he could to make her happy.

One result was that he showered her with presents—a fur tippet to keep her nose warm in the January frosts, an exquisitely painted fan to keep her cool in overheated rooms, books and flowers by the dozen to keep her amused and happy. When he produced a necklace of beautifully matched pearls on the evening of her first introduction to Society, she was overcome.

'Indeed, you are too good, Papa! You should not spend so much money on me!'

'My darling child, the pearls were your mother's. Who else should I give them to? And for the rest. . .' With a look of wry amusement, he went on, 'The Beaudon fortune falls short of the Sheldwood riches, I admit, but it is far from negligible. I am not the pauper your aunt undoubtedly led you to believe.'

'But. . .but they said you wanted to marry Aunt Cassandra for her money!'

'I did! And it's true that life would have been more comfortable if your mother had been given a dowry. But that is many years ago now. I have lived a fairly quiet life since your mother died, Francesca, and the Beaudon assets have increased. If you had permitted me, I would have been able to give you a London Season without the help of your Sheldwood inheritance.'

'Then I shall have no more qualms and will accept your gifts with great pleasure. You see, apart from Madame Elisabeth, no one has wanted to give me anything before.'

'Well, that situation will be remedied the minute you make your bow in Society! I prophesy that you will be showered with flowers and the rest.'

'Papa, you are a tease! I leave that sort of thing to Lydia. She is of an age to enjoy it.'

'You talk as if you were a hundred, Francesca. Twenty-five is not such a great age.'

'It is too old to look for romance. In any case I do not seek it, as you very well know.'

'My child, I was forty, and a rake past redemption, I thought, when I fell in love with your mother! But tell me. . .' Lord Beaudon paused. He was treading on delicate ground, he knew, but the temptation to gain Francesca's confidence was very strong. 'Have you never been in love?'

The response was too swift and too emphatic to be convincing. 'In love? No!'

'Not even with Freddie?'

Francesca's face was blank. 'Freddie who? Oh. . .that Freddie! Of course not. Who told you about him? Madame Elisabeth?'

'Don't blame her. I asked her if you had had any other friends, and she mentioned the episode with Freddie. She seemed to think your aunt had been unjust.'

'Well, I think so, too. I told Aunt Cassandra that I hadn't wanted to talk to him and, what's more, he hadn't spent more than five minutes in my company before she found us, but she wouldn't listen. She probably wanted to believe me wicked.'

Lord Beaudon gave an angry exclamation, but Francesca went on, 'You needn't worry, Papa. It's all in the past now; anyway, even at the time, I didn't care very much what she did—the worst part was having to listen to Mr Chizzle's sermons.'

'Why didn't you care?' He spoke so softly that Francesca found herself speaking without guarding her tongue.

'Nothing mattered very much at that time. . .'

'Were you so unhappy?'

'Yes.'

'Why, my child?'

Francesca walked away from him and stared out of the window. Her father held his breath as he watched her. If only she would confide in him!

When she finally spoke, her voice was flat and stiff, as if the words were being forced out against her will. 'I was not telling you the truth before. I did love someone once—or thought I did. A friend of Freddie's—also from Witham Court. Aunt Cassandra never knew about him. No one did.' Her mouth twisted in a bitter little smile. 'Except Freddie. Nothing of any consequence happened between us, but I thought my heart was broken. Silly, wasn't it? To break your heart over a rake—for that is what I discovered he was.'

She turned round and gave a wry smile, 'It's very rare to find a rake who really falls in love—Mama was luckier than she knew.'

Lord Beaudon smiled back at her. 'Your mama, Francesca, had her own anti-rake brand of magic. From the moment I saw her, my days of rakishness were over! And, in my opinion, you have the same magic—or could have, if you chose to exercise it. But. . .this man—how are you so sure that he was a rake?'

'He was staying at Witham Court. He gambled and drank. . .'

'He cannot be condemned on those grounds—they are not exactly unusual pursuits for a young man!'

'No, but. . . He made me believe he loved me. . .that I was beautiful. . .of value to him. Have you any idea what that meant to me, Papa? To be loved? After years of living without it?' Her father drew in his breath and shook his head in self-disgust. Francesca came over and put her hand on his arm. 'I understand now, Papa, really I do.

You mustn't blame yourself. You did what you thought was best.'

'But I should never have agreed to lose all contact with you, Francesca! However grieved I was at your mother's death, I should never have abandoned you so completely. I should have been there to help you when this man. . . What happened, my dear? Did you. . .did he seduce you?'

Francesca flushed and looked away. She said painfully, 'No, Papa. I was spared that folly. But not because. . .because I refused him. I was besotted enough to have given him anything he asked of me. No, I was saved from that last betrayal by his friend, who had come up the hill in search of him. We had to part before Freddie found us.'

'Freddie!'

'Yes, Freddie, Papa.'

Lord Beaudon decided to leave the question of Freddie for the moment. His daughter was talking of someone who had been much more important to her. 'This other man. . .?' He paused, hoping she would put a name to him. Francesca was silent, so he went on, 'You saw him just once?'

'No, we met the day after, too. But by then he had decided he. . .no longer wished to continue the acquaintance. Oh, he was plausible enough. He played the part of the romantic hero to perfection, pretending concern for me, telling me that he could offer me nothing, that he was poor, I was too young, that he had to go away. . . He was very plausible. He seemed as unhappy to leave me as I was to see him go.'

She stopped for a moment, then went on, 'And poor fool that I was, I was completely taken in. I believed him, Papa! I was unhappy, of course, but I was used to disappointment. And the thought that someone had loved me, really loved me, even if Fate and Fortune were against us, gave me courage to bear it. A latter-day Romeo and Juliet. . .I was really very young—and very naïve,' she added bitterly. There was a pause. 'Then a few days later I found out how he really regarded me. Freddie told me.'

She turned and lifted her head, gazing defiantly at her father. 'When my aunt found me with Freddie, I had just learned that my "Romeo" had boasted of his conquest to the others at Witham Court. I expect they repeated all the gossip to him, about my lack of fortune and. . .and all the rest. They had probably laughed about me. And after my "hero" had made his escape, Freddie came to see if he could be equally lucky.'

Lord Beaudon could restrain himself no longer. He swore comprehensively, then took his daughter in his arms and held her closely. 'My poor child! May Cassandra Shelwood rot in hell! Why the devil did I ever let her keep you?'

'She couldn't have stopped me falling in love, Papa. I did that all by myself.'

'But you wouldn't have been so vulnerable. Did you. . .did you never see him again? Not Freddie—the other man.'

'Oh, yes! As soon as he heard I had inherited the Shelwood fortune! He couldn't wait to come to see me again. I understand why—I knew he was poor, he had told me himself. But, on that occasion, even he couldn't bring himself to pretend he loved me. He talked of a "communion of spirit", was kind enough to offer me marriage as a form of protection from fortune hunters! He appeared to have no doubt that I would accept his offer. I was. . .humiliated by his assumption that I was stupid enough, still besotted enough to marry him!' Francesca's voice trembled. 'I am ashamed to remember what happened next, Papa.'

'Go on.'

'I have always tried to keep my feelings under control, whatever the provocation. I take pride in the fact.'

'I had noticed,' said Lord Beaudon drily.

'It was the only way to survive with Aunt Cassandra. But he. . .it was strange—it was as if I had no barrier to put up with him, whatever I felt. So when he tried to deceive me yet again. . .I tried to stay calm, to dismiss him with d-dignity, but. . . He stood there, Papa, so complacent, with such confidence! And I lost my temper. I can't remember exactly what I shouted at him, but I was unforgivably rude. I don't think he'll come back. I certainly never wish to see him again.'

'My child!'

'It's all right, Papa. It hurt at the time—it even hurt when he came back, though I knew him for what he was. I'm over it now. But that is why I want to marry someone. . .kind. Safe. Someone I can respect, but not anyone who will make me so stupidly fond. . .not ever again.'

But Francesca's wish never to see Marcus again was not to be granted. And once again, even after all the lessons on deportment and correct behaviour, she discovered that Marcus possessed the power to strip away her calm veneer, to reveal the tempestuously impulsive creature beneath. It was not a comfortable sensation.

On the few occasions she was left to her own devices, Francesca took to riding or driving in the woods and lanes round Packards. She was interested to visit the various farms on her father's estate and compare them with Shelwood. This was one interest that her father did not share with her, so, after an initial introduction to his agent, he left her to her own devices. Since she was always accompanied by her groom who knew the district well, Lord Beaudon's mind was easy.

On one such occasion she drove over to Brightwells', a large farm on the farther side of the estate, and was surprised to find that Samuel, her groom, was the younger son of the house. The family were delighted to welcome them both, especially as it was Mrs Brightwell's birthday.

When the time came for them to leave, Francesca could see that Sam's mother was disappointed not to have her son at the feast that was due to take place that afternoon, and insisted that Sam should stay. She could quite well find her way back to Packards without him. Thus it was that Francesca started off for home on her own—something she had been well used to at Shelwood.

The road was deserted, for the day was cold, though the sun was shining, but Francesca revelled in the fresh air, and the unexpected sense of freedom. In the enjoyment of her new life, she had not realised how much she missed some pleasanter aspects of her old one, when no one had been in the slightest concerned what she did. The road ran alongside the forest, and she slowed down to admire the huge trees that lined the way. She could see a small clearing off the road a little way ahead and decided to risk pulling in for a short while. But as she drew nearer, she saw that someone was there before her.

A carriage was standing on the edge of the forest, with a groom in livery in attendance. He had his hands too full to notice her—the horses were restless, and it was taking all his skill to keep them under control. Francesca was puzzled. What was such a splendid equipage—for the carriage was a handsome one, and the horses a magnificent pair of matched bays—doing here in this remote spot? She drew up behind the trunk of a large oak tree and watched.

Now she became aware that the noise of the groom's efforts to pacify his horses had been drowning other, more menacing, sounds. An altercation was taking place in the forest, and she could hear a girl's voice raised in distress. They were coming nearer, and Francesca heard the girl cry out.

'Leave me alone! You're hurting me! Leave me alone, I say!'

Francesca started up in her seat. What was happening?

Then a man's voice exclaimed in pain, 'Ouch! You little vixen! By God, I'll make you sorry for that, Charlotte!'

Two figures came out of the trees, a tall man, half-carrying, half-dragging a young girl towards the carriage. The girl was kicking and shouting, and the man's face was black with fury, his voice trembling with rage, but even so Francesca recognised him. With horror she realised that the abductor was Marcus! It couldn't be! Oh, dear heaven, surely it couldn't be! Even he could not stoop so low!

'Please don't make me go with you! I don't want to go with you!' The girl was sobbing with fear.

'Don't be such a fool, Charlotte! You know I'm stronger than you, so why keep on fighting me? It won't be half as bad as you fear!'

'It will, it will!'

'Oh get in, girl, and spare me these histrionics!' Francesca hardly knew Marcus's voice, it was so harsh. But what was she to do? She must do something to save the girl, but what? Marcus and the groom between them could easily foil any attempt at rescue.

But at the very moment when Francesca had decided to drive forward and risk the consequences, fate intervened. Some birds, which had been roosting in the trees above the carriage, suddenly flew up in a swirl of fluttering wings. One of the bays took strong exception to this and reared up, knocking the groom to the ground. Marcus let the girl go and ran to his servant's aid, ducking under dangerously flailing hooves to drag the man clear.

The girl, left unchecked for a moment, looked wildly round, obviously wondering which way to go.

'Quickly, girl! Here!' Francesca cried. With a sob of relief, the girl ran to the phaeton, and with Francesca's aid scrambled into it. Francesca gave her horses a crack of the whip and they careered off along the the high road, leaving Marcus still wrestling with his horses.

The girl sank back into the seat and burst into tears. Francesca glanced down sympathetically, but was too busy to comfort her. She was encouraging her horses to go faster than ever before, for she had seen the groom getting to his feet as they had passed the carriage. It was some miles to the next village and she must make every effort to get there before they were overtaken. It would not be long before the two men would set off after them, and her horses were no match for those bays! But as she whipped her horses to ever greater effort, her thoughts were in turmoil.

She had known that Marcus was a rogue and a fortune hunter, but this latest exploit was villainous! She could still hardly believe it. The girl was no more than sixteen— if that! But then, she reminded herself, she had been less than sixteen when he would have seduced her, a more willing victim than the girl beside her. Oh, Marcus! How could you, how could you be so wicked! And why am I foolish enough to be made so miserable by it?

She drove on, immersed in her own unhappy thoughts, till a small voice beside her said, 'I must thank you, ma'am.' The girl had recovered and was now looking at Francesca in grateful, if surprised, admiration. Francesca pulled herself together.

'I was glad to help you. . . Charlotte, is it? It was fortunate that I happened to be passing. But we are not clear yet, I am afraid. I shan't be happy till we have reached civilisation.'

Charlotte turned round and looked fearfully back down the road. 'I can't see anyone yet,' she said. 'Oh, please drive faster, ma'am! He mustn't catch me again.'

'I'll do my best. What is your name, child?'

There was a slight pause. 'Charlotte. . . Johnson, ma'am.'

Francesca glanced down. The dark blue eyes were guileless, but the girl was lying. She decided to let it pass for the moment. No doubt the child was shaken by her experience—her hands were trembling. What a fiend Marcus was! 'I think you may relax a little now, Charlotte,' she said calmly. 'My home is not far away. I shall take you there and then we shall decide what to do with you. Where do you live?'

Another pause. 'In London. I was waiting to take the stage coach to London. But he took all my money away from me and now I can't pay the fare.'

'You were travelling *stage* to London?' Francesca's hands tightened on the reins, but she spoke calmly. 'Forgive me, but I find that hard to credit. You mustn't be frightened of me, my dear. I shall help you all I can, but I must know the truth. Now tell me where you really live.'

'But if I do, you'll send me back! I can't go home again, I can't! I won't!' The childish voice rose in panic.

'Will your family not be worried about you?' asked Francesca.

'They won't care! They want to send me away, anyway.'

'Send you away? Where?'

'Back to the seminary. That's why I ran away.'

Francesca began to fear that this affair was not quite as simple as she had thought. Had Marcus encouraged the girl to run off with him? Or had she asked him to help her and then changed her mind when faced with the consequences—in which case Marcus might not be quite as villainous as she had thought? She shook her head impatiently—what was wrong with her? She was mad to try to find excuses for him! Whichever way it was, that scene in the forest had been very ugly. But. . .there was something odd about the affair. She drew up and turned to face her protégée.

'Charlotte—'

'Why have you stopped?' the girl cried, her voice shrill with fear. 'They'll catch up with us!' She reached over to take the reins, but Francesca took them firmly into her own hands again.

'Before we go on, I should like some answers, Charlotte. I would like to know your real name. I would like to know why you were on your way to London on a stage coach. And I would like to know the part played in all this by the man back there.'

'But he's coming! I can hear the carriage!'

'I have been thinking—he can't harm you while I am here. I know him, you see. He won't dare try to take you away again.'

'He will! Mama asked him. Oh, you don't *understand*—'

'You are quite right. I don't,' said Francesca, and watched with foreboding as the bays swept to a halt alongside the phaeton. Marcus handed the reins to the groom with a word, and strode over.

Chapter Seven

'Get down, Charlotte,' Marcus said grimly. 'Or, by God, I'll give you the hiding you deserve.'

Francesca rallied at these threatening words. 'One moment, sir!'

Marcus turned his attention to her. 'Good God!' he exclaimed. 'Francesca! Francesca Shelwood! What the *devil* are you doing here? And what the hell do you mean by racing off with this brat? Are you mad?'

Francesca did not allow herself to be intimidated by the outrage in his voice. She said coldly, 'I understand your annoyance at having your plans frustrated, sir, but surely your language is immoderate? Is this the manner in which you usually address ladies of your acquaintance?'

'Ladies of my acquaintance do not usually romp about the countryside unattended, interfering in matters which do not concern them. Now, I have better things to do than to bandy words with a madwoman, so if you will kindly remain quiet while Charlotte transfers to my carriage. . .'

Francesca was rapidly losing her temper. He was so dismissive, so coolly confident that she would do just what he asked! A madwoman indeed! She strove to keep calm as she said, 'I shall do nothing of the kind! The matter concerns me deeply, indeed it does. You forget that I know you for what you are, sir! How could I stand by and listen to this child's screams, watch while you dragged her to your carriage, and do nothing about it? I will most certainly not remain quiet. . .nor am I a madwoman!' In spite of herself, her voice rose on this last sentence.

She took a deep breath and went on, 'In fact, I fully intend to take her to my home and, after she has recovered from the fright she has suffered at your hands, I shall restore her to her family. You will now allow us to drive on, if you please.'

Marcus looked at her incredulously. He seemed ready to give her a blistering response, then his face suddenly softened and he burst out laughing. 'I see now what you think. . . Oh, Francesca, Francesca! Still leaping in where angels fear to tread? How refreshing to discover that the years have not changed you, after all!'

Puzzled by this extraordinary response, Francesca stared at him. The warmth of his tone, the memory evoked by these words transported her back to the day on the hill above Shelwood, to a world of sunshine and hope, of love and laughter. She gazed in fascination at Marcus, his face transformed into that of the young man of long ago. She began to smile in return, but then she remembered his betrayal so soon after, of her misery and disillusion in the weeks and years that followed, culminating in that cynical proposal at Shelwood.

'Nor have they changed you, Marcus,' she said bitterly. 'If I remember correctly, I was about this girl's age when I was unfortunate enough to meet you. But, unlike her, I had no one to protect me.'

He reddened, but said, 'Charlotte needs no protection from me.'

'That is a matter of opinion, sir! But I have no wish to waste any more time on a villain such as you. Make way, if you please!' And Francesca raised her whip.

Marcus leapt forward and took a firm hold of her wrist. They stared at one another in silence. Then he said softly, 'Charlotte, tell Miss Shelwood who you are.'

Charlotte had been gazing at them in wonderment, too interested in what was being said to attempt to run away. She said accusingly, 'She said her name was Beaudon!'

Francesca looked down at her. 'And you said your name was Johnson.' Charlotte was silenced.

'Are you going to tell Miss. . . Beaudon who you are, or shall I?'

Subdued, the girl said, 'Charlotte Chelford, ma'am.'

Marcus, still clasping Francesca's wrist, looked at her with scorn. 'Are you ashamed of your name, Charlotte Chelford? You have no reason to be. And, my girl, unless you mend your ways, it will be the Chelfords who won't wish to acknowledge *you*!' He turned his attention to Francesca. 'As for you, ma'am, I suggest you return to Packards—for that is where you must be staying if you're claiming the name of Beaudon—and be content that I don't pursue the matter further.' He dropped her wrist and turned back to Charlotte.

Francesca was bewildered. Marcus was certainly not behaving as a man discovered in a criminal act might be expected to behave. Had she indeed made a terrible mistake?

She looked at Charlotte, who suddenly clasped her hands together and exclaimed, 'Please, Uncle Marcus, *please* don't take me back to the seminary.' The expression in her eyes would have melted a heart of stone, but Francesca was too shocked to notice.

'*Uncle*!' she exclaimed. '*Uncle* Marcus?'

'Yes, madam busybody, I have the misfortune to be Charlotte's uncle.'

'Her uncle! Oh, heavens, I thought. . .'

'You thought. . .?'

'I was under the impression that you were. . .' Francesca paused, then she said miserably, 'It looked as if you were abducting her.'

'I thought as much.' He looked at her with a wry smile. 'You must tell me some time, Francesca, what I did to give you such a very low opinion of my character. Nine years is a long time to carry such a grudge, wouldn't you say?'

Francesca bit her lip and said nothing.

Marcus sighed, then looked at Charlotte, who was regarding them both with fascination. He went on, 'I would like to pursue the matter with you, but this isn't the time. My first concern must be to deliver Charlotte to her long-suffering mother—'

'To Mama? Not back to the seminary?'

'I shall see if I can persuade your mama to keep you at home—perhaps with yet another governess. You must promise to treat this one better than the others.'

'I can really go home again to stay? You're not sending me back to the seminary?'

'A ladies' seminary, however famous, is obviously even less able to deal with you than your family, you wretched child,' said Marcus severely. Then he spoilt the effect by adding, 'And I am sure your mama doesn't wish you to be unhappy. But you must promise me that there will be no more escapades, Carrie. Your mother has had enough to bear.' He waited until Charlotte nodded, and then he smiled. 'Now, get into the carriage and I'll take you home. Er. . .are you going to take your leave of Miss Beaudon?'

Charlotte took Francesca's hand and said earnestly, 'I do thank you, Miss Beaudon. Even though my uncle laughed at you, I think you were a heroine!'

Marcus laughed again. 'Things that might have been better put! Now get into the carriage, you minx!' Charlotte got down and went quietly enough across to her uncle's carriage. Marcus looked up at Francesca. 'Will you give me your hand, Francesca?' Almost without volition she extended her hand. He took it and held it while he went on, 'I apologise for my harsh words. You thought something was wrong, and you, being you, had to do something about it. Will you forgive me?'

She nodded, unable to say a word. He took a breath, hesitated, then said, 'Can't we be friends, Francesca? You are at Packards, I take it? May I call on you there?'

Francesca snatched her hand away. 'No!' she said violently. His face darkened, and she strove to speak more calmly. 'That is to say. . .I think it is better if we do not meet again. I have nothing to say to you. I may have been mistaken on this occasion, but my opinion of you remains the same.'

'This is ridiculous!'

'Good day, sir.'

He took hold of her wrist again, so tightly that it hurt. 'Take care you do not become like your aunt, Miss Beaudon! This obstinate prejudice against me is absurd, and when you are accepted into society you will discover just how absurd it is!'

'I do not expect to mix in the same circles as you, sir. Lady Forrest need expect no competition from me!'

He looked at her inscrutably, then he released her and shrugged his shoulders. He moved towards his carriage, saying, 'I do not intend to argue with you, but I must insist on one thing. We will go with you to the edge of the forest. You are not yet as familiar with this area as I am, and I assure you it is unwise for you to travel here alone. You should engage someone to accompany you if you intend to drive out much.'

Francesca did not bother to tell him that she already had a groom, nor that her father had already given her the same warning. She was desperate to escape from him. His presence was working the same old magic and she wanted none of it. She said curtly, 'Thank you. Good day, sir,' and whipped up her horses. The carriage followed her till they came to the village near Packards, then it swept past and went on its way.

Francesca found it impossible to put this encounter with Marcus out of her mind in the weeks that followed. Furthering her acquaintance with Marcus had never seemed so desirable, nor so dangerous. One moment she congratulated herself on having turned him away, and the next found her passionately regretting having done so.

For some time she had been ashamed of her extraordinary outburst at their last meeting at Shelwood. It had been unworthy of her. Hurt and angry herself, she had been unpardonably rude, had insulted and enraged him. And in the forest she had given him further reason to be angry with her. But he had seemed willing to overlook it all, to be prepared to begin again, had offered her friendship. . . Had she misjudged him?

Then Francesca would scornfully revile herself for being so spineless. Of course she hadn't! It was all perfectly simple. She had a fortune. Marcus had not. It wasn't at all difficult to see why he had been willing to overlook her mistake, had smiled instead of frowning, had offered her friendship instead of expressing justifiable anger at her interference. Not at all difficult. He was still hoping to marry the Shelwood fortune.

But, under any circumstances, friendship was the last thing she wanted from him. She could hate him for what he had done. She could, if the circumstances had been different, have loved him with all her heart. But friendship? Never! She must obliterate the little scene in the forest from her mind, and forget him. And sometimes, in the bustle of preparations for her introduction to the great world, she even occasionally succeeded.

If Francesca's introduction to Society was not quite as sensational as her fond father had prophesied, it was certainly very satisfactory. Mrs Canfield, true to her word, arranged several small gatherings during the early months of the year to give the girls some experience, and Society's approval of Miss Beaudon and Miss Canfield was immediate. Some less charitable souls wondered aloud if Mrs Canfield had offered to sponsor tall, blonde, elegant Miss Beaudon because she knew what an effective contrast the girl provided for her own lively, dark-haired daughter, but Mrs Canfield was generally so respected that these remarks were ignored.

They were invited everywhere. Mrs Canfield had the entrée to even the highest circles, and, in addition, Society was highly intrigued that Richard Beaudon should reappear after so many years with a daughter in whom he clearly took so much pride. London's hostesses were eager to learn all they could about the legendary Rake Beaudon, and Mrs Canfield was subjected to many an inquisition. She was her usual discreet self, merely saying enough to establish that Lord Beaudon was a reformed character, interested only in seeing his daughter take her rightful place in society.

'I never thought I should live to see Rake Beaudon doing the pretty at an occasion like this,' said an elderly dowager to Mrs Canfield one evening at Almack's. 'He would have died of boredom in the old days. And how he persuaded the patronesses to receive him, I cannot imagine.'

'Come, Lady Clayton, you should show more charity,' said Mrs Canfield with a teasing smile. 'I can answer for the fact that he has reformed. It must be a good twenty-five years since Lord Beaudon scandalised London society.'

'And what has he be doing since then, I'd like to know? I suppose the chit really is his daughter?'

'Most certainly she is, ma'am!'

'Well, there's no need to get on your high horse. You're too young to remember Rake Beaudon in his prime. There's nothing he wouldn't have dared. But I suppose you wouldn't be sponsoring the girl if there was anything amiss—and she is remarkably like him. Where's her mother? And who was she?'

'Lady Beaudon died some time ago, but she was a Shelwood before she married.'

'Shelwood? I've not heard of them.'

'They're quite a respectable Buckinghamshire family, but they always lived very quietly. I don't think they ever came to London.'

'Hmm. I expect the Shelwood girl was an heiress— Rake Beaudon wouldn't have married her otherwise.'

'On the contrary, I understand that Sir John Shelwood cut his daughter off without a penny when she married Lord Beaudon. He approved of his son-in-law even less than you.'

'Oh, I didn't disapprove of Beaudon, my dear. Like all the rest of us, I fell in love with him, but my mother had more sense than to let him near me. And it looks as if he hasn't lost the art of pleasing even after all these years— just look at Sally Jersey, she's positively flirting with him! He is still very handsome, of course. So is the girl—pity the Beaudon fortune is so small.'

Mrs Canfield smiled but did not contradict Lady Clayton. The world would eventually learn that Francesca's fortune was not limited to what her father could give her, but meanwhile she should be given time to find the man of consideration and honour she desired to marry. Once the extent of her fortune was known, she would be pursued by other, less noble characters.

This conversation was one of many similar ones, but since Mrs Canfield kept her counsel, Francesca and Lydia were free to enjoy the popularity which their own charm brought them, and susceptible gentlemen in Society were soon debating which lady was more worthy of their devotion—the divinely fair Miss Beaudon or the vivaciously dark Miss Canfield.

They were invited everywhere and met everyone of note. Everyone, that is, except Lord Carne. He was apparently away, for Society saw nothing of him, and it was rumoured that he was employed on some Foreign Office business in France. Lydia and Mrs Canfield were disappointed, but the name meant nothing to Francesca and, though she sympathised with Lydia, she was personally unaffected by his absence.

'I know you wish me to meet this paragon, Lydia, but surely, if he is as eligible as you say, he would regard me with indifference?'

'But Lord Carne is not like that at all, Francesca! He is the kindest of men—is he not, Mama? And whatever Mama may say, I think you would be an ideal match for him. Oh, why doesn't he come? I do so wish he were here! He promised to dance with me at my début!'

'I'm sure he will keep his promise to you, Lydia,' said Mrs Canfield with a sympathetic smile. 'But you must try for a little patience, my dear—the season has hardly started yet. And it does not become you to be gazing round every five minutes, as you were last night at Lady Carteret's, to see if Lord Carne is present.'

'No, Mama.'

Francesca took this conversation to heart, for she too had been guilty of such behaviour, though it had not been to seek out Lord Carne, nor had it been with Lydia's eager anticipation. Wherever she went, she was unable to

prevent her eye from wandering through the crowds, looking in apprehension for a tall lithe figure, to stop herself
from listening for the deep, warm tones of the man she
had dismissed so summarily from her life. Marcus.

She smiled ruefully. Once, she remembered, she had
passionately wished to be powerful, rich and beautiful
enough to give him a set-down. Well, she was now rich
enough, and though she would never consider herself
beautiful, others admired her. But did she have the power?
Could she give Marcus the set-down he deserved? She
doubted it. She was not certain how to deal with him at
all when they met in Society—as they surely would. But
her training in difficult social situations was not put to
the test. To her great relief, she told herself, she never
saw him, however diligently she watched and listened.

Apart from this, Francesca found that she was enjoying
London life, though after a while she began to wonder
whether she would ever find the husband she sought. Mrs
Canfield saw to it that she was introduced to a number
of respectable gentlemen, and one or two of them seemed
more than ready to regard Miss Beaudon as a future wife.

But though Francesca acknowledged their worth, she
found it impossible to take any of them seriously. Mr
Caughton was both respectable and reasonably rich, but
the poor man was very dull! Lord Banford was more
amusing, but he brayed like a horse—she couldn't possibly live with that. Sir Jeremy Sharp was handsome
enough if you liked blond men, but she found his uncritical
admiration definitely cloying. Though she had no intention of falling in love again, the prospect of living in
intimacy with anyone she had met so far appalled her—
she was apparently more difficult to please than she had
thought!

Meanwhile, the approval of the world around her was
balm after all the years spent as an outcast, and it was

very pleasant to go to balls and routs, to walk, drive and ride in the Park, to visit the shops whenever she wished, and, above all, to be accepted for her own sake. So she decided to put aside the question of her future, and enjoy for the moment all that life in London had to offer.

This state of affairs was not to last much longer. One evening at the theatre with her father, Francesca became aware that she was being stared at by a lady and gentleman a short distance away, and when she turned to see who it was she recognised Lady Forrest and Freddie. Though it was a shock, Francesca looked away again as indifferently as she could. But apparently it was not enough to put them off.

'Forgive me, but have we not met before?' Lady Forrest had come over, followed by a reluctant Freddie. She was smiling, but her eyes were appraising Francesca, as if she could not quite believe what she saw. Then her look shifted to Lord Beaudon and the smile became more practised. This, her admiring gaze told him, was someone worthy of her attention. Lord Beaudon remained unaffected. He had taken in Lady Forrest's opulent charms and Freddie's slightly seedy air, and lost no time in removing his daughter from both.

'I rather think not,' he said coldly, and, taking Francesca's arm, led her firmly away. Francesca gasped at this snub, but was quite content to go with him.

'You didn't know them, did you?' he asked after they were safely back in their box. 'They're certainly not the sort you ought to know. Raffish, both of them.'

'We were never introduced, if that's what you mean, Papa,' said Francesca. 'I. . .have come across them when they visited Witham Court.' He gave her a sharp look, and she nodded. 'The gentleman was Freddie. Lady Forrest I met more recently when she was on her way there. I have no desire to know either of them any better. Thank you for rescuing me—I had no idea you could be so. . .so. . .'

'Ruthless? Oh, I know all the ways of dealing with undesirables, my dear. I was one of them myself in the old days! But if I'd known who that fellow was, I might have been considerably less courteous.'

'*Courteous*? Is that what you call it?' asked Francesca with a laugh that caused her father to smile in return. 'Then I'm glad you didn't know who he was. And I'd far rather forget all about both of them.' And in her enjoyment of the play afterwards, she did indeed forget the encounter.

But the damage had been done. Charlie Witham was told of the incident when Lady Forrest next saw him.

'I could *hardly* believe it, Charlie. It was Lord Beaudon with her—I asked Freddie. What a *rude* man he is, for all he's so handsome! But it *must* be Fanny Shelwood, it *must*. What a *transformation*!'

'A little beauty, give you my word,' said Freddie. 'Good mind to take up where I left off, money or no money.' This enthusiasm did not please Lady Forrest.

'She's still as skinny as a rake, of course,' she said coldly. 'And basically as plain as ever, I suppose. But her clothes! Where did she get the means to dress herself at Fanchon? And the pearls she was wearing were worth a small *fortune*. I am *dying* to know, Charlie. Didn't you say that Lord Beaudon was her father? Is he really foisting his love-child on the *ton*?'

'He's capable of it. But it don't sound like his sort of caper. I wonder whether we've been wrong all these years. . .I'll see what I can find out, Charmian. I'll put Withers on to it right away.'

Withers worked to good effect, and such details as were not available through official documents he ferreted out elsewhere. Charlie Witham could hardly wait to spread the news. An heiress loose in London, with such a colour-ful story behind the scenes! A long-lost father, a vengeful aunt, poverty, deprivation and the sudden acquisition of enormous wealth. . . In no time, the whole of London was humming with the details of Francesca Beaudon's past history. And, what was more to the point for some of them, her present riches.

Poor Francesca became an object of universal sym-pathy, curiosity, and ambition, inundated with invitations on every side, pursued relentlessly by every gazetted for-tune-hunter in London. Her father was furious, and he, Mrs Canfield, Lydia and a small circle of true friends rallied round to protect her. But their powers were limited. Short of remaining indoors, there was no way Francesca could avoid the unwelcome attentions of gentlemen who had ignored her when they thought that the Beaudon for-tune was all she could look forward to.

The self-control she had learned as a child helped her to remain calm, in public at least, but her simple pleasure in London life was now at an end. It was almost the last straw when Marcus reappeared in London, and she found that all her brave resolutions had not diminished in the slightest her confusion of feelings about him. And it seemed inevitable that their meeting should be just as unexpected, every bit as unconventional as their former encounters.

Francesca had had enough! It was too bad! Evenings that had been so delightful just a few weeks before were turn-ing into nightmares. She had looked forward to visiting Carlton House ever since Mrs Canfield had described its splendours. Besides, whatever they said about the Prince Regent, he was the leader of London Society, and it was an honour to be invited to one of his balls. But she had been sadly disappointed. The atmosphere was stifling in the crowded rooms, and though the furnishings were every bit as magnificent as Mrs Canfield had said, Francesca found them slightly overdone.

The Prince himself was not at all as she had imagined him—handsome, witty, and regal. Instead she was faced with a corpulent gentleman, whose clothes were too tight and too elaborate, and who was so heavily complimentary to her that she blushed in spite of her famous cool reserve. He insisted on holding her hand for far too long, and then introduced her to a tall, saturnine gentleman who was standing near by, whose cold eyes were appraising her in a manner which caused her to feel rather like a horse complete with a price tag stuck to her forehead.

'Lord Coker has been asking who the beautiful young lady in the blue dress is, Miss Beaudon. He's a great friend of mine so—may I tell him?' the Prince asked with a roguish look.

'Of course, sir. I am honoured,' was Francesca's dutiful reply.

'Miss. . .Beaudon? Charmed t'meet you,' drawled Lord Coker with marked lack of interest. There was a slight pause then, somewhat puzzled, Francesca curtsied and moved away. She joined Mrs Canfield and Lydia, and together they went through to the ballroom.

'You look serious, Francesca. Was the Prince Regent not as you imagined?'

'It is always strange to meet someone so famous in the flesh, ma'am,' was Francesca's diplomatic reply. 'But tell me about Lord. . .Coker, was it?'

Mrs Canfield looked disapproving. 'He is a great friend of the Prince, of course. But I would regard him as an undesirable acquaintance for my daughter. He can be charming. . .'

'I did not find him so.'

'No, he did not set himself to please you, did he?'

Francesca laughed. 'Why on earth should he?'

'It is said he is in search of a wife. And Lord Coker's wives are always rich.'

'Mrs Canfield! How many has the poor man had?'

'Save your sympathy for the two first Lady Cokers. Neither of them was a happy woman. Francesca, I am very content that Lord Coker appeared to ignore you. Do not seek his acquaintance. He is a dangerous man to cross. The Prince Regent is capricious, but at the moment Lord Coker is undoubtedly enjoying his favour, and it gives him a great deal of undeserved power.'

Francesca could hardly believe that her friend, normally so moderate, so restrained in her judgements, could be so harsh. But she soon forgot Lord Coker in her enjoyment of the conversation and dancing that followed. Later on, however, when she was sitting quietly, half-hidden in one of the many alcoves, his indifference to her was accounted for.

Lord Coker and a companion came strolling through the room, observing the dancers. They did not notice Francesca behind them, and through some trick of the acoustics in the room their conversation was perfectly audible to her. Wine had perhaps made them less cautious than they might have been.

'Why on earth you've dragged me away from the best run of luck I've had in weeks, just to watch all this cavorting, I cannot imagine, Coker! What the devil are you at?'

'I need to find the demned Shelwood filly. I've been looking for her all night, but I haven't seen a trace! How can I fix my confounded interest with her if I don't even meet her?'

'Of course you've met her! Prinny introduced you not an hour ago. Damned civil of him, if you ask me.'

'When? Which one was she?'

'The tall blonde girl in blue.'

'That's Beaudon's daughter.'

'She may be Beaudon's daughter, but she's the Shelwood heiress all the same. Shelwood was her grandfather.'

'The devil he was? So she is an heiress, after all. Damn it! I was looking for someone called Shelwood, and when the Prince introduced us, I thought he was amusing himself at my expense with the Beaudon filly. You know his way. Confound it! I may have made a slight error there.'

The other chuckled. 'You were more than a touch uncivil to the lady. You'll have to exercise all your famed address to reinstate yourself when you do find her.'

'You think I can't?'

'Miss Beaudon doesn't look like your usual empty-headed debutante. You might find it harder than you think.'

'A wager, Felton?'

'On what? That you'll marry her?'

'I intend to do so, of course. But at the moment, my aim is to get her to dance with me.'

'Oh, I shan't bet on that. All you'd have to do is to ask Prinny to present you to her as a partner—and he'd do it for you, too! You're very much in favour at the moment.'

'I won't ask him to present me, and I shall dance with the girl before the supper interval. Will you take me on?'

'That's only half an hour away. . . You won't do it, Coker! Five guineas that you can't.'

'Fifteen minutes would be enough, but we will leave it at the half-hour. And we'll make it ten guineas.'

'You won't do it, y'know. Miss Beaudon is well known to be difficult to please, and you started off very badly.'

'I'll do it with ease, and enjoy it. The ten guineas are as good as mine. But first we must find the chit. Getting her away from Maria Canfield will be the hardest part. You seem to know something about the heiress, Felton. Tell me about her. . .'

Chapter Eight

They wandered away and Francesca was left to fume alone in her alcove. To be the subject of such a conversation, to hear men making a wager on her future behaviour disgusted her, and she spent some minutes recovering her temper. Her first impulse was to find Mrs Canfield and then leave Carlton House, but cooler reflection persuaded her that this was impossible. What reason could she possibly give for such discourtesy to her royal host? That one of his closest friends had insulted her? Impossible!

Besides, it was said that Lord Carne was coming to Carlton House on his return from Paris and Lydia had been in high spirits all day because of it. She could not deprive the girl of her chance to meet her hero again. No, flight was not possible, so she must simply find Mrs Canfield and stay close to her for the rest of the evening—that might be protection enough.

Unfortunately, her plan was foiled from the outset. She saw Mrs Canfield at the far end of the room and got up to join her. But she had gone little more than a few paces when she was confronted with the very man she hoped to avoid.

'Miss Beaudon!'

Francesca looked coldly at him and nodded.

He smiled. 'I have looked for you everywhere. I wish to explain. . .'

'You must excuse me, Lord Coker. I am on my way to join Mrs Canfield.' Francesca made to walk past him.

'Then I will accompany you. It is hardly fitting that such an exquisitely elegant young lady should walk unprotected through these crowds.' He put up his glass and surveyed the scene with a look of contempt. 'One wonders how some of them got past the flunkeys.'

'It really isn't necessary. . .'

Taking Francesca firmly by the arm, he said, 'Come, Miss Beaudon. I see your friend only a few yards away.'

As they threaded their way through the throng, Lord Coker said, 'You are right, of course. Explanations are tedious. We will dispense with them. Ah, Mrs Canfield! I have your lovely protégée here, but I am in something of a dilemma.'

'A dilemma, Lord Coker?'

'You see, the Prince Regent, in his infinite wisdom and kindness, has asked me to look after one of your charges during the supper interval. But I hardly dare take Miss Beaudon away from you without first asking your permission. She is too modest to agree without it.'

'I assure you, Lord Coker—'

Ignoring Francesca's protest, he went on, smiling all the while with great charm at Mrs Canfield, 'Or should I offer to look after your lovely daughter, instead? The Prince would not wish me to ignore his orders entirely, you see.' He raised one eyebrow.

'But I. . . I. . . It is too much honour, Lord Coker. The Prince is very kind, but—'

'He likes his own way, too.' Lord Coker's smile grew a little steelier. Mrs Canfield threw a desperate look at Francesca as he went on, ''Pon my soul, ma'am, the choice is a difficult one. A golden goddess like Miss Beaudon here, or. . .' he turned to Lydia, who was standing by her mother looking awed at being addressed by the great Lord Coker '. . .Miss Canfield—a bewitching naiad in green. And so delightfully young.'

Lydia blushed and looked down, but she was smiling at his flattery.

Mrs Canfield stiffened and Francesca said hastily, 'I believe Lydia is already engaged for the supper interval, sir.' She looked at Lord Coker with delicate disbelief. 'But if the Prince has commanded—'

'I assure you on my honour he has, Miss Beaudon.' He looked at her, daring her to challenge his words. 'Do you wish me to take you to him?'

Francesca gave him a level look. 'I would not put you to so much trouble. I am sure the Prince is a loyal friend.'

'Then shall we go?' He offered her his arm; after a moment's hesitation, she curtsied to Mrs Canfield and took it.

Francesca was thinking hard as she walked away. She found it galling that Lord Coker was about to win his wager so easily. The minute they joined the throng on the ballroom floor he would be ten guineas the richer, and she would have helped him to it. Was there a way in which she could prevent his leading her on to that floor in the next half hour? She would certainly try.

'But, sir,' she said, smiling as charmingly as she could, 'did you not say that the Prince wanted you to take me to supper?'

He stopped and looked down at her. 'I did.'

'Then should we not go to the supper room rather than the ballroom?'

'I think not,' he said calmly. 'I am very self-indulgent, Miss Beaudon. I cannot deny myself the pleasure of a dance with you—indeed, a waltz with you. Come.' He would have walked on with her, but she removed her arm and stood where she was.

'Please, Lord Coker,' she said with another delightful smile. 'Do not indulge yourself at my expense. I am an indifferent dancer, but I love to talk—you have been described to me as one of the best conversationalists in London. And in addition, I am really very thirsty.' She looked at him under lowered lashes in what she hoped was a beguiling manner.

His thin lips twisted in a complacent smile at her pleading tones and he took firm hold of her arm. 'My dear,' he said, 'we shall talk all you wish. We have much to say to one another, I am sure.'

'Then—'

'But we shall dance first.'

Francesca felt her control slipping. 'I don't wish to dance, sir!'

His grip on her arm was cruelly tight. 'Nonsense, of course you do.' When she still pulled against his grip, he said softly, 'I can't believe you wish to make a scene here, my dear. Think what damage it would do you and your friends. . .' and without waiting any longer, he swept her into the circling throng.

Francesca endured, rather than enjoyed, the dance that followed. Lord Coker was expert enough, but, without holding her too obviously close, his grip on her waist, and in the twists and turns of the waltz, was both intimate and cruel. Nor did he release her afterwards. Before she realised it, he was leading her out of the ballroom.

'Lord Coker! Stop! Where are we going?' she cried, as they went through long doors into an apparently empty passage.

'You wished for refreshment? This is a less crowded route to the supper room. We shan't lose ourselves— I know Carlton House like the back of my hand.'

Suspicious, but unable to argue, Francesca allowed him to lead her down the passage. It was lined with furniture and *objects d'art*, but she was not allowed to linger.

They went through a hall, then along another passage and finally arrived at an entrance guarded by two flunkeys. At a nod from Lord Coker, they opened the doors and Francesca was led into one of the loveliest rooms she had ever seen. Furnished in blue velvet with touches of gold, the room was dominated by a magnificent chandelier. Forgetting her suspicions, she walked into the room, gazing at the pictures and ornaments, all in exquisite taste, which filled it. She was speechless with admiration.

'I see you like it.' Lord Coker had come up behind her and put his hands on her shoulders. Startled, she moved away and turned to face him.

'Thank you for showing me such a beautiful room, sir. Now, if you please, I should like to join the others in the supper room.'

'In a while,' he said.

'Now!'

'Come, Miss Beaudon. You surely don't imagine that I would take all this trouble to be alone with you just to show you a room! You expressed a very flattering wish for my. . .conversation. I thought we should manage better if we were private.' He took her hand and kissed it. 'The admiration you demonstrated for me before we danced has encouraged me to hope for even more.' He smiled with arrogant confidence.

Francesca moved towards the entrance. The doors were shut. Refusing to panic, she said coldly, 'Lord Coker, I think you mistake me. I am not in the habit of listening to anyone who tries to coerce me. I insist that these doors are opened immediately!'

'Admirably said! Well, I will let you go—'

With a sigh of relief, Francesca put her hand on the

ornate handle of the door. She was pulled back ungently and held in his arms.

'After you have heard me out.'

'Let me go!' she cried, struggling in vain to free herself. 'You must be mad, sir!'

'Not mad—merely in love.'

If Francesca had not been so frightened and angry, she would have laughed at the lack of any real feeling in these words. He could not have made his motive plainer. But the situation was none the less serious. Fear of this man, fear of the scandal should she be discovered in this private room with him, anger at his arrogance and conceit—all were fighting for supremacy. Anger won. She leaned back as far as she could and said coldly, 'If you do not release me this instant, Lord Coker, the world shall know you for the villain you are. I am not entirely without protectors.'

'My intentions are honorable, Miss Beaudon. I wish to marry you. And, if you were to spread tales about me, then you overestimate your influence in Society. The world saw you laughing and flirting with me in the ballroom. You came willingly enough. No, my dear. Telling the world would not harm me, and it would ruin you. Come, you shall listen to what I have to say—how much I admire you, and how ardently I wish you to be my wife. We shall forget your harsh words.' He pulled her head towards him and kissed her.

Outraged, she snatched up an ornament from the console table nearby and hit him with it. The vase shattered and he staggered with the blow. For a moment she was free. She fled to the far corner of the room, praying that the door she had seen there was not locked. It opened at her touch and she raced through and locked it from the other side, just as Lord Coker, snarling with rage, reached it. He was cursing her comprehensively and threatening her with ruin and destruction.

Francesca did not wait to hear. She fled through a second door and a third, forced herself to walk swiftly but calmly down a staircase thronged with people. But though their presence offered some protection, she doubted she could control the trembling in her limbs much longer. She must seek out some quiet place where she could recover. The doors at the far end of the conservatory opened into the garden, and Francesca made for these, desperate for fresh air and solitude. She snatched a glance behind her.

Lord Coker was at the far end, by the staircase. He was consulting a footman, who shook his head and pointed in the other direction. She must escape before he turned and saw her.

Abandoning decorum, Francesca slipped out and fled in a panic down the garden. A bank of bushes lay to her right. She stopped, gave another rapid glance behind to make sure that she was unobserved, then darted to the side—and ran straight into the tall figure of a gentleman, who had apparently been enjoying the air, and indulging in a cigar. The unexpected force of the collision caused him to stagger, but he threw his cigar away and held her firmly in his arms until they had both regained their balance.

With no surprise at all, Francesca heard the deep, warm, familiar tones say, 'Why! What a pleasant surprise! I thought you never wished to see me again, Miss Beaudon.'

It was too much. Francesca gazed up at Marcus in horror. It was humiliating enough that there had been a witness to her unseemly behaviour and headlong flight, but although she was somewhat overwrought by her scene with Lord Coker, she could have controlled her feelings with anyone else. But that she should meet Marcus again in such circumstances. . .it was too much! She burst into tears.

After an initial stiffening of surprise, Marcus gathered her more firmly to him and held her until gradually her sobs subsided and she was able to speak.

'You shouldn't. . .I must ask you. . . Please let me go. I'm sorry to make such an exhibition of myself.'

He released her instantly. 'What happened?' he said curtly.

For one moment Francesca was tempted to tell him. The feeling of security, of comfort she had experienced in his arms, was very seductive. But another moment's thought stopped her. If she told Marcus what had occurred in the Blue Velvet Room, he might involve himself on her behalf. Lord Coker was a powerful man. He would take it very badly if Marcus, whom he would regard as a nobody, questioned his behaviour. She had no wish to see Marcus hurt.

Even worse, Marcus himself might look embarrassed and make some excuse to leave her. That would mortify her beyond bearing. So she said, somewhat lamely, 'It. . .it was so hot in there. I was overcome.'

'Francesca, I'm not a fool. It must have been more than that. Considerably more to have so discomposed you. I have never seen you in tears before.'

The proximity of this man, and the events of the night, loosened her tongue. Her reply was almost involuntary.

'Haven't you?' she asked wryly. 'I assure you I have shed many in the past. But then, you were not there to see.'

They stared at one another, and as they looked the old magic took hold of her. When Marcus grasped her arms and drew her to him, she did not resist. And when he held her even more closely, she did not pull away, but buried her head in his shoulder. The sense of being where she belonged was immediate.

Oh, Marcus, she thought in despair, why do I feel this closeness with no other man? Is this why I have refused all the others? Why I regard them as second-best, though I know them to be good, kind men, so much more worthy of my regard than you could ever be. They would never hurt me as you have hurt me, yet I can feel nothing for any of them. What have you done to my life, Marcus? Why did we ever meet?

'Let me look at you, Francesca.'

She lifted her head. He was as handsome as ever, but in the dim light reflected from the windows of Carlton House he looked sombre, threatening even. The dark blue eyes were shadowed, the beautiful mouth set in harsh lines. A chill went down her spine and she shivered. His hold tightened.

'Tell me what happened to put you in such a panic.'

'I. . .I can't. And I must not stay here like this. Please let me go, Marcus.' He did not immediately release her and with a sudden flare of spirit she wrenched herself out of his arms and said angrily, 'This won't do! I must be mad! I don't intend to escape from one seducer, merely to fall into the arms of another!'

'Damn you, I'm no seducer!' he said fiercely. 'Of all the pig-headed, obstinate women—'

Francesca interrupted what promised to be a notable loss of temper by turning away to start back to the house, but she stopped short when she saw the tall figure of Lord Coker in the middle of the lawn. It was impossible to avoid discovery. Her pale blue dress was luminous in the darkness.

'Well now, what have we here? The lovely Miss Beaudon, no less.' The words were harmless enough but the tone was malevolent. 'Running away was very foolish, my dear. It only arouses the hunter in every male. Or did you know that already, you witch? Did you expect me, perhaps? You have certainly chosen a delightfully secluded spot.'

Lord Coker advanced towards her, and Francesca felt caught in a snare, unable to move. 'Shall we continue our highly interesting conversation, Miss Beaudon? Or shall we move on to other delights? Payment, let us say, for my injuries.' His white teeth gleamed in the darkness as he smiled. 'I promise you, I shan't let you get away so easily this time.'

Marcus took a step forward, though he was still in shadow. The movement caught Lord Coker's eye, and he said softly, 'The devil! So it wasn't modesty alone which caused you to flee my arms with such drastic determination, but an assignation in the garden. Well, well, well! The virtuous Miss Beaudon has more of her father in her than I thought!'

'Coker!' said Marcus curtly. Francesca put her hands to her cheeks. The confrontation she had feared was about to take place, and it was bound to prove disastrous for Marcus. Physically he was more than a match for his lordship, but he had nothing like Coker's political power and influence.

'What the devil—?' Lord Coker stopped in his tracks and stared in surprise, not unmixed with annoyance, at the tall figure before him. His eye turned to Francesca, then back to Marcus. 'I see! Not without protectors, you said. With some justification. No wonder you appeared so indifferent to my charms, my dear. This is a conquest any young lady would be pleased to flaunt.' Turning to Marcus, he drawled, 'I congratulate you on your turn of speed, my dear fellow. When was it you got back from Paris?'

'A few hours ago,' said Marcus curtly.

'One wonders when you've found the time to fix your interest with Miss Beaudon here. But one quite sees why. She has little idea how to behave but she's reasonably handsome—and so is her fortune. . .'

Marcus said softly, 'I don't think I understand what you mean, sir.'

Francesca was chilled by the menace in his voice.

The two men stared at each other for what seemed an eternity, then Lord Coker gave a laugh. 'I meant no harm. You must forgive my very natural chagrin at being denied a chance of furthering my acquaintance with one of the most desirable young ladies in London. Especially at being cut out by a man who hardly needs Miss Beaudon's. . .assets. You're as rich as a Nabob yourself. But what a stir this will create! The Nonpareil indulging in secret meetings in the gardens of Carlton House!'

'If I hear anything said linking Miss Beaudon's name with mine, you will hear from me, Coker. So guard your tongue.' This was said so peremptorily and so coldly that Francesca gasped and looked anxiously at Lord Coker. Had Marcus no sense? To address one of the the Regent's favourites in such a manner was to court disaster. But to her complete bewilderment, instead of threatening Marcus, as she would have expected, Lord Coker remained silent. What was going on?

Marcus offered her his arm and continued, 'Now I will finish what I was doing, which was to find Miss Beaudon and escort her back to her chaperon, before her absence from the ballroom is remarked on. As a close friend of her host, you will no doubt be shocked to hear that the behaviour of some villain or other forced her to seek refuge in the garden. . . Certainly the Prince would be furious at such an insult to a guest of his. Indeed, if he knew who the culprit was, he might even withdraw his favour from the fellow. Silence all round is called for, I believe.'

'Quite!' snapped Lord Coker.

'Good. Now, you will excuse us, I am sure, Coker.'

'I shan't forget this, Carne!' Then, with a lowering

glance at Francesca, Lord Coker gave a cursory bow, turned on his heel and strode up towards the house.

Marcus watched him go. Then he looked at Francesca, who had withdrawn her arm from his and now stood staring at him, a frown on her face.

'Did you wish me to challenge the fellow, Francesca? I'm sorry if I disappointed you, but I thought you would prefer to avoid the inevitable scandal if I did. Coker won't harm you again.'

'No, no! The matter is best forgotten. But. . .'

'But what?'

'Lord Coker called you Carne!'

'Yes, he did. Why are you surprised? It is my title.'

'B-but. . . That is impossible! Lydia talks of Lord Carne all the time! She cannot sing his praises loudly enough.' The incredulity in Francesca's voice was too much for Marcus.

He laughed out loud, then said solemnly, 'You must make allowance for Lydia's partiality. She adored her father and I was his friend. She will learn the truth in time.'

'But it's not only Lydia! Mrs Canfield. . .my father. . .all the rest. They all speak well of you! Indeed, they all admire you!'

'Mrs Canfield cannot think more highly of me than I do of her. Your father. . .I haven't yet met him, I believe. And as for the rest. . .' He shrugged his shoulders, and looked at Francesca with one eyebrow quirked. She was still shaking her head in disbelief.

His lips twitched and he went on gravely, 'I assure you that I am Carne. I inherited the title somewhat unexpectedly a few years after we first met.'

'But Lord Carne is rich, and you. . .you—'

'I was poor. Quite right. I inherited wealth together with the title. One doesn't normally mention such things, Francesca but, since we are talking so very openly, I will admit it—I am an extremely rich man. Rich as a Nabob, as Coker said.'

'I. . .see. That would account for some of it, I suppose. . .'

Marcus sighed and said ruefully, 'My popularity, you mean? I am sure you are right, though I know of no one else who would point that out with such brutal frankness. You don't mince matters, do you?'

Francesca did not hear him. She was still struggling to come to terms with this startlingly new situation. 'But it doesn't account for the admiration of the rest. I have heard good people—people I respect—talking well of you, describing you as a man of character.' She shook her head again in bewilderment. 'I cannot understand it.'

Marcus found that he was enjoying himself immensely. His voice was unsteady as he replied gravely, 'I can't account for it myself. It is gratifying to hear of it, of course. But don't worry, Francesca. I shan't suffer from conceit—not while you are there to redress the balance.'

At this Francesca stiffened and said accusingly, 'You are laughing at me, Lord Carne!'

He smiled and said, 'Only a little. It is quite refreshing, believe me, to find a lady in London who does not hang on my every word, whether it makes sense or not. But it is time to take you back to Mrs Canfield. Coker won't talk, at least not for a while, but others may notice you have been out of sight for too long. Shall we go back?' He offered his arm again and, with some reluctance, Francesca took it.

As they walked slowly up the lawns to the house, Marcus said, 'There must have been some considerable change in your fortunes, Francesca. Am I to understand that you and Lord Beaudon are now reconciled? He acknowledges you as his daughter?'

'He never denied it. It was my aunt who. . .refused to

believe that he had married her sister, and the neighbour-hood, including the Witham Court set, took its lead from her. But she was. . .mistaken.'

'Mistaken? I doubt that.' Marcus flashed her a sceptical look, but she didn't see. Her mind was in turmoil. She had to ask, even though the subject was painfully embarrassing. 'Lord Carne, when you came to Shelwood. . .after my aunt had died. . .and. . .and offered for me. . .'

'Yes?' His tone was not encouraging, but she struggled on.

'Were you as rich then?'

'I told you. I inherited everything about four years ago. Why do you ask?'

Colour rose in Francesca's cheeks. How could she explain, when she didn't even know herself why it was so important?

He waited a moment, then drawled, 'I am not asking whether you have changed your mind, Francesca. The moment for that is past. But would your answer have been kinder, if you had known I was rich? Would you have treated me differently?'

'Of course I would!'

The look of cynicism on Marcus' face increased, but Francesca did not see it. She was not only totally unaware of the effect her words had on him, she hardly noticed indeed what she was saying, absorbed as she was in her own thoughts. Her resentment, her anger, the manner in which she had rejected him, had all been based on the belief that he would be marrying her for her money. Now she had just discovered that she had made another mistake about him—a more disastrous mistake than any of the rest. Whatever his motives in coming to seek her out at Shelwood, acquiring her fortune had not been one of them.

She had not only been shamefully insulting, she had been grossly unjust to him. Though she could still hardly believe it, this man beside her, whom she had called a rake and fortune-hunter, a seducer and abductor, was in fact a polished leader of society, universally spoken of as a man of integrity and wealth. An offer of marriage from him must be regarded as a signal honour. Mrs Canfield had called him a target for all the matchmakers in London. 'You have a better chance of marrying the man in the moon!' her father had said.

But, in that case, *why* had he come to Shelwood? Had she been wrong about his feelings? Had he genuinely been in love with her all those years ago? And had his love been re-awakened when he saw her again on the road to Witham? Her eyes softened as she stole a glance at him, a tentative smile on her lips. But he did not respond. If anything, his face grew colder.

She took herself to task for idly dreaming the impossible. How could he possibly have fallen in love with her again? In her old clothes covered in mud and weeds after clambering out of that ditch, she had hardly represented any man's ideal. He hadn't behaved as if he admired her, and he certainly hadn't spoken like a man in love when he had asked her to marry him. Indeed, she had had the impression that she had hurt his dignity, not his feelings, in refusing him.

But, *if it was not to gain a fortune, why had he come at all?* She *had* to know. She turned to ask him, but was astonished to see that he was, in fact, regarding her with an expression of tired cynicism.

'Why. . .what are you. . .? Why are you looking at me like that, Lord Carne?' she stammered.

'I suppose I had hoped for something better.'

'Better? What do you mean?'

'You made your opinion of me perfectly plain when you refused me at Shelwood. I was surprised at your vehemence, but I accepted that you did not like me enough to marry me. I was disappointed to hear you say just now that, if you had known I was rich. . . But it's of no consequence. I had thought you would be different, that's all. Come, let me escort you to Mrs Canfield.'

The colour rose in Francesca's cheeks, but, restraining her impulse to answer him angrily, she said in her coolest tones, 'You think I would have accepted you had I known you were rich, whatever my opinion of your character?'

'Have you not just said so?'

'Indeed, no! You asked me if I would have *treated* you differently, had I known you were rich, Lord Carne, not whether my answer would have been different.'

'Aren't you splitting hairs?'

Francesca was losing the battle to stay calm. She said with a snap, 'Do you find it so impossible to believe that any woman could refuse an offer from the great Lord Carne? Allow me to tell you, my lord, that I find you impossibly conceited!'

'You have found me so many things in the past, Francesca, none of them flattering, that your insults now have very little power to offend me.'

His words reminded her that she owed him some apology. She took a deep breath and said formally, 'I have behaved very badly on several occasions, I know, and I have been at fault in jumping to conclusions about you. I now regret many of the things I have said, especially in the library at Shelwood, and I hope you will forgive me.'

He looked at her impassively, then nodded. 'Let it all be forgotten.'

'Not. . .not quite yet. There is something I still do not understand. I now know that your motives for coming to Shelwood were not what I thought. But. . .I am still puzzled. Why. . .why did you ask me to marry you after my aunt died?' Francesca held her breath, as she waited for his reply. It was not immediately forthcoming, so she went on, 'You did not appear to be in love with me—indeed, you said as much at the time.'

Marcus hesitated. He had broached this conversation impulsively, cynically almost. His pride had been badly hurt by her scornful refusal of him, and he wanted to hear her admit that she had been wrong to refuse such a splendid offer. So far she had not obliged him, and he now regretted opening the subject at all. His innate honesty compelled him to answer truthfully. 'Your situation seemed so hopeless. I cannot say that I was in love with you, but I was not in love with anyone else, either. I remembered our past association and thought we could build on that—'

'You were sorry for me,' said Francesca, cutting him short. She had known in her heart that he was not in love with her, but his words nevertheless had given her a pang. But no sign of this appeared as she said, 'Pray say no more, sir. Whatever the misunderstandings were—on either side—it was fortunate that they prevented us from entering into a marriage which could only have led to misery for both of us.'

She took a deep breath. It was all too painfully embarrassing. This conversation should never have started in the first place. He had been sorry for her! Sorry! The great Lord Carne willing to perform another of his charitable acts, to make a lovesick, idiot of a girl happy at last! Oh, no! There was no going back. She had been a fool to think otherwise. And if she wished to have any self-respect, any peace of mind, she must avoid him in the future, as far as that was possible.

'You still haven't told me what your answer would have been, Francesca.'

'You can hardly expect me to do so.' They had nearly reached the garden doors. 'I can't—I don't—' She was stammering like a schoolgirl! Francesca took a deep breath and began again. She said coolly, 'Lord Carne, pray let us forget what has been said tonight. I hope you will excuse my behaviour in the past. I have clearly misjudged you. In future. . .' She stopped, unable to continue.

Marcus regarded her with another slightly cynical smile. 'You will be kinder? Would like us to meet in order to explain how you have changed? Perhaps often?'

'What do you mean?'

'You are quite right, of course. "Marcus" was not good enough for you. But it cannot do you any harm at all to be seen in the company of Lord Carne, an eminently eligible member of the *ton*, the object of every match-making mama in Society!'

Francesca felt another surge of rage, but her training stood her in good stead. They were now in sight of other people. Her expression was calm and her voice low as she said, 'You were wrong, Lord Carne. It seems that even I cannot redress the balance of your conceit, nor, sad though it is to see it, have I any wish to do so.

'I was about to thank you for your protection tonight, and to say that I am ashamed of the things I said to you on that memorable day in the library. And, though your enormous self-esteem makes it unlikely you will believe me, I was also about to say that having made our peace, we should avoid each other as far as possible in the future. Because of the past I could never be easy in your company.'

They were now at the foot of the stairs. She raised her voice and said politely, 'Thank you for fetching me from the garden, Lord Carne, but pray do not let me keep you from your friends any longer. I am sure I can find Mrs Canfield for myself.' Then she gave a small curtsy and made her way up the stairs.

Chapter Nine

Marcus watched her go with a slight smile on his lips. Francesca wished to avoid his company, did she? He was not all convinced that he wished to avoid hers. You could say what you liked about Francesca Shelwood—or Beaudon, as she now was—conversation with her was never dull. Stimulating, appealing, infuriating—but never a bore. From what she had said, there was no danger that she regarded him as a prospective husband.

That was as well, for though he had sometimes been tempted to take a bride for the sake of the Carne name, the thought of marriage bored him beyond measure. The closest he had ever come to being in love—deeply in love—had been with Francesca herself all those years ago. But he had forgotten her in the time that followed, and he was now a very different man from the callow youth who would have thrown everything away for love.

His rash and quixotic gesture in offering for Francesca when her aunt died had resulted from a remnant of feeling for her, a sense of responsibility for her welfare. It had been very ill-judged. Thank God she had refused him! As she had said, they would both have regretted it.

But perhaps, for old times' sake, it would amuse him now to cultivate her a little, introduce her to his friends—

she might well find a reasonable match among them. The Beaudon fortune could not be very great, but not all the members of his circle were on the hunt for an heiress. One of them was sure to find her suitable—but who?

Marcus frowned. Some of them were sticklers—would they be put off by Francesca's behaviour? She could be very impulsive. . . But how could she know how to behave? Her training at Shelwood had not prepared her for life in Society. She was intelligent, she would learn. . . And she had been upset tonight by Coker's treatment of her. . .

Marcus's frown deepened. Coker might be one of the Prince Regent's gambling cronies, but he was a scoundrel all the same. What had he been up to with Francesca? It was out of the question, even for Coker, to think of making her his mistress, but the Beaudon fortune was hardly large enough to tempt him into marriage. His two previous wives had both been considerable heiresses.

Marcus shook his head decisively. Whatever lay behind Coker's interest in Francesca, he was certainly no fit companion for her; if no one else would stop the connection, then it was up to him to do so. . .she was much too good for Coker! The frown on Marcus's face gave way to a smile as he thought of Francesca. How lovely she had looked, even in her agitated state! Yes, he owed it to the past to keep an eye on her interests in London. She might yet make a reasonable match.

But when Marcus began to review his circle of acquaintance, he was surprised to find that the thought of any of them marrying Francesca repelled him. They made excellent friends, but each one of them lacked some quality or other which he considered essential for her happiness. Richard Caughton was a steady, kind fellow and he certainly wasn't hanging out for a rich wife. But it had to be said that he sometimes was rather a dull dog—Francesca would be bored with him in a month.

Vincent Tatham was much more the type for her—amusing, witty, polished. . .but would he cherish her when she was ill or unhappy? It was doubtful—he could be a bit of an unfeeling brute.

Monty Banford? Never! His taste was for a full-blown, obvious sort of beauty, and his mental processes were equally unsubtle. He would never appreciate Francesca's elusive charm.

What about George Denver? Now he was a distinct possibility. Plenty of address, nice little property in Kent, a very good fellow all round. . .but no, it wouldn't do! George simply wasn't up to her weight—she would walk all over him, and despise him for allowing it. He couldn't submit poor George to that. Who else was there? More names occurred to him, but each had something amiss. Devil take it! There wasn't one of them fit to marry her! Not one!

Irritated with his lack of success, Marcus decided to consult his sister. He had asked her once before to help him with Francesca without much success, but the present situation was very different. Francesca was now perfectly respectable. Her fortune might be only moderate, but she was worthy of any man's consideration as a wife. Lady Chelford was bound to think of someone—her circle of acquaintance was wide and comprised some of the most respectable families in England. But when he broached the subject, his sister's reaction was not what he had expected.

'My dear Marcus!' she exclaimed. 'Where have you been all these weeks?'

'In Paris—as you very well know. Why is that to the purpose?'

'Why should you imagine that Miss Beaudon needs

any help from me to find a husband? The idea is absurd!'

'Come, Sarah! You can surely help me this time! Miss Beaudon is no longer a penniless nobody. She is perfectly respectable now, with the Beaudon name and fortune behind her. It shouldn't be that difficult to think of someone who would be prepared to marry her.'

Lady Chelford's eyes narrowed. 'I am positive I can find at least a dozen, if not more! But. . .before I go any further, Marcus, tell me why you regard Miss Beaudon's future as your concern?'

'Damn it, I feel responsible for the girl!'

'I know you do, Marcus. But what puzzles me is *why*! You said you were sorry for her in the past, but Miss Beaudon no longer has the slightest need for your pity. She is a very fortunate young woman.'

'Sarah—'

Lady Chelford swept on. 'And unless you are about to declare a directly *personal* interest in her, Marcus—'

'You know I don't think of marrying anyone at the moment.'

'Then I suggest that you leave Miss Beaudon, together with her father and Maria Canfield, to sort out her future for herself. Good heavens, man, Francesca Beaudon could take her pick of London society!'

'That is surely a trifle exaggerated? She is beautiful enough, but the Beaudon fortune is modest—'

'Modest! Marcus, you have been out of London too long! Did you not know? The girl was her grandfather's heir. She has a personal fortune of seventy thousand pounds, and a large estate in Buckinghamshire. There isn't an eligible man in London who wouldn't give his eyebrows to capture the Shelwood heiress!'

'Her grandfather's heir. . .' Marcus was stunned. 'The devil she is!' There was a pause, then he said slowly, 'She said something about it that time in the library, but

I ignored it. . .I thought she was telling me a tale. . .' He fell silent again. 'An heiress. . .'

'A considerable one. She is, of course, courted and flattered wherever she goes. In fact, it is perhaps as well that you are not considering her for yourself, Marcus. You might find it difficult to get near her!' This was said with a touch of malicious amusement.

Marcus felt unaccountably irritated. 'I had no idea. . . Well, you're right for once. She certainly doesn't need my help to find a husband. What a ridiculous idea! Quite mad. I'm glad I spoke to you, Sarah—I was close to making a fool of myself.' He went to the door, then stopped. 'I don't know why it is,' he said angrily, 'but that girl has the knack of causing trouble wherever she goes!'

'What on earth do you mean?'

'She rushes about knocking me into streams, falls into ditches, reviles me for trying to help her, romps through the forest interfering in my concerns, and now—'

'We cannot be talking of the same person, Marcus! Miss Beaudon has charming manners! What is more, she is known for her detachment and poise. As far as I know, she has never put a foot wrong in matters of propriety.'

'Ha! You don't know her, Sarah!'

'No, I obviously don't. Nor, if what you say is true, does the rest of society! Tell me more about this creature.'

But Marcus recollected himself. Charlotte had willingly agreed to say nothing about what had happened in the forest, and now he had very nearly revealed the ridiculous story himself! 'No, no! It's of no consequence. It all took place in the very distant past, when. . .when she was still a child. Though I cannot believe she has changed as much as you say.'

'You will see for yourself. But if you have no wish to marry her, then you must leave her alone!'

'You need not say anything more, Sarah. I will certainly

leave her alone! I wash my hands of her. Completely. The rich Miss Beaudon can choose a husband whenever she will without my aid!'

He left at that point in what seemed remarkably like a fit of temper. Lady Chelford stared at his departing figure in astonishment. Marcus was the soul of patience and calm. She could not remember when he had last slammed a door like that. What had got into him?

Then she raised an eyebrow, and started to smile. Perhaps. . .just perhaps, her brother might be deceiving himself. How delightful that would be! Marcus was a very dear brother, always ready to help in any difficulty, and she was truly grateful to him. But there was no denying that, since he had come in to the title, he had been disgracefully spoilt. He had had his choice of Society's beauties for far too long. It would do him no harm at all if he was attracted to someone who did not fall over herself to win him.

Marcus may have washed his hands of Francesca, but he could not help observing her as she danced and conversed, as she took part in all the many events which made up the London Season. And, to his surprise, he soon saw that his sister's account of Francesca's conduct in society was perfectly correct. Francesca knew how to behave rather better than most her contemporaries, in fact. In spite of the persistent attention of so many members of the *ton*, she bore herself with dignity and grace. And in the face of their flattery and obvious admiration, she remained detached, even politely amused.

He could never find anything in her manner to fault. He was amazed. Her collapse into tears, her agitation and loss of temper in the garden at Carlton House—these had been completely out of character for the Honorable Francesca Beaudon as Society knew her. He had never liked Coker, but now he found it difficult to address the man with any degree of civility, for he was sure Coker was to blame.

In this he was wrong. Lord Coker's behaviour had merely set the scene. Marcus remained unaware that he himself had been the real cause for Francesca's distress. It did not occur to him that few people would ever be permitted to see her as he had seen her that night, that he was one of only two people in the world who could break through the wall of reserve to the vulnerable, passionate girl behind. London society approved of Miss Beaudon, but would have laughed to scorn the idea that her heart was not always ruled by her head.

The longer Marcus studied Francesca, the more puzzled he became. She was an enigma. It was not that she was beautiful in her fine dresses and fashionable hairstyles— that came as no surprise to him. He had always seen beyond the shabby clothes and the wilful refusal to attempt any personal adornment. The fineness of her bone structure, the clarity of her gray-green eyes, even the gleam of dark gilt hair—he had noted all these on their first acquaintance.

Her beauty was less obvious than those of vivacious charmers such as Lydia Canfield—or in her different sphere, Charmian Forrest. Francesca Beaudon's attractions were for a connoisseur's eye, someone who appreciated a more subtle play of colour and line. Her beauty was wasted on the general herd, yet he had seen it from the first.

But he had always been aware of a mysterious line of communication between them. It was there whether they wished it or not, something quite out of their control. He had known when she was worried and distressed, whatever she actually said to him—it had produced an irrational desire to help her. But now this ability to read her mind, to know her true feelings, had vanished without trace. Francesca had closed him off, and Miss Beaudon was as proper, as reserved with him as she was with everyone else—a pattern of decorum, grace and charm.

He had not been aware how much he valued the warmth, the freedom that had previously existed between them, until they were no more. Damn it, she could be what she liked with others—they did not know what she was truly like. But he—he missed the laughing, impetuous. . .*real* girl he had fallen in love with on the hill above Shelwood!

Then there was the question of her fortune. At first, Marcus was strongly irritated by the thought that Francesca was rich. He had made a fool of himself that day at Shelwood with his offer of marriage. Mistress of a large fortune and with her own father to look after her, Francesca could well manage without Lord Carne's solicitude then—and now. She was far from needing his help.

But, as Marcus watched Francesca dancing, walking, driving with some of the most eligible bachelors in the town, he began to change his mind again. However little Francesca realised it, she *did* need him! Her fortune was a very real source of danger to her, putting her at risk with all the sharks and self-seekers at loose in the polite world. Lord Beaudon, much as he loved his daughter, had been away from London too long to recognise all the pitfalls, and he was quite clearly not in the best of health.

The obvious fortune-seekers were soon chased away, it was true, but one or two more apparently respectable characters, friends of the Prince Regent such as Lord Coker, or charmers, such as Sir Anthony Perrott, whose engaging manners hid their cold-hearted ambition—men such as these were cultivating Francesca. She even seemed to be enjoying their company!

It became obvious to Marcus that something more was needed. And who better was there than Marcus himself? He had the entrée to all levels of society, from the Prince Regent down. He knew Francesca and he knew both the world she had moved in in the past, and the world she moved in now. However little she would thank him for it, protecting her from her own folly, until she found the right sort of man, was the least he could do. Marcus was filled with a sense of satisfaction at this clear call to duty. Perhaps on the way he would find that missing girl.

It was not long before Francesca realised that avoiding Marcus was impossible. His close friendship with Mrs Canfield and Lydia made meetings between them inevitable; to her annoyance, she soon saw that Marcus was making no attempt to avoid her—on the contrary, he seemed to regard her as part of the Canfield family, to extend to her his patronage and protection. He did nothing to single her out, made no special effort to engage her in other than general conversation, but she was conscious all the time of his presence, and frequently of his eye on her.

The Canfields were delighted when he accompanied them to balls and concerts. They accepted with pleasure his invitations to rides in the park, excursions into the country, expeditions to places of interest, and Francesca was always included. However reluctant she was, she found herself forced to accept more often than she wished.

'But why will you not come, Francesca?' cried Lydia on one occasion. 'Hampton Court is delightful. You will enjoy it much more than staying in town!'

'Lydia, do not press Miss Beaudon. Perhaps she has the headache and wishes for a little peace and quiet. Your chatter can be very tiring.' Mrs Canfield's voice was calm, but she was looking anxiously at Francesca.

'Oh, no, ma'am. I like to hear Lydia talking.'

'Then do come!' Lydia put a pleading hand on Francesca's arm. 'Lord Carne's carriage is extremely well sprung, and I shall see to it that you have all the cushions and parasols necessary to keep you comfortable. And I shall not say a word more than you wish to hear, I promise. Please, Francesca! It isn't the same without you.'

'But Lord Carne is an old friend of yours. He cannot wish to see me making a fourth on every excursion you make!'

'Nonsense! He likes you.'

'Lydia!' Mrs Canfield's voice held a warning and Lydia said no more.

But later, when they were alone, Mrs Canfield said quietly, 'Francesca, forgive me for what I am about to say. I only wish to spare you difficulty or embarrassment. Though you have not acknowledged it, I. . .I have the impression that you and Lord Carne knew each other in the past. Am I right?'

Francesca hesitated. She owed her friend the truth, but was reluctant to reveal the extent of her previous acquaintance with Marcus.

'Believe me, I do not wish to pry, but if it distresses you to be in his company, you have only to mention it. I shall perform the impossible and find a way of silencing Lydia.'

Francesca smiled. 'You are very kind, ma'am, but I truly enjoy Lydia's conversation. She is so. . .so artless, and so loving. How could I not enjoy her company? But you are right—I have met Lord Carne before. Briefly. In Buckinghamshire.' She paused. 'It was many years ago, before he succeeded to the title, so his name meant nothing to me when Lydia spoke of him. I only recognised him when he came back from Paris. I hope you don't think that I deliberately deceived you?'

'Of course not! And you are not disturbed to meet him now? I sometimes have the impression. . .'

Francesca had confided as much as she was prepared to. 'It is kind of you to be concerned. But I was a mere child when we first met, so our acquaintance was. . .was not important.' Her tone was so casual that Mrs Canfield was satisfied. No one could have guessed from Francesca's demeanor then or later how much she resented Lord Carne's constant attendance.

His presence agitated her, roused feelings which she preferred to forget—how could she conquer this stupid weakness for him, when he was always there, his dark blue eyes watching her, his voice a constant reminder of those hours on the hill? But once again, she had cause to be grateful to the hard school of her earlier life, which enabled her now to reveal nothing of this as she walked and talked, listened and smiled with every appearance of serene enjoyment, though her famous reserve was a trifle more apparent.

The presence of Marcus was not the only cause for unease. Francesca was becoming increasingly concerned about her father. His decision to support her during her London Season had delighted her and, since the news of her wealth had spread, she had been grateful for his protection from the worst of the fortune hunters. But he was not robust, and his exertions were having an effect on his health.

However, he dismissed her concern with a laugh. 'Nonsense, child! Watching your success has taken years off me! And though there are not as many old friends left in London as I would have wished, I manage to have a very pleasant time of it. I like that fellow Carne, by the way. Not at all the dull sort of stick I expected from Maria

Canfield's eulogies. You could do a lot worse for a husband.'

It said much for Francesca's control that though the rose in her cheeks increased a fraction, she reminded her father calmly that, as he himself had once said, Lord Carne was out of her reach.

'I'm no longer so sure of that. He's forever in your company.'

'He is a close friend of the Canfields, as you very well know, Papa.'

'But it's my impression that his eyes are on you a good deal of the time, not the Canfields. Perhaps you've caught his fancy—should I sound him out, d'you think?'

'No, Papa! Believe me, that is the last thing I want you to do.' The vehemence in her voice caused Lord Beaudon to raise an eyebrow.

'Protesting too much, Francesca?'

Francesca pulled herself together. 'The truth is, Papa, that Lord Carne and I do not. . .are not. . . The fact is, we have little in common. I have too much regard for Mrs Canfield to express this openly. It would hurt her, I know. And I am also aware that his. . .patronage is valuable to all of us. But I have to confess that my feeling towards him is best described as indifferent.'

Lord Beaudon regarded her in silence for a moment. There was more to this than met the eye. Once he would have taken her words at face value, as deceived by her cool control as the rest of the world had been. But now his instinct told him that, whatever she felt for Lord Carne, it was not indifference. Could Carne possibly be the man she had been in love with? Surely not! Carne was no rake, and he was a most unlikely crony of Charlie Witham. But there was something. . . Lord Beaudon resolved not to pursue the matter with Francesca, but to wait and observe.

'Is Carne to be at Lady Huntingdon's tonight?' he asked.

'I believe so. Why do you ask?'

'She usually sets up some card tables for those who don't wish to dance—I thought I'd invite him to a game, that's all. Nothing like a hand of cards to get to know a man.'

'Papa—'

'Oh, I won't mention your name, girl. Why should I, if, as you say, you have no particular interest in him? No, Carne seems to me to be a sound fellow—I'd enjoy making his better acquaintance. You surely don't wish for my company in the ballroom, do you? You'll be safe enough at Bella Huntingdon's—and Maria will be with you.'

'Are you sure you wouldn't prefer to rest this evening? I have no particular wish to go out—we could have a peaceful time together. . .'

'Francesca, it is my dearest wish to see you happily settled with a man you can respect. You won't find a husband if you sit at home keeping company with your papa!'

'I'm no longer so sure that. . .that I want to marry anyone. I seem to have met most of the eligible men in London, and there isn't one with whom I could spend the rest of my life. . .except you, Papa,' she added with a twinkle.

'Nonsense, girl. You must just keep on trying! Now off you go—put on the new dress I saw arriving today. Another from Fanchon, wasn't it? What colour is it this time?'

'White and green—I think you'll like it. Lydia was in raptures over it. Papa, I cannot begin to tell you how well your choice of sponsor has suited me. Maria is so very kind, she and I seem to agree on practically everything.

And Lydia is a darling. It is *my* dearest wish to see *her* safely established!'

'Young Tom Endcombe seems very attentive.'

'He does!' She paused. 'He's pleasant enough, I suppose. . .though. . .in my opinion, Lydia needs someone more mature, someone who would look after her. Still, Maria seems to approve of him. If I could see Lydia happily settled, I wouldn't care about the rest of the Season. You and I could return to Packards and enjoy some country air—and some country hours. You may not need a rest, but I'm certain that I do!'

'Rubbish, Francesca! In any case, I must return to Paris some time soon.'

'To Paris? I had rather forgotten Paris. You. . .have responsibilities there?'

'I must talk to you about Paris. We'll have a chat tomorrow—there's something I've been meaning to tell you.'

'What is it?'

'Tomorrow,' said Lord Beaudon firmly. 'Tonight we both have to change for Lady Huntingdon's ball. I am expecting to be stunned along with the rest of London by my daughter's new dress.'

Francesca's appearance in the doors to Lady Huntingdon's reception room caused many a man's heart to beat faster. Tall and slender in a simple slip of white silk, with an overdress of delicate green gauze draped with all the cunning of London's foremost dressmaker, she was a vision to take one's breath away. Her hair was wound with pearls and pale green ribbon, its dark gilt coils echoing the gold and pearl embroidery of her dress. Her eyes were silver-green in the candlelight, and she was smiling at Lydia as they entered the room a little way behind Lord Beaudon and Mrs Canfield.

She was quite unconscious of the impression she was making. Her attention was on Lydia, and her smile was full of affectionate warmth, very different from the polite mask with which she fended off her suitors. And at least one man found himself suddenly, disconcertingly, so stunned that he forgot everything else—much to the irritation of his companion.

'I say, Carne, old fellow—you might answer when a friend asks a perfectly civil question!'

'What was it, Monty?'

'I asked you if you was thinkin' of dancin' tonight. Lady Huntingdon usually sets up a damn good card room. Care for a game later?'

'I. . .don't know. Ask me later. I have to give the Canfields some of my time tonight. I promised Lydia a dance.'

'Nice little girl. A bit young for you, though.'

'There's nothing to it. You know that, Monty. Her father was a friend of mine, and I like to please Lydia and her mother for his sake.'

'He was a friend of mine, too, but that don't mean I have to dance attendance on his widow. Not at a ball! Anyway, Beaudon was asking if you'd be in the card room tonight. He wants a game.'

He had his friend's full attention. 'Beaudon? I wonder why?'

'I expect he likes picquet. I see the divine Miss Beaudon has arrived. By Jove, she's in looks tonight—it's almost enough to make me change my mind about blondes. I've always thought her a touch insipid.'

'Insipid!'

'Yes—Lydia Canfield is usually far better looking than the Beaudon girl. But tonight. . . Let me know about the cards, won't you?'

'Yes, yes. Excuse me, Monty.'

Not without difficulty, Marcus made his way over to the Canfields, who were surrounded by a crowd of admirers.

'Lord Carne! There you are! You remember your promise?'

'Lydia!' Mrs Canfield shook her head as she greeted him. 'You must forgive her, Marcus. She is a little excited tonight.'

'Her high spirits do her no harm in my eyes, Maria. She looks delightful. A new dress?'

'Yes! And I think it is the prettiest I have ever possessed. Francesca helped me to choose it.'

Marcus looked at the white dress with its coquelicot ribbons. 'Miss Beaudon chose well.' Then he turned to Francesca and bowed. 'Miss Beaudon.'

The smile which had so enchanted him from across the other side of the room had disappeared. Francesca's face expressed polite interest, nothing more. She looked beautiful, but remote. Marcus felt a sudden surge of impatience. He wanted to pick up the woman and shake her until her eyes sparkled with feeling again, until she smiled at him with the same affectionate warmth, until her lips parted to laugh with him, talk to him, revile him even, with her old passionate involvement. . .

Damn it, he wanted her to show some feeling towards him, some acknowledgment of their old bonds! This. . .statue was not the real Francesca. What had happened to her? But his own face revealed none of these thoughts.

He said calmly enough, 'Lydia, I have been looking forward all week to the dance you promised me. May I?'

He possessed himself of all three ladies' cards and filled in his name. Lydia was delighted, Mrs Canfield protested but was overridden, and Francesca found herself unable to object without appearing rude. That would show her— she couldn't escape waltzing with him tonight! And he'd written his name down twice. Satisfied, he offered Lydia his arm and took her in the direction of the music. As they went along, he noticed that Francesca was already surrounded with eager partners.

'Do you really like my dress, Lord Carne? It's from Fanchon.'

Marcus suppressed a smile at the awe in Lydia's voice, and assured her that he thought it very charming.

'It's a present from Francesca. She is so good. I love her dearly. People often say she's cold, you know. But I have never found her so, and nor has Mama. You don't find her cold, do you?'

'I think Miss Beaudon is very fond of you, Lydia. And who would not be?'

Miss Canfield laughed and blushed and for a while their conversation turned to other things. But just as they were leaving the floor, Lydia said suddenly, 'I wish she was happier—I sometimes wonder if she is in love.'

Marcus was startled. 'In love? Who?'

'Francesca, of course. Well, people often seem to be unhappy when they're in love, don't they? But I've watched her very closely, and have never had the slightest hint as to who he might be. I suppose she spends more time talking to Lord Denver than to anyone else. He's very kind, of course, and certainly very handsome. Mama likes him a lot, I know. But Francesca. . .I don't know. She certainly doesn't seem to encourage him—nor anyone else, which is strange when everyone knows that the object of the Season is to meet and marry someone you like.'

'It isn't always that easy, Lydia.'

'I suppose not. You haven't found anyone yet, have you? You know, I once hoped that you and she would become attracted. But it would never have done. I've given that idea up.'

'I'm relieved to hear it. But what makes you say so?'

'Well, most ladies of our acquaintance fall over themselves to attract your attention, Lord Carne. No, don't smile at me, you know it's true. But Francesca seems so reluctant to talk of you that I sometimes wonder if she doesn't like you. She's always very. . .quiet when I mention your name. I suppose she could hardly admit to me that she doesn't like you. And yet. . .'

'Yet what?'

'Oh, I don't know. Tell me, do you know Lord Endcombe's son, Tom?'

Marcus had been more intrigued by that 'yet' than he could show, but he had to drop the subject of Francesca, and exert himself to show interest in the present object of Miss Canfield's volatile affections. He did this to such good effect that Lydia returned to Mrs Canfield, very well pleased with her distinguished partner.

Marcus then turned to Francesca, who was just joining them. Ruthlessly stepping in front of a gentleman who was about to claim her hand, he said with a charming smile, 'I think you promised this one to me, Miss Beaudon. It will be the first time we have enjoyed a waltz together, I believe.'

Chapter Ten

They walked towards the ballroom together, and many who saw them thought how well-matched they looked— Lord Carne, tall and distinguished, and the elegant Miss Beaudon. No one could have guessed from their air that Marcus was far from feeling as assured as he looked, nor that Francesca was bracing herself to put other, less conventional, occasions in Marcus's arms out of her mind. She had always known it would be difficult and for this reason had always avoided dancing the waltz with him. But now she had to face it.

The music began, the couples swept on to the floor. Francesca concentrated with determination on the steps of the dance and stepped into Marcus's arms. They circled once, twice, with utmost decorum, the correct distance set and scrupulously maintained between them.

Marcus eventually said in a carefully polite tone, 'The orchestra is, I believe, excellent.'

'And the floor not excessively crowded,' responded Francesca, with equal care.

There was another silence while they negotiated the corner of the room. Then, 'Lydia looks well, I think.'

'It is a very pretty dress.'

'Very pretty.'

Another silence, while they each searched for something unexceptionable to say. Marcus could bear this artificiality no longer. He said abruptly, 'Do you dislike me so much, Francesca?'

Francesca missed a step. 'What did you say?' she asked in astonishment.

'I asked if you disliked me so much that you cannot bear to talk to me even as much as ordinary courtesy would demand!'

'How can you say that? I have talked as much to you as I would to anyone else!'

'Then I can only pity your partners. Perhaps they are so dazzled that they find nothing to criticise.'

'By my wealth, you would say. They are at least civil, Lord Carne.' Francesca's voice was cool but perfectly calm. In the old days she would have flared up to challenge him.

'But I claim the privilege of an old friend to speak the truth.'

'Truth is a double-edged weapon, Lord Carne. It is better not unsheathed without good cause. Tell me, is it your opinion that Lydia and Lord Endcombe's son will make a match of it?'

'Lydia is still very young. It's early days yet for her to be making her choice, but I find nothing to object to in young Endcombe. He's harmless enough. You, on the other hand, seem to be very reluctant to make any man happy—or am I behind the times?'

She stiffened, but still remained perfectly calm as she said, 'Mrs Canfield has told me much of your generosity to her family since her husband was killed. This must give you some right to take an interest in their future...'

'Let us say nothing of that! Peter Canfield was a very good friend to me.'

'But you have no privilege as far as I am concerned.

Nor do I propose to discuss my future with anyone who has so little claim to an interest in it, Lord Carne!'

'For God's sake, Francesca, stop this Lord Carne business! You called me Marcus once. Let me ask you again. Do you dislike me so much that you refuse to recognise any bond between us at all?'

'There isn't one. Not any longer.'

'Then I am simply another member of the crowd to you? Look at me, Francesca, and tell me it is so, if you can.'

Francesca's hand trembled in his. She was pale, but her calm air did not desert her, and she looked at him fearlessly as she said, 'You ask too much. It would be uncivil to tell you that I dislike you, and I have already been too uncivil in the past. In any case, how could I. . .dislike you, when you have been so attentive to all of us? But I will not feed your vanity by confessing to anything but a memory.'

'Of what?'

'Of. . .of someone in another life, a man called Marcus, who once said he loved me. I am not sure he even existed, except in a girlish fantasy. Now I would prefer either to talk of something else, or to go back to Mrs Canfield.'

The waltz had come to an end, but neither of them was aware that the music had stopped. They stood staring at one another, each challenging the other, unheeding of the curious looks they were attracting.

'This will not do!' said Marcus with determination. He took Francesca's arm and led her off the floor. But at the doors of the ballroom he turned away from where Mrs Canfield and Lydia were waiting, and marched her in the direction of the garden. Francesca pulled herself free. She was pale, but still calm.

'I do not wish to go into the garden, Lord Carne. Please take me back to my friends!'

'But I want to talk to you, Francesca.'

'I can imagine what you wish to say and have no desire to hear it. In any case, Lady Huntingdon's ball is not a fit place for such conversations.' Her tone was still measured, her air still remote.

It was the last straw. Marcus took her arm and walked her willy-nilly further into the garden. They would not be overheard here. Then he took both her hands in his. He said angrily, 'Francesca, I cannot bear to see you like this. I have seen statues who have more animation! You may deceive Society with your touch-me-not airs, but you cannot deceive me. I know you too well. What has happened to you?'

'When will I manage to convince you that you do not know me any longer? You take too much on yourself. I am not, and never was, your responsibility, Marcus.' Her voice rose as she spoke, and he could see that she was breathing less steadily.

'Ah, a touch of emotion at last! And you called me Marcus!'

Francesca bit her lip, and turned away from him. He was absurdly pleased to see it—the first round was his. There was a long way to go before she would smile at him with the same unguarded, affectionate warmth which Lydia had evoked, but he would not rest until she did. And he had at least cracked her unnatural composure. He exulted in the thought. He, of all the men in London, still had the key to that other Francesca—one which the polite world had never seen or even suspected, but a girl he had once loved.

'Francesca,' he said softly, seductively.

She tore herself out of his grasp. 'No! I won't listen to you!' she cried. 'I don't know why you are doing this—amusement, curiosity, pique—but whatever it is, it is not kind! You broke my heart ten long years ago, Marcus—

you see, I am not afraid to confess it. I understand your reasons—better now than I did then. But you left a lonely and unhappy girl behind you, and there were times when I was not certain I would survive the treatment. But I managed.

'It has taken me all that time since to learn common sense, but I have done it, too. I will not now throw all those lessons aside! I will not go back to what I was, not for you, not for any man in the world! I tell you, I *will not* listen to you!' Francesca dashed a hand across her eyes, turned abruptly away from him and head bent, went back into the house.

He would have followed her, but was stopped at the door by a familiar figure.

'Marcus, old fellow! Well, upon my word—still pursuin' the fair Francesca, eh? More worth the effort now, ain't she? My word, what a difference a few years can make.'

'Freddie! What are you doing here?'

'M'cousin brought me. Respectable chap, and devilish dull, but he got me an invitation, so I suppose I have to be grateful. The wine's not at all bad. Have you had some?'

It was clear that Freddie had indeed enjoyed the wine. His face glowed with good humour.

'Freddie, you must excuse me. I have to—'

'I'll come with you, Marcus. Truth to tell, there aren't many familiar faces in the crowd. I'm not sure I'm all that *grata* to most of them.'

The last thing Marcus wanted was Freddie Chantry's company, especially at this moment, but it was like trying to get rid of a puppy who wants to play. The years, he thought grimly, had done nothing for Freddie's sense.

'As a matter of fact, I was a touch surprised to see you with Miss Beaudon, Marcus. Especially coming in from the garden,' he added with a knowing look.

'I had something to say to her in private.'

'Of course you had! Talking all the way through that waltz, too. We all wondered what was going on. If you don't mind my saying so, old chap, the ballroom ain't the sort of place to try that sort of thing. Bound to set the tabbies miaowing. I shouldn't be a bit surprised if the odds on Denver didn't lengthen even more after tonight. . .'

'Odds on Denver? What do you mean? What has George to do with anything?'

Marcus spoke so brusquely that Freddie took a step back. 'Sorry, Marcus. Thought you'd have known. They were saying in the clubs that Denver's the most likely man to succeed with our heiress.'

'Denver!'

'Oh, it was never by any means a sure thing. The lovely Miss Beaudon don't show much by way of feeling, do she? But there's no one else she showed any preference for at all. Till tonight, that is.'

'Denver! She'd never have him!'

'Why not? Denver's very presentable. Plenty of address with the ladies, knows how to please, easygoin'. . .not short of the dibs—nice little estate and an income to go with it. She could have done a lot worse. What's wrong? A friend of yours, ain't he? But of course, if you and the charmin' Francesca have decided to take up where you left off at Shelwood, that's a different matter. . .'

Marcus' face darkened. 'Forget about that time, Freddie! You don't know what you're talking about.'

'Silent as the grave, old chap. But if you don't want gossip now, you shouldn't appear so dead to the rest of the world when you're dancin' with her. And you shouldn't make off into the garden and upset the famously self-possessed Miss Beaudon!'

There was no difference in Marcus's manner as he made his escape, but he was disturbed. He did not really believe that Francesca was attracted to Lord Denver. Of course she wasn't! He had been frequently in her company in the past weeks, with and without George. There had been nothing to indicate any special affection between them. It had been an unwelcome surprise to hear what the clubs were saying, though. . . And the new Francesca did not wear her heart on her sleeve. . .but George Denver? Impossible!

He made his way slowly through the ballroom, where he was less than delighted to see Francesca, apparently quite recovered, dancing with the same George Denver. He watched them, somewhat sourly, for a few moments, then went on into the library, where card tables had been set up. Here he found Lord Beaudon in an otherwise empty room.

'Carne! You couldn't have come at a better moment. I've just won handsomely from Standish, and am ready for another victim. Care for a hand of piquet?'

Marcus agreed readily enough but, as they played, the mind of neither man was totally on the game in hand. They talked, casually, about the West Indies, the politics of Europe, and Paris, but each was interested in learning more about his companion than the state of the world. They had an enjoyable game, which Lord Beaudon won by a narrow margin, then by common consent they wandered on to the small balcony that overlooked the ballroom. Francesca was dancing again with Lord Denver.

'Your daughter appears to be enjoying life in London, sir,' said Marcus.

'What? Oh, Francesca! Yes, yes, I believe she is. Though she sometimes finds the fuss and attention a touch tedious.'

'Tell me, Lord Beaudon, do you find London much changed after your long absence?'

'Society never changes, Carne. The mixture is very

much as before.' There was a slight pause, then he added, somewhat deliberately, 'I am surprised to see Chantry here tonight, though. I'd have thought our hostess more discriminating.'

'Oh, Freddie's harmless enough.'

'Friend of yours, is he? In that case I apologise, of course. He's generally seen with the Witham crowd. You a friend of Charlie Witham's, too?'

'I. . .I know him, let us say.'

'Ever been to Witham Court?' Lord Beaudon asked idly.

'Yes.'

'Lovely place—at least, it was in my day. Is it still?'

'The place itself is lovely, but it has deteriorated a lot in recent years. It badly needs some attention.'

'Is that so? You know it well, then?'

'Hardly,' said Marcus. 'I've only stayed there twice.' He looked at his companion with a slight frown. 'It's next door to Shelwood, of course. I expect that's why you take such an interest in it? Surely your daughter could tell you more about it than I?'

Lord Beaudon looked back at him blandly. 'She seldom talks about her life at Shelwood, and I haven't questioned her, Carne. But it's never a good thing to have a neglected estate on one's doorstep. I am quite certain that Shelwood itself is in perfect condition. My late sister-in-law would not have permitted otherwise.'

'I am certain she wouldn't. I hear it is in the hands of a manager at the moment. Does. . .does Miss Beaudon intend to return there at the end of the Season?'

'I suppose that depends. . . She might decide to live with me—or she might take a husband.'

'Yes, of course.'

The eyes of the two men followed the graceful twists and turns of the throng below.

'She seems to be difficult to please, my Francesca. She doesn't say much, but I rather think she's had any number of offers.'

'She's a beautiful woman.'

'I agree, though we needn't beat about the bush, Carne. She wouldn't be half as beautiful to some eyes if the Shelwood estate wasn't in the frame, too.'

'That's inevitable, I suppose. But she need not concern herself about them. There are many other, more honorable men,' said Marcus, adding casually, 'George Denver for one.'

'Yes, Denver. He seems quite taken. And she certainly seems to spend more time with him than with most of the others. Except yourself.'

'Me? I enjoy Miss Beaudon's company, of course, but it would be more true to say that I spend time with the Canfields. And since they share a house with her, it is natural. . .'

'Of course, of course. Quite natural. Another hand of piquet?'

'I am promised to Mrs Canfield for the supper interval. Perhaps later?'

'I'll come with you, Carne. Perhaps Francesca will be free to accompany her father.'

'I doubt it.' The two men watched as Lord Denver escorted Miss Beaudon off the ballroom floor. She was smiling as they disappeared through the doors and Marcus suddenly frowned and turned back to the library. Lord Beaudon was standing in the doorway, and Marcus was surprised to see him looking rather stern. He looked as if he was debating something in his own mind, but in the end he smiled and said, 'Shall we go?'

Though he badly wanted to speak privately to Francesca again, Marcus was given little opportunity that evening.

During the supper interval she kept close to her father, or talked to Lord Denver. And when he returned to claim the second set of dances he had written in to her programme at the beginning of the evening, she was not to be found. When he finally tracked her down, she was talking to Lady Clayton, who was regaling her with tales of her father's exploits in London twenty-five years before.

'Lord Carne! You must forgive me,' Francesca exclaimed brightly. 'I had to repair my dress, and by the time I had finished the dances had started. I am afraid I assumed you must have found another partner. You will think me very uncivil, but I assure you the repair was necessary.'

'In that case, how can I not forgive?' He bowed. 'Lady Clayton.'

'I suppose you've come to take this charming young woman away from me, Carne?'

'I am sure Lord Carne will excuse me if I do not go,' said Francesca. She turned to Marcus. 'Lady Clayton has been telling me such stories about my father.'

'My attractions apparently outweigh yours, Carne!' said the dowager with a malicious smile. 'What will you do?'

'Give in gracefully, I hope, ma'am,' said Marcus. 'Your stories are renowned. May I hear some, too?' He sat down on the chair at Francesca's side.

Lady Clayton's black button eyes took note of the colour rising in Francesca's cheek, then switched to Marcus, whose countenance was impassive. 'Of course you may, Carne,' she said. 'Though what the younger generation is coming to I cannot imagine. A ball is an occasion for dancing, not listening to an old woman's tales!'

'But since my present dancing partner is at your side, I shall be forced to spend the next half hour alone—

unless you take pity on me. Or are your tales unfit for my unsullied ears?'

Lady Clayton cackled with pleasure. 'I could tell you tales that would make your hair stand on end, Carne. . .but I won't. Indeed, I've just about come to the end of my repertoire.' She turned to Francesca. 'I'm a touch tired. I hope you won't mind, my dear—you must ask your father for the rest. Take her for some refreshment, Carne. The child looks flushed.'

'I. . . I. . . What about you, Lady Clayton?'

'I shall be perfectly happy here, Miss Beaudon. Look, here comes my son—he'll take care of me. Thank you for listening to my tales.'

'I enjoyed them. May I hear more another time?'

'Of course, of course. Call on me whenever you have the time. Bring your father! I wasn't allowed to have much to do with him in the old days.'

As they walked away, Francesca said, 'I do not need refreshment, Lord Carne. I should like to find my father, if you please.'

Marcus looked at her determined face. 'Very well. It seems I shall have to wait for a more suitable opportunity to continue our discussion.'

'I have told you! I do not wish to discuss anything with you. Why will you not leave me alone?'

'I cannot. I cannot let matters rest as they are at the moment. I will not let you shut me out, Francesca. But there's no time now to pursue the matter—I will call on you tomorrow or the next day.'

There was no time for more. Lord Beaudon was just a few yards away. Marcus bowed and left her.

Francesca spent a sleepless night. For some mysterious reason of his own, Marcus was determined to reawaken feelings in her that she thought she had conquered. And, in the small hours of the morning, she faced the unwelcome truth that, if Marcus chose to exert the inexplicable power he had over her, she would be powerless to stop him. The thought filled her with dread. She had sworn that she would never again be as impulsive, never as subject to her emotions, that no man would ever hurt her again! Never! She had made herself invulnerable. But not to Marcus, seemingly.

What should she do? Was flight the answer? Madame Elisabeth had returned to her cottage in Shelwood after Francesca and the Canfields had come to London—perhaps she should do the same? The idea was appealing. She could occupy herself running the Shelwood estate—there was much she would like to try. Marcus would hardly pursue her there.

But. . .what would her father say if she fled to Shelwood? They had learned to love each other again during these months at Packards and in London. He had sacrificed his comfort, his life in Paris to be with her. What would he think if she abandoned all their plans?

In the end she decided to go back to her original plan of finding a husband and an establishment of her own. It was undoubtedly what would most please her father. But marriage was a solemn step—one she could not undertake lightly, and for all the offers she had received, there was not one which had tempted her.

Francesca threw up her hands impatiently and took herself to task. This was absurd! At least three or even four of the men who had offered for her were men of honour and consideration. And now there was George Denver. . .more than moderately well off, handsome, quite amusing. Why was she being so difficult to please? She was a fool! She shivered. Unless she did something soon, Marcus would make an even greater fool of her! On this frightening thought, Francesca lay down and finally fell asleep.

The next day, Francesca's desperate desire to find a way out of the trap that was closing round her, assumed even greater urgency. In the afternoon, Lord Beaudon arrived, demanding to have a talk with her. But he had not come, as she thought, to talk of Paris.

'I've been thinking about Carne,' he began abruptly. 'He's Freddie's friend, isn't he? The one you fell in love with years ago. The rake.'

Francesca was too startled to put up much of a defence. 'How. . .how can you say so?' she stammered. 'Everyone knows that Lord Carne is the pattern of honour and decency. No rake.'

'Don't prevaricate, Francesca. I am right, aren't I? Aren't I?'

'Yes, but—'

'Then he shall marry you!'

'No!'

'He won't need much persuading. I had a word with him last night at the ball. He's very intrigued with you. He could hardly take his eyes off you. He'll marry you after I've had a word with him. You still love him, don't you?'

'Papa, you mustn't! You don't know what you're saying. No, I don't love him!'

'It's my belief you do. And you obviously haven't anyone else in mind for a husband. Carne would be an excellent choice.'

'I could not possibly marry Lord Carne, Papa. The idea is absurd. I won't let you approach him.'

'Couldn't stop me if I've made up my mind.'

'Please, Papa, please do not say anything to Lord Carne!'

'Why not, Francesca? Are you afraid he will refuse?'

'Yes. But I would be even more afraid if he agreed.' The words had slipped out before she could stop them.

Lord Beaudon regarded her for a moment. 'I find that very curious, Francesca. I can't believe he's a monster. He seems a very civilised sort of fellow. . .why should you say a thing like that? Unless. . . My child, I want to help you all I can, but I must know the truth. What is it about Carne that frightens you?'

Francesca gave a little shrug of resignation. Then she took a deep breath and said stiffly, 'Lord Carne has already asked me to marry him.'

'Well, then. . .?'

'Last year. At the time I thought he was hoping to make his fortune by marrying me, and I refused him. I told you about it.'

'But that's ridiculous. He's a very wealthy man himself.'

'I. . .I didn't know that at the time.'

'But now you do know.' Lord Beaudon frowned. 'But I don't understand—if he was rich, why did he want to marry you? He must have been in love with you, Francesca!'

'No. He was sorry for me. He felt some lingering sense of responsibility because he had abandoned me all those years before.'

'Rubbish! No man chooses a wife because he is sorry for her!'

'You're wrong, Papa. It's just the sort of thing Lord Carne would do. He is very involved in charitable works of every kind.' Francesca's tone was bitter.

'Well. . .it's just possible, I suppose.' Lord Beaudon sounded far from convinced. He went on briskly, 'But even so, that is no reason to reject him now. He's no fortune hunter, and you no longer need his pity or his money. Your pride wouldn't be hurt. It's perfect!'

'I *will not* marry Lord Carne, even if you managed to persuade him to make me the offer,' said Francesca fiercely.

'He would make a kind, considerate husband, Francesca. Isn't that what you were looking for?'

'Papa, don't you understand? I once loved Marcus to distraction. I could not now marry him for less. Kindness, consideration, friendship even—these are what I might seek in any other man. But not Marcus! Never Marcus. . .I could not be content with so little from him!'

'I see.'

'If it will make you happy, Papa, I will marry someone else—of your choosing, if that is what you wish.'

Lord Beaudon shook his head. 'I think you would be making a grave mistake, my dear. I must consider. . .'

'But I have your promise that you will not approach Lord Carne?'

'Oh, yes. That wouldn't answer. Not at the moment.'

He was still looking preoccupied when he left a few minutes later. Neither of them had thought of mentioning Paris.

Francesca's next visitor was Lord Denver. When he came in to the saloon, she was standing at the window, staring down into the street.

'Miss Beaudon! I hope you are well?' His voice, cultivated, resonant, with a pleasant timbre, expressed concern.

Francesca pulled herself together and turned to welcome him. 'Lord Denver—how pleasant to see you. I am quite well, thank you.'

'You look a little pale. . .'

'That is because I was too idle to go out for my walk this morning. And you?'

'Oh, I'm always perfectly fit. I rather hoped you would

come for a drive with me. I have the carriage outside.'

Francesca was about to refuse, but then changed her mind. 'I'll get my bonnet,' she said.

Lord Denver handled the horses with considerable skill through the crowded streets, then they drove out to pleasantly green parts of the town that Francesa had not seen before. His conversation was undemanding, but revealed facets of his personality she had not previously noticed.

He made her laugh with his account of the difficulties in running a family home that had its origins in a Norman castle, and had hardly been improved since, and she was impressed by his love of the countryside and his considerable knowledge of its flora and fauna. He was attentive without being obvious, and they returned to Mount Street perfectly in charity with one another. Francesca's spirits were considerably improved, as she thanked him.

'You. . .you mentioned that you had sketched some orchids near Shelwood,' Lord Denver said. 'May I see the sketches some time?'

'Would you like to see them now? I have them in my room here. You must not expect too much of them, Lord Denver—they have no great artistic merit. But I tried to capture the main characteristics of the plant.'

He made some complimentary response and she left him in the saloon while she fetched her drawings. When she returned he was speaking to Lydia, who had just come in from her ride. Her hat and veil had been discarded, revealing dark curls and glowing cheeks. Her eyes sparkled with laughter as she described some event at the previous night's ball. She was a picture of life and animation.

'Francesca! Lord Denver here swears that I must be teasing him. Tell him, if you please, what happened to

Lady Portman's wig! Did it or did it not catch in Sir Rodney Forrester's coat button?'

'I assure you it did, Lord Denver.'

'You see?'

'I was wrong to doubt you, Miss Canfield. I wish I had been there to see it.'

'Francesca had to take me away before I disgraced her by laughing out loud. But I think she was just as hard-pressed. And now you must excuse me. I have to change my clothes. Mr Endcombe is taking me to Somerset House, and I hardly think these will do.' Lydia curtsied and left them.

'A charming girl,' said Lord Denver, still smiling.

'She's a darling.'

Lord Denver looked at Francesca quizzically. 'You speak with rare warmth, Miss Beaudon. Miss Canfield is fortunate to have aroused such affection.'

'She deserves it.'

'And I? Could I hope in time to deserve a little of your affection?'

Francesca was unprepared for such a direct approach. She was still holding her sketchbooks and fingered them nervously as she replied, 'You have been very kind to me, Lord Denver. But I. . . I. . .'

He smiled. 'I spoke out of turn. Forgive me. Dare I hope you will come to the Lady Marchant's with me tonight? You did say you would.'

'Of course. I shall be pleased to.' She spoke warmly, relieved at avoiding a tender scene.

'I will call for you. Till tonight.' He took his leave without any further attempt to approach her.

And that evening he was once again the charming, considerate man she was growing to like. They left Lady Marchant's early. When they arrived at Mount Street,

Francesca was so much in charity with him that she invited him in.

'You left the sketches behind when you went this afternoon. They are still on the table—I told the servants to leave them.' They went into the salon. 'Here they are!' As she held the book out to him, the cover, worn with age, gave way and the contents fell to the floor. They both bent to gather them up, but Francesca froze as she recognised one of the sketches—a small orchid that had been flowering just ten years ago up on the hill above Shelwood. Sunlight on water, leaves against a blue sky, happiness such as she had never known before or since. . .

'Miss Beaudon! Francesca! You are not well! Let me help you!'

Francesca did not hear. She was staring at the sketch, overcome by a feeling of such pain and loss that she could not move. Then she became aware that someone was gently raising her and helping her over to the sofa by the window.

'Shall I ring for a maid?'

She looked up. Lord Denver was at her side. 'No. No, thank you. It was only a moment's weakness.'

'You were pale when I first called this morning. I have overtired you—the drive was too long.'

Francesca forced herself to speak normally. 'No, it was not that. I probably over-exerted myself at Lady Huntingdon's ball. I am perfectly well again now. Thank you for your concern, Lord Denver. You are very kind.'

'I should like to be much kinder to you, Francesca. Indeed, it is my very ardent wish that you would give me the right to cherish you for the rest of your life.'

The pain in Francesca's heart eased a little at the sincerity of his tone. 'Cherish' was a comforting word. She even managed to smile.

'Francesca? Would you. . .could you ever consider marrying me?'

She looked into the brown eyes so close to her own. True, faithful, kind, considerate, honourable. . .the temptation was very strong. If she married Lord Denver, she would be safe forever from Marcus, and the torment he could cause, safe from herself. Why did she find it so difficult to take the final step?

'You are very kind. I am honoured, Lord Denver. But I. . .I'm not sure. . .'

'Say yes, Francesca! I know I could make you happy.'

'I. . .I would need time to think. . .'

'But you will at least give me leave to hope?'

'I. . .yes, I will.' He snatched her hand and kissed it fervently.

'You have made me the happiest of men, my darling!'

'But—'

Neither of them had noticed that the door was open, nor that a tall figure was coming through it.

'Forgive me for interrupting you like this. The matter is urgent, or I would not have intruded on what is evidently a private moment.' Marcus was very pale, and he spoke in clipped tones. 'Your father is ill, Francesca. I have come to take you to him.'

Chapter Eleven

Francesca put her sewing down and looked over to the
bed. Her father was restless. She went over, and gave him
a sip of water, speaking to him softly. But he did not
respond, and eventually she sighed and laid him back
against the pillows, which were piled high behind him.
She went back slowly to her chair by the window and
picked up her sewing again. Dr Glover had assured her
that his patient was making good progress, but it was
difficult to believe him. For three days now, ever since
he had been taken ill at White's, Lord Beaudon had been
lying helpless, unable to talk or move without assistance.

'But he hears you, Miss Beaudon!' Dr Glover had said.
'He may not always understand the words, but a familiar
voice is a lifeline to him. You must talk to him, let him
know you are there.'

This Francesca had done. She had spent most of each
day in her father's room and at night she had the room
next to his, ready to be fetched at a moment's notice. The
outside world had not existed for her. All her attention
and energies had been directed towards the figure on the
bed, willing him to recover. She had talked to him often,
dredging her memory for details of their life on St Marthe
and the people there—her mother, Maddy and the rest.

Talk of London had seemed to distress him, and Francesca had avoided mentioning it, though she had wondered what the cause was—her father had always seemed so content with his life in the capital. Mrs Canfield, when asked, had seemed to think it might have something to do with the events at White's immediately before Lord Beaudon's collapse, but had not been able to tell her more precisely. Francesca had not pursued the matter—there would be time for that later. For the moment, she was content to concentrate on ensuring her father's recovery.

There was a gentle tap at the door and Mrs Canfield came quietly into the room. 'You have a visitor, Francesca. I'll sit with your father while you see him.'

'Who is it?'

Mrs Canfield shook her head and put a finger to her lips. 'I think you should go down and see for yourself.'

Puzzled, Francesca got up and after a quick glance at her father she went downstairs. Marcus was waiting for her in the salon. Shocked, Francesca turned to go back upstairs.

'No! Francesca, wait! I have to know how your father is.'

'You could have asked Mrs Canfield.'

'She thought I ought to see you.'

Francesca looked at him in astonishment. 'Maria wanted me to see you? Why?'

Marcus did not immediately reply. He strode about the room, looking most unusually ill at ease. 'Damn it, I don't like this,' he said savagely. 'I don't like it at all. Why the devil couldn't Maria have dealt with this?'

'What are you talking about? I don't underst—' Francesca drew in her breath and gripped the chair in front of her. 'It's about my father, isn't it? You were with him at White's. You know what happened. Were you the cause of his attack—is that it?'

'No, on my honour! But. . .but I was involved.'

'*What happened,* Marcus?'

'Your father was very angry at something he heard. He was about to challenge someone when he. . .when he fell ill.'

'Go on,' said Francesca. 'I want to hear everything, Marcus. Was it you he challenged?'

'No. It was Coker.'

'*Coker!*'

'We were all there at White's—your father, myself, Monty Banford, some others, and. . . Coker. And the Witham crowd. You don't want to hear this, Francesca.'

'Yes, I do!' she said fiercely. 'My father is lying upstairs helpless. He might even die. I want to know it all!'

'We'd all been drinking, but Witham and Freddie Chantry more than most. They hadn't seen your father— he was at a corner table. They started talking about the old days, about the parties at Witham, and how your grandfather had tried to stop them. One thing led to another and Freddie mentioned you. . .and me.'

'What. . .what did he say?' Marcus looked uncomfortable, and she added bitterly, 'No, you needn't tell me— I can guess. I know what he thought of me—he made it plain enough at the time.'

'But how could Freddie have said anything to you? He never saw you.'

Francesca looked at him derisively. 'Oh, but you're wrong, Marcus! He sought me out a few days after you left. On the bridge where I first met you. I think you must have given him a false impression of my. . .availability.'

'*What*?'

'Freddie and the others were very impressed with your account of my charms. The night after we met. I suppose you had to tell them? Anyway, he thought he could console me for your defection.'

'Good God—I never knew! Francesca, I swear it wasn't like that at all!'

'I deserved it. I had behaved like a w-wanton.' Her voice revealed self-condemnation. 'I deserved it all. But now my father has suffered because of it.'

'How could you possibly have deserved anything like that? What happened?'

'With Freddie? I was shocked and frightened, of course. Whatever impression I may have given you, I was. . .very innocent. My life had been rather isolated. He tried to kiss me, and I couldn't get away from him. That was when my aunt found us. She thought the worst, of course. I was in disgrace for a considerable time.' She gave him a twisted little smile. 'Wasn't that an ironic turn of Fate? The right punishment for the wrong man.'

'By God, if I'd known that I'd have throttled him! You have to believe me, Francesca, I had no idea of all this! Not till this moment.'

'No,' she agreed. 'How should you? You were away fighting for your country, weren't you? I expect you had already forgotten me. But why are we talking of this? It all took place a long time ago. Are you going to tell me what happened at White's? Was that when my father came into it, when Freddie told his tale?'

'Not then, no. I lost my temper and knocked Freddie down. I realised afterwards it was the wrong thing to have done. It only made the whole affair more public—it would have been better to take him outside quietly and deal with him there. But. . .I was in a rage. Freddie apologised when he came to, and withdrew what he'd said. Even then, if it had been left there, it would have been forgotten. No one takes much notice of anything Freddie Chantry says.'

'But Lord Coker was listening.'

'Yes. He sneered at Freddie for apologising. He never forgets an injury. He said he had seen us in the garden at Carlton House, and that anything Freddie had said was perfectly true. You can imagine the rest.'

'And?'

'I turned on him, but your father just swept me aside. He went up to Coker and demanded he withdraw his words. By God, Francesca, your father was impressive! I've never heard Coker so spoken to before.'

'But getting in a rage is bad for him! He shouldn't have done so. Why didn't you stop him?'

'I couldn't. No one could. And he didn't seem to be in a rage. He was cool. Icy. Very much in the grand manner. Coker couldn't bear it. He lost his head and went for your father.'

'Good God!'

'I hauled Coker back, but your father had already fallen. When I got to him he was unconscious. I thought. . .I thought at first he was dead.' He paused. 'You know the rest. Tell me, how is he now? I hear Dr Glover gives some hope?'

'I believe he is improving. There are more signs of consciousness than there were. What happened to Lord Coker?'

'He. . .er. . .nothing.'

'Tell me, Marcus! I shall ask someone else if you do not.'

'He objected to the way I had handled him. He was right. I hadn't been gentle. He challenged me.'

'To. . .to a duel? But they're no longer allowed!'

'I said I'd meet him wherever and whenever he wished. And I'd have been glad to. But the Prince got to hear of it, and Coker's now in disgrace. I hear he's talking of going abroad for a while.'

Francesca got up and walked about the room. Marcus's eyes followed her.

'And now?' she said finally. 'What are they saying now? About us?'

'It's forgotten, Francesca. And you needn't worry about Denver. I've seen him and made it clear that there's nothing in it. He. . .he was with you when it all happened, of course. I'm sorry I had to interrupt you.' He paused. 'I must wish you happy. I suppose this business with your father has delayed any official announcement?' Francesca looked blank. 'Of an engagement.'

Francesca hesitated. Then she said, 'Yes. Nothing can be settled until I am sure Papa is on the mend. What did you tell Lord Denver?'

'That he was a lucky man.' Their eyes met. Then Marcus looked away and walked to the window. 'A very lucky man.'

There was silence in the room. Francesca broke it.

'I must get back to Papa,' she said nervously. 'I'm sure he misses me when I am not there.'

'I should like to see him when he is fit to receive visitors. I'd like to reassure him that all is well.'

'Of course. I'll send you a message. And. . .thank you for telling me. Maria was right to insist.' She went to the door, but stopped, the handle in her hand as he said,

'Francesca!'

She turned slowly but stayed where she was, her back to the door. 'Marcus?'

'Do you love him?'

Francesca flushed painfully. 'He is a good, kind man—'

'Good God, I know that! But it wasn't what I asked. Are you in love with him?'

'There are different kinds of love, Marcus—'

Marcus muttered something incomprehensible and strode over to her. He looked at her for a moment, then swept her into his arms and kissed her hard, a passionate, deep kiss which made no concession to propriety or

féminine weakness. Her response was instinctive—
immediate and overwhelming. He grunted with satisfaction and kissed her again, more deeply than before. When
he finally released her, she would have fallen if he had
not supported her. He said with grim satisfaction, 'Is that
the kind of love you feel for Denver?'

Francesca's eyes filled with tears. She lifted her arm
and hit him as hard as she could. Then she opened the
door and ran up the stairs as if all the demons in hell
were after her.

As Marcus left the house and strode down the street, his
cheek was burning from Francesca's blow. But he was
unaware of it. His feelings were in turmoil. He felt
anger—with himself, with Francesca, with his long-dead
uncle, with the world at large. He felt regret—bitter
regret—for the pain and humiliation he had caused
Francesca all those years ago. It had been all so much
worse than he had ever suspected. Even more bitterly did
he regret his carelessness in throwing away something he
should have cherished beyond everything else.

But above all, his overmastering feeling was desire—
a passionate desire to return to Mount Street, to take
Francesca in his arms once more, to feel again her total
response to his kiss. Why had he never before realised
that Francesca was the one woman in the world for him?
The one woman in the world with whom he felt complete?
Why had he deceived himself for so long—complacently
seeking suitable husbands for her, smugly protecting her
from fortune hunters, when he should have been claiming
her triumphantly for his own? He had been stupid
beyond belief.

But recognition had come too late. Because of his own
wilful, incomprehensible blindness, Francesca now
belonged to someone else. To one of his best friends, in

fact. It was too much to bear. He shouted for a bottle of brandy when he arrived home, and spent the rest of the day in his room, completely failing to drown his sorrows. However, Marcus was made of stern stuff.

The next day, in spite of a bad hangover, he recovered a measure of reason. Though Francesca appeared to be lost to him, he could still be of service to her. His position in Society gave him power to protect her, to stifle any remarks which foolish gossips might venture. His friendship with the Canfields gave him every excuse to visit Mount Street, and once Lord Beaudon was well enough, he could visit him, keep him entertained during his convalescence. There might well be business that needed attention, matters which could not be entrusted to an unmarried female.

He grew happier at the thought that he could still help Francesca in all sorts of ways. It did not occur to him that these services might be better performed by her betrothed. When the thought did occur to him, he dismissed it. Denver was a good fellow, but simply not up to it.

The next time Marcus visited Mount Street he was told that Miss Beaudon was unable to receive him. And the next. When he asked Mrs Canfield to help him, she looked extremely uncertain.

'I don't know what was said the last time you were here, Marcus. But Francesca was very upset. I think you cannot have presented the affair at White's as tactfully as you should.'

'I know she was distressed. That's why I must see her—to put matters right.'

'She's with her father. I'll go up and ask her. But don't place too much confidence in my efforts. She is very determined.'

'How is Lord Beaudon today? Is he well enough to receive visitors?'

'He will be very soon. He still cannot speak, but he understands what we say, and can now nod or close his eyes in reply. It is a great improvement.'

She went away, but returned a few minutes later, shaking her head. 'I cannot prevail upon Francesca to see you. I have never known her so obstinate. I am sorry, Marcus. Perhaps in a little while. . .?'

Marcus set his jaw. 'Will you let me know when Lord Beaudon is ready to see people? I might at least be permitted to visit her father. Does Denver come often?'

'He is very attentive. But Francesca really does not have a great deal of time, you know. She is with her father most of the day, and rarely sees anyone other than myself and Lydia.'

'Is she getting fresh air?'

'I do my best to persuade her. She occasionally consents to go for a drive with Lord Denver, but it is not enough.'

Marcus looked at her curiously. She seemed unaware of any official link between Francesca and Denver. And though he had spoken to Denver himself several times, there had been no further mention of a betrothal. Damn it, he thought irritably, what was wrong with the man? He ought to have been here all the time, shouldering Francesca's burdens, making sure she had enough rest, exercise, fresh air and generally exerting his right to take care of her! What was the man made of?

Or—his heart gave a great leap at the thought—was it possible that he had been mistaken in what he had heard that fateful evening? Was there still a chance of winning Francesca, after all? Somehow or other, he must, he would find out. But to do that, he would have to see her, and at the moment that was apparently impossible. He would wait. She couldn't refuse forever.

None of these thoughts showed, however, as he said in his usual calm manner, 'I see. Well, I place my confidence in you, Maria. You have said you will let me know when Lord Beaudon is well enough to see me. Francesca need not be there if she does not wish. Is she. . .is she well?'

'She looks pale and tired, I'm afraid. It's natural—her nights are frequently interrupted. Once or twice I have found her sitting in her father's room wide awake, even in the small hours. It isn't at all necessary for her to do so—he sleeps quite well now, and, in any case, the nurse is always present. I think she herself finds it difficult to sleep.'

Marcus nodded. The sooner he sorted out this business of Francesca's engagement, the better. It was clear that she was urgently in need of someone to look after her.

The summons to Lord Beaudon's bedchamber came a few days later. Marcus set off for Mount Street in a frame of mind that was a good deal happier than on his previous visit. He had used the time to good effect. A convivial evening with Denver had established that the engagement was a tenuous one—more an agreement on the lady's part to consider an offer, rather than a commitment to accept.

Lord Denver was sanguine about the outcome. Francesca had treated him with more kindness than any of her other suitors, and, what was more, she had assured him that no one else, not even Marcus with whom her name had been linked, had a right to greater hope.

Marcus listened, filled up Denver's glass, and pitied him from the bottom of his heart. If his friend had succeeded in winning from Francesca a firm committment to marry him, then Marcus would have been forced to step aside. But as it was. . . Denver had no idea of Francesca's true nature. Her passion, her laughter, even the strength of her character were unknown to him. If he ever did manage to discover them, they might even come as an unwelcome surprise. No, there was no doubt whatsoever—Francesca would be wasted on this kind, conventional. . .ordinary man.

So Marcus went back to Mount Street, determined to set about persuading Francesca that she was his and his alone. His plans suffered a setback when he was told once again that Francesca would not meet him. Undaunted, he asked to see Lord Beaudon and was conducted up the stairs to a large bedchamber on the second floor. Francesca was nowhere to be seen, but Lord Beaudon was awake and watching with a fierce eye. Marcus greeted him fearlessly, then sat down and proceeded to give him a clear account of what had happened since the evening at White's. Lord Beaudon nodded once or twice, but still seemed unhappy.

'What is it, sir?'

The pale lips mouthed, 'Madeleine. P-Paris.'

'I don't understand. Can you repeat it?'

'Mad-M-Madeleine. Want you to go.' He moved restlessly when he saw that Marcus was still looking puzzled. 'Francesca. Fetch Fran. . . Francesca.'

Marcus went to the door and told the servant to bring Miss Beaudon. She came a few minutes later. When she saw Marcus, her step faltered, but her eyes went to her father. Marcus was shocked at her appearance. She looked as if she had not slept for a week.

'He was asking for you,' Marcus said. 'I'll leave you with him.'

There was a grunt from the bed. Francesca hurried over. 'What is it, Papa?' she asked urgently. 'Are you in pain?'

'Ca. . .arne. Stay.'

Marcus came back to stand on the other side of the bed. 'I'm here, sir. What can I do?'

'Pa. . .aris.' Lord Beaudon's eyes went to Francesca.

'Mmm-eant to tell.' He frowned and said suddenly, 'Madeleine.'

'That's what he was saying before,' Marcus said softly. 'Do you know what it means?'

'Madeleine. . . I don't—Papa! Do you mean Maddy?'

Lord Beaudon nodded, a smile of relief on his worn face.

'Do you know where she is?'

'Paa. . .ris.' Exhausted with his efforts to speak, Lord Beaudon closed his eyes.

'Papa! Papa!' There was no response. The eyelids did not even flicker.

'Leave him, Francesca. Let him rest.'

'But you don't understand! It's Maddy! He wants to tell me about Maddy.'

'He can't tell you anything more for the moment. Look at him.'

Lord Beaudon was lying perfectly still, eyes shut, his face pale and sunken. He was sound asleep.

'He'll tell you more when he wakes up. You'll have to be patient. Who is Maddy?'

'My nurse. On St Marthe. She came with me to England, but my aunt sent her away. I have always wondered what became of her.' A tear rolled down her cheek. 'He's known all the time, and never told me.'

'Come and sit down. Your father won't wake for a while. He's exhausted.' He led her to her chair by the window and sat her down. He looked at her white face, the dark shadows under her eyes, saw that her hands were trembling, and had some difficulty in stopping himself from taking her in his arms to give her comfort. He would almost certainly be rejected. Instead, he called the servant and ordered some wine to be sent up. When it came, he persuaded her to drink some. A little colour came into her cheeks. Then he drew another chair up and set himself to soothe her shattered nerves.

'Now tell me about Maddy. Her real name is Madeleine? It's a pretty name. My nurse was called Mrs Rolls. My sister and I called her Roly-Poly. And she was.'

'Maddy wasn't fat. She was a beautiful woman.'

'Tell me about her.'

Francesca seemed to have forgotten their last devastating meeting. She sat passively while he held her hand and encouraged her to talk about her life on St Marthe.

'Mama was ill after I was born. I don't know what she had, but it meant she had to rest a lot. Maddy was engaged to look after me, when I was just a few weeks old.'

'She took the place of your mother?'

'Oh, no! I spent a great deal of time with Mama—and Maddy was there, too. Mama had a huge bedroom with a veranda overlooking the sea. It was full of white draperies. I remember thinking how pretty they looked fluttering in the breeze—the Trade Winds, I suppose. No, Maddy and Mama were friends. They laughed a lot.'

'Who was Maddy? Where had she come from?'

'I'm not sure. I think she had lost her own family in a hurricane. She was a Creole. They were both so beautiful, Mama and Maddy. Mama was blonde and little, with dark brown eyes, but Maddy was quite tall. She had black hair and a skin that looked like the petals of the magnolias that grew at the side of the house.'

Marcus blinked. Privately he wondered how Lord Beaudon had dealt with the problem of an invalid wife and a raven-haired beauty as his daughter's nurse. It was as if Francesca could read his mind.

'I expect you're wondering about Maddy's position in our household. She was my nurse, of course. But later, when I got older and used to think about the time on St Marthe, I often wondered how my father viewed her. At the time I had no high opinion of him, so I assumed the worst. But one thing I was always sure of, even as a child. My mother and Maddy loved one another. Whatever happened, they were friends. And Maddy was as unhappy as I was when my mother died.'

'Whatever the truth of it, your father must have placed your comfort above his own. He sent this Maddy to England with you.'

'Yes, he did, didn't he?' She sat for a moment in thought. 'I didn't see a lot of him on St Marthe—or at least, I don't remember seeing him much. But since he came back, I have talked to him a great deal. I am quite sure now he was devoted to my mother.'

'When did your mother die?'

'When I was five. More than twenty years ago.'

'And you have never seen or heard of Maddy since she left Shelwood.'

'Not till today.'

'Then we must find out where she is. Your father clearly knows.'

'I think. . .I think she might have gone back to stay with him. Which would mean that she was in Paris now.'

'We shall see.' He took her other hand in his and bent forward. 'I'll help you all I can.'

Francesca looked up at him, then seemed suddenly to realise who he was. She snatched her hands away from him and jumped up. 'Thank you, but I don't need your help. I can send for Maddy myself as soon as I know for sure where she can be found.'

'Your father seems to regard me as necessary.'

'He is sick.'

'And therefore not to be listened to?'

'I told you, I don't need anyone!'

'What about Denver?'

'Oh. Oh, yes. He'll help me. If I need him. I must

ask you to go now. My father will soon wake.'

'In that case I must stay—to take my leave of him.'

Francesca said nothing, but moved away to the side of the bed. Once again Marcus stood on the other side. Their eyes met.

'Can't you forgive me?' he said.

'I. . .find it hard. I find it hard to forgive myself.'

'Don't say that! You have nothing, nothing at all, to forgive yourself for! Let me start again, Francesca. I've been all kinds of a fool, but you must believe me when I say that I've come to my senses at last.'

'I. . .I owe something to Lord Denver.'

'George Denver isn't the issue between us. You know that. Can you compare what you feel for him with your feeling for me? Can you forget what happened the last time we met?'

Francesca shut her eyes. When she opened them again, they were full of pain.

'Yes,' she whispered. 'Yes, I can. I will. I won't let myself remember. I don't want any part of it. Please go, Marcus!'

'I know I hurt you in the past, and I cannot say how much I regret it. But can't you bring yourself to trust me now? Please, Francesca!'

She started to shake her head, then looked at him uncertainly, confusion in her eyes. The sincerity in his voice had had an effect. 'I. . .I. . .I don't know,' she said at last. 'I don't know. I can't think at the moment. It's all been too much. You'll have to excuse me.'

He saw that she was at the end of her tether and grew angry with himself for pushing her too far, too quickly. 'It's all right, my dear,' he said swiftly. 'I'll wait. At least you haven't refused to think about it. But don't shut me out completely. I'll leave you to say your farewells to your father. I'll come again as soon as he wishes.'

He took his leave of her and went out. Francesca watched him go. Neither of them had noticed that Lord Beaudon's eyes were wide open, and that he was studying them both, straining to hear what they were saying. By the time Francesca turned back to the bed, his eyes were shut.

Chapter Twelve

Marcus cancelled most of his engagements and came back at an early hour the next day, without waiting for a summons. Lord Beaudon had made it clear that he was to help Francesca in the business of 'Maddy'. That 'Maddy' was important to both of the Beaudons was reason enough in Marcus's mind to abandon any obligations to the rest of Society.

When Mrs Canfield saw him arrive, she shook her head and intercepted him before he had set foot on the stairs.

'May I have a word with you, Marcus?'

He hesitated, then good manners prevailed. They went into the salon.

'Why are you here?'

'To see Lord Beaudon.'

'You are very good, I know that. Who should know better? But do you not think you are being a little. . .unwise, Marcus?'

'Unwise?' he asked with a touch of hauteur.

'The gossip has been silenced for the moment. But do you not think your frequent visits—your very frequent visits—might provoke more? You know what London is like. I am venturing to speak to you like this, Marcus, because I am very fond of both you and Francesca. She has enough to bear at the moment without becoming the topic of more speculation.'

'Lord Beaudon has conveyed that he wants my help in some way, Maria. I am here to see if he can make his wishes clearer. I shall probably not even see Francesca.'

'Is there no one else who can aid Lord Beaudon?'

'Apparently not. Not even Denver.' This was said with a certain degree of satisfaction.

'You realise that your readiness to help may lead others to read more into your relationship with Lord Beaudon's daughter than you might wish?'

'That is not possible.' Mrs Canfield's eyes widened. He smiled ruefully and said, 'I had not intended to say as much to anyone yet. Certainly not to Francesca herself—but I think I may rely on your discretion, Maria. You are the first to know that when all this is over, I intend to ask Francesca to marry me.'

'Marcus! This is very sudden. I had no idea—'

'Do you think she will?'

He waited for her answer with more anxiety than he was willing to reveal. Maria Canfield must be more in Francesca's confidence than most.

'I. . .I don't know,' she said slowly. He had the impression she was choosing her words carefully. 'You have a powerful effect on her, of that I am certain. I know you two met in the past, but Francesca has never talked about it to me. I suspect she has painful memories of it.' He would have spoken, but she went on, 'That must remain between you. I do know that she has set her mind on marrying someone. . .less dangerous to her peace of mind than you appear to be.' She paused, then added, 'Lord Denver is devoted to her.'

'He would never make her really happy, of that I am sure.'

'How can you say so? It is my opinion that Lord Denver

is everything a young girl could hope for. Indeed, I could have wished. . . But no matter.'

'That's just the point, Maria! George Denver is the best of fellows—a man couldn't ask for a better friend. He would make an excellent husband for a young girl— someone like Lydia, for example. But Francesca is not a young girl! She is an intelligent, strong-minded woman. In a very short time they would each be disappointed in the other. Francesca would be stifled, burdened by his concern, his desire to protect and indulge her. She could not maintain the image she presents to Society throughout years of marriage. Not without doing violence to her true character. And, ultimately, Denver would be made unhappy by her desire for independence, her strong views, her appreciation of a good argument—her passion, her impulsive ways. . .'

'Francesca? Impulsive?'

'You see? Even you, who have lived with her all these months, do not know the real woman.'

'And you do?'

'I know Francesca as I know myself. She is part of me, as I am sure I am part of her.'

'These are strong words, Marcus,' said Mrs Canfield, looking at him as if she had never seen him before. 'And I think I know you well enough to know that you do not use them lightly. But. . .have you considered this? Francesca may well not wish to be the real woman you claim to know.'

'What do you mean?'

'From the time Francesca Beaudon first came to Packards, she been single-minded in the pursuit of one ambition.'

'To find the sort of husband she thinks she wants. I know that, Maria.'

'That is not what I meant. Finding that sort of husband—a man like Denver, for example—is merely a symptom. Her real ambition is to protect herself from the kind of hurt she suffered in her earlier life. Her aunt's treatment of her was, from all accounts, unbelievably cruel. And, though I cannot imagine you meant to, I suspect you, too, hurt her—badly. Now she seeks calmer, kinder waters in her relationships. She allows herself affection—look how fond she is of Lydia. And her love for her father has deepened over the months. But strong, passionate feeling? I doubt if she will ever allow it to rule her.'

Marcus frowned and swung away to the window. He was silent for a minute. Then he said harshly, 'What you say merely makes me more determined. Given time, I know I could make her love me—as she should love someone. Anything else would be a denial of her true nature.'

Mrs Canfield looked at him thoughtfully. Then she smiled and said, 'In that case, I wish you success. I am quite sure that, if Francesca allowed herself to fall in love with you, she could not be in better hands. Will you take a little advice?'

'Of course.'

'Do not press her at the moment. She has enough to cope with. Act as the good friend I know you can be. This business with Lord Beaudon gives you an excellent opportunity.'

'So you've changed your mind—you approve of my visits?'

'You are always welcome, you know that, and now that I understand your real feelings, I will do all I can to promote your interests—we shall ignore gossip and speculation. And now I think Lord Beaudon has waited long enough.'

Marcus kissed her hand. 'If you can help me in this

matter, Maria, you will have more than repaid any trifling
service I may have done you in the past—ten times over!'

'I have to say that I never thought to see you in this
state, Marcus. I had quite given up hope that you would
ever marry.'

'Oh, I shall! And Francesca Beaudon will be my bride.
You will see!'

When Marcus entered the bedchamber, Lord Beaudon
was once again alert. He was looking at the door, an
expression of anxiety on his face. When he saw Marcus
he relaxed visibly.

'Good morning, sir.' Lord Beaudon inclined his head
and lifted his hand—shakily, but a movement all the same.
In response to the gesture, Marcus sat down by the bed.
He wasted no time on niceties—Lord Beaudon's strength
was limited and must be used on more important matters.
'You were telling me about someone called Madeleine—
Maddy. Is she in Paris?' Lord Beaudon nodded, looking
at him anxiously, and Marcus continued, 'She was your
daughter's nurse?' Another nod. 'You have been. . .look-
ing after her since she was sent away from Shelwood?'

A slight grin twisted Lord Beaudon's mouth as he
nodded, then the worried look descended again.

'You wish me to send a message to her. Should she be
sent for?'

This time there was a distinct frown.

'Fetch her myself?'

Another frown. The wrinkled hand on the cover
clenched in a gesture of frustration, as Lord Beaudon tried
to speak.

'Easy, sir, easy. It will come. Don't force it.'

'Don't understand. Hu. . .hurr-rry. Age—' Marcus was
puzzled again, but waited patiently. After a moment, Lord
Beaudon tried again. 'Age. . .nt!'

'Your agent? In Paris?' An impatient shake of the head. 'In London? You wish me to speak to your agent in London.' Lord Beaudon sank back with a sigh of satisfaction. 'I'll do it at once. Does Francesca know who it is, where he is to be found?' A tired nod. 'I shall find her and ask. Ah, here she is.'

Francesca came in with an older man, obviously a doctor. She was very formal as they greeted one another.

'Your father has requested me to visit his agent, Miss Beaudon. Could you give me his direction?'

Francesca looked at her father, who nodded slowly. 'Of course. I have it downstairs.'

'Then I shall wait downstairs. Do you wish your agent to come to see you, sir?'

The doctor intervened. 'If I may interrupt? I think that would be most unwise. Lord Beaudon should not exert himself as much as he has done already. He should not have any visitors at all.' His look at Marcus was severe.

Marcus smiled charmingly back. 'I am a family friend, sir. I venture to suggest that Lord Beaudon will be easier in his mind if someone he trusts is looking after his daughter, and his business affairs.' Ignoring a small gasp of indignation from Francesca, he turned to the figure in the bed. 'May I see the agent on your behalf, sir? I will report what he says.'

Lord Beaudon nodded. A close observer would have said that he was smiling.

Marcus returned later that day, but asked to see Miss Beaudon rather than her father. She came into the salon reluctantly.

'Don't look like that, Francesca. My reason for wishing to see you is perfectly legitimate. How is your father? I thought he looked brighter this morning.'

'He fell asleep again after you left. But in general he

seems to be improving by the hour. His ability to speak is slowly coming back to him. Why did you wish to see me?'

'I sent for Loudon, the agent, and your father's affairs are all in hand. There are a few papers for him to put a mark to when he is ready. But the news I was initially sent for—the news of Maddy—is not very satisfactory.'

Francesca sat down. 'What is wrong?'

'Your father rents a house in a fashionable quarter of Paris. Maddy lives with him there.'

'What is wrong with that? I'm sorry he concealed Maddy's presence for so long from me, but there's no reason to condemn—'

'I have made no such comment. Your father's affairs are his own. Don't jump down my throat, Francesca. I'm trying to help.'

'Well, what is wrong, then?' she asked, less than graciously.

'The house in the rue du Luxembourg has been closed. Maddy has disappeared.'

'What?'

'I wasn't able to make a great deal of sense out of what Loudon said. But it appears that when your father decided to spend the Season here in London, he sent a large sum of money to Maddy, care of his steward in Paris. This was for household expenses, including the rent on the property, which fell due last month. It, apparently, wasn't used for this purpose. The owners' agent has been trying to get in touch with your father for the past week.'

'But what has happened to Maddy?'

'Loudon doesn't seem to know.'

'But this is terrible! She must be found. I couldn't bear to lose her again after all these years. And my father. . .what will my father say?'

'That is precisely why I am consulting you. He must

be told, but gently. You must calm yourself, Francesca.'

'Yes, yes, of course. We must not alarm him. I will be calm.' She took several breaths, then said, 'It would be better if I had a plan of action to suggest to him. What can I do?' She paused again, then said with decision, 'I shall go to Paris.'

'You! Don't be absurd! What could you do in Paris? No, I must be the one to go.'

'It is you who is being absurd! Maddy doesn't know you, you have no connection with the Beaudons—what would the world think if Lord Carne were to race off to Paris in search of Miss Beaudon's former nurse?'

'It's better than having them wonder why you were allowed to go in search of Rake Beaudon's mistress!' He looked at her with a flicker of amusement in his eyes, asking her to share the joke. Her lips trembled into a reluctant smile, but she soon grew sober again.

'I'm serious, Marcus. I must be the one to go. I had already sent for Madame Elisabeth to help us with Papa. She should arrive any minute. I think I could persuade her to come with me, and I shall find a reliable courier to look after us.'

'You are still talking rubbish, Francesca. If you insist on going, I shall accompany you, of course.'

'You will not! How could I possibly allow it? What a field day that would make for the gossips!'

For a moment Marcus was tempted to declare himself. As Francesca's acknowledged fiancé, he could escort her, suitably chaperoned, on her father's business without arousing too much censure. But a moment's thought put a stop to the impulse. If Francesca refused him, as she well might, there would be an end to all communication between them. And she needed him at this moment more than ever before. He must find a way round the problem, not meet it head on.

'Your father will be wondering what has become of you. And of me. Francesca, shall we declare a truce for now? Before we launch into any schemes, it might make sense to find out exactly what your father wants.'

Francesca looked at him as if her mind were only half on what he was saying, and he wondered what she was plotting. But he was pleasantly surprised when she said, 'I agree. But I think we must tell Papa the truth. Evasion or pretence would only worry him more. His speech may be impaired, but his wits are as sound as ever.'

They went up to Lord Beaudon's bedchamber.

'I'm that glad you've come, ma'am. His lordship has been fretting this half-hour!' The nurse sounded and looked flustered. It was obvious that Lord Beaudon had been a difficult patient.

'Papa! I'm sorry I wasn't here. I. . .I was delayed.' Lord Beaudon made a dismissive movement with his hand. His eyes went to Marcus. As usual, Marcus wasted no time on formality, going straight to the point, as he knew Lord Beaudon wished.

'Good evening, sir. You are looking better. I've done as you asked. Loudon and I have sorted out most of your outstanding business, as you asked—and there are papers for you to sign.'

'Madeleine?' Lord Beaudon's speech was distinctly clearer.

'What is it you wish to do about Maddy, Papa?'

'Want her to know. . .I haven't forgotten. Haven't seen her. . .three months. . .more.'

'Does she know about me?'

He nodded. 'Proud of you.'

'Why didn't you bring her?'

'Gossip. Didn't want. . .to spoil. . .your début.'

'Oh, Papa! Why didn't you tell me? How could you leave her?'

'Francesca.' Marcus had put a warning hand on Francesca's arm. Lord Beaudon's eyes followed the gesture.

'Fetch her now. With his help.'

'Whose?'

A smile lit the tired face on the pillow. 'Carne's, damn it.'

'I cannot do that!'

'Course y'can. Get engaged. Time anyway.' He closed his eyes and slept.

The stormy expression on Francesca's face was confirmation enough that Marcus had been right to be cautious. As soon as they were outside the door of Lord Beaudon's room, she turned on him.

'I know what you are thinking, but I assure you that I have never encouraged my father to believe that I wished to marry you! Indeed, it is the last thing I want!'

He glanced round expressively. 'Shall we discuss this in private, Francesca?'

'There is nothing to discuss! I have no intention of becoming engaged to you, Lord Carne!'

'You force me to tell you in something less than privacy that I have at the moment no intention of asking you to be my wife, Miss Beaudon!'

They were both so absorbed that they were not aware of Mrs Canfield until she said gently, 'Francesca, I'm surprised. What sort of discussion is this to be having on the staircase? Take Lord Carne into the salon.' Unseen by Francesca, she raised an eyebrow at Marcus as she passed them.

Marcus was fighting for survival. He said more calmly, 'Your father's interests are surely more important than our own for the moment. We can talk more easily downstairs.'

Francesca, still looking mutinous, allowed herself to be led into the salon. Here she marched past him and sat down defiantly in the window seat.

Marcus said carefully, 'Whatever my feelings, I should not have indulged in that piece of discourtesy upstairs. I apologise.'

Francesca said stiffly, 'I provoked you to it, Lord Carne. You have no need to apologise.'

'Very well. Now, can we forget it and continue with our efforts to solve the problem of Maddy?' His even tone and casual air were designed to reassure. Francesca relaxed a little. 'It is now clear that someone has to go to Paris, and that your father will not be content unless we go together. Whatever our own views on the matter, his are quite clear. He wishes us to be engaged.'

'And that would suit neither of us,' said Francesca with determination.

'Quite. But may I suggest that we do not tell him that? I am sure we could travel to Paris together without arousing comment if I went on official business and merely acted as your courier. I do have some unfinished Foreign Office business in Paris. Perhaps Mrs Canfield and Lydia would come with you?'

'Mrs Canfield has agreed to supervise the care of Papa. And Lydia should not be dragged away from London at the moment.'

'True. I had forgotten. Madame Elisabeth? I heard you say she was already on her way here?'

Francesca looked at him. Once again, he had the impression that he had only half her attention. 'It might work, I suppose,' she said slowly. 'How long would it take to arrange?'

'A few days.'

'Good!' Marcus looked at her in surprise. He had been

delighted that she had agreed with so little resistance, but had thought she would object to the delay—short though it was. 'I mean,' said Francesca carefully, 'that it is good that we have managed to settle on a solution.'

'What shall we tell your father?'

'He will be happy to know that we have agreed to go. We need not go into great detail.' She smiled wryly. 'He trusts you, I am sure.'

'Do you?'

'Trust you? Why, of course!'

'Do you, Francesca? Really?' He moved closer to her, absurdly pleased at her words. But she avoided him and went to the door.

'Papa must know what we are doing,' she said, and went upstairs.

Marcus followed her in silence. Very well, my girl, he thought. We shall see how we progress when you and I journey to Paris together. There will be occasions when I shall have you to myself—I'll make certain of it! And then. . .we shall see.

Marcus visited Mount Street only fleetingly the next day, and not at all the next. He and Francesca had seen Lord Beaudon and told him of their decision. He had congratulated them both and expressed his delight, though it was clear that this was shadowed by his anxiety about Maddy. Marcus had felt some compunction at deceiving Francesca's father, but comforted himself with the thought that, if all went well, he and Francesca would, in truth, be engaged by the time they returned to London.

What Francesca made of it, he was not sure. She had recently been more open with him, but now she retreated once more into reserve, and he found it difficult to guess what she was thinking. He was content to wait. He would have all the time in the world on their journey to

France to find a way back into her confidence.

So though he sent messages to Mount Street, he did not have time to see the Beaudons himself. He had been speaking the truth when he said he had unfinished business in Paris, but there were people in London he had to consult first. He spent an energetic two days making arrangements and gathering papers, making sure that their journey would be as comfortable as man could make it, and sending couriers ahead to prepare their reception in Paris. It was a demanding time; if he had not been buoyed up by the hope of finally persuading Francesca to trust him, he would have found it exhausting.

He was shocked and furiously disappointed when he arrived in Mount Street and found Francesca already gone.

'Miss Beaudon isn't here? Of course she is!' he said sharply to the hapless footman who had taken his hat and cane.

Roberts, the butler, came to the rescue. Dismissing the footman with a nod, he said, 'Mrs Canfield left instructions that your lordship should be shown into the salon. Would you come this way, my lord?'

Containing himself with difficulty, Marcus allowed himself to be ushered into the salon. He refused an offer of wine somewhat curtly, and waited impatiently for Mrs Canfield to arrive.

'Maria, what's this nonsense about Francesca?' he demanded as soon as she came through the door. Mrs Canfield was in an unusual state of agitation.

'Francesca set off for Paris last night, Marcus.'

'You cannot mean it!'

'I'm afraid I do.'

'Does her father know?'

'No. We haven't told him yet.'

'Why the devil did you permit such a thing, Maria?' His tone was peremptory.

Mrs Canfield stiffened. She said, 'I knew nothing of the matter. Francesca took advantage of the fact that Lydia and I were at the Scarborough rout party to escape.'

'Did she go alone?'

'No. Madame de Romain arrived yesterday and I assume she accompanied Francesca.'

'Two women! When did you say she went?'

'Last night.'

'My God! Two women travelling through the night along some of the most dangerous roads in England.' He paced restlessly through the room, then he stopped and turned. 'You must have suspected something! Why didn't you stop such a mad escapade? Or at least send for me!'

'Marcus, I make every allowance for your sense of shock, but you are being unnecessarily rude. I repeat—I had no idea, no idea at all that Francesca would undertake such a foolhardy enterprise. Nothing about her behaviour in the past would have led me to suspect it.'

'I told you that Francesca was impulsive and head-strong, and you refused to believe me. Oh, this is exactly like her! I should have anticipated it. Past experience should have taught me.'

'I can still hardly credit what you say. But I have come to agree with you, Marcus, that she needs a stronger man than Denver to control her. This will be a most unpleasant surprise for him. I believe him to be sincerely in love with her, but he will be shocked beyond measure at her behaviour.'

'Denver? Bah! He's too gentle a man for Francesca. Even I couldn't control her. No, with Francesca, you merely try to guard her from the worst of her follies, and love her for them. And hope that, with time, she will trust you enough to allow you power over her!' He had been talking almost to himself. But now he went on, 'So you see, Maria, I have to rescue her. I'll leave straight away, though it's impossible to catch them up before the packet sails. I wish you had sent for me sooner.'

'I did try to find you, but you were not at home. I could hardly send round the clubs for you!'

'I was with Stewart's man in the Foreign Office. Oh God, I hope she's safe!' He made for the door, then stopped. 'What about Lord Beaudon?'

'There's a note for him. I wasn't sure what to do, so I waited for you to come before giving it to him.'

'I'll take it. He's pushed her into this. If he hadn't been so hasty, we'd have managed very well. You'd better warn Glover to be on hand.'

But Lord Beaudon took what the letter had to say with remarkable fortitude. It did not mention the name Carne, but Francesca's reluctance to be in his company was clear in every line. When Marcus grew pale and clenched his jaw, Lord Beaudon chuckled. 'Don't worry. She'll have you,' he said. 'Patience. I suppose you're going to follow her?'

'I must. Though she does seem at least to have had the sense to supply herself with plenty of protection.'

The letter had been intended to reassure Francesca's father about her safety. She told him that she had used a reputable agent and she and Madame Elisabeth had found companions and guards for their journey. And they had letters of introduction, together with the addresses of some of Madame Elisabeth's old friends to help them in Paris.

'This is ridiculous!' Marcus burst out.

'Then be off to Paris and tell her so. And bring Madeleine back with you!' was Lord Beaudon's response.

Marcus wasted no more time. He was forced to take the travelling coach he had prepared with such care, for it contained all his papers, but it meant that progress was not as fast as he would have wished. But it was too late in any case to catch Francesca's party before they embarked for France, and the next packet was not till the following day. But, all the same, Marcus chafed at the delay. In spite of Francesca's reassurances he wanted to see for himself that she was safe and sound. And preferably under his own protection!

As Francesca travelled the long road to Paris, she occasionally allowed herself to wonder what the journey would have been like in Marcus's company. In different circumstances it could have been. . .idyllic. But she did not allow her mind to dwell on this for long, and not once did she regret her hasty decision to come to France without him.

Lord Carne may be everything Society said of him— totally honourable, completely dependable, absolutely scrupulous. But the Marcus that was lodged so unshakeably in her heart was none of these. The admirable Lord Carne would never attack a helpless female as she had been attacked in the salon at Mount Street. And elegant Miss Beaudon would never respond to any man at all in the abandoned manner in which she had responded, returning kiss for kiss, meeting passion with passion.

But Francesca and Marcus. . .ah, that was different! Neither reason nor respect for propriety, no sense of self-preservation or fear of hurt seemed to hold back this overwhelming force which could flare into life between them. Time had not affected it—at twenty-five she was as vulnerable to Marcus as she had been when she had given in to his charm when she was not even sixteen. She had managed to survive the experience of a broken heart once. A second exposure might well destroy her. The only way to guard herself was to avoid as much contact with him as possible. . .as she would.

*   *   *

They arrived in Paris early in the evening after an uneventful journey and went to a hotel not far from her father's house, recommended to them by connections of Madame Elisabeth. It was too late to pursue the question of Maddy that evening, so the two ladies retired early to their rooms and tried to get some rest.

The next morning they set off, armed with a street guide and Lord Beaudon's address. Though the rue du Luxembourg took some time to find, Lord Beaudon's house was soon identified. It was securely locked up. They tried knocking, and pulling the bell, but there was no response. When Francesca looked all round for someone to consult, the street was deserted.

'We are too early, Francesca. No one stirs here till midday.'

'Surely there must be some servant. . .?'

'Not in the front half of the houses, not before noon. Haven't you noticed that there are no street vendors about, either? Their cries are not allowed to disturb the peace of this neighbourhood till later in the day. If we return this afternoon, I am sure we shall find someone.'

Francescsa had to agree, and they returned, somewhat tired, to their hotel, where they went to their rooms to rest. But when Francesca called for Madame Elisabeth later in the day, she found that lady stretched out on her couch looking very frail.

'I am sorry, Francesca. I cannot walk another step today. Could we try again tomorrow?'

'Of course! You make me ashamed of myself, Madame Elisabeth. I dragged you all the way here without pause or rest, and then got you up early. . . Of course, you need rest. I have been unpardonably selfish.'

'Oh, no, my dear! You are anxious to find your nurse, I understand that. I shall be perfectly fit tomorrow, you'll see.'

Francesca sent for a chambermaid to attend to Madame Elisabeth. 'You must not allow me to stop you, Francesca,' said Madame Elisabeth. 'It is a beautiful afternoon—I am sure you would find someone to ask if you went back to the rue du Luxembourg.' She spoke to the maid in rapid French, then turned to Francesca. 'The maid says the streets are quite safe round here, but you must take care if you go further afield.'

Francesca thought for a moment. Then she said, 'I think I'll take the carriage, Madame Elisabeth. It's here in the stables, and the grooms are in the yard—I saw them as we came in. I just might want to go further, if someone tells me where Maddy can be found.'

'Of course. I'm sure you wish to find your nurse as soon as possible. You must be worried about her.'

'Are you sure you'll be all right? I'll get one of the chambermaids to stay with you if you wish.'

'No, no, that won't be necessary. A rest today and I shall be quite well again. And I am happy that you will be safe with the grooms we brought from England to guard you. They seem to have their wits about them. Off you go, my dear. And—*bonne chance*!'

The street was full of activity when Francesca arrived there for the second time. Nursemaids were walking the children, footmen were delivering notes and parcels, and next door to her father's house an elegantly dressed lady was just setting foot in her carriage. Francesca sent one of the grooms to knock at the door of her father's house and waited, aware of curious glances directed at her from all sides. The groom knocked once more, but there was still no response. Her heart sinking, Francesca left the carriage and went up to the house. The groom shrugged his shoulders and shook his head.

'It's no use trying there. They've gone.' Francesca's

French was far from perfect, but it was adequate enough to understand these words. She turned round. The speaker was about eight years old, and looking up at her with a child's curiosity. *'Tais-toi, Virginie!'* The nursemaid with the little girl took her hand and hurried her away.

Francesca looked helplessly round. The elegantly dressed lady, who had stopped to stare, got into the carriage and gave an abrupt order. The carriage moved off before Francesca could speak to her. A small crowd of footmen, other servants, street vendors and children had gathered at the bottom of the steps, gabbling rapidly. Francesca regretted that Madame Elisabeth was not with her. Her own French was not equal to this.

'C'est la maison de Milord Beaudon?' she asked hesitantly.

They all stared, then one of the footmen, taking pity on her, said, *'Oui, mais. . .* the little one is right, *mademoiselle.* The English milor' has not been here for months. More. And *Madame* was taken ill.' Francesca caught this last word—*malade* was ill.

'Where is *Madame* now?' she asked. The footman shrugged his shoulders. There was a discussion. At one point they eyed her uncertainly, then shook their heads.

'Please,' she cried. 'I must see *Madame*!'

They only shook their heads again. One woman—a street vendor from her looks—obviously disagreed with the rest. She harangued them in a French which was totally incomprehensible to Francesca's untutored ear. They replied in kind, and the footman ended the discussion with a decisive *'Non!'* Then he turned again to Francesca.

'I regret, *mademoiselle*, we cannot help you. Perhaps the embassy will advise you?'

Francesca thanked him, pressed a few sous into his hand and turned away disconsolately. She had the impression that they knew what had happened to Maddy, but had decided not to tell her. The speed with which they disappeared seemed to confirm this notion. She started back towards the carriage, and was just getting in when she heard,

'Psst! Psst, *mademoiselle*!'

Francesca turned. The street vendor was sidling up behind her. The groom attempted to push her away, but Francesca stopped him. The woman clearly had something to tell her. She was talking in some kind of patois, but when she saw that Francesca did not understand a word, she tried again, more slowly.

Francesca gathered that she was trying to give her an address, and eventually, after many false starts and failed repetitions, Francesca managed to say the address to the woman's satisfaction. She beamed with pleasure and held out a dirty hand. Francesca gave her some money, and they parted on good terms. As she hurried off down the street, the woman shouted something in a warning voice, but Francesca did not heed her. She was sure that *La Maison des Anges* in the rue Giboureau was where she would find Maddy. It sounded like a hospital of some sort.

Chapter Thirteen

After studying the street map one of the grooms had procured, Francesca saw that the rue Giboureau was some distance away in what looked like a prosperous district not far from the Bois de Boulogne. It should be easy to find. It was still early, so Francesca decided that, if she went straight there, she could see Maddy, find out how she was and still have time to get back to the hotel before it was too late. Then the next day, if Maddy's health permitted, she could set about making arrangements to convey her to England. Francesca gave the orders, and the carriage set off in the direction of the Bois de Boulogne.

The journey took longer than Francesca had anticipated, and it was almost evening before they reached the rue Giboureau. The road was lined with high walls, interrupted occasionally with tall, elaborately decorated iron gates. Francesca marvelled at tantalising glimpses of opulent houses set in lawns and flowerbeds behind them. If Maddy was in one of these, she was clearly being comfortably looked after—these mansions were like no hospital Francesca had ever seen.

'Miss Beaudon! Look!' One of the grooms was pointing at an elegantly discreet board set outside an open gateway which bore the legend *Maison des Anges*.

They drove up a short drive, lined with statues of nymphs in various graceful poses, to a beautiful house, built in the days before the Revolution. Broad steps led up to an imposing portico and intricately carved doors, and again there was an elegant board at the side which gave the name of the house. This time the board was surmounted by the head of a beautiful girl, her long, curling locks forming a frame for the whole.

Francesca rang the bell and then studied the board more closely as she waited. Flowers and leaves formed a background to the girl's head, all beautifully carved, and looking very lifelike—there were even a few insects on the flowers. Francesca saw that they were mostly bees— in fact, they were all bees. How strange!

'*Madame?*'

An exotic figure in Turkish costume was standing impassively at the door. He was at least six and a half feet tall with huge shoulders and a swarthy face half hidden by an imposing moustache.

Francesca blinked, checked the board, which still said *Maison des Anges*, and cleared her throat. In her coolest manner she said, 'I have come to see Madame Madeleine. . .' She stopped. What name would Maddy now be using? 'Madame. . .'

'*Je regrette. Madame Madeleine est malade.*' The deep voice expressed nothing but a detached finality. He started to close the door.

'Yes, I know she is sick,' said Francesca, raising her voice and speaking with all the authority at her command. 'I have come to her. Please tell her that Miss Beaudon, Miss Francesca Beaudon, is here. Meanwhile, I should like to see your. . .your *directrice*.'

'*Pas possible!*'

'Of course it is possible! Kindly let me in!'

'*Qui est-ce, Hassim?*' Hassim's tall figure completely

blocked the view into the hall, so Francesca did not see the owner of the voice until she appeared at her servant's side.

The man bowed. *'Une anglaise, Comtesse. Elle veut voir Madame Madeleine.'*

Though the Countess was in her fifties, she was still a beautiful woman. Her hair was grey, but fashionably cut, and her dove-grey dress, though sober in hue, was of heavy silk and trimmed with white lace. The figure revealed by the superb cut of her dress was still elegantly slender.

Francesca was impressed, but did not disguise her annoyance with this cavalier treatment. 'My name is Beaudon,' she said coldly. 'Until recently, Madame Madeleine was living in the rue du Luxembourg, in my father's house. I am one of her oldest friends. It surely cannot be that difficult for me to see her. Even if. . .' Francesca hesitated. 'Is she so very ill?'

The Countess looked disconcerted. 'Miss Beaudon? The daughter of Lord Beaudon? But you should not be here, mademoiselle! Please go at once!'

Francesca set her jaw. 'I have come from England to see my friend, and I am not going until I know how she is!'

'But you don't understand. . . Oh, *mon Dieu*, you mustn't stand here on the doorstep where anyone could see you. It is most unfortunate. Please go!'

'If you do not take me to see Madame Madeleine, *immediately*, I shall return with someone from the British Embassy.'

The Countess had been looking distinctly agitated, but at these words her lips curved into an ironical smile. 'It wouldn't be the first time one or two of them had visited me, *mademoiselle*, but they wouldn't bring *you* back here, I assure you.'

'What do you mean?' Francesca was growing angrier

by the minute. 'Surely even in Paris one may visit a sick friend in hospital?'

'A *hospital*! Is that what you think? Ah! Now I understand. . .a hospital! That explains a lot.' The woman turned her head away, but Francesca could have sworn she was laughing. It was too much! Exasperated, she turned on her heel and started down the steps.

'No! Wait, Mademoiselle Beaudon. I have changed my mind. You can see Madame Madeleine, if you promise not to stay too long. I think you are right. Your visit might do Maddy some good.'

Francesca swung round and stared at the Countess. *'Maddy?'*

'I, too, am a friend of Maddy's. An even older friend than you, I think. But please come inside. We can talk more comfortably there. If you will permit, Hassim will show your groom where to put the carriage. But you must be away from here before. . . Please do come in, Mademoiselle Beaudon.' When Francesca hesitated, the Countess said with a charming smile, 'You shall be perfectly safe, I assure you. Believe me, my sole object is to protect you. Let Hassim speak to your groom. We cannot leave the carriage in the drive for all to see. Come!'

Somewhat doubtfully Francesca allowed herself to be escorted inside.

Francesca had an impression of velvet and gilt, painting and statues, ormolu and boulle, as she walked into the grand entrance hall. Spacious rooms could be glimpsed on each side, and a broad staircase swept up in a wide curve to the first landing, its balusters supporting candelabras in the form of nymphs on either side. The house obviously belonged to someone of enormous wealth, though the furnishings were too opulent for Francesca's

taste. What sort of hospital was this? She looked doubtfully at her hostess.

'I shall take you straight away to Maddy. I think you
will be reassured when you see her. She has been ill, but
will soon be well again.'

Francesca tore her fascinated gaze from one of the
nymphs, on whose scantily clad bosom rested a small
carved bee, and said, 'But. . .why is she here, *Comtesse*?'

The Countess had started up the stairs, but now she
stopped. 'Do you not know? Your father has sent no
money to Maddy for the past three months—since he last
visited her, in fact.'

'But, indeed, he has! His agent in London. . .'

'Swears he has sent it? I thought as much,' said the
Countess, looking satisfied. She started up the stairs again.
'I said so to Maddy. Richard has not forgotten you, I told
her. And if she had not been ill, I think she would have
had more confidence in him, and pursued the matter.
There has been some trickery, I think. I never trusted her
steward, I'll swear he's to blame. But. . .why are you here,
mademoiselle? Why has your father not come in person?'

As Francesca explained the circumstances which had
led to her visit, they reached the top of the stairs and
started walking down a wide corridor with beautifully
carved and painted doors on either side. Once again the
theme was that of nymphs, bees and flowers, though here
some of the nymphs were disporting themselves with
more exuberance than decorum. Francesca blinked at one
spectacularly improper scene and hastily averted her eyes.
They passed a smaller passage leading off to the left,
which was hung with diaphanous rose and gold draperies.
The air here was scented with roses and a heavier, more
exotic perfume.

Francesca wanted to ask the Countess what it was, but
her attention was caught by a deep semi-circular alcove

a little way beyond the side passage. The walls were covered in dark red damask and in the centre was a small fountain. A white marble nymph was bathing herself in abandoned grace in the basin at its foot. Francesca felt the colour rising in her cheeks. The statues Lord Elgin had brought from Greece had been positively *chaste* compared with this. She hurried to catch the Countess up. 'I had no idea where Maddy was, otherwise I would have written to her long before this, *Comtesse*. Where. . .where are we?'

'You know where you are, Mademoiselle Beaudon. You are in *La Maison des Anges*.'

'Yes, but. . .' Francesca looked back doubtfully at the marble statue, but said no more. They turned into another side passage to the left, an altogether simpler affair with no doors, no draperies and only a faint scent of lavender.

'Maddy talks of you frequently. She loved you and your mother.'

'You have known her long?'

'We were children together.' They had now reached the end of the passage. The Countess turned and started to mount a narrow staircase. The scent of lavender grew stronger. 'We married more or less at the same time, had our babies more or less at the same time. Then the hurricane came to the island. . . We both lost everything. . .everything. We left the island after that— we could not bear to stay.'

'Maddy came to St Marthe. She was my nurse.'

'I know. And I came to France. But here is Maddy's room, *mademoiselle*. Wait here one moment.'

They had been talking so busily that Francesca had had no time to look around. She saw that they were now in a much plainer part of the house, and the door that faced them was uncarved and unadorned. The Countess went in and Francesca could hear her speaking rapidly, then an exclamation of joy in another voice—a well-loved voice from years ago. Questions and answers followed. She could make out none of the words, though there were echoes of the patois she had learned on St Marthe in her childhood. Then the Countess came out again.

'She is overjoyed to be seeing you again, but still weak—do not overtire her, Mademoiselle Beaudon. I have much to do, so I hope you will excuse me now. But. . .I *beg* of you, do not leave this room until I come to fetch you.' She led the way into a simply furnished room and then went out again. Francesca did not see her go—all her attention was on the figure in the armchair by the window. Maddy held out her arms and Francesca ran to her with a cry of delight.

Marcus arrived in Paris a little less than twenty-four hours after Francesca. He drove straight to Francesca's hotel, and found Madame Elisabeth alone in her room. From there he went to the rue du Luxembourg, and discovered that the house was still shut up and deserted. There was no sign of Francesca, but one of the boys in the street told him he had seen an English lady driving off in a big coach earlier in the day. He had no idea where they had gone.

Marcus went back to the hotel to find that Francesca had still not appeared, and that Madame Elisabeth was beginning to grow anxious for her. After doing his best to reassure the old lady, Marcus then went to the British Embassy and spent some time with a certain Mr Percy Gardiner, one of his closest friends there. What he discovered appalled him.

'Good God! Are you sure? *La Maison des Anges*?'

'Only too true,' said Mr Gardiner, looking at him curiously. 'Why are you so upset? The lady mean anything to you? No, that can't be so—Madeleine Lachasse is nearly old enough to be your mother, Marcus old dear.'

'She's nothing to me personally. I. . .I'm acting for a friend.'

Mr Gardiner looked sceptical. 'Well, you'd do better to tell your friend to leave *La Maison* well alone. Good Lord, I don't have to tell *you* what goes on there—apart from serving as a high-class brothel with some very peculiar practices, that is.'

'I have to get her out of there.'

'You mustn't go near the place, Marcus!' exclaimed Mr Gardiner, dropping his casual air. 'What the devil can you be thinking of? Don't touch it! Can't someone else fetch the lady?'

A vision of Francesca arriving at *La Maison des Anges* flashed through Marcus's mind. He shuddered. 'That's just what I'm afraid of. Er. . .has anyone else been asking about Lord Beaudon's *petite amie*? Today, or yesterday, perhaps.'

'No. . .I don't think so.'

'It's important, Percy. Could you ask around?'

Mr Gardiner came back a few minutes later with the assurance that no one had even mentioned the lady for the past few months. Marcus breathed a sigh of relief. Francesca had not yet learned Maddy's address. But in that case, where was she?

'What is all this about, Marcus? You can't seriously be considering visiting that palace of corruption! Think what it would do, man, if you were found there!'

'I know. But I must get Madeleine Lachasse out of the place as soon as possible—before anyone else goes looking for her.'

'I think you'd better explain.'

Marcus paused, then gave Mr Gardiner an edited version of his mission. Francesca's name did not figure in it.

'But damn it all, you cannot—you really cannot—be prepared to jeopardise all your work for the past year for the sake of this. . .this paramour! What is Richard Beaudon to you?'

'His daughter and I are betrothed,' said Marcus, stretching the truth a little.

'All the same. . . Wait here!'

Marcus spent the next few minutes arranging his thoughts. He was determined to go out to *La Maison des Anges* as soon as he was free of the Embassy, but knew that he was about to have a serious disagreement with people he had worked with in complete harmony over the last twelve months.

'What's this nonsense, Marcus? Don't be a fool, man. Of course you can't visit *La Maison*.' Marcus got to his feet and bowed to the distinguished-looking gentleman who now came in. Percy had wasted no time in bringing up the heavy guns. His friend gave him an apologetic glance, then went out, shutting the door carefully behind him.

'Good evening, Sir Henry.'

'Oh, good evening, good evening! No! It won't damn well be any sort of good evening if what young Percy tells me is true. Have you gone mad?'

Marcus gritted his teeth. 'No, but I can't see anything else to do. I have to get that woman out of *La Maison des Anges* as soon as possible.'

'The devil take it! Can't anyone else go instead?'

'No, sir. The matter is one of some delicacy. . .'

'To hell with that, Marcus! Look, if you are found anywhere near that hotbed of Napoleon supporters you'll. . .*we*'ll lose all credibility with the French government—you know that! Of all of us, you're the one man they really trust. An escapade like this would ruin months of work. I forbid you to go.'

Marcus grew pale. 'You'll have to forgive me, Sir Henry. I am not one of your staff. And I intend to go, as soon as I leave you, to fetch Madeleine Lachasse.'

'But *why*?'

Marcus was in a dilemma. The last thing he wanted was to bring Francesca into the discussion. She was at present loose in Paris, searching for her old nurse, and his blood ran cold at what she might do if she found out where the woman was. He placed no reliance on her sense of self-preservation. Impulsive, headstrong Francesca would once more rush in where angels would never dare to tread, but this time the consequences could be disastrous. For all its name, *La Maison des Anges* was no place for any kind of angel!

If that happened, then it would need all the discretion, all the skill at his command, to save Francesca from a catastrophic scandal. If it were once known that the Honourable Miss Beaudon had been found in one of the most notoriously wicked brothels in Paris, nothing—not a thing!—could save her from social extinction.

'*Why*, Marcus?'

Marcus was not to be rushed into a reply. He had no illusions—Sir Henry was perfectly capable of restraining him by force from visiting *La Maison des Anges*. That would hardly benefit Francesca. He must persuade, not fight.

'First, I should tell you, Sir Henry, that Lord Beaudon's daughter has agreed to marry me. . .'

'So London's most eligible bachelor has been caught at last? My congratulations, Marcus. But we'll give this news the attention it deserves later. At the moment. . .'

'That is the point, sir. Why I have to reach Madeleine Lachasse—tonight, if possible.' He took a breath. 'Madeleine Lachasse was Miss Beaudon's nurse, and Miss Beaudon herself is in Paris in order to take her back to England.'

'Good, good. So why can't we send one of the embassy

staff to fetch the Lachasse woman and deliver her to
yourself and Miss Beaudon? I'd like to meet her while
she's in Paris, by the way. She must be a real diamond
to have trapped you, Marcus.'

'I. . .I don't know where she is, sir.'

'What the devil do you mean?'

'Miss Beaudon is devoted to her nurse, Sir Henry. She
was in such haste to meet her again that she left London
ahead of me. However, Madeleine Lachasse was not at
the rue du Luxembourg house, so Miss Beaudon decided
to seek elsewhere. My worst fear is that she will find out
where the woman actually is, and visit her there. That is
why I wish to get to *La Maison* as soon as possible. Why
I will not trust anyone else with the mission.'

'But, good God, man! Surely no delicately nurtured
female would go near such a place!'

'Miss Beaudon can be a touch. . .impulsive, sir.'

Sir Henry frowned. 'Are you sure she's the right girl
for you, Marcus? Travelling alone to Paris, visiting all
sorts of queer places—she sounds like a bit of a hoyden.'

Marcus stiffened. 'She is everything I could wish for,
sir. She can be the soul of propriety. But where her loyalty
is concerned, she simply doesn't heed the cost. I consider
it my duty—and my deepest pleasure—to protect her
from her own impulsive generosity. But you are right—
her reputation is in some danger, and if it is to survive,
she needs my help tonight. I know I can rely on your
discretion, but the story is too dangerous to be trusted to
anyone else.'

Sir Henry sat in thought for a moment. Then he said,
'I suppose most of the men who go to visit the "Angels"
take care not to be recognised. It wouldn't be too suspicious if you were to muffle yourself up a little. Very
well! But. . .for God's sake, don't get caught! If you do,

we'll have to disown you, you know that. It will be the end of your work here.'

Marcus called again briefly at Francesca's hotel, only to find no news of Francesca, and Madame Elisabeth in a state of great anxiety. He refused all pleas that she should accompany him on his quest, claiming that she should remain where she was in case Francesca should return by herself. He did not reveal where he feared she might be.

He hired a fiacre to take him to the rue Giboureau—a slow business, but necessary to preserve his anonymity. When he finally arrived at the house it was getting late, though still early in the evening for its normal clientele. Hassim received him and asked him to wait in the hall till the Countess could be found. Marcus shook his head.

'I wish to speak to Madeleine Lachasse,' he said firmly. 'Take me to her, if you please.'

'*Madame Madeleine est malade.*'

'I know. Where is her room? Has she a visitor?'

Hassim glanced up. It was enough. Marcus leapt up the stairs two at a time, ignoring nymphs, candelabras, bees and the rest. At the first side passage he hesitated, and Hassim caught up with him.

'*Monsieur*!' He took hold of Marcus, but was pushed away so violently that he lost his footing and fell. Ignoring him, Marcus strode on past the alcove to the second passage. He paused to listen, then found his way to the small flight of stairs which led to the servants' quarters. At the top he could see a figure in a wine-red silk evening dress standing at an open door. She was speaking with emphasis to someone inside the room.

'Miss Beaudon, I beg of you, come away now. You have stayed far longer than you should. The evening visitors will be arriving at any moment. You *must not* be discovered here. I shall send Maddy to your hotel as soon as she is well enough, I promise you. That cannot be more than a day or two. Meanwhile, you must wait in patience, and not visit her here again.'

Francesca's back emerged from the room. For a moment Marcus could hardly breathe, he was so relieved to see her. Then he was overcome with sudden fury at her foolhardy, stupid, potentially catastrophic behaviour.

'I shall see you soon, Maddy. Very soon, I hope.' Francesca's voice was tremulous. The meeting had obviously been an emotional one. She went on, 'Then I shall take you back to England. Goodbye.'

'Miss Beaudon! Come! Quickly!' Exasperated, the Countess took Francesca's arm and ushered her out of the room, shutting the door behind her. She stopped suddenly at the sight of Marcus. He took a step towards her, but Hassim, who had just arrived, seized him from behind. With a roar Marcus turned on the Turk, glad to have an outlet for his rage.

'Hassim! No!'

'Marcus!'

The two voices spoke together. Hassim stepped back immediately and Marcus and Francesca faced one another.

'You fool, Francesca! What the devil do you think you are doing now? You unutterable fool!'

'Lord Carne!' The Countess took a step forward, then turned to her servant. 'Hassim, go back to the door. Don't let anyone up here till I tell you. Keep them below. And, don't say a word of this to anyone, you understand me?'

Hassim bowed and went in unruffled dignity downstairs.

'Lord Carne—this is a most. . .unexpected pleasure. May I ask what you are doing here?'

'Saving that. . .that. . .' Marcus could not find a suitable word. 'That idiot girl from her own folly.'

'It is no folly to visit a sick friend in hospital, sir!' said Francesca with spirit.

'*Hospital*!'

'That is what Miss Beaudon believes *La Maison des Anges* to be, Lord Carne.'

'Oh, God!' said Marcus.

'Quite,' said the Countess, her lips twitching in spite of her obvious concern. 'We are in rare agreement. Miss Beaudon must be removed from here as soon as possible. And you must go with her. It would not enhance *your* reputation to be found here, either.'

'I should have thought that would suit you very well, Countess Rehan. We have been enemies for long enough.'

'I do not regard you as an enemy, Lord Carne. My partners in this enterprise are your enemies.'

'I don't understand. What are you talking about?' Francesca looked from one to the other with a bewildered air.

'We haven't much time, Miss Beaudon. Lord Carne might explain—later when you are free of this house.'

'Why are you doing this for me, *Comtesse*?' asked Marcus abruptly.

'I am not a political creature. I may owe some loyalty to my partners, but my older loyalty—to Maddy and those she loves—must take precedence.'

'You have my thanks.'

The countess shook her head. 'We are wasting time, and we have none to waste. You must go as soon as you can. There is another exit at the back of the house, but you cannot reach it from here. We shall have to go back to the main corridor. Pull the collar of your cloak up round your face. Miss Beaudon, put this veil over your head.'

When Francesca appeared to be ready to argue, Marcus took the heavy veil and threw it over her. Then he took her firmly by the arm and said, 'Lead on, *Comtesse*.'

Sounds of conviviality could now be heard from some of the rooms, while others were silent. But the Countess hurried on, aiming for a small disguised door set into the wall at the top of the main stairs. They had almost reached it when she stopped short and uttered a cry of vexation.

Three men were slowly coming up the staircase. It was evident that they had dined—and wined—well. They held on to the baluster as they ascended, examining its decorations with exaggerated care and making bawdy comments on the nymphs. Though the Countess had cut off her cry as soon as she had uttered it, the men had heard her. They looked up.

She turned and pushed Francesca and Marcus back along the corridor. 'That idiot Hassim!' she whispered. 'Go back to the alcove. You can hide there. I'll see that they take the Harem passage.' Francesca and Marcus ran, soft-footed, back to the alcove, but just as Francesca was scrambling in behind the fountain, her veil caught in the statue's upturned fingers. Marcus swore and laboured frantically to release it. Then he joined her, pushing her further back into the niche. They heard the Countess greeting her visitors at the top of the stairs. 'Good evening, gentlemen. How may *La Maison des Anges* please you?'

'She's speaking English!'

Marcus whispered savagely, 'For God's sake hush, Francesca! Believe me, it's essential you keep quiet.'

'But—'

Marcus swore under his breath, then seized her and kissed her hard. Then he put his hand over her mouth and whispered, 'There are more of those if I can't keep you quiet any other way.'

'How dar—'

Marcus kissed her again. Then he said angrily, but still softly, close to her ear, 'This isn't a hospital, Francesca. It's a. . .a bawdy house!' Francesca gazed at him in shock.

He went on relentlessly, 'One of the most notorious in Paris. Now do you understand why you mustn't be found here?'

Francesca wanted to contradict him—wanted to reject the idea with horror, but she found that she couldn't. In a flash, she realised how well everything fitted—the Countess's anxiety to be rid of her, those nymphs, the rest of the exotic decor, even the name—a horrid irony. It was true! She hid her face in her hands in shame. No wonder Marcus was so angry. He put his arm round her.

'We'll come out of it,' he breathed into her ear fiercely. 'For God's sake, don't lose heart now.'

'I have a number of. . .temptations for the jaded palate.' The Countess was leading the men down the corridor. 'What is it to be?'

'We shall be guided by you, fair lady,' drawled a hatefully familiar voice.

It was as well Marcus had firm hold of Francesca. She jerked up in terror and clutched his arm. He nodded slowly. 'Coker,' he mouthed.

'Will it please you to come this way, milords?'

'Hold hard!' Another familiar voice. 'Am I dreamin' or what? Wasn't that Carne I saw just now, Countess?'

'You're drunker than I thought, Freddie,' said Lord Witham's voice. 'Carne? Here? Carne's a right enough fellow, but he's above being seen in a bawdy house—certainly not one with such a spicy reputation!'

'Well, that's what I would have said, Charlie,' said Mr Chantry with alcoholic dignity. 'But all the same. . .'

Francesca hid her face in Marcus's shoulder. Her hands clutched the cloth of his coat in fearful tension as disaster loomed.

The Countess said with the merest suspicion of censure in her voice, 'Is there something wrong, milords? Perhaps you would like to discuss the matter elsewhere? You must be disturbing some of my other guests. If you will follow me. . .?'

Her effort was wasted. Freddie said obstinately, 'I'm sure I wasn't mistaken. . .there's something about the set of Carne's shoulders. It was Carne, I'll swear.'

'Who is this Carne, milords?'

'A man of unimpeached virtue, my dear *Comtesse*— or so we've been led to believe.'

The Countess gave a low, delightfully incredulous, laugh. 'Unimpeached virtue is a rare commodity in *La Maison des Anges*. I doubt you'll find your friend here, milords. But come, I can find you something much more exciting—a rare beauty from Constantinople, three years in the seraglio of the Sultan, trained in all the arts. . . The story of her escape is itself a fantasy. She lives along this passage to the left of us. Come, breathe in the scents of the East, milords, and succumb to her enchantments. If you will follow me. . .'

But Freddie was not to be distracted. 'Later, Countess, later! You didn't know Carne in the old days, before he came into the title, Coker. Not nearly so respectable then, eh, Charlie? Remember those parties, what? I say! What a lark if it was Carne! I've got to see! He was standin' just down there somewhere. . . It almost looked as if he was tryin' to hide. . .' He suddenly shouted, 'Marcus! I say, Marcus, old chap!'

'Milords! Mr Chantry! You mustn't! This is an outrage! That part of the house is not for guests. Hassim! Hassim!'

The Countess' protests went unheeded. Freddie's curiosity had been aroused, and he was sufficiently intoxicated not to care for anything else. Charlie Witham joined in.

'Down there, you say, Freddie? Let's go and see. Excuse me, Countess.'

To Francesca and Marcus, the moment was one of undiluted horror. In the next few seconds they would be exposed, not only to Coker, who had no cause to love either of them, but worse, to two of the biggest scandal-mongers in London. Marcus pushed Francesca right back into the alcove. '*Stay here*,' he said softly, but fiercely. Then he opened his cloak, loosened his cravat and stepped out into the corridor.

'I heard the noise,' he said languidly. 'Is this the way to keep a house such as yours, *Comtesse*? I thought discretion was the keynote?'

'Milord, forgive me. I don't know what to say. . .'

'*Carne!* It *is* you! Well, I'm blowed! So this is what they call important diplomatic affairs? Affairs! They're affairs, all right!' Freddie gave a roar of laughter. 'Here to negotiate with the Sultan's favourite, are you?'

'Freddie. I wish I could say I was charmed to see you, but I really cannot do it. Do take yourself. . .and your two friends away. What a reputation you'll give the English!'

'Reputation! Well, that's cool! That's pretty cool!' said Witham.

'I hope you don't think that yours will survive tonight's revelation,' Lord Coker said, smiling unpleasantly. 'Even in London, one has heard of the infamous House of the Angels. It's a surprising place to find the noblest peer of them all.' His voice was full of malevolent satisfaction.

'Oh, come, Coker! Don't be naïve! We're men of the world, I hope? What will it gain you to chatter in London about what I get up to in Paris? It's not like you to be so childish.'

'It's hardly a matter for children. Or ladies—I wonder what Miss Beaudon would think of this?'

'You know my views—or you should by now—on hearing Miss Beaudon's name on your lips, Coker. I had hoped you learned your lesson. But surely not even you would soil any lady's ears with tales of brothels and the like! I'm sure the Prince wouldn't approve. Most ungentlemanly.'

'These things have a habit of getting around.'

'Well, well! I shall know who to blame if they do, shan't I? Freddie? Witham?'

The two gentlemen named responded to the sudden menace in Marcus's voice with eager assurances of their discretion.

'You can threaten them out of it, but not me.'

'You know, I've thought you many things, my dear Coker, but I never took you for a tittle-tattle before. Do your damnedest. The sticklers might disapprove of me for a while, but most of London will be amused—no more than that. Now, if you'll excuse me. . .'

'But why were you tryin' to hide, Marcus?'

'Freddie, you force me to be brutally frank. I didn't wish to meet you. I was on my way to some delightful, but unfinished, business. And now, if you'll excuse me. . .? *Madame la Comtesse* is no doubt anxious to provide you with some delights of your own. Goodnight, gentlemen!'

Marcus watched as the Countess ushered the three men down the Harem passage, then stepped back into the alcove. He let out a deep sigh.

'Marcus! Oh, Marcus!' Francesca clutched his arm.

'Wait! We're not quite out of the wood yet.'

'But I didn't know. . . What. . .what would happen if they found me here?'

Marcus's silence was eloquent. Then he said grimly, 'They won't. They mustn't. Let me help you put that veil on again. We must get out of here while we can.'

'I'm sorry, Marcus.'

He looked as if he was about to say something severe, but then changed his mind. 'The veil,' was all he said.

Francesca looked up at him and put her cheek against his. 'Thank you,' she said. 'Oh, Marcus, I do thank you.'

His arm tightened round her, but after a moment he put her away from him, and arranged the veil over her face.

'This is not the place,' he said. 'Let's get away from *La Maison des Anges*, and tomorrow I'll arrange for Maddy to come with us to England. Ready?'

Francesca lifted her head. 'Ready,' she said.

Chapter Fourteen

Francesca's carriage was waiting for them in the mews behind the house. They reached it without further incident, climbed in, closed the blinds and set off for the hotel. But just before they got there Marcus told the coachman to stop.

'I'll get out here,' he said. 'You mustn't be seen tonight in my company. Indeed, you should not be seen again in Paris. There's always the chance that Coker or one of the others might catch sight of you, and that would never do. Stay indoors till I get in touch with you.' He looked at her. His face was as stern as she had ever seen it. 'I will say nothing about tonight's escapade. Knowing you, it was fairly predictable. But I don't think I need tell you that the consequences could have been severe indeed.'

'I know,' Francesca said miserably.

His expression softened slightly. 'Don't look so cast down, Francesca. I think we have avoided detection. But you must now do exactly as I say until you are safe in England again. I shall not come to your hotel myself, but will contrive to send messages daily. And I will engage to have Maddy here as soon as she is fit to travel. Meanwhile, you will keep to the confines of the hotel. Do I have your promise?'

She nodded, unable to say a word.

'Good! Then I will bid you goodnight.'

'Goodnight, Marcus,' she said. Her manner was still subdued.

He sighed and said ruefully, 'You know, I find all this docility very alarming. I had expected at least a token resistance.'

'No doubt I shall eventually come about,' she said bitterly. 'But I begin to despair that I shall ever behave as I ought in any matter where you are involved.'

'The answer lies in your own hands, Francesca.'

'What do you mean?'

'Oh, no! I am not about to embark on any discussion or argument. Not here, not now. But some time you may like to reflect on our long acquaintance and perhaps view it in a different light. As I have. Goodnight.'

He bowed, had a short word with the driver and groom and was gone. The carriage started up again. Francesca pushed the blind aside and stared out, following the tall, lithe figure with her eyes until it disappeared into the darkness. Then she sat back, suddenly indescribably weary.

What had Marcus meant? Her behaviour tonight had been enough to give any decent man a disgust of her. She felt sick with horror at the thought of how Coker and the others would have behaved if they had seen her in that dreadful place. Thanks to Marcus, that danger had been averted, but what did he now think of her? His words had been enigmatic—in what 'different light' did he view her now?

These thoughts and others, equally tormenting, kept her awake for most of the night. Even the knowledge that she had found her beloved Maddy failed to comfort her. But the next morning, though her spirits remained low, she set herself to maintain a brave front before Madame

Elisabeth and to behave with all the circumspection that Marcus had advised.

As Marcus walked back to the Embassy he was equally heavy-hearted. He had saved Francesca from disgrace, but only at considerable cost to himself and his mission. His work in Paris was now irretrievably compromised, and only one course remained open to him. He did not relish his forthcoming interview with Sir Henry, but was determined to seek him out and inform him of the night's developments before anyone else could tell him.

The subsequent interview was every bit as painful as Marcus had expected. Sir Henry was famous for his patience and tact in dealing with representatives of other nations, but he did not waste either on his subordinates. Marcus was called every kind of fool in language that was as forceful as it was picturesque. He knew better than to offer any defence. Though in his own mind there was no question that he had acted in the only possible way, he could hardly expect Sir Henry to understand that.

'It's a damnable matter altogether! You know as well as I do that if anyone hears of this visit to the Countess Rehan's place, neither the French, nor any of our Allies, will trust you again.'

'I have thought of little else for the past two hours, sir. And though I did my best on the spot, it would be foolish to hope that Coker and the others will not spread the story—the tale of Lord Carne's lapse from virtue is too tasty a morsel.'

'Your personal reputation is your own affair. You could have visited all the bordellos in Paris every night for a month for all I care. But one of the most notorious centres for Napoleon's supporters in Paris! Why the devil did it have to be *there*?'

'Unfortunately—'

'Unfortunately!' roared Sir Henry. 'You ruin some of the most delicate negotiations we've been involved in for years, and you call it *unfortunate*! It's catastrophic, man!'

Marcus gritted his teeth. 'The consequences for Miss Beaudon could have been catastrophic, too, Sir Henry. She had to be rescued. But I am not belittling the quandary you and the rest of your staff are now in as a result. I deeply regret the necessity for my actions, and hope you will accept my immediate resignation from the mission. You shall have it in writing tomorrow.'

'I'll have it in writing tonight, Carne! Tomorrow the vultures may well descend on me. But no resignation is going to save this situation. Unless. . . How would it be if I saw Coker and the others myself? Explained the situation. . .' When Marcus hesitated he said impatiently, 'Well? Don't just stand there, tell me what you think.'

'Witham and Chantry are amiable fools. I think you could persuade them to say nothing—for the time being at least. Long enough for the effect to be diminished. But Coker. . .'

'Coker's a gentleman. I've never heard that he's unpatriotic. Fought at Waterloo, didn't he?'

'With some gallantry. There's nothing wrong with his courage. But. . .he has a personal animosity towards me, which might impair his judgement.'

'Balderdash! I'm surprised at your suggesting such a thing, Carne! No man of Coker's standing would indulge his own feelings at the expense of his sovereign's best interests. D'you doubt my ability to put it clearly enough? Is that it?'

'Of course not, sir.'

'Well, then. That's it. I'll send someone to fetch the gentlemen concerned as soon as they are. . .er. . .free. What the devil are you looking so doubtful about?'

'I wish you every success, Sir Henry. But. . .if Coker won't cooperate—'

'I'm sure he will!'

'But if not,' said Marcus desperately, 'then there's only one thing left for you to do.'

'What's that?'

'You'll have to disown me, vilify me. Say I'm in disgrace.'

'Don't be a fool, Marcus! I can't do that to you! You may have acted quixotically, but you're not a double dealer! Dammit, boy! I'm not going to spread lies about you!'

'You won't have to,' Marcus said with a grim smile. 'Just say you've sent me packing, and refuse to discuss the matter. Rumour will do the rest.'

'I can't do that to you, Marcus.'

'If Coker or the others do talk, it's the only way you can save your own position.'

Sir Henry was clearly uncomfortable with the idea, but he, too, could see the force of Marcus's words. 'Let's hope for the best,' he said gloomily. 'Write out that resignation and go to bed. I take it you'll be leaving Paris tomorrow—or today, rather. It's past midnight.'

'I can't guarantee that, but I'll go as soon as I possibly can. I have my own reasons for wanting to be away from here.'

Sir Henry was a skilful and experienced diplomat. A cosy chat in the Embassy library, a few carefully prepared half-truths, with a glass or two of superb Burgundy, and in no time at all Lord Witham and Mr Chantry had been persuaded that it was in their own interest, as well as that of the country, that they forgot the episode in *La Maison des Anges*. As Sir Henry ushered them out he was well satisfied with his efforts. But when he turned Lord

Coker was regarding him with a cynical eye.

'They're fools,' he said, 'to be satisfied with so little. If I'm to keep my mouth shut I want to know a good deal more than you told them, Sir Henry! How directly is Carne involved in these mysterious negotiations? Why is he so important?'

Sir Henry gave him a bland look. 'Why are you so interested? Most people would regard the request as reasonable, without any further detail.'

'Ah, but I have never been "most people". I flatter myself that my friendship with the Prince Regent gives me greater distinction.'

Sir Henry filled Lord Coker's glass. 'This. . .friendship. Am I right in thinking it is at the moment under a slight cloud?'

Lord Coker smiled. 'His Highness is sometimes forced to act in public against his private inclination. I shall return to London in the near future and you will see—he will receive me as warmly as ever. I amuse him. You may have confidence in me, Sir Henry. I shall have the Prince's ear again in a very short time. Now, tell me why you are so anxious to protect Lord Carne. I should have thought he was well able to take care of himself.'

'Hmm. . .' Sir Henry paused for thought. It was obvious that Lord Coker was not to be put off. His claim that he would return to the Prince Regent's favour was convincing. And there had been no sign of the animosity Marcus had spoken of. He made up his mind to be frank.

'Confidence is at the heart of Lord Carne's recent work for us. . .' And Sir Henry went on to explain the delicate balance of the negotiations, the importance of Marcus's known integrity, and the significance to the pro-Napoleon faction of *La Maison des Anges*.

'But if Lord Carne knew all this, why was he in the place at all?'

Sir Henry was in a quandary. He could not possibly betray the girl Marcus had gone to such lengths to protect. He blustered, 'How the devil should I know? Some woman, no doubt.'

'And you are asking me to remain silent about a man who knowingly put all these important negotiations in jeopardy for the sake of a woman? A harlot? The story gets better and better, Sir Henry. You've dismissed him, of course?'

'I didn't have to. Carne resigned that very night. But if it were known that he had been seen in the *Maison des Anges,* the damage to our position could be enormous.'

Lord Coker's interest was not in the government's position. He said thoughtfully, 'You would have to repudiate him instantly and publicly.'

'Even that might not be enough.'

'And people are so uncharitable. They would be bound to assume that he was guilty of much worse—double dealing, even.'

'I sincerely hope not.'

'You are being quite amazingly forbearing, Sir Henry. I wonder at you.'

'My chief interest is in saving our reputation with the French. But Lord Carne has done much for us in the past. He does not deserve the universal condemnation which would follow if his. . .indiscretion were revealed. I think you can see the force of my argument?'

'Oh, I can indeed, Sir Henry! I can indeed!'

Sir Henry Creighton was not a devious man. He accepted these words as an indication of Lord Coker's good faith. But he would have been much less happy if he could have seen the smile of satisfaction on Lord Coker's face as he left. He could not have known that he had just given Lord Coker a long-sought weapon.

*   *   *

It was two days before the Countess sent word that Maddy could undertake the journey to England. Both Marcus and Francesca greeted the news with relief. Francesca had grown heartily sick of the hotel and its small garden, but she had not dared to disobey Marcus's orders. As for Marcus himself—he had spent two of the most uncomfortable days of his life, not excepting his experiences at Waterloo. At least during the battle he had been kept too busy to be aware of anything else. Here in Paris, he was forced to stand on the sidelines while others did what they could to save the situation. His patience was sorely tried as he suffered sidelong glances, conversations that stopped suddenly whenever he came into a room and, worse than the rest, ribald remarks from one or two who had themselves paid visits to the Countess Rehan, men he had till now held in some contempt. Sir Henry was keeping his distance, but Marcus gathered from the few words they did exchange that the diplomat thought Coker would keep quiet. Marcus himself remained doubtful.

It was without regret that Lord Carne's party, consisting of two travelling coaches and their passengers, left Paris early one morning before the rest of the city was astir. No one was awake to remark on the sight of Lord Carne escorting a sick lady and her friends to England, though one or two might have wondered at the noble lord's hasty and discreet departure from the capital. Later, of course, when Lord Coker's poison spread, they knew the reason—or so they thought.

The journey was uneventful but not particularly enjoyable. Marcus drove his own carriage and, since it was more comfortable than the one Francesca had hired, the three ladies travelled inside. The second coach carried servants and luggage.

Francesca spent a good deal of her time with Maddy, talking of the old days on St Marthe, holding her when they travelled over rough patches of road, and generally exerting herself to make the journey as comfortable as possible. She was glad to do it, but it was a strain— especially as she found she was not sleeping very well at night. At the last stop before they reached Calais, Madame Elisabeth looked at Francesca's pale face and heavy eyes, and had a word with Marcus. As a result, Francesca was invited to travel outside for a while.

The fresh air was welcome after the close confines of the carriage, but as they travelled the last few miles in France, Francesca grew ever more dejected. Though Marcus had been perfectly courteous, and had taken pains to make sure she was comfortable, he had hardly spoken to her on their journey, and now when she was sitting right beside him, he was behaving almost like a stranger.

For the first time in their acquaintance, he appeared to find conversation with her difficult. He seemed to have something on his mind that he was not prepared to discuss. Never before had she felt shut out of his thoughts in this way, and the feeling was very lowering to her spirits.

Why on earth had she gone to such lengths to avoid his company on the journey to France? If this was the way he would have treated her, her efforts had been a waste of time! To think she had been afraid to travel with him, unsure of her ability to resist his charm, his claims to the old, closer ties between them, had feared that her feelings would once again overcome her caution. But now she perceived that such concern had been totally unnecessary. Marcus hardly seemed to notice she was there!

Perversely, she found herself wanting to be provoked and challenged in the old manner. . .yes, even flirted with. But. . .she stole a glance at him. Far from regarding her with affection, or even interest, he was frowning at the road ahead as if it held all sorts of unknown dangers.

Francesca grew more and more despondent. It was clear that Marcus now regretted having followed her to Paris! She couldn't blame him for that, though what she would have done without him she hardly ventured to think. All the same, she had not invited him to follow her, she thought resentfully—she had done her best to avoid his company! And when her father had pressed them to become engaged, it was she who had rejected the idea, not Marcus.

But she became gloomy again as she remembered that Marcus had afterwards stated with some force that he had no wish to marry her! And now she came to think of it, he had only pursued her and kissed her *after* he had witnessed Denver's declaration. That was it! He didn't want to marry her himself, but he didn't want anyone else to, either. He was a selfish, arrogant dog in the manger! She stole a glance at him. He didn't *look* like a selfish, arrogant dog in the manger. He looked like a man with a load of trouble on his back.

'Marcus?'

He looked at her apologetically. 'Forgive me. I was woolgathering. I'm afraid I'm poor company at the moment.'

'What is wrong?'

'Wrong? Why, nothing! I think we brushed through that business in Paris pretty well, do you not agree?'

'Are you concerned about Lord Coker and the others?'

'Not in the slightest. I doubt they will say anything, you know. Freddie and Charlie Witham are featherweights. They'll have forgotten about me by the time they get back to England. And Coker. . . What has he to gain? No, you mustn't concern yourself about Coker.'

'I think he will talk about. . .about *La Maison*—'

Marcus interrupted her before she could say any more.

'Don't ever mention that name again, Francesca! Not even to me. You must forget that you ever heard of the place, and you must make sure Madame Lachasse doesn't talk of it, either.'

Francesca looked at him with scared eyes. Marcus had sounded. . .frighteningly authoritative. When she nodded, he said more lightly, 'You need not concern yourself on my behalf. Coker gave his word to Sir Henry—he won't talk.'

'Sir Henry? Sir Henry Creighton?'

'Yes—apart from its. . .somewhat unworthy day-to-day business, the place you chose to visit is also one of the chief centres of pro-Napoleonic activities in Paris. My being found there might have prejudiced Sir Henry's position vis-à-vis King Louis and his regime. But I think we have managed to prevent that—Sir Henry saw Coker and explained.'

'And you trust Lord Coker? He hates you, Marcus. If he can do you harm, he will.'

'He may hate me, but he will hardly break his word. And. . .if he does. . .there's nothing wrong, if you'll forgive my mentioning it, in a man such as myself visiting a. . .a place which is not normally spoken of in the company of the ladies of Society.'

'You mean a bawdy house.'

'Precisely.'

'Have you been in the habit of it, Marcus?'

'What a question to ask! Really, Francesca! No, it is not something I have indulged in, if you must know. Now, if you would care to change the subject?'

'If Lord Coker's gossip won't do you any harm, why are you so. . .so abstracted? You haven't spoken a word since I joined you.'

He looked at her with a frown. Francesca lifted her chin and held his glance, refusing to back down. A glint of humour appeared in his eyes, the corner of his mouth twitched in the old, familiar, endearing way. 'You mean you feel neglected? Dare I hope that you would welcome my attentions?'

'Of course not! That is. . .I would welcome some attention, perhaps. More than I have been receiving from you in the past half-hour.'

'This is not what I have been accustomed to hear, Francesca. What has happened to the young lady who ran away to Paris rather than face my company on the journey?'

'Yes, well, things have changed.'

'Indeed, they have!' His face grew sombre again. 'I've been thinking. When we get to England I think you, Madame Elisabeth and Madame Lachasse should go straight to Packards. In that way, we might hope to avoid comment on your return, and any connection at all in the eyes of Society with me. I can see to it that your father joins you soon after. Both Madame Lachasse and your father need time to recover, and I am sure Packards is the best place for them. It would be natural for you to stay with them.'

'But. . .?'

'Yes?'

Francesca shook her head. She was disappointed, but could not argue with such an eminently sensible scheme, particularly as the only objection that occurred to her was that Marcus would not be there. It was plain that he did not desire her company in London. Pride came to her rescue. She sat up straighter and said brightly, 'I think you are right. And it will give me an opportunity to renew my acquaintance with Maddy. With one thing and another, I feel I have hardly spoken to her. Thank you, Marcus.'

He looked at her quizzically. 'Will you miss me?'

'A little, I suppose,' said Francesca airily. 'But I expect

Lord Denver and one or two of the others will visit us. It isn't far from London.'

He took hold of her chin and turned her face to his. 'I have other plans for Denver. Leave him alone, Francesca.'

This calm order—not even plans for her, but plans for Denver, indeed!—roused Francesca to challenge him. 'I do not think what occurs between Lord Denver and myself is any concern of yours,' she said somewhat coldly. 'I shall invite whom I choose to Packards.'

He laughed and kissed her briefly. Then, as she opened her mouth to speak, his eyes darkened and he kissed her again. In spite of herself, her response was as complete and unrestrained as it had always been. Even as her arms went round his neck, as she clung to him as closely as he was holding her, she had a fleeting moment of despair. Why was it that no caution, no memory of her grief and despair in the past, however painful, ever stopped her from responding to this man with all her stupid, unguarded heart?

Then she forgot everything as she abandoned herself to the feelings of delight, of bubbling joy, of excitement and desire which he could always evoke. The kiss went on, the horses dropped to a walk as his arm went round her, holding her more firmly to him.

He groaned, 'Francesca, Francesca! You've been trouble since the moment I first met you, but. . .kiss me again!'

For one glorious moment they forgot time and place, lost once again in the enchantment which had always held them in its spell. But then a plaintive voice coming from inside the carriage brought them startlingly back to earth.

'Lord Carne! Why have we stopped? Has something happened?' Madame Elisabeth's head was poking out of the window. Fortunately Francesca was not in her view.

'No, no! There is no cause for alarm, Madame

Elisabeth. Miss Beaudon was interested in the spire of the church over there. Er. . .shall we go on, Miss Beaudon?'

Francesca had been hastily tidying her hair and putting her hat back on. 'Thank you, Lord Carne,' she said calmly, suppressing a wild desire to giggle. 'It was most . . .interesting.' Marcus lifted an eyebrow and Francesca went scarlet. 'That is to say. . .'

'Good,' said Madame Elisabeth. 'I am glad to hear that Francesca has not lost her eye for detail. One can always learn something.' She put her head in again.

'Indeed, one can!'

'Marcus! Please don't make me laugh. You are cruel.'

'I am delighted to see you in a more cheerful frame of mind. You've been a little hipped since we left Paris.'

'I didn't think you had noticed.'

'Oh, indeed I had. It was natural, I suppose. But to return to our conversation before that. . .delightful interlude—I've more than made my point, I think.'

'Which is?'

'If you marry Denver, you'll spoil more than your own life, Francesca. Don't let him persuade you differently.' He turned to look at her. 'You must know I'm right.'

How could he even think of Denver at such a moment? Francesca's chief feeling was one of hurt and bewilderment. She had thought him as oblivious to the rest of the world as she had been. She had clearly been wrong. 'A delightful interlude'. Was that how he regarded it? 'A delightful interlude' sounded uncomfortably like 'Nothing much!'—his words to Freddie all those years ago on the hill at Shelwood. Had he. . .had he kissed her merely to prove a point?

With considerable self-discipline, she put her hurt on one side and sat up more firmly. Two could play at that game. 'I know nothing of the kind,' she said calmly. 'I don't know what particular point you wish to prove, Marcus, but that kiss—'

'Those kisses,' he murmured.

'Those kisses proved nothing at all. There's more to a good marriage than gratification of the senses. Comfort, ease, friendship—these have an important share, too. Please stop the carriage again—no! I will not listen to any more. I wish to rejoin Maddy and Madame Elisabeth inside.'

He hesitated a moment. Then his jaw set, and he did as she asked without further protest.

It took over a week to reach Packards, by which time Francesca's nerves were stretched to their limit. The conversation with Marcus before Calais was the last she had of any consequence with him. Once they reached the port he insisted that she stayed out of sight, and while he escorted Madame Elisabeth and Maddy on a short walk round the deck, Francesca was made to stay in the cabin. In England, too, she stayed inside the carriage, and when they drove through London he made sure the blinds were drawn. His precautions seemed ridiculously elaborate, but when she protested Madame Elisabeth refused to sympathise.

'For you know, my love, that it would not do for you to be seen in Lord Carne's company on a journey such as this. It is not as if you were betrothed to him. I think Lord Carne is being truly the gentleman in his concern for your reputation.'

'But I have you and Maddy to act a chaperons! It is ridiculous!'

'It may seem a touch excessive, I agree. But I have every confidence in Lord Carne's judgement.'

'Francesca, my honey—you are in love with this Lord Carne?'

'Oh, no, Maddy! He. . .he is a friend of my father's.'

'It don't look as simple as that to me. And I never heard no mention of this "friend" before. Tell Maddy, child.'

'I can't! I don't know!' Francesca sat back against the cushions. 'Did Lord Carne tell you that, Madame Elisabeth?' she asked morosely. 'That we were not betrothed?'

'Well, not precisely. I believe his words were that you had to wait until you had spoken to Lord Beaudon.'

'I knew it!' Maddy cried softly, clapping her hands together. 'He's a wonderful man—and he'll make just the right husband for my little Francesca!'

'You don't know, Maddy! You just don't know. . .'

'I know enough. A man don't sacrifice his whole career for just anyone. It's proof of something or other, and if it isn't love, what is it?'

'Sacrifice? What are you talking about, Maddy? There's no danger of that. Marc—Lord Carne says those men have been silenced.'

'You reckon they will stay so? I never met a man yet that don't gossip with his friends worse than any woman.'

'Well, there may be a little talk. . .but that won't do Lord Carne much damage. He said so himself.'

'We'll see, child. We'll see. Just remember what I said when the time comes—about his loving you.'

Francesca was to remember Maddy's words just a few weeks later. They gave her courage at a time when it was badly needed.

When their little party arrived at Packards, they found to their surprise that Lord Beaudon was already installed there. He was looking considerably better, and greeted his daughter and Marcus with delight. Maddy was conveyed to a comfortable room which had been specially prepared for her, and his welcome to her was a private matter, and took place behind closed doors. When he came down he found Marcus ready to leave.

'You're not going, my dear fellow, are you?'

'I'm afraid I must, Lord Beaudon. There are matters which must be attended to in London. I only came in order to make sure that your daughter and. . .her friends arrived here safely.'

'But when shall you come again, then?'

'I. . .' Marcus hesitated. 'I am not sure. Do you plan to stay at Packards for the rest of the Season?'

'I shall do so, certainly. Madame Lachasse will need my company during her convalescence in a strange country. But I am sure Francesca will come back to town, eh, my dear?'

'I thought I'd stay here for a while, Papa.'

'Nonsense! You'll return to London just as soon as you've recovered from your journey, and had a chance to talk to Madeleine. There's very little of the Season left, and you can come down again as soon as it is over. Now take your leave of Carne, my dear, then you can go and see if Madeleine is rested. I'll see you to your carriage, Carne.' He walked to the door.

Marcus took Francesca's hand to his lips and bade her farewell. Francesca said stiffly, 'I am conscious that I owe you a great deal, sir—'

'Say nothing of that. You owe me nothing, Francesca, except. . .'

'Yes?'

His voice dropped. 'Be very careful what you say about Paris. To anyone at all. Your reputation will be in shreds if—'

'You have no need to warn me! I shall be careful.'

'And. . .remember what I said about Denver. He's not for you.'

She snatched her hand away. 'We have already said enough to each other on that score, Lord Carne. Your efforts to protect your friend from. . .from my wiles are ridiculous! If Lord Denver chooses to visit me here, I shall be delighted to receive him. You I shall no doubt see next in London.'

His face was grave. 'Perhaps. We shall have to wait on events. Till then, live well and be happy with your beloved Maddy. That at least is something good which came out of our Paris adventure. Goodbye, Miss Beaudon.' He bowed and she watched him as he joined her father at the bottom of the steps. Sudden tears started to her eyes; with an impatient sigh she turned and hurried upstairs.

Lord Beaudon stared soberly at Marcus. 'Well?' he demanded. 'Am I to send an announcement to the *Gazette* or not?'

'I'm afraid matters are a touch difficult at the moment, sir. Much as I honour your daughter, I cannot at the moment ask her to be my wife.'

'I thought you already had, Carne!'

'A ruse, merely, to ease your mind. There's still some way to go.'

'What the devil is all this about, Carne? I expected that you at least would behave as a man of honour!'

'That is precisely what I am doing my damnedest to do, Lord Beaudon!' Looking grimmer than ever, Marcus got into the carriage and gave a curt command. The carriage rolled away, leaving Lord Beaudon staring after it.

Chapter Fifteen

When Francesca finally came back to London after three weeks at Packards, the town had a slightly faded air. It was very close to the end of the Season—a few less fashionable couples had already left for their estates, preferring the freshness of the country to the dust and smells of London in summer. The Prince Regent was still at Carlton House, playing cards with his cronies, riding, driving and taking part in the normal activities his gregarious nature demanded, but his household was preparing for the move to Brighton.

However, there were changes that could not be ascribed to the end of the Season. The Prince was again much to be seen in the company of Lord Coker, who seemed to have made his way back into royal favour. On the other hand, Lord Carne, who had previously been held in such general high esteem, including that of his royal master, now seemed to have fallen from grace.

There was a change, too, in the atmosphere in the house in Mount Street. Before Francesca's departure for Paris the three ladies—Mrs Canfield, Lydia and Francesca herself—had lived in happy harmony. But now the two Canfields seemed reluctant to indulge in the pleasant chats and exchanges of gossip which they had all previously enjoyed, and Lydia seemed ill at ease, avoiding Francesca's company whenever possible.

Francesca was hurt. She had expected a certain amount of coolness from Maria Canfield—after all, she had deceived her friend about her plans to go to Paris. But she would have expected that Lydia, whom she had come to love, would admire her for undertaking what would seem to her such an adventure!

However, she owed too much to the Canfields to allow this situation to continue, so she set herself to coaxing Maria Canfield into a better mood, and in the interest of regaining her friend's confidence she was more open than she had ever been about her reasons for leaving for Paris so suddenly.

'You know, better than most, how hard it was for me to learn to give my affection—even to someone like you or Lydia. Lord Carne once broke my heart, Maria. I did not wish to risk another such experience. A man like Denver would be so much. . .safer.'

Even as she said these words, she wondered fleetingly whether George Denver would ever have risked as much as Marcus had to save her from her own idiotic actions in Paris. He was essentially very conventional. Would he have turned away in shock—disgust even? She pushed the thought away and turned to her friend with a smile. 'But I am truly sorry I had to deceive you. I hope you will forgive me. Indeed, I value our friendship more than I can say. And I regard Lydia as a sister.'

For a moment Francesca thought Maria was about to refuse this olive branch, for she coloured up and looked distinctly uncomfortable. But then she held out her hand and smiled. 'I am glad you are back, Francesca. And I am sure that Lydia will be, too, when. . .'

'When what?'

'When she is feeling better.'

'Has she been ill? Why didn't you tell me?'

'Not exactly, no. Please—I should prefer to leave this subject till later. Meanwhile, believe me, I am your very good friend still. Er. . .what if I were to tell you that Marcus loves you? Would you still be determined to refuse him?'

'There are times. . .when I am afraid. Someone like Denver would be so much easier to live with. And he, at least, has already asked me to marry him, whereas Marcus has not. I don't know, Maria.'

'I see.' Maria Canfield's voice had grown cool again.

'How is he?'

'Denver?'

'No, Marcus.'

'We have not seen a great deal of him. He came once to tell us you were safely back, but since then he seems to have avoided us. Lydia is quite distressed. But now. . .'

'What is it?'

'I am not sure. There are whispers. . . Did you see much of him in Paris?'

'I. . .I only saw him once. Then he escorted us home— but that is between ourselves, Maria. Marcus does not wish it to be generally known.'

'Francesca, he loves you and is trying to protect you. Something untoward seems to have happened while he was there. It seems to have been something unsavoury, so I don't expect he said anything about it to you. But it has undoubtedly done Marcus harm in the eyes of the world.'

'What. . .what can it be?'

'I think it's better not to ask. It's one of those things that gentlemen talk about in clubs, but ladies are not supposed to know. It is all very strange. The Foreign Office seems to be involved as well. Denver is certainly privy to what has been going on, but he wouldn't dream of mentioning it to us.'

'Denver?'

Again, Maria's voice was restricted as she answered. 'Lord Denver has been very kind while you were away. We have seen quite a lot of him. His attention is all the more welcome since Marcus has not been seen much in company.'

Francesca was worried. It was clear that something of the business in Paris had become known. She must find out how much, and how seriously it was affecting Marcus. She regarded her friend thoughtfully. It was useless to question Maria—she would never have been told the scandalous details, the very idea was absurd. Denver was connected with the Foreign Office, he would certainly know. . .but would he talk? Almost certainly not to her. It was all extremely frustrating, but she was determined to find out, somehow.

Meanwhile, it intrigued her that Maria's interest was clearly not with Marcus, but with Denver. This was a new development, surely? It appeared that Denver's visits had been as frequent as ever, even while she had been away. What had been going on here during the past month? Her eyes widened as a thought struck her. Lydia and Denver? Was that possible? Of course it was! And it would explain everything!

What was more, Denver was exactly the sort of man she would have chosen for Lydia herself, and, if Lydia loved him, she would relinquish her own claim without a second's hesitation. But she decided to say nothing for the moment. She would soon meet him—and observe for herself.

Sure enough, Lord Denver called that very afternoon. Francesca noticed with interest that Lydia, always so open, so artless in her approach to visitors, gave him the briefest of curtsies, then picked up her embroidery again and stitched with unusual concentration. Maria was as courteous as ever, but was obviously tense, and her conversation was uncharacteristically forced.

Francesca grew increasingly confident that her suspicion of an attachment between Lydia and Denver was correct. She must act as soon as possible—Lydia's happiness was far too important to delay putting matters right. While she waited for Lord Denver's call to come to an end, she considered what she would say to him, and it occurred to her that she might even put some of it to good account.

So, when Lord Denver finally rose to take his leave, she said boldly, 'Lord Denver, if you have a moment, there's something I would like to discuss with you.'

The sudden silence was broken only by the small crash as Lydia's embroidery fell to the ground.

'Of course, Miss Beaudon.' Lord Denver's tone was gallant, but his smile was forced. Maria and Lydia bade him farewell, and if Francesca had not already had a very clear idea of what had been happening in her absence, she must have seen and wondered at Lydia's pale face, her haunted glance into Denver's eyes, her hasty and unusually clumsy exit.

'Do sit down, Lord Denver,' said Francesca affably, when they were alone.

'Thank you. . .I think I prefer to stand. You. . .you had something you wished to say to me?'

'Yes. I wonder if you could tell me what it is that they are saying of Lord Carne? I hear he is in some trouble.' When he looked surprised, she explained, 'He was kind enough to help me in France. I want to know what he is accused of doing there.'

His face pokered up, as she had thought it would.

'There's absolutely no truth in any of it,' he said. 'His friends need not concern themselves with it.'

'I should still like to know what it is. What is he supposed to have done?'

'It is nothing fit for a lady's ears, Miss Beaudon,' Denver said dismissively. 'I could not possibly repeat it. Was there something else you wished to say to me?'

'I see.' Francesca saw that, as she had suspected, he was not prepared to discuss it—nor would anyone else. She would have to try other means. 'Well, it will probably soon be forgotten,' she said airily. She saw the look of doubt on Denver's face, but did not pursue it. Instead, she went to the sofa and sat down. 'If you will forgive my saying so, Lord Denver, you do not look as pleased to see me as I had expected.'

'Of course I am. . .er. . .I am delighted, of course, that you are safely back in England. I hear that you found your nurse.'

'Yes, she is at present resting. You might meet her some day. When you come down to Packards.' Francesca looked with some satisfaction at Denver's reception of this semi-invitation. She was sorry for his discomfort, but it was no part of her plan to make things easy for him.

'Miss Beaudon, I. . .' He stopped.

'Yes, Lord Denver?'

'I. . .I. . .nothing.'

'Mrs Canfield tells me how well you have been looking after them both while I've been away. That was kind of you.'

'On the contrary, it was my pleasure,' he said sincerely, if a touch uncomfortably.

'I've been thinking a great deal about your proposal, you know.'

'Really?' he asked, apprehension in his tone. 'And what. . .what have you decided?'

'Well. . .I think we should deal very well together.'

'Miss Beaudon, I. . .'

'On the other hand. . .I am beginning to suspect that you are no longer as devoted as you once were. Am I right?'

'How can you say so? I have asked you to marry me, and am bound in all honour—'

'But I don't want you to be bound, Lord Denver. Not to me. I value your friendship, I enjoy your company, but I am not in love with you. I never said I was. In fact, if you will do me one small favour—which you will not enjoy—I shall willingly release you from any promises you may have made me. Then you will be free to approach Miss Canfield with an easy conscience.'

He looked astounded. 'But. . .but. . . How did you know?'

'No one has said anything, but I have eyes and ears, you know. And I am even fonder of Lydia than I am of you. I will wish you happiness with all my heart, and think you will find it, too. Lydia will make you a much better wife than I ever would.'

He came over and kissed her hand. 'Francesca, you are wonderful! Noble!'

'I'm afraid I am not that. You did say you would do me this favour, didn't you?'

'Anything, anything!'

'Swear?'

'Of course!'

'Then you will tell me exactly what they accuse Marcus of doing. In detail. All of it.'

He took a step back, looking horrified. 'I couldn't do that! You would be shocked.'

'You did promise. And—' her voice grew serious '—it may help to put right a very grave injustice which is being done him. You are his friend, Lord Denver. Trust me.

This is no mere female whim. You will not shock me. You see, I know most of it already.'

'Forgive me, but that is impossible. How could you have heard of such things?'

'Never mind. Tell me!'

He was reluctant, but hers had always been the stronger character, and he eventually told her all he knew. It was far worse than Francesca had feared. Coker had obviously spread his poison far and wide. Marcus had told her that he might be regarded askance by the more stiff-necked members of Society if his presence in the *Maison des Anges* became known, but she had had no idea that there was a more serious, political dimension to the affair, one which would ruin Marcus' career and expose him to the severest possible censure.

She was not shocked, but she was furiously, royally angry. To think that Marcus, who had behaved with complete integrity throughout, was being ostracised, calumnied, on the word of a scoundrel like Coker! She was speechless with rage.

Lord Denver looked at her white face. 'It has shocked you,' he said miserably. 'I knew it would. Can you ever forgive me?'

'I am not shocked,' said Francesca carefully, her voice trembling. 'Not in the slightest. The only part of it that I did not know already was that they were accusing Marcus of double dealing. How dare they? How could they?'

'But how *could* you know?'

'I was there,' she said, forgetting all caution in her anger.

'In Paris? I knew that, but. . .'

'In the *Maison des Anges*.'

'No, no! That cannot be! Miss Beaudon! Please! You must not joke about such a dreadfully serious matter. If you were believed—'

'I am more serious than I ever was in my life before, Lord Denver,' she said, interrupting him without ceremony. 'How do you suppose I know the name of the place? You were careful not to mention it.'

He sat down and put his head between his hands. 'Oh my God,' he said, appalled. 'What can you have been thinking of? I regarded you—'

'Oh, it all happened very innocently! I am not the fallen woman you obviously think me,' she said bitterly. 'My nurse was ill and had taken refuge with her friend, Countess Rehan. She. . .she is. . .'

'Countess Rehan's name is known to us.'

'Really?'

'Because of the connection with Bonaparte.'

'Of course. Well, I went to her. . .house to find Maddy. I was completely unaware of its nature, though I realise that that will not help me in the world's eyes. Marcus came there purely to rescue me, though I gather that a more sinister interpretation is now being put on his presence there. He has kept silent to save my good name.'

'I see. I never thought for one moment that Marcus was capable of dishonorable conduct, but I had wondered why he. . . This explains it.'

Lord Denver came over to her. He spoke somewhat stiffly, but with obvious sincerity. 'Marcus is right. Miss Beaudon, you have been good enough to release me without reproach from my commitment towards you. I owe you a great deal. I will naturally say nothing to anyone of what you have just told me. And, believe me, I am speaking as your good friend when I beg you not to let a hint of it reach the ears of anyone else at all. No one. If the world were to learn of your. . .unfortunate adventure, no excuse, no reason, *nothing* would be enough to save you from complete ostracism.'

'And what about the man who risked everything for me?'

There was an appreciable pause. Then he said, 'Marcus will come about. Things may not be quite the same, but the world will forget. . .eventually. I expect he will live at Carne for a while.'

'But it's so unjust!' Francesca was getting angry again. 'He's a man of integrity, of honour. He enjoyed universal admiration and respect. And now they are accusing him of treachery, double dealing, hypocrisy and all the rest! How can he bear it?'

'He'll have to.'

'This is Coker's doing.'

'I think it must be. Though the rumour has not been ascribed to any particular source.' He cleared his throat. 'Mrs Canfield will be wondering what has become of us. May I. . .?'

'Take your leave? Of course. You have been honest with me, Lord Denver, and I appreciate it. I do not need to wish you luck, but I *will* wish you happy. May I make a suggestion?'

He looked as if he was wondering what further dreadful request she was about to make. 'What is that?'

'The decision is yours, of course,' she said reassuringly. 'But it might be a good idea to take Lydia and her mother to Kent on a short visit to your estates. They will be looking especially beautiful at this time of year.'

Relieved, he said, 'I think it an excellent idea. But. . .why do you suggest it? I assume you wish them to be out of London. Why? What are you planning to do, Miss Beaudon? Nothing rash, I hope?'

'That is my affair. But I will say that I cannot rest until justice has been done.' She held up her hand. 'No, do not argue. My mind is made up.'

Lord Denver regarded Francesca with a peculiar mixture of doubt and awe, as if she had suddenly grown two heads. Was this the stately, reserved Miss Beaudon, the woman of elegance and propriety whom he had admired for so long? He began to think he had had a lucky escape. A certain amount of liveliness could be very attractive, but Francesca Beaudon was suddenly revealing herself to be headstrong, imperious, passionate and foolishly scornful of convention—not qualities to be looked for, in his view, among the gentle sex.

But he softened towards her as she gave him one of her warm, enchanting smiles, and said, 'But my friends would be better out of it. So take them to Kent as soon as you can.'

'Are you quite sure I cannot persuade you to think again? I suspect that you are about to take a catastrophic step.'

'Lord Denver, I have to tell you that there is only one man who could ever have the slightest influence on my actions. And in this instance, though I am now certain that he loves me more than I deserve, and believes he is acting in my best interests, I will not listen even to him. I *must* do what I can to re-establish him in the world's eyes. Do not waste your time on me—you would do better to look after Lydia.'

'I think I will. She would be safer out of London for the moment. I'll see if she and her mother could possibly set off tomorrow!'

Mrs Canfield and Lydia were easily persuaded to leave London the next day. Lydia was over the moon with happiness—it simply did not occur to her to refuse Lord Denver's sudden invitation. Maria was a little surprised, but saw some reason in Francesca's argument that London would gossip less about the change in Lord Denver's affections if the happy couple were already out of town.

Once the Canfields had departed, Francesca sent a note to Marcus, requesting him to visit her. He sent a reply back with her man. It was unfortunately impossible for him to come to Mount Street in the near future. This was a setback, but one which Francesca had foreseen.

Undeterred, she set about preparing for the last great event of the season—a rout ball at Northumberland House. She dressed with unusual care. This would probably be her last appearance in Society, and she intended to bow out looking as lovely, as elegant as she had always looked. Her dress of silver-threaded gauze over a white satin slip, the diamonds in her hair and round her arms, the silver dancing slippers—all combined to re-create the image with which she had first impressed London, and to give her the courage she felt she might need.

Her final task before setting out was to write another note to Marcus to be delivered later in the evening. By the time he received it, she would already be at the ball.

At Northumberland House, she had a word with one of the footmen, who listened to her request impassively, received with lofty condescension the generous douceur she slipped into his hand, and only expressed his amazement much later to his particular crony in the back hall.

London was delighted to see Miss Beaudon in such looks, asked kindly after her father, and gave not the slightest indication that they knew anything of her sojourn in Paris. Everyone had assumed she had gone to Packards to prepare the place for her father. Francesca smiled, parried a few questions about the Canfields and Lord Denver, and danced a great deal.

The world had till now only seen the image Francesca had so carefully created for them—the image of an elegant, coolly disciplined cipher. But now, at long last free of the anxieties and fears of the past, as certain as she could be that Marcus loved her more than she had ever thought possible, she had decided to take the future into her own hands. She felt as truly rich, beautiful and powerful as she had ever wished to be—free to be more herself than ever before.

She glittered like a star, dazzling her partners with her wit and raillery, and seeming to float on the air, so graceful and carefree were her steps. Society was enchanted, and she was surrounded with eager admirers all competing for her favours. Francesca smiled at them, danced with them, bewitched them—and gave them not another thought.

As the hour advanced, all her attention was on the doors to the ballroom. A sigh of satisfaction escaped her as she heard sounds of slight altercation—Marcus had arrived, without, of course, an invitation. However, her footman friend soon intervened and within minutes Marcus was inside the ballroom, regarding her with a baleful stare. It was a quarter past eleven.

No sooner had the set of dances finished than he claimed her and, ignoring the protests of her partner, swept her off to one side. He began without ceremony, forced to keep his voice low, but sounding fierce, nonetheless. 'What the devil are you thinking of? I forbid you to do this!'

Francesca gave him a brilliant smile. 'On the stroke of twelve, Marcus. A dramatic time for a dramatic revelation. Appropriate, don't you think?'

'But it won't do any good. And it will do you irreparable harm! For God's sake, don't do it, Francesca, I beg of you!'

Francesca returned the nod of an acquaintance who was dancing by before she answered him. 'You didn't tell me everything, did you, Marcus? That you could be accused of betraying your trust, letting your country down, all for the sake of a night's indulgence at a brothel. You didn't tell me that.'

'Don't use that word in this company, for God's sake!'

'They can't hear us—they think I'm flirting with you. Why didn't you warn me what might happen?'

'Sir Henry assumed from what Coker said that he would remain silent. He was mistaken. And I did warn you that there might be some disapproval.'

'You didn't mention ostracism, social disgrace.'

'What does that matter? The important thing is that you should be saved from ruin.'

She put her head on one side and looked up at him. 'You keep trying to save me from ruin, Marcus. Why, I wonder?'

He hesitated, then said, 'We cannot possibly discuss such matters here in the middle of a ballroom. Let me take you home.'

'Oh, no! I've taken a great deal of trouble to get you here tonight. Leaving before I've done what I set out to do is out of the question. But I will let you take me on to the balcony here. For a minute or two.' Oblivious once again to the curious glances being cast in their direction, they moved out on to the balcony overlooking the gardens.

'Well, Marcus? Tell me why.' After a pause during which he remained silent she went on, 'Can it be that you love me? Really love me—enough to marry me? Or has my behaviour finally given you a disgust of me?'

'I love you,' he said wretchedly. 'You must know that. I think I've loved you ever since I first saw you on the hillside at Shelwood. But. . .marry you? I'm not sure I can.'

She lowered her head to hide the amusement in her eyes. 'I *have* given you a disgust of me,' she said mournfully. 'Impetuous, rash, foolhardy, found in. . .bawdy houses and the like, and worst of all. . .a wanton. I have never been able to behave as I ought when you kiss me.'

'Francesca! If you only knew what it does to me when we kiss. How could anything so wonderful give me a disgust of you?'

He took a step forward, but she turned away, shaking her head. 'You love me, you kiss me. . .but you won't marry me. Why not, I wonder? Are you a rake, after all? Surely not!'

He set his jaw and was silent. The new Francesca was not to be put off. She had a very clear idea of the situation between them and the knowledge gave her confidence to continue. She gave a sad little sigh. 'I see I shall have to abandon the last vestiges of maidenly behaviour. But after all, why shouldn't I? It will be of little consequence tomorrow. I have nothing to lose.'

'Don't say that!'

'Why ever not? It is true. And. . .though I cannot like it, Marcus, you have forced me into a most unconventional situation. I find myself having to ask *you* to marry *me*. You see, I'm giving up all pretence at behaving as Society expects. The Honourable Francesca Beaudon is about to disappear forever tonight. I hope she will be replaced with a besottedly happy Lady Carne. But if you. . .if you refuse me, then Miss Shelwood-Beaudon of Shelwood, spinster and recluse, will appear in her place.'

'Francesca, I love you. There is nothing I would desire more than to be able to marry you, but how can I? It is as you say—I am in disgrace. I cannot ask you to share that.'

'At last!' Francesca dropped her wistful air and said briskly, 'Marcus, you are being ridiculous. If that is the only barrier to our marrying, then the sooner I am in disgrace, too, the better. Thank you, that is all I wanted to know.' She started towards the ballroom.

He caught her arm. 'I will not let you do this!'

'You cannot stop me!'

'Oh, yes, I can—by force if necessary!'

Francesca wrenched herself free and ran into the huge room full of people. It was five minutes before midnight. Marcus followed and made his way purposefully through the crowds towards her. He caught her arm again.

'Carne!'

Francesca and Marcus, absorbed in their struggle, had not noticed the appearance of a number of personages in the double doorway. Foremost among them was the Prince Regent. At his side was Lord Coker.

'Sir.' Marcus released Francesca and bowed. The Prince's face was thunderous.

'What the deuce do you think you're doing here? Are you all right, Miss Beaudon?'

Francesca curtsied. 'Thank you, sir. Yes.' She found it hard to hide her satisfaction at this turn of events. Marcus could hardly stop her now.

'It seems that Carne finds it impossible to keep his hands off the ladies, sir,' Lord Coker said, with a sneer. Francesca turned on him in a flame.

'Lord Carne's attentions, however forceful, are more welcome than yours were on a similar occasion, Lord Coker! If I remember correctly, I had to break a vase over your head before you would leave me alone.'

A moment of stunned silence was followed by unmistakeable sounds of amusement among those present. Lord Coker turned sallower than ever, and said viciously, 'I can hardly believe that the Prince Regent is interested in the antics of someone who prefers the advances of a man such as Carne, Miss Beaudon. I must assume that you do not know the truth about the gentleman. . .'

'As it happens, I know the truth better than anyone here—'

'Francesca, I forbid it,' said Marcus urgently. 'Sir,

I beg you. . . Miss Beaudon is not herself. . .'

'And whose fault is that, Carne?' asked the Prince in a voice of ice. 'The behaviour we observed as we came in was not the sort to reassure a lady. A few weeks ago, we would have sworn you were incapable of such disgraceful conduct. As it is. . .you would be well advised to make your apology and go. Indeed, I am not sure why you are here at all.'

Marcus was white. The Prince's tone had been cutting, and the rebuke both public and powerful. It was the worst yet of the consequences of his Parisian débâcle.

'Sir, let me explain—' Francesca began.

'It is not at all necessary, Miss Beaudon,' said the Prince, smiling at her. 'You cannot be held to blame in this matter.'

'That's not what I meant, sir. I wish to make it quite clear why Lord Carne is innocent of the charges at present in circulation against him.'

'Francesca!'

'Really, sir, what can this woman know of such matters?'

Marcus's despairing cry and Lord Coker's contemptuous question came together.

The Prince looked at them both dispassionately. Francesca saw for the first time those qualities in him which made him royal. 'My lords, you will allow me to deal with this in my own way, if you please! I agree, Coker, that Miss Beaudon is probably not aware of the true nature of Lord Carne's. . .indiscretions—I am not prepared to call his conduct worse than that at the moment—but the lady's manner seems to me to carry conviction. It intrigues me.'

Marcus took a deep breath and approached the Prince. 'Sir, Miss Beaudon is overwrought. She does not know what she is saying. Send her home, I beg you.'

The Prince looked at him, a frown on his normally amiable face. 'You know, Carne, what intrigues me most of all is why you do not wish me to listen to the lady.'

'Miss Beaudon is impulsive and quixotic, sir.'

'Are you trying to save Miss Beaudon against herself? I find that hard to believe. And I have small inclination to listen to someone I should much prefer not to have to meet—at the moment.'

'Oh sir, please do not speak so, I beg you!' cried Francesca. 'You cannot know it, but you are being truly unjust to Lord Carne. He does not deserve your disapprobation.'

'Now why do you say that, Miss Beaudon? How can you possibly know why Carne is in disgrace?'

'I was in Paris at the time. Lord Carne escorted me back to England.' An audible sigh went up from the company.

The Prince looked grave as he said, 'I am not sure that you would be wise to go any further, Miss Beaudon.'

'I must! I went at my father's request to deal with some urgent business. He was unable to go himself—if you remember, sir, he was taken ill at White's a little while ago. I believe he was attacked there.'

With a glance at Lord Coker, the Prince said, 'Go on.'

'Lord Carne followed me there. He was of the opinion that I might do something foolish. And I did. I went, in error, to a place where no lady should ever be found. I will not mention its name, but Lord Coker apparently knows it well.'

Lord Coker laughed contemptuously. 'This is a farrago of nonsense, sir! The lady is clearly making this up in a ridiculous attempt to reinstate Carne. She must be besotted. Why waste your time with her?'

'I find myself for once in agreement with Coker, sir. Miss Beaudon is ill—let me take her home. Come, Francesca.' Marcus took her arm again.

Francesca shook him off and took a step forward. 'I *will* speak! The Prince deserves the truth.'

The Prince Regent regarded the slender figure in white and silver, who had just spoken with such passionate conviction. 'The situation is unusual. I think I'd like to hear what Miss Beaudon finds so important, that she risks her own reputation.'

Marcus groaned and turned away.

Francesca said, raising her voice a little so that everyone who wished could hear, 'Lord Carne came to rescue me from a place in Paris which was not only morally undesirable, but one which he knew to be politically dangerous. I had gone there in all innocence, but if I was seen there, particularly by anyone who knew me, my reputation would be soiled beyond repair. On the other hand, if he was seen there, his own reputation and his career in politics would be destroyed forever. He chose to take that risk. In the event he was seen. By Lord Coker, who has no cause to love him, and who, I assume, has been behind the campaign to blacken his name.'

'I still say this is nonsense! Carne has put her up to this! No lady would ever go near—'

'The *Maison des Anges*? But I was there, Lord Coker! I saw you and two others coming up the stairs, I heard the salacious remarks you made about the statues there, and I listened as the Comtesse Rehan offered you the. . .attentions of a lady who had once been a. . .a Sultan's concubine.' A scandalised gasp from those present, followed by murmurs of protest, caused her to pause. But she put up her chin and went on bravely, 'I was hiding in the alcove, trembling with fear of discovery when Mr Chantry and Lord Witham defied the Countess and came to look for Lord Carne. Is that enough?'

'Good God!' Lord Coker turned away from her. 'What sort of woman are you?'

There were more murmurs and a general withdrawal from Francesca's vicinity.

Marcus swept the crowd with a glance of scorn. Then he said, 'True, loyal and fearless. Strongminded to the point of obstinacy where the happiness of those she loves is concerned. Lord Coker would be fortunate indeed if such a woman ever stooped to do so much for him. Ask her to tell you why she was in Paris.'

'My dear Carne, I will do no such thing!' Lord Coker said loftily. 'The sooner Miss Beaudon realises her presence here is embarrassing us, the better.'

Francesca's public acknowledgement of her catastrophic mistake had taken more out of her than she had expected, and she was now suffering from reaction. She was trembling, but she faced the Prince Regent proudly and her voice was clear as she said, 'Sir, I assure you, it was always my intention to relieve Society of my presence after tonight—I have no wish to embarrass anyone.'

The Prince frowned, then said, 'Lord Coker was overhasty. I should like to hear why you were in Paris, Miss Beaudon, even if Lord Coker doesn't.'

'I had a nurse as a child whom I loved very dearly. My father sent me to find her and bring her to England. But when I went to her house, I was told she had been taken ill. She had sought refuge with her only friend in Paris, a lady who happens to be the *directrice* of. . .of. . .the place where Lord Carne found me. I had no idea of its nature. I cannot imagine what would have happened to me if I had been found there by anyone other than Lord Carne. He behaved throughout with integrity and honour.'

Her voice shook with the intensity of her feelings as she went on, 'And it is wrong, cruelly wrong, that he is being made to suffer for my folly, and another's malice.' She swallowed. 'Forgive me, sir, I. . .I cannot say any more. It has been too much. Too much.' She curtsied hastily and hurried out of the ballroom.

'Follow her, Carne. Look after her.' As Marcus turned to obey, the Prince Regent added, 'And, Carne. . .I should like you to come and see me as soon as you can.'

Marcus bowed and left the room.

He caught up with Francesca as she hurried down the stairs to the entrance hall. 'You were magnificent!' he said.

'Please. . .don't say anything. Now that it's all over, I find I am not nearly so brave as I thought. The look on some of those faces. . .'

Francesca's carriage was waiting at the doors. They got in, and Francesca gave way to her tears. Marcus took her in his arms.

'Hush, Francesca, my love. Why are you crying? You must compose yourself—we have some unfinished business, if you remember. You asked me a question tonight, and I still have an answer to give you.'

'Oh, what must you think of me?' she sobbed.

'If you will stop ruining my coat, I will tell you. Here, let me.' He tenderly wiped her face with his handkerchief.

'How do I know that you're not just sorry for me?' Francesca sobbed, tears breaking out afresh. 'You were once before.'

'You're being absurd! Come, Francesca. Pull yourself together. You must know that I love you beyond words. More than my career, my reputation, my life! If I had realised all those years ago what you would come to mean to me, I could have saved us both a great deal of inconvenience and unhappiness. Do I need to tell you that you're the only woman in the world for me? Look at me, Francesca. Did you mean it when you asked me to marry you? Or were you just playing with my affections?'

'Oh, Marcus!' She looked up, laughing through her tears.

'We'll go down to Packards tomorrow. Then we shall marry as soon as it can be arranged. And after that I'll love you, and treasure you, all my life.' He tilted her face to his and kissed her gently. Then he looked at her; in the dark blue depths of his eyes was all the love, honesty, humour and passion that belonged to this man she loved— had loved for so long. She smiled at him. Then, as he kissed her again, less gently, she laughed for joy, and threw her arms round his neck, responding as she always did—and always would.

It was quite some time after the carriage had drawn to a halt in Mount Street before Lord Carne handed Miss Beaudon out and escorted her to her door.

'Till tomorrow,' was all she said as she gave him her hand. He took it to his lips.

'And all that it brings.'

'Disgrace, ignominy, rejection from Society?'

'Possibly, but why should that worry us? If the world does find it impossible to forgive us—though I suspect that sadly that will not be the case—then we shall have peace to enjoy each other, and more than enough to occupy us at Carne and at Shelwood. But you did your work too well tonight—I think the Prince Regent is disposed to be kind.'

'I could think of something else to shock them all, if that is your wish?'

Unheeding of the groom patiently waiting by the carriage, and of the butler standing in the hall, Marcus laughed delightedly and caught her in his arms again. 'I have no doubt that life with you will always hold shocks, my love—you seem unable to avoid them—but they should be confined to your long-suffering husband. He's used to them. Leave Society to shift for itself!'

Epilogue

It had been a beautiful day, and now in the early evening a slight breeze had got up, bringing a welcome freshness to the warm air. Shelwood glowed in the mellow autumn sunshine, as the field workers returned to their homes. The crops were in, the barns and granaries were full. They could be reasonably certain of a safe, comfortable winter. They knew themselves to be fortunate. Shelwood was not only a prosperous estate, it was a happy one.

They smiled as they saw the little party approaching them. On their way back from Madame Elisabeth's, no doubt. Miss Fanny was hanging on her lord's arm like a bride, not a matron of four years! And Lord Carne looked as proud as any man could of his growing family—three bonny young bundles of mischief as they were. Little Miss Verity was the worst of the three of them, too, for all her angelic looks! There were those in the village who could remember Miss Fanny's mother in the old days. From what they said, this one was just such another.

It had been a lucky day for Shelwood when Miss Fanny had returned with a new and handsome lord for a husband, though they could wish that the family spent more time at the Manor. But Lord Carne had his own estates in Hertfordshire to look after, and it was said they also usu-

ally spent a month or two every year in London, visiting
King George that had been Prince Regent for so long.
But every summer they spent two or three months at
Shelwood, visiting, walking, catching up with the news
in the villages and farms. A proper lady, Lady Carne was.
And her husband was a very gentlemanly gentleman.

Yes, Shelwood was the happiest place to be in
all England.

AN INDEPENDENT LADY
by
Julia Byrne

Julia Byrne lives in Australia with her husband, daughter and a cat who thinks he's a person. She started her working career as a secretary, taught ballroom dancing after several successful years as a competitor, and, while working in the History Department of a Melbourne university, decided to try her hand at writing historical romance. She enjoys a game of cards or mah-jong, usually has several cross-stitch projects on the go, and is a keen preserver of family history.

Look for

THE VIKING'S CAPTIVE

Coming May 2003

Chapter One

'*Good God!* What next?'

The exclamation, though uttered with barely suppressed impatience, was not explosive enough to disturb the mid-morning quiet pertaining in the reading room at White's Club.

One did not, in fact, give vent to explosive exclamations while one was within the dignified portals of a gentlemen's club. Especially when one was the possessor of an old, distinguished title, who took pains to shield from the unwary the fact that he'd inherited every one of the fierce predatory traits that had enabled his ancestors to seize and hold the title in the first place.

The outburst did, however, reach the ears of the fair-haired gentleman lounging in a comfortable leather armchair set at an angle convenient for private conversation.

'Something amiss, Marc, old fellow?' Viscount Eversleigh enquired idly from behind the *Morning Post*. He turned a page. 'Good Lord, a third robbery at Bristol. Situation's getting right out of hand.'

Marcus Benedict Rothwell, Seventh Earl of Hawkridge, clenched his fingers around the letter in his hand and fixed what he could see of the Viscount with a look of narrow-eyed purpose.

'My sister, Augusta,' he began in ominous tones, 'writes to inform me that her butler has taken to falling down drunk every evening while serving dinner; Lucinda has run off to Gretna Green with a half-pay officer; and young Crispin has broken his neck by overfacing one of his father's prize hunters.'

'Dashed inconsiderate,' mumbled Eversleigh. 'I suppose you'll have to post down there and sort everything out, as usual.'

Marc straightened the letter with a snap of his wrist. 'She concludes with the news that your grandfather has finally been gathered to his ancestors after making a new will leaving his fortune to the cook and her husband.'

'*What?*'

The *Morning Post* flew through the air and landed in a small avalanche of paper. Eversleigh sat up with a jerk.

'Ah.' Marc smiled with fiendish satisfaction. 'I trust I now have your full attention, Pel?'

'You do, but that was a damned nasty way of going about it.'

'Inaccurate, too, if I recall your grandfather's cook.'

Eversleigh shuddered. 'I should say so. Wouldn't surprise me if the old boy did turn up his toes after one of her dinners. Can't see him leaving her more than a pension, though. Tight-fisted old bastard.'

'Oh, surely not.'

'Of course he is. Why the devil d'you think I'm hanging out for a rich—?' He caught the gleam in Marc's usually cool grey eyes and grinned. 'You'll have the ancestors spinning in their sepulchres, casting aspersions like that. Stiff-necked lot, the Eversleighs. Not a bastard among 'em. But never mind that. I take it you don't really need to dash off to Gretna, or attend Crispin's funeral?'

The gleam vanished. 'The only funeral I'm likely to attend in the near future is that of my grandmother's latest protégée.'

'Ahh.' Eversleigh nodded as one upon whom light has dawned. Then he frowned. 'Hold on. Thought her ladyship'd sworn off impecunious poets. It was a poet, wasn't it? Wanted her to perch on that rock off the beach at Hawkridge so he could write an ode to a mermaid. Dashed idiotic notion. The tide comes in at that spot before you can blink. Remember the time we were caught—'

'I remember,' Marc informed him, ruthlessly interrupting this excursion into their shared boyhood. 'In the case of the impecunious poet, you're a year out of date. After I sent him packing, we had the artist who was starving in a garret. He needed a profession until he made his name painting portraits; my grandmother decided she needed a secretary to take care of all those plaguey details such as letters of credit and bank drafts.'

'Aha.'

'Indeed. Fortunately, her banker noticed the artistically embellished figures on several transactions and contacted me. He'd never approved of a dowager countess managing her own affairs and was convinced that Grandmama had dropped a rein or two.'

The Viscount looked dubious. 'Very independent old lady, your grandmother. Wouldn't like to be the one to tell her she can't tool her own carriage anymore.'

'You'll be happy to know I don't have to perform that particular task.' Marc glared at the sheets of paper in his hand. 'My dear grandmama is now wide awake to the wiles of struggling artists. Her new companion possesses no skills in that direction at all.'

'There you are, then.'

'Augusta, however, imparts no such assurance that Mrs Chantry—Mrs Amaris Chantry, if you please—won't offer to restore the paintings in the long gallery, while appropriating more portable articles of infinitely greater value.'

'Oh.' A short pause ensued. Eversleigh raised a delicately

enquiring eyebrow as he bent to gather up the *Morning Post*. 'Someone offered…'

'Six months ago. A most charming gentleman rented the old Smitton place and promptly joined the Society for the Beautification of Our Village. That, according to Grandmama, immediately put him beyond reproach.'

'Bloody hell!' Eversleigh jerked upright again, leaving the paper to its fate. Sheer horror was stamped on his pleasant features. 'Is that crowd of gossiping old biddies still running amok? One of 'em tanned my hide with her walking cane when I hit a cricket ball through the vestry window twenty years ago. Thought they'd be safely underground by now.'

'Apparently they're still tottering about on walking canes. Grandmother, who's the Society's patron, met Mr Bartle at one of the meetings and was much impressed by his knowledge of history. He purported to be a scholar of art who specialised in the restoration of old paintings.'

'Was he?'

'We never found out. The first painting was taken down, laid on a table and surrounded by an impressive number of bottles and brushes. After two days of working in the strictest seclusion to minimise the danger of ruining the painting, Mr Bartle departed with several silver candlesticks, a handful of snuff boxes, and the first countess's pearls, which for some insane reason were draped over the statue of her husband on horseback.'

Eversleigh laughed. 'Nice to know nothing's changed at Hawkridge since I've been in France.'

'Unfortunately that's not quite true. Mrs Chantry is now in residence. She's a widow.'

'Not exactly a criminal offence, old fellow.'

Marc stared grimly at the letter in his hand. 'There's no mention of Mr Chantry, his style or profession, or how he met his end. The only facts to be gleaned from the crumbs of information scattered between page after page on Lucinda's wilful behaviour and the delicate state of Crispin's health are that Grandmama met Mrs Chantry when she visited Bath a few weeks ago.'

'Dare say she might. Place is full of widows.'

'Mrs Chantry is a *young* widow. "Tragically young",' Marc added, quoting directly from his sister's letter. "Such a sad situation. Left almost destitute. Forced to earn her own living. And you know what sort of living might be forced upon a penniless girl as lovely as Mrs Chantry." He scowled at the missive again. 'How the hell does Augusta know about things like that?'

Eversleigh grinned. 'I hate to tell you this, Marc, but your sister has been a married woman for quite some time. Not that I can imagine Nettlebed drumming up the energy to carouse with widows—young or otherwise.'

Marc ignored this judicious pronouncement on his cheerfully indolent brother-in-law. 'Unfortunately Augusta's worldly knowledge doesn't extend to Mrs Chantry's parents. They appear to be shrouded in mystery.'

'Probably dead too.'

'Oh, that's a great comfort to me, Pel. I hope you're not going to offer the same explanation when I inform you of the lack of former employers in our widow's history.'

'Perhaps she's been widowed only a short time. You know, Marc, before you go racing off to Devon to tear the destitute Mrs Chantry from beneath your grandmother's wing, you might consider that she really is a young widow left tragically bereft.'

'Have you ever heard of a widow named Amaris?'

This demand gave Eversleigh pause. He pursed his lips and bent his mind to grave consideration of the matter.

'No,' he finally pronounced. And grinned. 'At least, not the type of widow who hires herself out as a companion to elderly ladies.'

Marc did not feel inclined to share his friend's amusement.

'Exactly. The veracity of this particular widow's tragic past also comes into question when I tell you that she and my grandmother met when Mrs Chantry almost fell under the wheels of Grandmama's coach.'

'Good God, how did she manage that?'

'She was faint with hunger. More likely it was the performance of her life. She could've saved herself the trouble. Grandmama wouldn't care if she was treading the boards. We've had poets, artists, restorers. Why quibble at an actress?'

Eversleigh nodded in gloomy agreement. 'Knowing your grandmother, she's probably fascinated. Like to tread the boards, herself.'

'Not at her time of life,' Marc vowed, rising to his feet. 'Pel, you'll have to convey my apologies to the Scatterthwaites. I was supposed to attend their ball tonight, but I'll be otherwise engaged.'

'Ask Goring over there to convey both our apologies,' Eversleigh suggested, rising with alacrity. 'I'll be otherwise engaged, too.'

Marc lifted a brow. 'You're coming with me?'

'Of course I'm coming with you. Urgent family business.'

A look of amusement crossed Marc's face. 'Scatterthwaite's daughters are worth twenty thousand a year. Each.'

'I'm not that desperate. Besides, you might need help removing the widow. All very well to toss poets through the library window. You can hardly do the same to a female.'

Marc muttered something that sounded distinctly like 'Why not?' Tossing Mrs Amaris Chantry through the library window would, he decided, go a long way towards relieving his exacerbated feelings.

The situation was getting out of hand. There were far too many people in the world who were prepared to take advantage of his grandmother's affectionate, generous nature. And since no one else seemed capable of doing anything about it, he would have to step into the breach.

A rather nasty sense of inevitability threatened to hover over him. Rather like a sword about to fall. If he didn't want to spend the majority of his time evicting confidence tricksters from his ancestral home he would have to think very seriously about supplying the dowager with a companion of impeccable lineage and proper notions of conduct.

Said companion would also need to be kind enough to tolerate Lady Hawkridge's frequently maddening ways, intelligent enough not to bore him witless within a week, and attractive enough to make facing her across the breakfast table every morning a not impossible task.

In other words, it was about time he made another attempt to supply himself with a wife.

The prospect didn't fill him with delight. The last two attempts, while not exactly disasters, had been crowned by a conspicuous lack of success. Fortunately, only one had been a public lack of success. The other he'd always regarded as more of a lucky escape.

The thought of either situation recurring made him scowl so ferociously that Lord Goring, when cornered, didn't voice even a mild protest at having to face Lady Scatterthwaite and her daughters and inform them that two of the *ton*'s most eligible bachelors would be missing from a ball put on especially to lure them into their coils.

'If only I could decide where to put the Society. Really, Amy, I am quite at my wits' end.'

Mrs Amaris Chantry looked up from the pile of letters she'd been sorting as the Dowager Lady Hawkridge burst into the library like a small, plump, mauve-clad whirlwind.

Her ladyship was armed with a feather duster.

Amy had no idea why her employer felt obliged to dust since there was a maid assigned for the mundane task, but she'd been living at Hawkridge Manor for a full month now

and was quite inured to her ladyship's habit of starting conversations while still *en route* to her auditor.

She also had no trouble following Lady Hawkridge's ram-
bling discourse.

'The winter parlour would be charming now that we have
some sunshine after all that rain, but if Mrs Tredgett should
attend, she'd be sure to take offence. On the other hand, the
drawing-room is far too large, and so *dauntingly* formal that
persons such as Miss Pucklenett will be quite overcome.'

Lady Hawkridge took an agitated turn about the library and
fetched up in front of the lectern upon which reposed the family Bible, an imposing tome of ponderous proportions in which
were recorded the arrivals and departures of several generations of Rothwells.

Her ladyship looked at the duster in her hand and waved it
in a vague sort of way over the vellum-bound volume.

'I don't know why the Society's meeting couldn't be held
at the Vicarage as usual,' she went on, her cherubic face
marred by a frown. 'I know the younger girls aren't well, but
they won't be running in and out of the parlour, will they?'

'Ahh.' Amy nodded in complete understanding. 'Mrs ffollifoot has begged that you'll hold the Society's meeting here.
I suppose no one else has volunteered. In that case, ma'am,
have the drawing-room made ready. Miss Pucklenett positively *delights* in being overcome. Think what a treat it will
be for her.'

'Good heavens, you're quite right.' The dowager looked
much struck by the notion. 'Poor thing. I suppose she doesn't
have a great deal to look forward to. Not that the Mayhews
ever treat their staff with anything but the greatest consideration.'

'As do you, dearest ma'am.' Amy rose from her seat, a
warm smile curving her mouth as she crossed the room to her
employer. 'However, I doubt that Mary will view with any-

thing but the greatest *dismay* the fact that you're doing the dusting.'

'Well, I thought of the drawing-room earlier, but I couldn't remember when we'd last used it. And there always seem to be so many rooms to dust.' Her ladyship looked at the duster again and aimed a swipe in the general direction of a shelf of books. A small cloud of dust motes danced in the air.

Amy stifled a sneeze. 'Even so, ma'am—'

'Now, don't scold, Amy dear. I've a perfectly good explanation.' The dowager paused, then added in accents of doom, 'Chicken-pox.'

'Ohh.'

'It's all the fault of the Vicar's wretched offspring. I hope I'm sympathetic towards children in their sick-beds, Amy, but not when they infect my maids.'

'Perfectly understandable, ma'am. Poor Mary. Would you like me to ask Mrs Cubitt if we should send for the doctor?'

'I don't think housekeepers believe in pampering the maids, but if anyone could persuade her, it would be you. And, after all, I did send for dear Dr Twinhoe when the boys caught the chicken-pox. Not that it did any good. I was hoping he'd give them a draught that would keep them in their beds, but he said the most we could hope for was that they wouldn't run about infecting everyone else.'

'A daunting thought, ma'am.'

Her ladyship shuddered. 'I suppose we should've been grateful that Pelham was visiting here when they both came down with it, but they were the most dreadful patients. Marc and Lord Eversleigh, you know. At least, he's Eversleigh at the moment. When that bad-tempered, gout-ridden old fool is finally pushed into the family vault, he'll be the Earl of Colborough.'

'Er, bad-tempered, gout-ridden…'

'Old fool,' confirmed her ladyship, brandishing her duster

with vigour. 'I said old fool and I meant it. Have *you* had the chicken-pox, Amy?'

Amy blinked. 'Yes, ma'am.' And every other childhood ailment known to mankind.

Fascinated by the unaccustomed ire emanating from her employer, she dismissed childhood ailments and probed delicately. 'I collect you're speaking of the elderly gentleman who lives in that house on the other side of the cove.'

'There is no *gentleman* on the other side of the cove.' Lady Hawkridge glared at the duster in her hand, hefted it and charged at a nearby armchair like a knight going into battle. 'Only an old fool who said our Society was a bevy of cackling hens who— Oh, heavens! The Society!' The duster was suspended in mid-air. 'What am I thinking of? Why must Mrs ffollifoot leave it to the last minute to change her plans? We'll have to write notes and— Amy, do you think…?'

'Of course, ma'am. It will take only a few minutes to dash off a quick note to everyone and there's plenty of time before the meeting for the notes to be delivered. Please don't fret about it.'

Lady Hawkridge beamed. 'Dear Amy. So dependable.' She abandoned the assault on the armchair and began to circle the room, flicking the duster over bookshelves and occasional-tables as she passed. Several small ornaments rocked wildly. Amy rushed to avert disaster.

'So kind,' Lady Hawkridge continued, oblivious to the guardian angel of ornaments following in her wake. 'And with all those letters to answer, too. I don't know where I'd be without you, Amy dear. My eyes aren't as good as they once were, you know, and I receive such a volume of mail that I fear they would be quite worn out if I had to deal with it myself.'

Since Lady Hawkridge had, that very morning, espied a rare wildflower blooming on the cliffs several hundred yards away from Hawkridge Manor, Amy had no trouble identifying this remark for the kindness it was.

Gratitude filled her heart, causing tears to well behind her eyes.

She would never cease to thank the benevolent providence that had prompted the Dowager Countess of Hawkridge to call for her carriage that day four weeks ago instead of summoning a chair to negotiate the hilly streets of Bath.

Amy didn't like to think about what might have befallen her if she herself hadn't been on that particular street at the same moment. The thought only had to creep to the edge of her mind to have her flesh turn cold and shivery.

She'd been down to her last shilling. The future had loomed like a crouching malevolent beast, waiting to drag her back into a pit of black despair from which she could never escape.

'Sometimes,' the dowager confided, pausing in her progress to peer at the pile of letters on Amy's desk, 'I wonder if Marc was right when he accused me of indiscriminate patronage of the arts. Oh, dear, that looks like his writing.'

Amy shook off her memories and returned to the desk to pick up the unopened letter she'd laid aside. An arrogant black signature was slashed across one corner of the envelope.

'I thought it might be, ma'am, since the letter is franked by Hawkridge.' She handed it over. 'The only other letter concerning artistic matters this morning is a request for a donation to establish a retreat where a group of sculptors can fashion statues of humans in their, ah, natural forms.'

'Oh, dear, I don't think Marc would approve of that.'

Amy was sure of it. Not that she objected to his disapproval in this particular instance, but she also possessed the uncomfortable suspicion that he wouldn't approve of her either.

She could hardly blame Hawkridge. After hearing the sorry tale of the dowager's previous experiences with people whom she'd taken under her kindly wing, Amy had decided that Hawkridge would immediately assume her to be the latest in

a long line of hucksters out to fleece his grandmama of as
much as possible in the shortest possible time.

Rehearsing speeches of explanation in the event that she
ever met the Earl had not resulted in a feeling of confidence
that such a meeting would be pleasant. Hawkridge did not
appear to be filled with tolerance and understanding for his
fellow human beings.

While the dowager broke the sealed envelope with a distinct
lack of enthusiasm, Amy glanced up at the portrait of the Earl
that hung over the mantelpiece.

Eyes the colour of sleeting rain stared back at her from
beneath level black brows. There was something about those
eyes—something the artist had tried to capture, only to have
it remain elusively out of reach. Something...

Amy shook her head. The more she tried to pin down the
expression, the more it slipped away.

She turned her attention to his other features. Even at the
age of twenty they were forbidding; the straight blade of his
nose, the high razor-sharp cheekbones and chiselled jaw putting Amy forcibly in mind of the savage Indian warriors fortunately residing in the American colonies. The air of fierce
pride and masculine arrogance was echoed in the way he
stood, leaning with careless grace against the shoulder of a
huge black horse. He held the reins loosely in one large, ele-
gantly-shaped hand, even though the horse looked as if it was
about to take a chunk out of anyone foolish enough to approach.

Amy felt a familiar shiver slide down her spine. The same
shiver she experienced every time she gazed at the painted
image of the Earl of Hawkridge. The portrait had been done
fourteen years ago, so Lady Hawkridge had informed her,
upon the Earl's succession to his grandfather's title, but Amy
had no reason to believe that those years had mellowed the
arrogant, handsome face or softened the hard, unsmiling line
of his mouth.

The thought wasn't comforting. Even more disturbing was the fact that the painting had the unsettling effect of distracting her from her work at odd moments during the day. Too often she found herself searching those stern features for signs of the boy who'd been catapulted swiftly and tragically into manhood.

The transition seemed to have been complete.

She could, of course, have used any of the other rooms that comprised the sprawling maze that was Hawkridge Manor. Lady Hawkridge had kindly instructed her to avail herself of whatever room took her fancy.

Amy had chosen the library.

And she was honest enough to admit that she'd chosen the room because the portrait fascinated her. She wished it didn't—fascination, unwilling or otherwise, did not augur well if she ever met the original—but that didn't alter the fact.

She was utterly enthralled by the image of the Earl of Hawkridge.

Her only consolation was that she was unlikely to be confronted by the real thing any time soon. The Manor might have been the Earl's boyhood home and principal seat, but it was a long way from London where he apparently preferred to spend his time.

Amy could only be grateful.

She was still busily counting her blessings when the sound of carriage wheels on gravel wafted through the open windows of the library.

'Oh, heavens!' The dowager looked up from her letter. 'You don't think Mrs ffollifoot has sent notes to everyone and they're arriving already, do you?'

'I doubt it, ma'am. Perhaps Mrs Cubitt has sent for the doctor, after all. Would you like me to find out?'

'If you would, Amy. Oh, dear, if it isn't one thing, it's another. Even dear Mr Tweedy would be rather in the way when I'm so distracted. And this afternoon everyone will want tea and there's Mary with the chicken-pox—'

With the dowager twittering behind her, Amy crossed the room with determined strides. Whoever was arriving would have to be informed that this was not a convenient time to visit. Even if it was 'dear Mr Tweedy' who, in her opinion, was going to prove rather too dear for the dowager's purse.

She reached the door, yanked it open, and gave a squeak of shock as a dark figure loomed over her.

The Earl of Hawkridge stood on the threshold.

The real one.

Amy stumbled back several paces and blinked. It wasn't an illusion. Hawkridge was standing there in the flesh. The impact on her senses was all that she'd feared. After one gasp of dismay, she stopped breathing.

Chapter Two

'Good heavens! Marc!'

The startled exclamation came from his grandmother, not the lady he'd almost bowled over in the doorway.

Marc spared the youthful unknown a quick glance. Fortunately, she'd retreated in a hurry—before he could indulge an utterly insane impulse to catch her about the waist and hold her against him instead of letting her bounce off.

It was not an auspicious beginning. If she was his quarry, several alternatives to ejecting her were already springing to mind. All rendered him distinctly uncomfortable.

Reining in his suddenly wayward thoughts, he manufactured a smile for his grandparent and bent to kiss her cheek. 'Good morning, Grandmama.'

'Marc, what a lovely surprise. I've been wanting you to meet dear Amy for weeks, and here you are.'

'Yes.' He straightened, erasing the smile when he turned to dear Amy. The first thing he noted was the bare fingers of her left hand. He dropped his voice to a tone well below freezing. To his extreme annoyance, it was the only thing about him enjoying that chilly temperature. 'Here I am.'

Mrs Chantry shivered slightly. His satisfaction at the betraying motion was small consolation for the effect she was having on him. It was also brief.

Her chin went up. She thrust out her other hand with equal defiance. 'How do you do, my lord?'

'Mrs Chantry,' he acknowledged, and made the monumental mistake of enclosing her hand in his.

Two wildly opposing impulses assaulted his brain with startling speed. Her hand felt so small in his, so soft, he wanted to cradle it as if he held the finest crystal, while at the same time he was rocked by an equally strong urge to rap his fist against the pointed little chin aimed so pugnaciously at his chest.

Damn it, his plans didn't include letting his victim know she'd thoroughly distracted him from his mission.

Triumph didn't appear to be Mrs Chantry's first reaction to the hard grip of his fingers, however. When he finally managed to release her, the colour in her face, already an interesting shade of pink, burned hotter. She continued to meet his gaze, but defiance was fighting a rearguard action. She looked guilty—as guilty as original sin.

She also looked as tempting.

Marc continued to study the blush suffusing Mrs Amaris Chantry's cheeks while he fought temptation. The faintest hint of lavender water, overlaying warm female flesh, that wafted to his nostrils didn't help the endeavour.

There was no doubt about it. His grandmother's latest companion was going to be trouble.

More than trouble, he concluded grimly, subjecting the total picture to a comprehensive appraisal. She was potential disaster clad in a cream muslin gown the exact tint of skin that threatened to make his mouth water. An elegant primrose spencer, puffed of sleeve and ruffled at the throat, clung like a lover to small, round breasts that *did* make his mouth water.

Resisting the urge to swallow, he jerked his gaze upward. Hints of the same golden hue as her spencer showed in the rich tawny hair coiled in a neat twist atop her head. He clenched his fingers around the whip still in his hand to stop himself reaching out and tugging at that too-neat coil.

It would have been easy; she barely topped his shoulder.

Eyes narrowed against a vision of silken hair flowing over delicate curves, he lowered his gaze again, and decided that instant lust had overturned his brain. He, who had never waxed lyrical about a woman, found himself in danger of drowning in sable-fringed pools of the clearest, purest crystalline green he'd ever encountered.

And he'd encountered a few. He'd certainly encountered enough to suspect that subtle artifice had been employed to enhance lashes that were much darker than her hair. He would have been happy to prove the theory, but he was too busy being drawn into the beguiling depths of those eyes.

Fathomless eyes that told him their owner had seen too much and hadn't liked much of what she'd seen. Eyes turbulent with defensiveness and defiance, set beneath gently arched brows, and dominating a face too piquant to belong to a diamond of the first water, but so finely drawn his fingers itched to touch the petal-soft skin, to trace the fragile bones beneath.

There was an air of innocence about that face; she looked…untouched. Which was ridiculous. She'd been married, so she was hardly untouched. And if her title was a courtesy one, she'd look even less innocent. And yet, those eyes held an expression that, despite the wariness, despite the shadows that spoke of knowledge hard won, lacked that indefinable something that said 'favours for sale'.

For the first time Marc found himself wondering if she really was what she purported to be. A young widow forced to earn her own living.

The possibility was unexpectedly annoying. Annoying, he admitted wryly, because in that first instant of seeing Mrs

Amaris Chantry, he'd pictured her in another position altogether.

Such as under him. In a bed.

He suddenly realised his grandmother had been twittering
the whole time he'd been standing as if he'd been bowled over
by the Royal Mail, and he hadn't listened to a word she'd
said. He vaguely recalled such hopeful phrases as 'delightful
company', 'so kind', 'so ready to help…'

'And you'll be happy to know she doesn't approve of me
setting up a retreat for naked sculptors.'

That got through. Marc's gaze snapped briefly to his grandmother's impossibly innocent face. She beamed at him. He
decided to take charge of a rapidly unravelling situation.

'I'm relieved to hear, Mrs Chantry, that you don't approve
of people sculpting while naked.'

'Oh! That isn't…I mean…'

From the corner of her eye Amy saw Lady Hawkridge's
lips twitch, and cursed both her employer and the new wave
of colour rising to her cheeks. She'd meant to behave with the
sort of dignified maturity that would convince the Earl she
was fully suited to her position here, and instead was blushing
and stammering like a schoolgirl.

It was all Hawkridge's fault, of course. The way he'd
pounced on her in the doorway before she'd had any warning
was enough to overset the staunchest nerves.

Not that he was exactly like his portrait. In fact, as far as
she was concerned, the portrait had a great deal to answer for.

The reality was very much taller for one thing. She had to
tilt her chin up in what was sure to appear a challenging angle
to look him in the eyes. And there didn't appear to be much
daylight between him and the doorway. In any direction.

She tried to tell herself that his elegant greatcoat, adorned
with several capes, added to the impression of overwhelming
size, but it was clear that Hawkridge's tailor did not need to
use an inordinate amount of capes to fill out those broad shoul-

ders, or emphasise the width of chest that met her gaze when she lowered her eyes.

She lowered them further, hoping for something to lessen the impact.

Hope died a swift and ignominious death. Hawkridge's buckskins clung to the long powerful muscles of his thighs in a way that caused her own legs to go unaccountably weak. As for his topboots, she could have climbed into one and disappeared.

A slight movement had her gaze climbing upward in time to see his left hand clench about his whip, as though he was contemplating using it on her. She wasn't surprised; in a mind-numbing burst of knowledge she'd realised precisely what that long-ago artist had so lamentably failed to capture.

Hawkridge might appear civilised; he might dress with the kind of fashionable elegance that drew the eye; he might even behave with civility in polite company. But his instincts were those of the warrior he resembled.

She should know, Amy thought, bracing herself to confront the fierce glitter in those piercing grey eyes. She'd fought enough battles of her own not to recognise another iron-clad will when she met one head-on.

'I see you noticed the absence of a wedding ring, my lord,' she stated, recklessly taking the offensive into enemy territory. 'I had to sell it.'

She didn't appear overly distressed by the circumstance, Marc decided. In fact, her air of youthful innocence was in direct contrast to the cool self-possession that dropped over her like a cloak after she'd looked him up and down. That wide-eyed examination had had its inevitable effect. He was glad he'd left his greatcoat on. The garment hung open, but if he turned slightly away from his grandmother she wouldn't see his unruly body ignoring the commands of his brain for the first time since his youth.

He didn't intend to hide his reaction from Mrs Chantry; he

wanted her shaken out of that surface calm. But she appeared not to notice.

Given that his buckskins moulded his form like a second skin, even a mild male response would have been obvious. Mrs Chantry was either so innocent her marriage was a tale of fiction, which might account for the guilty secrets in her eyes—her mysterious husband had been a eunuch, a possibility he dismissed out of hand—or she had turned her back on a positively brilliant career on the stage.

'Now, Amy, I'm sure there's no need to go into all that,' soothed Lady Hawkridge, jabbing him in the ribs with an un-subtle elbow when he opened his mouth to find out.

His glare was met with a guileless smile. 'I'm so glad you're here, Marc, dearest. Augusta is having such a difficult time with Crispin. You know what young boys are like. Not that you ever listened to anyone, but Crispin thinks you're an out-and-outer, so he may listen to you, and heaven knows poor Nettlebed can't—'

'If Nettlebed took a good look at his son instead of taking Augusta's word for it that the brat is delicate, he might do better,' Marc grated, annoyed at the digression.

He saw a flash of approval in Mrs Chantry's eyes, and raised a brow. 'It seems you agree, Mrs Chantry.'

She looked a little self-conscious. 'I wouldn't presume to pass judgement, my lord, when I have no experience with youths.'

'You've never been employed as a governess in your, er, career?'

'No, sir. My place here with Lady Hawkridge is my first position. Um…that is…'

'As a companion,' he murmured.

Her lashes flickered, telling him the shot had hit home.

Not so innocent, then. That untouched, barely-out-of-the-schoolroom appearance must be invaluable to her. He wondered what the hell she was doing as a companion to an elderly lady when she could be earning a fortune in another, more horizontal, position.

No, better keep his mind off the horizontal plane.

'Then I trust the duties of a companion are more to your taste, Mrs Chantry,' he added smoothly.

She tilted that defiant little chin at him again.

'Indeed they are, my lord. And speaking of duties—' Taking a deep breath, she stepped forward, rather in the manner of one about to herd sheep. 'I'm sure you and Lady Hawkridge wish to enjoy a tête-à-tête, so if you'd be so kind as to escort her to the drawing-room, I'll continue with the morning's tasks. Notes,' she added when he raised a brow. 'We're holding a meeting here this afternoon of the Society for the Beautification of Our Village. Chicken-pox at the vicarage, you know. I'm sure the ladies will be agog at your presence, if you mean to join us, that is, but first I have to let them know and…'

She finally ran down through lack of air.

'Yes, indeed,' seconded his grandmother valiantly, taking his arm and tugging.

Before he could argue, Marc found himself back in the hall. The lady he'd come to evict sent him a sweet smile and gently shut the library door in his face.

He glared at the wooden panels an inch from his nose. 'Correct me if I'm wrong, Grandmama,' he began in arctic tones, 'but was I just ordered out of my own library?'

'Of course you were, dearest. You can't expect poor little Amy to write notes to everyone with you looming over her shoulder. You tend to do that a lot, dear. Looming, I mean. You should put a stop to it.'

He gritted his teeth. 'Grandmama, you and I need to have a long talk.'

'How lovely.' Completely undaunted by the prospect, Lady Hawkridge began to steer him towards the drawing-room, waving a feather duster over a vase of flowers as they passed. Several petals floated to the floor.

He decided not to ask.

'I want to hear all the London gossip. You know, Marc, you should convey those interesting little tidbits that we all wish to hear in your letters, instead of warning me against unlikely disasters as if I'm in my dotage.'

'I know you're not in your dotage, Grandmama, but—'

'Now sit down, dearest, while I see what needs to be done. Oh, dear, I do hope Amy is right. Poor Miss Pucklenett. She likes to be daunted by drawing-rooms, you know. It's very sad.'

Marc divested himself of his greatcoat while he counted to ten.

'If Miss Pucklenett is another of your lame ducks—'

'Really, Marc, if you ever paid attention to anything other than my affairs, you'd know that Miss Pucklenett has been the Mayhews' governess forever. And I do not collect lame ducks.'

He couldn't help smiling. 'Of course you do, love. Look at the way you let Pel and me run wild all over the place when we were boys.'

'That,' declared the dowager with dignity, 'was a different matter. You were our grandson—well, you still are, of course—and after that terrible... Well, Pelham had lost his parents, as you had.' She wielded the duster with considerable violence. 'What else could one do when that silly old fool at Colborough Court took no interest in his only grandchild?'

Marc's expression turned wry. 'Colborough lost a son and daughter-in-law, too, Grandmama.'

'Yes,' admitted her ladyship. 'Indeed, he was never quite so irascible until that dreadful day, but to criticise anyone who tries to go about their lives as best they may, although he never goes out himself, is perfectly intolerable.'

'Ah.' Marc grinned. 'Old Colborough still refers to your Society as a bevy of cackling hens.'

His grandmother muttered something unintelligible as she continued to attack various articles of furniture with the duster. There appeared to be no logic to her progression. He wondered if he should point out that several priceless antique urns imported from China by his grandfather were in imminent danger of shattering.

'Grandmama, forgive my ignorance on such matters, but why are you dusting?'

The dusting was suspended, saving the urns from their inevitable fate. 'Marc, are you feeling quite the thing, dearest? Surely you heard Amy·say that chicken-pox is everywhere. Mary caught it. So unfortunate, but I'm sure she didn't do it deliberately.'

'Mary being one of your maids.'

'Yes, so you see why Amy and I are in such a pucker.'

The thought of Mrs Chantry in a pucker held a certain appeal. Especially the sort of pucker that sprang in vivid detail to his suddenly fertile brain. His body approved of the fantasy, too.

Annoyed, Marc shoved his hands into his breeches pockets and began to pace. 'Mrs Chantry did not strike me as the sort of person who gets into puckers. On the other hand, for a minute or two there, she did look decidedly guilty.'

'Guilty!' His grandparent glared at him as if he'd accused *her* of nefarious activities. 'What a dreadful thing to say. Poor little Amy. Guilty of what, pray?'

'I don't know, although after the antics of your former secretaries, nothing would surprise me. I merely meant that Mrs Chantry looked at me as if she expected to be evicted in the same manner as that idiot poet and was prepared to fight me every inch of the way.'

'Well, I should think so,' declared the dowager in indignant accents. 'The very idea! Tossing poor little Amy through the library window.'

'Poor little Amy appears to be an enigma,' Marc stated, pausing in his perambulations and fixing his grandmother with a stern eye. 'What precisely do you know about her?'

'Lots of things,' claimed the dowager somewhat defiantly. 'But I don't intend to talk about Amy while you pace about like a tiger ready to pounce on everything I say.'

'All right.' Raising his hands in a gesture of compliance, Marc strode over to a sofa and flung himself on to an over-stuffed cushion. 'There. I won't even loom.'

His grandmother beamed. 'That's much better. Now let me see. Well, Amy reads beautifully. Such verve. Such passion. Such—'

'Yes, it doesn't surprise me to learn that her acting skills are superior.'

Her ladyship's approving smile vanished. 'Marcus, you are becoming extremely cynical, which I take leave to inform you is not an attractive trait. Just because we had that *tiny* bit of trouble with Mr Bartle…'

'Not to mention Ambrose the Artist and that fool poet.'

The dowager had the grace to blush. 'Poor dear Florian. At least he didn't try to rob me.'

'No, he pestered you with attentions, as if you'd marry a man younger than your own grandson. I suppose I should be grateful I only had to toss him through the window instead of chasing after him as I did Bartle to retrieve those damned pearls.'

Lady Hawkridge hung her head, reminding Marc of a chastened schoolgirl standing before a hatchet-faced governess. Even the duster drooped. He felt like a brute.

'Grandmama, I'm sorry.' Rising, he curved his hands around his grandmother's shoulders and squeezed gently. 'I wouldn't distress you for the world, but there's no blinking at the fact that your very nature makes you a target for spongers. If you want a companion I'll find you one. In fact—'

'But, Marc, dearest, I've already found my own companion.' Restored to animation by that indisputable fact, the dowager whisked herself out of his hold and continued her whirlwind circuit of the room. 'I can't imagine why I didn't employ a lady before. Dear Amy is so obliging, so willing, so sweet-natured, so—'

'Who was her husband?' he demanded bluntly, hoping to extract one solid fact from what threatened to become a panegyric on Mrs Chantry's sterling qualities.

The result was a stare of the liveliest astonishment. 'Why, dearest, whoever do you think? Mr Chantry, of course.'

Marc sat down again and put his head in his hands.

'There, there, dear.' The dowager flitted up to him and patted him consolingly with the duster. 'You must be tired. Such a long journey from Town. You should go straight to your room and lie down.'

'Grandmama, I don't need to lie down.' He stared in resignation at the smear of dust on the shoulder of his coat. 'Although I might soon become a candidate for Bedlam. I meant, *what* was Mr Chantry? For all you know, he could have been anything from a respectable businessman to a thief from the stews.'

'Oh, my goodness, how that does take me back. My old nurse, you know. Whenever we had cherries for tea we'd play a game by counting the pips. Rich man, poor man, beggarman, thief. Whatever came last was the man one would marry. Oh, my.' The dowager sighed.

'I'm trying to elicit some facts here, Grandmama, which are not likely to be found in the nursery. So far you don't know who Mr Chantry was, what he did, or when he died. I've never even encountered the name. How old is Mrs Chantry, by the way?'

'Good heavens, I've never asked. And neither will you. Really, Marc! The thought of asking a lady her age.'

'Stow the righteous indignation, Grandmama. Mrs Chantry, for all her elegance and poise, appears extremely young. I'd be surprised to learn she's much above twenty.'

The dowager appeared much struck. She blinked in surprise and gave the matter considerable thought. 'Do you know, Marc, I think you're right. Not that I've wondered, you understand, but now that you mention it, Amy does seem young. When you take a *close* look, that is. And yet, her manner is quite poised, isn't it? One would naturally assume she is older.'

'Probably what she wants you to think,' Marc muttered. 'What about her financial situation? Augusta claimed she was destitute, and she certainly looks as if a puff of wind will blow her over, but she's dressed in the first style of elegance.'

'Well, of course she is. Do you think I'd let my companion go about in rags? Naturally, I gave Amy a little money on account so she could replenish a sadly depleted wardrobe.'

'A little money on account.' Marc nodded grimly. 'Now we're getting to the hub of the matter. How much money?'

'Very little,' declared the dowager triumphantly. 'I tried to persuade Amy to take more, but she wouldn't hear of it. She said she was more than capable of fashioning her own gowns from materials bought from the village draper. And I must say she was right. She has so many useful accomplishments. Why, she can even cook. Such a comfort when Mrs Pickles might be struck down with chicken-pox at any moment.'

'A comfort, indeed. I note that the gown she cleverly fashioned isn't in funereal black. Quite the contrary.'

'Primrose,' stated her ladyship, 'is a very *pale* shade of yellow, and when partnered with cream, is perfectly proper for a young widow out of mourning. Besides, Amy wears her dark green pelisse when she goes out. She made that, too.'

'Hmm. What about more conventional accomplishments?'

His grandmother fixed him with an innocently inquiring eye. 'Do you mean things like torturing the pianoforte or the harp, throwing paint at a canvas, singing that reminds you of cats howling?'

Marc grinned before he could stop himself. 'My remarks after the last crowd of debutantes Augusta paraded before me.' Rising, he seized his grandparent in a fond embrace that lifted her clean off the floor. '*Touché*, love. If I promise not to interrogate you any further about Mrs Chantry, will you let me stay?'

'As if you need to ask to stay in your own home,' protested Lady Hawkridge in somewhat muffled accents. 'You know I'm always delighted to see you, but only if you promise not to intimidate poor little Amy.'

'I promise I won't intimidate Mrs Chantry,' he repeated obediently, setting the dowager on her feet. He decided he could safely make such a promise. If Mrs Chantry had nothing to hide, a few questions shouldn't bother her.

Besides, she didn't appear to be easily intimidated.

Amy leaned against the library door for a good five minutes, both hands clamped over her heart to stop it from leaping clean out of her chest. She seemed to be having a great deal of trouble breathing. No doubt both conditions were caused by relief that she hadn't been hurled forth before she could state her case.

She'd never met anyone more intimidating. She could hardly believe she'd actually faced down the Earl of Hawkridge—the real one—and won a reprieve.

Aided and abetted by the dowager.

The admission had her frowning. She stopped pressing her shoulders to the door as though Hawkridge might burst through it again at any moment, and pondered the point.

For one who had opened her grandson's letter with considerable reluctance, her ladyship had looked inordinately de-

lighted to see the author. Hawkridge, himself, seemed as fond
of the dowager. The brief smile he'd given his grandmother
had almost startled Amy into peering from him to the portrait
to see if she'd mistaken his identity. The fact that she was still
standing here, instead of sailing through the library window,
was added proof that Hawkridge cared enough about his
grandmother not to dismiss her latest companion out of hand.

On the other hand, he could be biding his time.

Amy set her lips in a determined line. It was one thing for
her to know how woefully unsuited she was to be residing in
a gentleman's house; Hawkridge had no right to look at her
as though she'd had a fistful of purloined trinkets in her possession.

Although now she came to think about it, he hadn't looked
at her in *quite* that way. His eyes had certainly been hard, and
unnervingly intent, but...

Amy shook her head. She suspected it would be a great deal
less wearing on her nerves if she *didn't* try to remember the
precise expression in Hawkridge's eyes when he'd looked her
up and down. Or anything else about him.

Fascination with a portrait was safer.

She glanced up at the painting as though to confirm that
comforting conclusion, and waited for the familiar shiver to
slide down her spine.

Nothing happened.

Amy frowned and stared harder at the painted image.

Her spine stayed perfectly free of shivers.

Then realisation struck her with the force of a thunder clap.

She was looking at the portrait of a boy. The boy she'd
sought all along; matured, even hardened by recent bereavement, but defined by his very youth, the promise of his full
strength and manhood still ahead of him.

The man who'd towered over her in the doorway had ful-
filled that promise and more. But greater physical strength
alone didn't set the man apart from the boy. The difference

was in the harnessing of that strength, and the fierce will that drove it. He'd learned to conceal the warrior within. Probably enough to escape detection by most of Polite Society. And it was that—the sheer impact of intense masculinity under ruthless restraint—that was utterly overwhelming.

No wonder he'd taken her breath away.

Amy shivered, unable to stop her errant mind from wondering if Hawkridge's control ever snapped to reveal the man behind the polished façade. And if it did, what would happen if she was in the immediate vicinity when an explosion occurred?

The questions had an unfortunate effect on her senses. She thought of the way Hawkridge had loomed over her in the doorway and her legs trembled. She remembered the piercing glitter in his eyes when he'd looked her up and down and her wits threatened to scatter to the four corners of the room. She remembered the sheer size of him and every nerve in her body quivered, shivered, and generally behaved in a manner that was alarmingly unfamiliar.

Alarm was not something with which she wished to become re-acquainted. She had to put a stop to this right now. If she wanted to keep the safe, peaceful existence she was beginning to carve out for herself she was going to need every wit she possessed. Legs would be useful if she had to flee. And her nerves would just have to return to fascination with a portrait, because peace and safety were of more importance to her than fascination with an Earl.

Or any other peer of the realm.

For that matter, they were of more importance to her than fascination with a male of any description.

Amy straightened her shoulders. With that fact resounding in her head she should soon recover her own façade. Heaven knew she'd worked hard enough to perfect it. She would simply stay out of Hawkridge's way until she was sure it was solidly back in place.

Or, she thought, fixing the painting with a narrow-eyed glare of accusation, until she'd better prepared herself to face the subject of a disastrously incompetent portraitist, who had been lamentably lacking in foresight.

Chapter Three

With the praiseworthy goal of avoiding Hawkridge in her sights, Amy set out for the village of Ottersmead as soon as her notes were written.

She anticipated a pleasant outing. Ottersmead was a peaceful place, perfectly suited, she'd decided on her first visit, to the restoration of jangled nerves.

Situated on a spectacular part of the Devon coast, it was sufficiently removed from the post road so that constant traffic did not disturb its sylvan setting, but was still within easy reach of the summer resort town of Teignmouth.

As villages went, Ottersmead was larger than most. A dozen or so genteel shops and houses fronted on its main street, at one end of which stood the Vicarage, a half-timbered edifice surrounded by a very pretty rose garden that dated from Tudor times. The Green Man, a respectable hostelry capable of accommodating the occasional visitor in comfort, presided at the other end of the street; a well-attended market was held on the first Thursday of every month; and the whole was encircled by several fine estates, all of which had been owned by the same aristocratic families for generations.

The residents of Ottersmead were justly proud of their village, none more so than the Society for the Beautification of our Village, and Amy was perfectly happy to assist their efforts at beautification by delivering her notes in person. Especially when the task coincided with her desire to escape from the house.

After despatching a footman to deliver notes to those members of the Society who resided outside the village proper, Amy stepped out at a brisk pace. The sky was a bowl of deep cerulean blue, the sun shone, and the blustery wind she encountered on the road overlooking the rolling swells of the Atlantic was invigorating enough, she hoped, to blow a disturbingly persistent image of Hawkridge out of her mind.

Even a temporary lull would be beneficial. She might be able to convince herself that she'd blown the Earl's impact on her out of all proportion.

The wind had other ideas. Hawkridge materialised at her side as if deposited there by insidious forces of nature, and long before the village, nestled in its crescent-shaped bay between the arms of the surrounding cliffs, had so much as come into sight.

'Mrs Chantry,' he acknowledged in a polite voice that bore no resemblance whatever to his chilling tones of earlier. 'I hope you don't object to my accompanying you.'

'Of course not, my lord.' Amy ordered her heart out of her throat, whence it had jumped at his sudden appearance, and wished she'd had the courage to tackle the path down to the beach. Once on the sand, she would have been invisible to anyone on the cliff top.

Not that it mattered. The tide was in. Though the beach was accessible further along, at this particular point during high tide the waves lapped against the cliff. It was a shame she'd never learnt to swim.

'Thank God you're not one of those females who objects to walking at a smart pace,' he observed, matching her speed without effort. 'I need to stretch my legs after the drive from London.'

Amy stared at him suspiciously. Why was he being civil? He didn't look civil. In fact, he looked distinctly dangerous with his black hair ruffled in the breeze, his coat open and his hands stuffed into his breeches' pockets. Even his cravat appeared to have been released somewhat from its precise folds.

She blinked at him. It was difficult to be sure without actually peering, but the top button of his shirt appeared to be unfastened. The elegant gentleman had been replaced by a brigand. All he needed was a cutlass and earring.

Amy frowned. She didn't approve of pirates.

Unfortunately, disapproval was having little effect on her heartbeat and breathing. Both usually steady functions had accelerated to a disturbing rate.

'You must have left town before dawn, my lord,' she managed to say, surprised she could speak at all, let alone string coherent words together. Her mind scurried to and fro, marshalling arguments, readying her defences—wishing she didn't have an almost compelling urge to study him. Just to make sure she hadn't exaggerated his dangerous qualities, of course.

'Actually, we left yesterday evening and spent the night on the road.'

'Oh. We?' she added when something more seemed called for.

'I drove down with Lord Eversleigh. Colborough's heir.' He jerked his head at the pile of stone perched above the sea on the opposite side of the cove.

'Ah, yes. Lady Hawkridge mentioned Lord Colborough only this morning.'

A swift, unexpectedly wicked grin crossed his face. 'Not by name, I wager.'

'Er…no.' Amy swallowed in an attempt to ease the sudden constriction in her throat. By what bird-witted piece of logic had she considered Hawkridge dangerous when unsmiling? That grin was lethal. Some misguided woman should have

married him years ago to save her sisters from galloping heartbeats and irregular breathing.

'I thought not. Grandmama and Colborough enjoy open
warfare so much I've often wondered why they never made a
match of it.'

Still grappling with the image of that wicked, slashing grin,
not to mention the unnerving thought of Hawkridge in the role
of husband, Amy struggled to uphold her end of the conversation. 'Lord Colborough and Lady Hawkridge have long been
acquainted?'

'Since childhood. When my grandfather died I thought mu-
tual loss might eventually draw them together, but Colborough
become a virtual recluse.' He sent her a swift glance. 'Grandmama was widowed six months after my parents and Lord
Eversleigh's drowned in a boating accident. The shock was
too much for my grandfather.'

'I don't wonder at it,' she murmured, compassion momentarily diverting her. 'When Lady Hawkridge told me...' She
shook her head; the task of conveying sympathy for such a
tragedy was utterly beyond her. 'There's really nothing one
can say, is there?'

Hawkridge's mouth took on a cynical curve. 'The perfect
answer. All right, Mrs Chantry. How much?'

If he'd snatched her up and dangled her over the edge of
the cliff, Amy couldn't have been more stunned. The change
was so sudden, so incisive, that for a moment she couldn't
think. Then a surge of heat shot through her.

Oh, he was good. Lull the victim into a false sense of security, then strike. But though her very fingertips tingled with
shock, this was something she could fight.

'I have no intention of leaving Lady Hawkridge's employ,
my lord, unless she dismisses me.' She schooled her features
to cool composure. 'No matter what incentive you offer.'

'You didn't even pretend to misunderstand me.' A brow

lifted. 'Unexpectedly refreshing. But what made you think I was offering to buy you off, Mrs Chantry?'

She looked up at him. 'What else would you mean by "how much"?'

He raised his brow again; the sardonic gleam in his eyes all the answer she needed.

This time the surge of heat was so intense she wondered she didn't levitate straight off the ground. She looked away quickly, cursing her fair complexion that showed every change of colour, and reminded herself that Hawkridge could well be trying to provoke her into giving notice.

'I doubt a man would offer to buy a woman he dislikes. But the answer is still no.'

'I admire your restraint,' he murmured, watching her. 'Those offers were blatant insults, but though you refused both, you weren't shocked into retaliation.'

'Women in my position become accustomed to insults, sir.'

'Women in your position. Do you mean widows?'

'Not necessarily.' She met his gaze head-on. 'Single women, also, may be subject to offers of an insulting nature, even…even hounded…' She broke off, tilting her chin but looking away again. 'It's the way of the world when a woman has no male protector. However, the reason I didn't react as you may have expected is that I know your offer sprang from concern for Lady Hawkridge.'

'Indeed? To which offer do you refer?'

Amy set her teeth. 'The one to buy me off.'

'And when I implied otherwise?'

'I don't believe your implication was meant to do anything more than goad me into impulsive behaviour.'

'An interesting thought,' he murmured.

She clenched her hand around her reticule.

'Careful,' Hawkridge advised, glancing down when a sharp crunch sounded. 'Mrs Tredgett, for one, won't appreciate receiving a crumpled note.'

Amy concentrated on not throwing her reticule at him. A lady did not cast missiles at a gentleman. Even when the gentleman was not behaving like one, didn't look like one, and managed to make her feel very unladylike indeed.

'Perhaps I should make it quite clear from the outset, my lord, that I have no intention of robbing Lady Hawkridge, or of sponging off her. That should render unnecessary any more offers you may have in mind.'

'You come straight to the point, don't you, Mrs Chantry?' He smiled. 'I like that.'

'I'm merely following your example, sir. Besides, under the circumstances, I see no virtue in prevarication.'

'Good. Then I can be equally blunt.' His smile vanished. Eyes the colour of arctic ice bored straight through her. His voice went as cold as fog rolling in across a very dark sea. 'My grandmother tends to see only good in people. She's also kind-hearted and generous to a fault. While those qualities endear her to her family and friends, they also lay her open to disillusionment and hurt. I will do anything, Mrs Chantry— *anything*—to see that she is *not* hurt.'

Amy swallowed. The knowledge that she wouldn't hurt her benefactress for the world didn't prevent chills sprinting up and down her spine at the menace in Hawkridge's tone. A less determined companion would probably flee in total disorder.

A less determined companion wouldn't, for instance, dream of teaching him a lesson in determination.

She wiped the scowl from her face and replaced it with a sweetly approving smile. 'What can I say, my lord, except that your sentiments do you credit.'

His eyes narrowed to glittering slits. Amy decided that teaching Hawkridge a lesson in determination was probably not a good idea while they were negotiating the steep road down to the village. She wanted to arrive in one piece.

She infused her voice with the tone of gentle reason, and tried again. 'Only time will prove that I would never betray

Lady Hawkridge's trust, sir. Indeed, I'm more grateful to her than I can ever explain.'

'Try,' he bit out, obviously unmoved by gentle reason.

She sent him a fulminating glare. 'I doubt you would understand what it's like to be down to your last shilling, having spent everything else on appearing presentable so as to gain *respectable* employment.'

This blunt statement seemed to give her opponent food for thought. After a hard-eyed appraisal, he strode along beside her for some distance in silence.

Amy tried to calm the turbulent gyrations of her stomach. There was no reason to be nervous. Hawkridge hadn't dismissed her; she could withstand the odd insult or two. What else could he do to her?

The question had an unfortunate effect on her senses. They scurried about as though seeking refuge from a threat. Such frantic exercise was not conducive to rational thought. She had to keep her wits about her, because she was quite certain that the next salvo wouldn't be long in coming.

'You were not left in fortuitous circumstances, I take it, Mrs Chantry.'

Amy smiled grimly to herself and decided that brevity of reply was her only recourse. 'No.'

'You have no other family?'

'No.'

'I find that difficult to believe. You're little more than a girl. Where are your parents?'

'Dead.'

'Grandparents?'

'I… Dead.' It seemed a safe guess.

'Hmm. Stonewalled. I'm almost afraid to ask. Er…former employers?'

She looked up, startled by the hint of dry humour. Then looked quickly away when the gleam in his eyes sent a sizzle of heat through her veins. 'N-none.'

There was a slight pause. She could feel those light grey eyes aimed at her like twin rapier points. 'You know,' he said at last in a conversational tone she didn't trust for a minute, 'you intrigue me, Mrs Chantry. Every one of my instincts tells me you aren't what you seem. And yet I can't make up my mind about what it is you do seem, or what it is you are. Or even if it's the other way about.'

Since he'd rendered her almost cross-eyed trying to work that out, Amy judged it prudent to remain silent.

'However,' he continued, still in that pleasant tone that caused her to snap back to instant attention, 'it's patently obvious that you dislike, lying.'

Heat stung her cheeks; it was useless hoping he'd think it was the natural colour caused by a walk in the brisk wind. 'I'm not lying, my lord. I've never been a companion; therefore I cannot produce any previous employers to speak for me.'

'Perhaps I should warn you, Mrs Chantry, that I have little patience with people who even fiddle with the truth to suit their purposes.'

Her eyes flashed. She lifted her chin, but pressed her lips resolutely together.

'Well done,' he acknowledged softly. 'Whatever else you are, you're familiar with battle tactics. Was your husband a military man, Mrs Chantry?'

Amy's breath caught. Her mind went blank.

'Uh…no.'

'A professional man, perhaps?'

'No.'

He sighed. 'It would really be a great deal less wearing on both our nerves if you'd simply tell me.'

She doubted Hawkridge even had nerves. 'Does it matter?' she demanded, goaded into more than monosyllables.

'I don't know,' he shot back. 'Does it?'

He'd cornered her. Why on earth hadn't she foreseen questions about her husband? Probably because most people hesitated to ask such questions of a young widow, she answered herself. Hawkridge clearly had no such scruples.

Not that any amount of warning would have improved the situation. He was right. She hated lying. Even fiddling with the truth made her feel wretchedly uncomfortable. But she had no choice.

'My husband…invested in certain enterprises,' she finally conceded. And almost collapsed in relief when she saw salvation, in the person of a lady, emerge from the gates of a small estate on the outskirts of the village.

She barely managed to keep her gasp of thankfulness silent. Her acquaintanceship with the estate's chatelaine, Lady Ingham, was of the slightest, but that didn't prevent her from transforming her rigid features into a bright smile of greeting.

'Damn and blast,' muttered Hawkridge, clearly not sharing her feelings on the matter. He scowled. 'Kitty always did have the habit of interrupting at the wrong moment.'

At the sound of his voice, the lady in question looked around. Amy was just hoping her smile didn't appear too desperate, when her rescuer let out a most unladylike shriek of delight and launched herself at Hawkridge.

Amy ground to an astonished halt as Hawkridge not only withstood the assault, but swooped Lady Ingham into his arms and, laughing, his scowl quite banished, twirled her around.

Her ladyship didn't appear to find anything strange in his behaviour. She hung on for dear life and laughed back at him. 'Marc, you wretch, where did you spring from? Oh, heavens, put me down. We're shocking Mrs Chantry.'

Eyes gleaming, Hawkridge set his assailant on her feet and glanced in Amy's direction. 'Mrs Chantry's been at Hawkridge for several weeks, Kitty. She must know you're a hoyden by now.'

'Alas, it's true,' acknowledged Lady Ingham with a rueful smile for Amy. 'But I'm sure you know how it is between old friends, Mrs Chantry. Poor, dear Ingham, though,' she burbled before Amy could answer. 'Such goings on at the gates. He *would* be shocked.'

'How is Ingham?' enquired Hawkridge, a distinctly indulgent smile in his eyes.

Amy could only stare at him in amazement. Was this the same man she'd started out with? She hadn't suspected he was capable of laughter, let alone playful gestures such as twirling a lady around.

Something fluttered inside her as she wondered what it felt like to be locked in those strong arms. Though not necessarily be twirled. If Hawkridge wrapped her in his arms, she strongly suspected her head would spin without any assistance.

The thought paralysed her. Instead of seizing the opportunity to escape, she stood there like a stuffed owl, wondering why she was tingling all over as if she really was enveloped in his embrace.

When Lady Ingham started down the steps built into the cliff opposite her gates with a gay word of farewell and a promise to visit, she was quite incapable of doing more than respond with a weak smile. Fortunately, her ladyship noticed nothing amiss; she was engaged in waving to a little boy who was already industriously at work on the pebbled beach below, assisted by his nurse.

Amy could only be thankful.

'You look as if you'd like to follow Lady Ingham, Mrs Chantry. The beach here is wide enough to walk on without the discomfort of wet sandals. Would you prefer to stroll along the shore?'

And risk looking like a helpless female by clutching the railing all the way down that precipitous descent?

'No!' she uttered with such force that his brows shot up. When colour flooded her cheeks his expression went unnervingly intent.

'A...another acquaintance since childhood, my lord?' she

managed to ask in a voice that showed a lamentable tendency to squeak. Forcing her legs into motion, she started walking.

'Yes, as a matter of fact.'

He sounded intrigued. Which was even more nerve-racking.

Then he glanced up and his mouth took on a sardonic curve. 'And aren't you fortunate, Mrs Chantry? Here comes a second saviour in the person of my brother-in-law.'

Relief was plainly writ large on her face. Amy didn't care. Lord Nettlebed's appearance outside the Vicarage was clearly a gift from On High. Quickening her pace to something perilously close to a run, she greeted him with outstretched hand and every sign of pleasure.

Quite forward behaviour in a mere companion.

'How do you do, Mrs Chantry?' Nettlebed asked, cordially shaking hands. A smile lit his hazel eyes. 'Just the day for a pleasant stroll, isn't it? After all the rain we've had, you must be glad to get out of the house.'

She now had serious doubts about that.

'Mrs Chantry prefers to stride,' Hawkridge put in, gripping his brother-in-law's hand. 'Good to see you, Bevan. How is everyone?'

'I thought Augusta gave you that information in expensive detail,' Nettlebed returned drolly. 'You don't appear to have lost any sleep over it, however. You're looking disgustingly fit, Marc.' He let his gaze rest on Hawkridge's less-than-sartorially-arranged cravat. 'If a little informal.'

Hawkridge shrugged. 'I was interrupted in the middle of changing.'

An image of Hawkridge ripping off his cravat promptly flashed into Amy's mind. It was immediately followed by a picture of him shrugging those powerful shoulders out of his coat...hooking a finger in the neck of his shirt...ripping...

The pictures stopped right there—mainly because her brain had frozen in shock.

Beside him, Marc felt her stiffen and decided his reply had

given the game away. His quarry had finally realised he'd followed her, regardless of what he'd been doing at the time.

She ought to count herself lucky he hadn't got further along in the task of changing into more comfortable attire, he thought grimly, because when he'd caught sight of her heading for the cliff road at a pace strongly reminiscent of escaping prey, sheer predatory instinct had taken over.

He'd shot out of his room and bounded down the stairs without a thought for what he was wearing.

For all the good it had done him. Far from obtaining answers, he had several more questions resounding in his brain.

Not least of which was why he experienced a damned painful surge of arousal every time Mrs Chantry aimed that pointed little chin in the air.

'Well, be prepared for a lecture on the proper country attire for gentlemen,' Nettlebed continued, in blissful ignorance of his companions' emotions. 'If, as I presume, you're on your way to call on your sister.'

'I'll drive over later this afternoon,' Marc growled. Then mentally kicked himself when Nettlebed's brows rose lazily at his brusque tone. 'I don't anticipate a lecture, however. As soon as Augusta is informed that I intend to stay at Hawkridge for a week or so, she'll start planning a ball or some such nuisance.'

His brother-in-law was successfully diverted. 'We're already in an uproar over the party we're holding tomorrow night,' he said dryly. 'For God's sake, don't put the idea of a ball into Augusta's mind. She thinks a social whirl will distract Lucinda from the young man we've had haunting the place since she returned from that damned—please excuse me, Mrs Chantry—that exclusive Bath seminary.'

Beside him, Mrs Chantry stiffened again. Marc sent her a swift glance, wondering what had set her off this time. There was a tiny line between her brows, but she didn't appear shocked at Nettlebed's language or the fact that he was discussing family business in her presence.

Then she seemed to shake off whatever had arrested her attention and smiled at his brother-in-law.

'Please think nothing of it, sir. Lady Nettlebed has been kind enough to confide some of her worry to me. Although… I didn't know Miss Nettlebed had met Mr Chatsworth while she'd been at school.'

Nettlebed nodded gloomily. 'You'd think a Young Ladies Academy would take better care, wouldn't you? God knows, they charge enough.'

Her answering nod was so full of sympathy anyone would have thought she had teenaged children herself.

Marc found himself grinding his back teeth, a reaction that gave him a severe jolt. He knew Nettlebed doted on Augusta; even if that hadn't been the case, he suspected Amy was smart enough not to cast out lures to anyone in his presence. But for some odd reason he wanted to tell Nettlebed to keep his problems with Lucinda to himself.

'I can perfectly comprehend your feelings on the matter,' Amy said, startling him until he realised she and Nettlebed still had their heads together like a couple of anxious matrons. 'But speaking of family concerns, you must have a great deal to discuss with Lord Hawkridge. I'll be on my way.'

'Can't be late delivering those notes,' Marc muttered, not knowing if he was more incensed with Amy or himself. He fixed his brother-in-law with a look of heavy meaning. 'You on your way back to the Park, Bevan?'

His lordship remained annoyingly uncooperative. 'No, not really,' he said vaguely. He waved a hand at the residence behind him. 'Had to drop in at the Vicarage. Place is full of chicken-pox. Augusta hasn't had it, nor has Lucinda for that matter, so the task fell to me to do the civil. Didn't realise it was so demanding. Feel like I've had the wretched illness myself, all over again, after listening to Mrs ffollifoot.'

Marc resigned himself to the inevitable. 'A pint at the Green Man should disperse the mists. Come on—' he sent Amy a faintly menacing glance '—Mrs Chantry is in a hurry to be gone.'

She tipped her chin up. 'Only as far as the other end of the village, my lord.'

As a challenge it was without equal. Annoyance exploded into outright male wrath. When she'd exchanged polite fare-wells with Nettlebed, he deliberately stepped between them, speared her gaze with his, and taking advantage of a passing barouche, issued his own challenge. 'Don't cross swords with me, Mrs Chantry, unless you're willing to take the consequences.'

She flushed; her eyes widened. Then she drew back and lifted her chin at him again.

'So now you're resorting to threats, my lord. I can only wonder, given your opinion of me, why you didn't simply dismiss me out of hand this morning. It would have saved us both from an unpleasant walk, not to mention—'

'I can't dismiss you out of hand,' he interrupted through his teeth. 'Grandmama would be extremely upset. And you know damn well I won't distress her.'

She affixed a smile to her face that made his fingers itch. 'Now why would I presume that, sir? I try to reserve judge-ment about a person until I'm somewhat better acquainted with him.'

Marc inclined his head in grim acknowledgement, and de-cided to leave his opponent in possession of the field before he did something he'd regret. Such as throwing her over his shoulder in full view of the village and carting her back to Hawkridge where he could kiss that cat-with-the-cream smile right off her face.

'Your point, Mrs Chantry.' He lifted his hand and, against every sane instinct, touched her cheek briefly in a parody of a fencer's salute. His blood surged in his veins. She was as soft as mist. And as elusive.

'However,' he continued, 'there is another reason why I won't dismiss you out of hand. I intend to know you better, also. To that end we'll continue this conversation on our way back to Hawkridge. You have twenty minutes to deliver your missives before meeting me back here.'

She had delivered her missives in considerably less time.

Amy was still thanking Providence for her narrow escape as the members of the Society began filing into the drawing-room later that afternoon. She was also quaking in her little kid sandals. Defiance had taken on a rather dangerous aspect.

Not that she'd actually agreed to the time limit arbitrarily set by Hawkridge. She'd simply turned on her heel and stalked off; the prospect of another conversation with him, in twenty minutes, not to mention the suddenly unbridled workings of her mind, enough to spur her to unprecedented speed. Never had notes been delivered so fast. She'd been on her way back to the Manor practically before the recipient of the first missive had taken it from the tray presented by her housemaid.

Amy was sure she was still unbecomingly flushed from her uphill dash when Miss Pucklenett paused beside her in the drawing- room doorway, hands clasped to her bony breast.

'The *drawing-room*,' she uttered, justifying Amy's assertion that she would be quite overcome. She seemed oblivious to the elegant, burgundy-draped windows, the magnificent marble fireplace or the exquisitely rendered ceiling murals for which the Manor was famous. 'How *kind* of Lady Hawkridge. How *gracious*. Just as though I was a real person. And she is even staying to attend the meeting.'

Amy suppressed a smile. 'She is the Society's patron, ma'am.'

'Yes, yes, my dear, but patrons aren't required to attend all the meetings, you know. How shall we ever be able to convey our gratitude, our awareness of the very great honour, our—?'

'For heaven's sake, Clara, sit down and keep your tongue between your teeth until your wits catch up with it,' Mrs Tredgett commanded, living up to her reputation as the village dragon. Prodding her friend onwards with her walking cane, she sailed into the room. 'Real person, indeed! What do you think you are? A ghost?'

Miss Pucklenett was too busy being overcome by her surroundings to take offence. Amy doubted she would have resented Mrs Tredgett's stringent comments in any case. The Society's ladies had all known each other for years and, while not members of the upper echelons of local gentry, being made up of the Vicar's wife, various minor squires' relics, one or two governesses and the doctor's sister, were perfectly content with their place in the scheme of things.

Amy was more than happy to be included in their number. It was several steps up from the last social strata she'd occupied, no one frayed her nerves with awkward questions, and there was no reason for her imagination to run riot—unlike its behaviour in the company of certain other persons.

Half an hour into the meeting, however, she was forced to concede that Lord Colborough's opinion of the Society for the Beautification of Our Village had some justification. All of five minutes had been spent on the tricky question of how many ornamental ducks would be ordered from the stonemason to adorn the village wall separating the beach from the gravelled walk optimistically known as the Promenade. Everyone was happy to agree with Lady Hawkridge's suggestion of six, each smaller than the preceding one. The motion thus carried unanimously, the ladies settled down to the main business of the day—gossip.

When Lady Hawkridge was summoned from the room by her butler a few minutes after the tea-tray had been brought in, the gossip promptly swerved to include her grandson.

'I saw it with my own eyes, my dears.' Mrs ffollifoot, as befitting her position as the Vicar's wife and the Society's usual hostess, picked up the teapot and, ignoring Amy's claims as the dowager's deputy, poured tea for the guests. 'There was Hawkridge in the middle of the road, in full view of anyone who happened along, *cuddling* Lady Ingham.'

'*Shameless!*' Miss Twinhoe, a spinster of indeterminate age who kept house for her brother, leaned forward, nose twitching like an eager foxhound.

'*Shocking!*' Miss Pucklenett's skinny form, clad in drab grey wool, quivered with excitement.

'*Scandalous!*' Mrs Tredgett snorted. 'But just like him,' she added, in the tone of one who is an expert on the subject.

'And he then continued on his way with his cravat positively *mussed.*'

'Oh, heavens! Mussing a gentleman's cravat! Whatever was Lady Ingham thinking of?' quavered Miss Pucklenett. 'Why, if dear Mrs Mayhew were to *think* that one of her daughters would behave in such a forward fashion, I would expect to be turned off without a character and end my days in destitution and poverty.'

'There is no need to indulge in exaggeration, Clara,' Mrs ffollifoot admonished, returning the teapot to its stand. Everyone ignored their cups of tea. 'Especially as you are still with us despite Miss Mayhew's attempts to attract Lord Hawkridge last winter.'

Miss Pucklenett had not spent all her adult years as a governess without learning to think fast on her feet. 'Miss Mayhew was no longer under my authority at that time, Eliza,' she declared with dignity. 'And in any case, it was Lady Ingham who encouraged dear Amabel to, er, pursue the Earl.'

'Should've known it was useless,' stated Mrs Tredgett. 'But Kitty Ingham never did have much sense. Not surprised she was cuddling Hawkridge. After all, they were—'

'They weren't cuddling,' Amy burst out, unable to stay silent another minute. She was intervening for Lady Ingham's sake, she told herself. Hawkridge was perfectly capable of looking after himself. 'I was there, since Lord Hawkridge kindly offered me his escort into Ottersmead. Lady Ingham's greeting might have been, er, enthusiastic, but it was perfectly innocent.'

'Yes, yes, my dear Mrs Chantry, we all know that.' Mrs ffollifoot clucked her tongue in affront at having her story stripped of scandalous connotations. 'But it's the *look* of the thing. Dear Mr ffollifoot was grievously shocked, and I could only be thankful Lizzie and Jane were safely in their beds and unable to witness such a hoydenish display, although one could wish that Lizzie hadn't contracted chicken-pox at this particular time.'

'Afraid young Mayhew might sheer off,' muttered Mrs Tredgett in an aside to Amy. 'Shouldn't think so. Dull as dish-water, poor boy. Give me a red-blooded male like Hawkridge any day.'

Amy swallowed. The thought of Hawkridge demonstrating red-blooded maleness was not something she wished to dwell upon.

'I'm sure Lady Ingham meant no harm,' she managed to say weakly, resisting the urge to press a hand to the fluttering in her stomach. 'And Lord Hawkridge's cravat was already mussed because he came chasing after…uh…I mean…'

Everyone sat forward, eyes fastened on her with avid expectation. Amy gazed back at them, her mind unnervingly blank. 'The wind blew it,' she finally got out in a desperate rush.

The ladies sank back in their seats with a collective sigh of disappointment.

Miss Twinhoe recovered first. 'A kind-hearted person such as yourself would naturally say so, Mrs Chantry,' she said, nodding approval at Amy. 'Oh, no need to colour up, my dear. *Your* demeanour is exactly as it should be. I was saying so only yesterday to Miss Pucklenett, wasn't I, Clara? There are several young ladies who would do well to follow your example, but while Hawkridge is in residence you may be sure we'll have all manner of forwardness. Encouraged, I might add, by his own sister, Lady Nettlebed.'

'Not to mention Lady Ingham,' put in Mrs ffollifoot, whose disapproval of that damsel seemed to be increasing in leaps and bounds. 'One would think Hawkridge could have his pick of the London debutantes, without her throwing every eligible lady in the county at his head.'

'I daresay she wishes his lordship to be as happily settled as herself,' suggested Miss Twinhoe. 'They were engaged, you know,' she added, for Amy's benefit. 'But Miss Ashcroft, as she was then, broke it off, practically on the day of the wedding. Such a scandal.'

'Never understood why,' grumbled Mrs Tredgett, obviously annoyed by her lack of comprehension. 'Hawkridge has wealth, an old, distinguished title and is indecently good-looking into the bargain. What more did the girl want?'

What, indeed?

Amy thought of the affection and easy camaraderie between Hawkridge and Lady Ingham and wondered the same thing. Why *had* Kitty Ingham broken her engagement? And, more to the point, why had a man of Hawkridge's predatory nature accepted the blow?

'His lordship doesn't strike me as the type of man to accept being jilted,' she murmured, unable to resist her curiosity on that particular point.

'Well, he is, after all, a gentleman, my dear,' Mrs ffollifoot informed her, getting her revenge by assuming Amy was ignorant of gentlemanly behaviour. 'What else could he do?'

The question continued to exercise Amy's mind for several minutes. Graceful resignation didn't appear to be Hawkridge's style; perhaps he'd cared so much for Lady Ingham, he'd wanted her happiness despite the cost to himself.

The thought caused a strange pang in her heart. It was immediately followed by a sensation closely akin to fear. Why should she care about his feelings? Hawkridge meant nothing to her; except as a dangerous opponent who had a dismaying habit of invading her mind at inconvenient moments. She would put a stop to it. After all, it was the portrait that had fascinated her; she would simply renew her efforts to avoid its subject.

Unfortunately for this sensible plan, she returned her attention to the conversation to find that Hawkridge was still its main topic.

'Yes, indeed,' Miss Pucklenett was saying. 'I've always found him to be the perfect epitome of gentlemanly behaviour. So gracious. Such manners. So very charming.'

Mrs Tredgett apparently felt compelled to throw in a dash of realism. 'A holy terror when he was a boy.'

'Poor orphaned lad. Quite helpless to do anything,' murmured Miss Twinhoe, shaking her head.

Amy very nearly shook hers as well. A holy terror she could believe, but charming? The perfect epitome of gentlemanly behaviour? *A poor helpless orphan?* Were these ladies *blind*?

'Of course, you don't know anything about that, Mrs Chantry, since you've only just met his lordship.' Mrs ffollifoot sent her an acid smile. 'He always comes down especially to investigate her ladyship's companions.'

'I'm sure it's very touching that he cares enough about dear Lady Hawkridge to assure himself of Mrs Chantry's suitability,' declared Miss Twinhoe hurriedly. 'Not that there can be any doubt about that, my dear.'

'Very protective,' stated Mrs Tredgett. 'Runs in the family.'

'And one must remember that the previous companions were *men*.' Miss Twinhoe made the pronouncement with all the air of one discussing wild and dangerous beasts, whose behaviour could be counted upon to be vastly different from that of more civilised beings.

'Very true,' agreed Miss Pucklenett in hushed accents. She glanced around and lowered her voice still further as though about to divulge a hideous secret. 'And we all know of the Unfortunate Habits that effect certain persons of the Male Persuasion.'

Since the entire Society had several times been regaled with the sorry tale of their friend's long-ago *tendre* for her father's curate, and the scoundrel's subsequent elopement with the daughter of a wealthy tradesman, everyone nodded sagely. A few seconds of silence ensued while respect was paid to the demise of Miss Pucklenett's youthful aspirations to the wedded state.

By the time it was judged proper to continue, Lady Hawkridge returned to the drawing-room and conversation became general.

Amy sat back and contemplated her cup of tea. She completely forgot about her resolution to keep Hawkridge out of her mind; several vastly contradictory images of him were whirling therein in dizzying array. She didn't know which was predominant. The gentleman gracefully accepting his *congé*—her imagination still balked at that one. The boy on the verge of manhood, struggling with bereavement. The rakishly dishevelled, wickedly grinning pirate on the cliff top. Or the relentless interrogator who seemed determined to uncover everything she'd prefer to forget.

And beneath it all, waiting, was the warrior she sensed as surely as she recognised the less-than-civilised side of herself.

A warrior, she suspected, who was going to be more than a little annoyed that she'd eluded him that afternoon.

Chapter Four

Amy attached a tiny lace cap to her upswept hair, checked her appearance one last time in her mirror, and reminded herself that she'd survived worse fates than confronting an irate male across the dinner table. Even one who loomed in doorways, arrived on cliff tops without warning, and asked a lot of questions.

She was prepared. Hawkridge wouldn't take her by surprise again.

Buoyed by that thought, she cracked open her bedchamber door and peered cautiously through the aperture. No one appeared to be looming. Her spirits brightened considerably. Since there were no cliff tops in the house, and she'd rehearsed several pithy answers to a variety of possible questions, the evening might not be so bad after all.

Releasing her pent-up breath, she stepped into the passageway, her head half-turned to close the door.

'Good evening, Mrs Chantry.'

'*Aaagh!*' Amy whirled and cannoned into her door. Unfortunately, in the shock of the moment, she hadn't had time to latch it. The door flew open under the impact. She felt herself reeling backwards and squeaked in dismay.

An arm taut with sinew and muscle caught her about the

waist and hauled her to safety against a powerful male body. Except that safety was not the first word that sprang to mind.

Amy squeezed her eyes shut as her head spun like a fair-ground maypole gone mad. Thank heavens they weren't on twirling terms, she thought wildly. She was having enough trouble coping with the masculine heat and power enveloping her.

She was released before she could melt completely. Senses still whirling, she leaned against the wall, a hand to her heart, and summoned a thread of a voice. 'Thank you, my lord.'

When he didn't answer, she forced her eyelids open. Grey eyes blazed into hers, glittering with enough heat to scorch her pale rose silk evening dress right off her trembling form. 'I mean...' She jerked herself upright. 'So now you've added creeping up on people to the list!'

The muscles in his jaw locked; the flames abated. He shoved his fists into his pockets and glared back at her. 'List?'

'Never mind,' said Amy crossly. She peeled herself away from the wall and started toward the stairway. With luck, her legs would feel steadier than limp muslin by the time they got her there.

It was going to be rather more difficult to erase the fierce intensity in Hawkridge's eyes from her mind. Just for an instant the civilised mask had been ripped aside. He'd looked at her as if he'd been a brigand in truth. A brigand about to throw her to the floor and ravish her.

The shocking part had been the primitive thrill that had coursed through her at the thought.

'I'm sorry if I startled you,' he bit out, not sounding sorry in the least. 'I was on my way to enquire if you'd been unexpectedly struck down by illness since you didn't keep our appointment in the village.' He slanted a mocking glance down at her. 'Chicken-pox, perhaps.'

Amy had no attention to spare for sarcasm. 'Appointment? Oh, yes, appointment.' She tried for a tone of airy unconcern—and resisted the temptation to clutch the balustrade with both hands as they started down the wide sweeping staircase that led to the hall.

'Yes.' He fixed her with a pointed stare. 'The appointment we made before you delivered your notes, Mrs Chantry.'

'Oh, dear, perhaps I misheard you, sir. As I recall, Mrs Mayhew's carriage rattled by at that precise moment. Your words must have been drowned out.' Feeling a little steadier when he didn't challenge this flimsy excuse, she summoned up a polite smile. 'I hope you didn't wait long.'

His smile was equally polite, and a great deal more dangerous. 'Not at all,' he purred. 'I was right behind you all the way back to Hawkridge.'

She gulped, her entire back tingling as if he was stalking behind her at that very moment. The gleam in his eyes had her straightening her spine with an almost audible snap. 'Indeed? In that case, I'm surprised you didn't catch up with me so you could continue your interrogation.'

His smile became even more polite. 'Actually, it was my intention to continue our conversation, but I became distracted by the view.'

She tripped over the bottom step. 'The view?'

Hawkridge steadied her with a large hand beneath her elbow. 'Yes. It was quite fascinating.'

Amy's brows snapped together. 'One would have thought you're quite accustomed to the view, my lord. You've lived here most of your life.'

'Indeed, but there's always something new to be seen, don't you find?'

At this moment, she would be happy to see Lady Hawkridge and a dinner table surrounded by servants.

'But there's no harm done. If you're determined to remain here, Mrs Chantry, we'll have plenty of opportunity for convivial walks to the village.'

'Convivial—' Amy set her teeth. 'Very true, sir. I do trust, however, that you'll refrain from interrogation, at least while we're toiling uphill.'

'Next time we'll take the horses,' he assured her, and bowed before ushering her into the withdrawing-room where the family traditionally congregated before dinner.

Lady Hawkridge was seated before a cosy fire, reading the *Morning Post*. She looked up as they entered. 'Horses?' she queried, putting her paper to one side. 'No, no. Much too large. But, you know, Amy, I'm beginning to have my doubts about those ducks. Perhaps we should have more fully considered Miss Twinhoe's suggestion of dolphins.'

Marc eyed his grandparent with caution. 'Dolphins?' He glanced at Amy as she seated herself at the other end of the dowager's sofa. The faintest of smiles was playing about her mouth. His eyes narrowed. The little wretch knew what his grandmother was twittering about and wasn't above letting him flounder.

'I think you might find the waters around here a little short of dolphins, Grandmama,' he essayed.

Lady Hawkridge stared at him in bewilderment. 'Good heavens, Marc, what has that to say to anything? Were you expecting Mr Brinwell to catch a real one?'

'Er, if you want a dolphin, yes.'

Amy stopped resisting the smile fighting to break free and decided—with great magnanimity, she thought—to come to his rescue.

'Lady Hawkridge refers to the ornamental ducks the Society is commissioning from the stonemason, sir. To adorn the sea-wall in the village.'

He stared at her, thunderstruck. 'Good God! *Ducks*?'

His grandmother took umbrage at his tone. 'Well, you must admit, Marc, that ducks would be more appropriate than horses!'

'I was talking about riding, love,' he returned, feeling quite incapable of further explanation.

'Oh. Well, in that case I suppose it will have to be the ducks. Although a nice dolphin, in the act of frolicking, would have served as a back-rest if anyone wished to sit upon the wall and drink in the view.'

'How odd,' Marc murmured. He propped his shoulders against the mantelpiece, folded his arms and smiled down at his grandmother. 'Mrs Chantry and I were discussing views only a moment ago.'

Amy glared at him. She had heard enough about views.

Her tormentor hadn't, apparently. 'Perhaps, in the pursuit of searching out interesting views, Mrs Chantry, you'd like to ride tomorrow morning? It promises to be a fine day.'

Amy took up the tablecloth she'd been hemming the evening before and stabbed her needle grimly into the linen. 'I'm here to work, my lord, not jaunter about—'

She stopped as if someone had struck her across the throat, her gaze riveted to the newspaper beside her. Between one heartbeat and the next the withdrawing-room at Hawkridge Manor vanished, and she was catapulted into the past.

'Oh, Amy, dear, you've pricked your finger.'

The dowager's voice came to her from a great distance. Amy shook her head and wrenched herself back to the present.

'It's nothing, ma'am.' She stared at her finger, forcing herself to study the tiny wound so she wouldn't have to look at Hawkridge. She didn't dare look at him. She knew he was watching her. She could feel the sudden tension in him, the coiled waiting stillness of the hunter. 'See. The merest trifle.'

'Only one drop of blood,' her ladyship agreed comfortably. 'But it always gives one such a start. Now, where were we? Ah, yes, jauntering about—'

She was interrupted when the butler entered to announce dinner. Amy breathed a sigh of relief. With luck, Hawkridge might put her abrupt silence down to the sting of her needle.

It seemed he must have; the tension emanating from him

abated, and he stepped forward to take his grandmother in to dinner.

Amy followed, hoping that by the time they sat down, her employer's notoriously flighty memory would have forgotten about jauntering.

'You know, Amy, jauntering about the countryside puts me in mind of something,' Lady Hawkridge continued, slaying this hope in one fell swoop. She smiled fondly at her grandson as he held her chair for her. 'While Marc is here to escort us, we should go out and about a little more. You've scarcely met anyone since you've been at Hawkridge, and there's no reason for you to be so retiring because you're my companion. Quite the contrary.'

Amy contemplated, without enthusiasm, the bowl of chicken soup presented to her by Pickles. She had just lost her appetite. 'I'm a widow, ma'am.'

'Yes,' murmured Hawkridge, seated at her right. 'Remember, we don't know the precise date of Mrs Chantry's bereavement, Grandmama.'

He was sent a quelling look. 'Oh, dear, I'm so sorry, Amy. I assumed, since you're out of mourning, that your loss was over a year ago.'

'Well, as to that, you are right, ma'am, but—'

'Then there's no reason why we can't indulge ourselves with a little jollification,' declared Lady Hawkridge, a pleased smile replacing her frown. 'Augusta's party will do nicely for a start. Nothing formal, you understand; merely a gathering of friends to amuse Lucinda until she makes her come-out.'

'But—'

'Now, Amy, you know Augusta will be happy to see you. Why, she was saying only the other day how she values your judgement, how impressed she was by your good sense, how—'

'That's very kind of Lady Nettlebed, I'm sure, but—'

'And no more nonsense about being a companion. That is merely a circumstance; *you* are perfectly presentable.'

'Thanks to your generosity, ma'am. And please don't think me ungrateful—indeed, I'll never be able to repay your kindness—but I'm perfectly happy in the company of Miss Pucklenett and Miss Twinhoe and—'

Her ladyship clucked her tongue. 'Goodness me, no, that won't do. Worthy ladies though they are, you can't wish to end up keeping house for a doctor, even if he is your brother, or losing your wits every time you see a drawing-room.'

'A depressing fate,' concurred Hawkridge, finishing his soup and sitting back in a casual sprawl that managed to look extremely dangerous. He contemplated Amy from beneath half-lowered lids. 'But we've yet to ascertain, Grandmama, if Mrs Chantry has a brother. And if so, is he a doctor?'

Amy met the challenging glitter in those grey eyes with uptilted chin. 'The answer to the first of those questions, my lord, is no. Which leaves the second redundant.' So pleased was she with that reply that her appetite promptly returned. She applied herself with gusto to the second course of lamb cutlets braised in a mint sauce.

'There you are, then,' declared the dowager. She waved a cutlet in the air in triumph. 'If Amy doesn't have a brother, we don't need to worry about him.'

'You relieve my mind, Grandmama.'

Her ladyship was too busy making plans to suspect sarcasm. 'And it isn't as if you're going to be waltzing with every gentleman who crosses your path, Amy. That *would* be too forward in your present circumstances. However, a lady always knows precisely how to behave, and since you're very much a lady, I have no qualms on that account. There can be no objection to your attending Augusta's party. Don't you agree, Marc?'

'No objection,' he muttered.

Mrs Chantry aimed that pointed little chin at him again. She appeared torn between reluctance to embark on a social whirl and indignation at his tone. Her feelings on the subject were the least of his problems, however. He was glad he was sitting down, a napkin over his lap. Apart from his usual reaction to that distinctly feminine challenge—a response that was becoming disturbingly familiar—her mutinous expression re-animated a vivid mental picture of the view he'd found so fascinating that afternoon.

The sight of her pert, rounded little derriere swaying agitatedly back and forth as she'd sped up the hill in front of him had aroused several rather heated fantasies. He'd wanted to curl his hands around those tantalising globes, to stroke, to caress, to savour that uniquely feminine softness.

And that was only the start.

Once the seed was sown, his mind had proved disastrously fertile. The delicately curved ankles revealed every few seconds by the violent upward flipping of her skirts hadn't rendered the trip any less painful. Something had to be done before Mrs Chantry caused permanent damage.

The first step was to get her away from the house again.

'And since you now have Grandmama's approval in the matter of jollification, Mrs Chantry, there can also be no objection to us riding together tomorrow morning. Shall we say ten o'clock? You'll notice there are no carriages rattling by, so I'll expect you to the minute.'

Amy blinked at him, her wits momentarily suspended. It wasn't Hawkridge's somewhat menacingly uttered rider that bothered her; she had just discovered a rather significant gap in her education.

She must have looked as blank as she felt, because Hawkridge raised a brow. 'You do ride, Mrs Chantry?'

'Er, no.'

The dowager looked vaguely surprised. 'You don't ride, dear? Well, not every lady cares for horses, you know.'

Amy thought quickly. An instant's silent debate had her

abandoning the idea of following her ladyship's lead. If Hawkridge thought she didn't care for horses, he was perfectly capable of marching her down to the stables and introducing her to the animals, regardless of her feelings on the matter. Her reply had to be prosaic.

It also had the advantage of being the truth.

'It isn't that. My mother and I did live in the country for a time, but I was so young I scarcely remember it. Then we moved to town.'

'Ah, so you did have a mother, Mrs Chantry.'

'Marcus!' His grandmother bent a severe frown upon him. 'That was very rude. Pay no heed to him, Amy.'

'I don't intend to, ma'am.' Amy took her time over the last mouthful on her plate, placed her knife and fork neatly side by side and set her lips in a prim line. 'I've already learned that your grandson does not always behave like a gentleman.'

'Yes, I know. And nothing can be done about it. Though if the gossip one hears is the truth, several ladies have attempted the task.'

'I would be obliged to you both if you'd stop discussing me as if I'm not here,' Hawkridge stated. He raised an ironic brow at Amy. 'My apologies if I seemed rude, Mrs Chantry. Such was not my intention.'

She sent him a sidelong look, gently mocking. 'I believe you, my lord. You seem to manage the feat without any prior intent at all.'

Lady Hawkridge choked and lifted her napkin hastily to her lips. 'Oh, dear.' She coughed discreetly. 'That last mouthful must have gone down the wrong way.' Ignoring her grandson's abruptly narrowed gaze, she beamed at Amy. 'Have you finished, Amy, dear? Perhaps we should leave Marc to his port. It might improve his mood.'

Amy rose from her chair as though propelled by springs. 'An excellent idea, ma'am.'

Hawkridge sighed and stood also. 'Given the female conspiracy to which I find myself falling victim, I feel I should accompany you. Merely to defend my character, of course.'

'If you say so, dearest.' Lady Hawkridge patted his arm as she passed him. 'I'm sure Amy will be glad of your company. I don't know how it is, but every time I attend one of the Society's meetings I feel…quite…exhausted…afterwards. Oh, dear…'

To Amy's dismay the dowager began to wilt. To her horror, her ladyship didn't stop at wilting. Before her very eyes, Lady Hawkridge transformed herself from a still-spritely elderly lady to one whose air of enfeeblement was positively ghastly.

A tiny, claw-like hand reached, shaking pitifully, for Amy's arm; she leaned heavily, her weight quite disproportionate to her suddenly shrunken size. Her voice quavered with the weak tones of one croaking out last wishes. 'Perhaps you wouldn't mind ringing for Giddings, Amy? To assist me up the stairs.'

'I'll certainly ring for Giddings, ma'am, but first allow me to escort you to your room.' She would have hauled the dowager towards the door in her haste, except that Lady Hawkridge drooped even more. Amy had to grab hold of her ladyship with her other hand to prevent her from slithering all the way to the floor.

'No, no, Amy, dear. I know you won't take it amiss, but I'd like to have Giddings. When one is overtaken by the wretched weakness engendered by advancing years, one needs long-familiar faces about one.'

'I'm sure that's quite understandable, ma'am, but—'

'And it would take such a load off my mind to know you'll keep Marc company on his first night at home.' Blue eyes lifted pleadingly. 'He likes a cup of tea, you know, and who will pour it when Pickles brings in the tea-tray if you're upstairs with me?'

'Well, as to that—'

The bird-like claw patted her arm. 'I knew I could depend on you, Amy, dear. So kind. Thank you.'

Amy sent a frantic glance at Hawkridge. He had taken up his post against the mantelpiece again, arms folded across his chest, and was watching the performance with a smile of unholy amusement in his eyes.

Which was all very well for him, she thought frantically. What if the dowager really was overcome by exhaustion, unlikely though it seemed? It was part of her job to see to her ladyship's comfort, to accede to her wishes.

'Would you please ring the bell, my lord,' she directed, glaring at him when he grinned.

'I already have. Giddings should be here at any second.'

The door opened on his words. Giddings bustled in, apparently not at all surprised to see her mistress in an advanced state of decrepitude.

'There, I knew how it would be after all that dusting,' she scolded. 'Now just leave her ladyship to me, Mrs Chantry. I'll have her put to bed and resting in a trice.'

'So kind,' croaked the dowager, waving feebly. With a smile for Hawkridge and Amy that appeared to take the last of her rapidly dwindling stores of strength, she tottered from the room, supported by Giddings.

Amy could only gaze after her employer in awed admiration—until a chuckle from the vicinity of the fireplace reminded her of the remaining company.

'What convinced you that Grandmama wasn't about to expire in your arms, Mrs Chantry?' Hawkridge pushed himself away from the mantelpiece and crossed the room to a table that held a decanter and several crystal glasses. He poured himself a small measure of brandy and turned to face her.

Her gaze rested thoughtfully on the glass in his hand. 'For some odd reason, my lord, I can't imagine you drinking tea.'

He raised a brow.

'It would be far too civilised.'

'You consider me uncivilised?'

'I'm sure you can be perfectly civil, my lord.'

A smile touched his mouth. 'That wasn't quite what I asked.'

When she didn't answer, the smile turned wicked. 'Your unspoken accusation is positively reverberating in the ether, Mrs Chantry.'

She wasn't going to rise to that bait either.

He laughed softly. 'We'll reserve the discussion of my un-civilised tendencies for a later date. You still haven't answered my original question. Quite an innocuous one, I thought.'

She narrowed her eyes at him. 'After my first shock, sir, I realised you weren't at all worried about your grandmother's health. Nor was Giddings, come to that. The conclusion was obvious. However, a companion doesn't argue with her employer.'

'And you are a very proper companion, aren't you, Mrs Chantry?'

'I hope so. However, I have no obligation to be a companion to you, my lord. I'm sure you're quite capable of amusing yourself until you retire, so I'll wish you good—'

'But my grandmother expressly asked you to keep me company, Mrs Chantry.'

Amy paused, one foot half-suspended from the floor. 'That was part of her act, as I'm sure you're aware.'

'Yes. I did wonder if your lack of concern sprang from instant recognition of a superlative performance. Merely a fleeting thought, you understand.'

She stifled a sigh, returned her heel to the floor and looked back over her shoulder. 'Since I've never had the opportunity to attend a playhouse, my lord, I'm glad the thought was merely fleeting. My answer to your query as to my lack of concern was the simple truth, no more, no less.'

'Excellent. Why don't you sit down so we can explore some more simple truths together?'

The notion of exploring anything with Hawkridge caused a tremor to ripple through her. Amy turned very slowly. He stood watching her, one brow raised, the half-smile playing about his lips holding amusement, a hint of appeal—and an unnerving amount of charm.

Fascination stirred; tantalising, teasing. Curiosity tip-toed in its wake.

Miss Pucklenett had been right. He could be charming. How many guises did he use to mask the fierce intensity that was evident only in the stillness with which he waited and the intent glitter in his eyes?

It was probably foolish to ask the question, let alone stay in the expectation of an answer, but hadn't she prepared herself for this very situation? Her earlier evasiveness had only aroused Hawkridge's predatory instincts. If she gave him nothing to sink his teeth into—another tremor rippled through her—he might cease his questioning.

Perhaps Lady Hawkridge, knowing her grandson, had reached a similar conclusion and created the opportunity.

Amy swallowed, walked over to a chair and sat down. 'Very well, my lord. I can see you won't be content until you've completed your interrogation.'

'Not at all, Mrs Chantry. I'm merely endeavouring to make polite conversation. It's what one does after dinner, you know.'

'You appear to need practice at it, sir.'

He laughed aloud at that, the sound causing a *frisson* of sensation to feather over her skin. For some odd reason she found herself holding her breath until he'd strolled over to the sofa opposite her armchair and sat down.

'Then let us practice, Mrs Chantry, by all means. I see yesterday's news is at hand to assist us.' He retrieved his grandmother's discarded newspaper and, sending her a swift glance, began to read. '"Another shocking robbery at Bristol. Last night thieves broke into a gentleman's residence, tied the terrified occupants hand and foot, including the unfortunate servants, and proceeded to ransack the house. This newspaper considers transportation too lenient for such scurrilous rogues.'' What do you think, Mrs Chantry? Should the wretches be hanged when they're laid by the heels?'

He glanced up as he spoke—and immediately narrowed his eyes on her face.

Thank God she'd had that warning earlier. Even so it was a struggle to force her frozen features into an expression of mild interest. Only sheer determination to hold on to her place here had her managing the task.

'A very frightening experience,' she remarked, neatly dodging a debate on transportation or hanging. If Hawkridge suspected such a discussion had the power to disturb her, he wouldn't rest until he knew why. 'But there's no need to delve into the newspaper for a topic of conversation, my lord. I'm quite happy to answer your questions.'

'Hmm.' Hawkridge tossed aside the *Morning Post* and crossed one booted foot over his knee. He still watched her narrowly, but the expression in his eyes turned ironic. 'Why do I get the feeling I'm not going to learn much?'

'Why should you wish to, sir?'

'A good question,' he muttered. 'When I do learn more, I might have an answer.'

'Well, unless you're still labouring under the misapprehension that I'm here to fleece Lady Hawkridge and so must possess a shady past—'

'No,' he interrupted. 'Actually, having had the opportunity to observe you further, Mrs Chantry, I believe you're genuinely fond of my grandmother. Under those circumstances, I can't imagine you cheating her.'

'Oh.' Amy flushed. The very small, very scared part of herself that was always wary, relaxed some of her defences. 'Thank you, sir. In that case—' She made to rise.

'However, I am interested to learn how it comes about that a lady of your tender years finds herself completely alone in the world.'

Amy dug her fingers into the arms of her chair, resisted an urge to grind her teeth, and sat back.

Hawkridge smiled faintly. 'You say you have no family living. What of your husband's relatives?'

'I don't know, my lord.'

His brows shot up. 'You don't know?'

'My husband never mentioned his family.' She shifted slightly. 'Perhaps I should make it plain that my marriage was very brief.'

'I see. I'm sorry to hear that, Mrs Chantry.'

'Yes. And since my own mother died only a few weeks before I le—er, lost my husband, I was forced to find some means of support.'

He studied her somewhat thoughtfully, making her nerves jump as she wondered if he'd noticed her slip.

'It must have been very frightening to be left alone like that. Were there no friends you could turn to? You mentioned living in town. Surely somewhere in London…'

'My mother and I lived in Branscombe, sir.'

When he lifted a brow, she added, 'It's near Cheltenham.'

'Ah.' Another smile touched his mouth. 'Too small to possess a livery stable, no doubt.'

Amy frowned. 'Really, my lord, are you still wondering why I don't ride? Why on earth would you belabour such an insignificant point?'

'A grave fault, I know, but insignificant points sometimes have a way of turning out to be crucial.' His smile turned apologetic. 'Your family, for instance. Are you quite sure there's no one?'

'No one.'

A quizzical gleam came into his eyes. 'No one *at all*? No aunts, uncles, third cousins in the fourth degree, crusty old great-uncles living in seclusion?'

Amy had to smile. 'None that I know of, sir.'

'Who was your father, Mrs Chantry?'

'No one with any connections who might have come to my aid, if that's where this is leading,' she said somewhat drily. 'He was merely the son of a vicar, destined to follow his father into the church.'

'Destined? I take it from that, he didn't do as expected?'

'No.' She shifted again and tried to relax muscles that were drawing tighter with each question. She had nothing to hide about her parents. Not compared to the rest. 'Unless one has private means, the remuneration for newly ordained curates is not enough to support a wife and family. However, my father had fallen in love with my mother and wished to marry her immediately, so he left home to find other work. My grandfather disowned him.'

Hawkridge frowned. 'A rather extreme method of bringing your father to heel.'

'But quite common, my lord. Even in your own circle.'

He inclined his head. 'Indeed. Although the laws of inheritance protect elder sons. And some of us...' He hesitated; his gaze shifting to the fire. 'Some of us are fortunate enough to have parents who care about their offspring.'

His brows drew together. He sent her a swift glance before getting to his feet and bending to place another log on the fire. 'So, what happened to your parents in the end, Mrs Chantry?'

Amy barely heard the question; her attention was suddenly riveted to him. He straightened, but stayed where he was, staring down into the flames. She wished she could see more of his face than a half-profile. That fleeting moment had left her strangely shaken. He'd spoken quite matter-of-factly about his parents' deaths that afternoon. But just now...had the mask slipped again? This time to reveal vulnerability? Was he aware of it—or was he using it to lure her into confiding in him?

'Mrs Chantry?'

Amy started and glanced up. She hadn't even been aware that her gaze had fallen to her hands, gripped tightly in her lap, but now her senses were painfully alert, and almost…waiting. The quietness was so intense she felt Hawk-ridge's presence as if they were touching, although he wasn't particularly close. The fire flickered lazily, sending wisps of smoke drifting up the chimney. The clock on the mantel ticked, sonorously, as though time had slowed in the silence of the room.

The entire house seemed to wait for her answer.

'They eloped,' she murmured, throwing off the odd notion that, in that moment, her life had stilled, before moving on in another, unknown, direction. 'Mama told me they travelled about for some time, seeking work, and then my father died of a fever a month before I was born.'

Hawkridge frowned. 'And your mother returned home?'

'No, my lord. Apparently my maternal grandfather was also lacking in sympathy.' Her chin went up. 'Possibly because my parents didn't manage to get themselves married during their travels.'

'I see.' He was silent for a moment, then added, 'Inconvenient of them.'

The gentle humour eased some of her tension. Amy smiled wryly. 'They were both under age. Without their parents' consent, any marriage would have been illegal.'

'Unlike your own, Mrs Chantry.'

'Yes.' She made a sound that wasn't quite a laugh. 'I made sure of it.' And had regretted it ever since.

The abrupt silence that followed had her entire body tingling. She hadn't said those last words aloud, had she? No, that wasn't why she was suddenly frozen where she sat.

He'd done it again. Distracted her, slipped under her guard and—

She came to her feet with a rush that almost sent her chair toppling backwards. Her hands fisted at her sides. 'Oh, you are an excellent interrogator, my lord. I noticed it this afternoon, but apparently the lesson didn't last long enough. How dare you imply that I'm masquerading under false pretenses, that I wasn't married at all?'

He stepped forward a pace, brows drawing together. 'Before you whip yourself into a fit of the vapours, Mrs Chantry, I implied no such—'

'Yes you did! Your statement was deliberately designed to trip me up. To…to…trick me into confessing—'

She stopped short, clamping her lips shut on the rest.

His voice went very soft, very gentle. 'Confess what, Mrs Chantry?'

Amy shuddered and made a desperate grab for her composure. What was she doing? If she wasn't careful, she *would* be confessing everything.

She pushed away a sudden insane desire to do just that. Pushed it away violently.

'I was speaking metaphorically, my lord.' She took a breath; let it out. 'If you have any doubts about that, I'd be perfectly happy to go upstairs and fetch my marriage lines for your perusal. Perhaps *that* will put an end to your questioning.'

She wheeled about on the words, but Hawkridge was beside her before she'd taken a step. He caught her above the elbow, his long fingers completely encircling her arm. Amy gasped once, then went very still. Even her breathing stopped. His hand felt hard and warm, his fingers terrifyingly strong against the softness of her inner arm.

She shivered, threw off the sensation of having been captured, and turned, brows raised in haughty enquiry. The expression apparently needed practice; Hawkridge gentled his grip, but he didn't release her.

And his eyes were glittering, intent on her face.

'That won't be necessary, Mrs Chantry. I was merely remarking that your parents' experience no doubt influenced your own. I didn't mean to discompose you.'

Her chin lifted. 'You didn't, sir. I was objecting to your methods. Now, if you don't mind…'

He ignored the tug she gave her arm. His voice went even softer.

'You, on the other hand, are definitely discomposing me.'

'That, my lord, is not my concern. I'm sure a man of your intelligence will be able to think of a solution. Good evening, sir.'

Amy jerked her arm out of his grasp as she spoke, and swung about with a flip of her skirts. Somewhere in the back of her mind she was aware of Hawkridge's narrow-eyed gaze on her as she stalked towards the door. No doubt he was contemplating the view again. She hoped the defiant twitch of her hips accurately conveyed her mood.

Unfortunately, she had not accurately assessed his reaction. Instead of eyeing the view from a distance as he'd done that afternoon, Hawkridge crossed the room with the speed of lightning, slammed his hand flat on the door, and banged it shut before she'd opened it more than an inch.

Amy whirled, and promptly plastered her spine to the panels behind her. In front of her Hawkridge loomed, one arm extended past her shoulder, his hand still holding the door shut, so close she could feel the brush of his clothing against hers, could feel him breathe. His face was taut with annoyance, and something else that sent heat rushing through her veins.

She swallowed. Breathing was well nigh impossible. Masculine purpose and power swirled about her in crashing waves.

And yet she wasn't afraid. Furious, fascinated, befuddled. But not afraid.

Which was enough to spur her to a woefully belated protest.

'Really, my lord, I believe I've answered quite enough—'

'Not even half of them,' he grated. His free hand came up to capture her face. He leaned closer until Amy was sure she was going to merge either with him or the door. Both were hard, utterly unyielding; of the two the door was safer.

But Hawkridge was far more potent. His rain-coloured eyes glittered into hers, sending rational thought to the four winds.

His long fingers moved, tilting her face up to his and sending a fresh wave of heat swirling through her.

He lowered his head until his breath washed over her lips. 'You haven't answered the most important question of all, Mrs Chantry.'

'But...' Her voice was a breathless squeak. 'Aren't you satisfied *yet*?'

'Far from it,' he growled softly. 'I intend to alter that unhappy situation.'

Before she could make any suggestions, his mouth came down on hers.

Chapter Five

Hunger surged through him, insatiable, ravenous. He forgot Amy was smaller than he, forgot she was weaker. Holding her captive with the weight of his body, Marc parted her lips and plundered.

She gave a muffled squeak of protest, but the roaring of his blood was louder. She tensed with resistance; he felt only the first instant of startled surrender.

Soft. Sweet. Slender. Almost fragile against him, but quivering and intensely alive.

The sensations tore through him in such rapid succession that for the space of several pounding heartbeats he was oblivious to the fact that Amy was fighting him. No longer resisting; really fighting. Her hands were fisted against his chest and she was shoving, struggling, straining to free her mouth.

The jolt cleared the mists from Marc's mind. He jerked back, stunned by his own behaviour. He, who had always taken care to control his more primitive instincts when dealing with women, had assaulted his grandmother's companion like a marauding barbarian.

He stared at her, wondering why she wasn't screaming the house down. Her eyes were huge in her flushed face, her breasts heaved. Her lips were parted and trembling; moist and reddened from the force of his, they were a temptation he didn't dare linger over.

He wrenched his gaze from the luscious sight, released his hold on her, and stepped back.

And was promptly snapped back another pace by a teeth-jarring right to the jaw. The blow was hard enough to blur his vision. Marc blinked—and decided not to shake his head. It wouldn't be wise while his brain was rattling.

'You *bastard*!'

Amy was calling him a bastard? She had obviously been rendered completely irrational with shock.

He blinked again and revised his opinion. His grand-mother's proper companion had vanished. In her place was a quivering bundle of sheer feminine fury. Her eyes flashed green fire, the sparks threatening to ignite another explosion of wrath at any moment. Her entire body shook. He could almost feel her blood pulsing, hot and fast, beneath her skin.

His body, shocked momentarily under control by her blow, hardened again with a rush that nearly doubled him over.

He cursed, and slammed the cage shut on instincts that had always been savagely reined.

'Mrs Chantry,' he began. And couldn't think of another thing to say.

His victim didn't have the same problem.

'I may be illegitimate, my lord,' she raged. 'And beneath the other women of your acquaintance because of it, but that does not give you the right to use me for your amusement the minute you learn the fact!'

Whirling, she pulled the door open, whisked herself through the aperture and slammed the door shut with the full force of her arm.

Marc winced as the reverberations shook the room. A small painting hanging beside the door fell to the floor with a crash. The windows rattled in sympathy. The din didn't help the ringing still going on in his ears.

God, what had he done? The kiss itself wasn't such a crime. After all, he'd been driven mad all day by the paradox presented by Amy's innocent appearance and the wary knowledge in her eyes…he'd been so aware of her he'd practically felt her every move…the last provocative flip of her skirts had been the final straw… Was it any wonder he'd kissed her?

But his timing had been absolutely appalling.

'Bloody hell!'

Marc turned abruptly and began to pace. He strode the length of the room, wheeled and started back. He wished there was something in his path so he could kick it aside. He was painfully aroused, frustrated, and furious with himself.

Mrs Amaris Chantry was a tantalising mixture of knowledge and innocence, but she *was* innocent.

At least, innocent of the type of career he'd suspected. No enterprising widow with an eye to the main chance would have reacted with such fury to a mere kiss.

Marc groaned aloud. 'A mere kiss' didn't begin to describe the sensations aroused by the feel of her mouth beneath his. Damn it, she'd even tasted innocent. Innocent and sweet; almost virginal. He was too experienced not to recognise the genuine article.

Especially when it hit him in the face.

He stopped pacing and cautiously felt his jaw. Where the devil had Amy learned to throw a punch like that? She might be young, and heart-breakingly vulnerable, but she wasn't defenceless. She'd fought back. She'd treated him to the cutting edge of her tongue.

She'd yielded. For one tiny infinitesimal second, her mouth had trembled and softened beneath his.

Was that why she'd reacted so violently, when his earlier insults had elicited no reaction at all?

Something deep within him was suddenly alert; a sleeping predator abruptly wakened.

He started pacing again, fast. He was still aroused, still frustrated, still furious with himself. But beneath it all, a fierce elation was beginning to burn.

He hadn't frightened her. For three or four mind-spinning seconds he'd given his instincts full rein, and Amy had neither swooned, shrieked nor thrown a fit of the vapours. Every eligible lady his sister had dangled in his way over the years would have indulged in one of those options.

His last fiancée had treated him to all three.

His grandmother's mysterious companion had matched him. He'd have preferred a passionate response to his kiss rather than a blow to the jaw, but she'd matched him.

He stopped pacing, and stared, eyes narrowed in thought, at the door. Somehow he had to find a way out of the disastrous pit he'd dug for himself. Because it was suddenly, vitally, imperative, that he discover everything he could about Mrs Amaris Chantry.

Amy had packed and unpacked her single bandbox three times in an agony of indecision before she realised the futility of the exercise. Not only did she have nowhere to go, she had no way of getting there.

And how could she repay her kind employer by creeping out of the house like a thief in the night?

The answer was simple. She couldn't.

Frustrated, and inexplicably on the verge of tears, she kicked her bandbox under the bed and paced to the window. Her agitated reflection stared back at her.

What was she going to do?

The night-shrouded woods glimpsed beyond the south lawn didn't provide an answer.

Amy stalked back across the room and sat down on the bed.

An instant later she was up and pacing again. She couldn't sit still; she felt as if all her nerves were dancing on the surface of her skin. None of the practised, calculated embraces from her husband before their marriage, nor the perfunctory pecks that had come later, had prepared her for such an onslaught of sensation.

The mere memory of the fierce pressure of Hawkridge's mouth on hers caused lightning to streak through her all over again. He hadn't asked, he hadn't persuaded, he hadn't even seduced. He'd taken as if he'd had the right.

How had she so badly miscalculated as to credit him with *any* civilised propensities? The man wasn't a warrior. He belonged in a cave.

Amy shivered and wrapped her arms about herself. Outrage aside, it wasn't Hawkridge's primitive tendencies that worried her—one could get very primitive when food was handed out where she'd been.

What caused her entire being to quake with alarm was a persistent, nerve-tingling vision of herself sharing the cave with him.

Amy sank down on her bed and put her face in her hands. This was the result of fascination with a portrait. Present her with the real thing and she promptly lost her wits, and reverted to some rather uncivilised behaviour herself.

Heat flooded her cheeks as she remembered her actions, her *words*. No lady would have behaved like that. She had sunk herself utterly beneath reproach—and she'd been doing so well. Her only consolation was that no one else had witnessed her lapse. She doubted Hawkridge would inform his grandmother of the encounter. The dowager had obviously retired to her bedchamber in the sadly mistaken belief that Hawkridge wouldn't attack her companion the minute her back was turned. He wouldn't be likely to disillusion her.

Especially when the entire episode was all his fault.

That thought provided an effective antidote to self-castigation. Amy sat up straighter and frowned at the opposite wall.

It was no use sitting here wallowing in mortification. The situation could have been worse. She might have succumbed to the wild torrent of excitement that had swept through her the instant Hawkridge's mouth touched hers; she might have let him sweep *her* away to realms as yet unexplored.

But she hadn't been swept away. She'd escaped. And now she wouldn't think about it again. She wouldn't think about the heat and power of his body, the hard, thrilling demand of his mouth. She'd do what she had always done. Put it out of her mind and go forward.

But...forward to where? Why should she be driven from the only safe haven she'd known—although safe was a moot point at the moment? Still, Hawkridge wouldn't be staying forever. Surely she could cope with his presence for a few days.

Planning how to do so provided a welcome distraction. Amy bent her mind to the task. Avoiding Hawkridge was proving unexpectedly difficult; given his conqueror's response to any challenge, she doubted the situation would improve. But she could ensure she was never alone with him. Even if it meant joining the dowager in her quest for jollification.

Embarking on a social whirl was, after all, more ladylike than another bout of fisticuffs.

Amy glanced down at her hand and flexed her fingers. Her knuckles felt somewhat bruised. So, for some strange reason, did her heart.

She pushed the notion aside. Naturally she felt shaken. It was a perfectly normal reaction, but nothing to do with her heart. Now that she was calmer, she'd get undressed, climb into bed, and contemplate ways and means of sticking to the dowager like a shadow. And then she would go to sleep.

Dreamlessly.

Doing so shouldn't present a problem. What with one thing and another, it had been a rather exhausting day.

Her careful planning came undone the minute she knocked on Lady Hawkridge's door the next morning, only to be informed by Giddings that her ladyship had left the house to pay morning calls on several tenants.

Amy stared at Giddings in surprise. It was Lady Hawkridge's custom to take breakfast in her bedchamber before summoning her companion to discuss the day's activities. Amy then left the dowager to the ministrations of her dresser while she, herself, attended to any secretarial duties that fell to her lot. What on earth had possessed her employer to deviate from her usual course?

When she put this question to Giddings, that worthy individual launched into a monologue on the miraculous recovery enjoyed by the dowager after a good night's sleep.

Amy wished she could make the same claim. Thanks to a restless, dream-filled slumber, she had woken considerably later than her usual time. To find herself abandoned.

There was only one thing to do. Cutting short Giddings's earnest speech on the restorative properties of sleep, she descended the stairs in search of Pickles. The way the morning was shaping up, Hawkridge was probably lying in wait in the breakfast parlour. She would have a tray sent in to the library.

It took some time to put this plan into action. When she finally located Pickles, who was putting away billiard balls that looked as if they'd been rather violently cannoned all over the billiard table, he reproachfully informed her that no one had touched the tea-tray he'd borne into the withdrawing-room on the previous evening. And Mrs Pickles had especially baked Amy's favourite macaroons.

Amy adjourned to the kitchen to soothe Mrs Pickles's wounded feelings. She accomplished the task by letting Mrs Pickles ply her with bread and butter dripping with honey, followed by a cup of coffee, while Mrs Cubitt provided a homily on missing meals when she needed to build up her strength.

Consequently, the imposing clock in the hall was solemnly striking eleven by the time Amy carried a second cup of coffee into the library—after first ascertaining that Hawkridge wasn't lying in wait for her there.

He wasn't. Amy breathed a sigh of relief and locked the door. She wasn't precisely sure about the propriety of locking an Earl out of his own library, but that didn't prevent her from defiantly turning the key.

She made sure the windows were latched for good measure.

Then, refusing to so much as glance at the portrait above the fireplace, she marched over to a shelf of books and commenced work.

Since her normal duties took up very little time, she had asked Lady Hawkridge to let her sort and catalogue the vast collection of tomes acquired by various Rothwells over the decades. It was a task she relished. For years the only book she and her mother had possessed was a tattered Bible; access to all the books she could read was a feast to one starved of formal learning.

Amy settled down to the search she'd been conducting for over a week. So far, she was forced to the conclusion that no Rothwells had felt it expedient to purchase treatises or papers on the laws pertaining to marriage. Perhaps Parliamentary Acts would help—if she could find them.

She was so intent on her quest that when a section of shelving beside the fireplace began to swing inwards with a particularly blood-curdling groan of ancient hinges, she merely glanced around in mild surprise.

Every drop of blood stilled in her veins as mild surprise turned to shock.

Hawkridge strolled out of the dark cavern beyond the opening, contemplated the locked door for precisely two seconds, then looked at her, brows raised. 'Good morning, Mrs Chantry.'

Amy stared back at him, both hands clutching a heavy book to her breast. It was no use asking how he'd got in; the answer was perfectly obvious. She searched wildly for something else to say.

'You deserved to be locked out, my lord.'

As an opening remark it was rather undiplomatic, if true.

He retaliated with a faintly menacing smile. 'Well, now we're both locked in.'

Her eyes blinked wide.

Before she could think of a solution to her dilemma, Hawkridge glanced down, frowned, and flicked a large spider off his sleeve. It landed on the floor with a plop and scuttled under the desk.

Amy gazed after it in consternation. She was locked in with Hawkridge and a spider. A large spider. Things were getting worse.

'And the only way out,' he purred, as though reading her mind, 'is the spider-infested way I came in.'

She shuddered.

'But don't worry, Mrs Chantry. Fortunately for you, I do occasionally succumb to the odd chivalrous impulse.' He pushed the bookshelves closed and walked across to the door.

Amy shuddered again as the hinges protested with another nerve-shattering screech. Then watched in astonishment as Hawkridge unlocked the door.

'That takes care of the proprieties,' he remarked and turned to face her.

She gazed owlishly back at him over the top of her book. It seemed to be getting heavier, but its bulk gave an illusion of protection. Hawkridge might have succumbed to a chivalrous impulse, but he was between her and escape. She clutched her burden tighter.

'However, we'll leave the door closed for the moment. I wish to speak to you alone, Mrs Chantry—'

She took a step back.

'—to apologise.'

Amy's jaw dropped.

He gave a short laugh. 'I thought that might be your reaction. You know, Mrs Chantry, I believe you've been guilty of the same crime as myself.'

'What?' Oh, thank goodness. She'd finally relocated her voice.

'Prejudgement.'

'Oh.' She considered the charge. 'Well, perhaps, my lord, but—'

'And,' he continued inexorably, 'as if that isn't bad enough, your method of retaliation last night was rather unexpected. For a lady.'

Amy blushed to the roots of her hair. 'I am fully aware of that, sir, but I take leave to tell you that you did not behave like a gentleman.'

A rueful smile curved his mouth. Coming forward, he touched his fingertips to her cheek. 'I know,' he admitted gently. 'In fact, my behaviour was atrocious, and I do beg your pardon for it.'

Amy froze at the brief touch; her mind reeled. Hawkridge's evident sincerity startled her as much as his unexpected appearance. Despite all her resolutions, she felt a softening inside. There was something rather disarming about a man who admitted he was wrong, without making excuses for it.

She groped for some sort of response. 'Well... Thank you, my lord. I mean...I accept your apology. That is...so long as you promise—'

'I never make promises I might not be able to keep,' he murmured, still in such a soft tone that his meaning took a moment to register. When she levelled a suspicious glare at him, he smiled wickedly. 'Perhaps I should make it clear that I'm not apologising for kissing you, but for my appalling lack of finesse during the process.'

'What! But... That... You...'

She stopped before she spluttered herself to a complete standstill, and tried again. 'Really, sir, if you think that sort of apology is sufficient, you're fair and far out. I told you last night that I won't be used for your amusement and—'

'I was not,' he stated with great precision, 'using you for my amusement.'

'Indeed?' She tilted her chin at him. 'Was last night the way you treat all the ladies of your acquaintance?'

'No,' he admitted ruefully. 'But not for the reason you're probably thinking.'

'Hmph!' Her chin went higher. 'Clearly, you have more respect for them. What else am I to think?'

Every trace of amusement vanished from his eyes. He lifted his hand and taking her chin between thumb and forefinger, gave it a little shake. 'Let me make one thing very clear, Mrs Chantry. I *do* consider you to be the equal of the other ladies of my acquaintance, regardless of your birth. Furthermore, I had no thought last night of repaying your confidences by insulting you.'

She blinked at him.

His gaze dropped briefly to her lips before he released her. 'I kissed you for another reason entirely, which we won't go into at the moment.'

'We won't? No.' She shook her head. 'Of course we won't.' Her mind seethed with possibilities. Only one made sense. He was going to offer her a *carte blanche* without the insult of 'how much' attached to it.

The thought should have horrified her. She should have felt affronted at the very least—although logic told her she could hardly expect a more respectable offer. Instead, a shiver that felt very like anticipation brushed her skin.

'However,' he went on, the amused gleam returning, 'I did derive some benefit from last night's salutory lesson.'

Still grappling with her horrifying lack of horror, Amy could only stare at him.

He grinned. 'I've finally discovered what your husband did.'

She went utterly still; shock blanked out everything. For a

minute she couldn't even think. Then, very slowly, she turned and carefully returned her book to its place.

'Oh?'

The sudden intensity of his gaze was palpable. 'Do you know, Mrs Chantry, you've gone quite pale. Why should that be?'

Amy took a deep breath and forced her features into an expression of unconcern. 'It...must be my shock at your powers of deduction, sir.'

When he didn't answer, she risked a glance at him. She couldn't do much about her lack of colour; every drop of blood in her veins had plummeted southwards along with her heart. 'Well? What did my husband do?'

After another long, nerve-racking moment of contemplation, Hawkridge started to grin. 'He was a prize-fighter.'

Amy's colour returned in a rush. She wished she could sink through the floor in mortification. Failing that, she would have been happy to sink into insensibility, but even as she wondered how to achieve that helpful state, the devilish gleam in Hawkridge's eyes saved her. To her utter astonishment, she giggled.

Then clapped both hands over her mouth and stared at him over the tops of her fingers, her eyes as round as saucers.

And in that moment he knew.

This was the one. This was the woman he'd been waiting for.

A wave of sheer primitive possessiveness hit him with all the force of a raging torrent. He wanted to reach out, snatch Amy into his arms and carry her off to a cave somewhere. The sheer violence of the need startled him. And he *knew* how ruthless he could be.

Fortunately, common sense reasserted itself. The nearest cave was some distance away. He suspected that long before they reached it, Amy would have reacted to his primitive tactics with another blow to the jaw. It wasn't the response he wanted.

He pushed ruthlessness back into its cage, took a deep breath, and smiled.

Amy lowered her hands very slowly. For a minute there, she'd wondered if she really was going to swoon away for the first time in her life. Something had flashed into Hawkridge's eyes. Something so fierce, so utterly implacable, she'd frozen like a rabbit staring into the eyes of a hawk. Unable to see anything else. Unable to hear. Unable to feel anything but the frantic beating of her heart.

Then the expression was gone. He smiled, and a completely inexplicable feeling of happiness welled up inside her. Before she could contemplate the wisdom of such a response, she found herself twinkling back at him.

'That statement, sir, was extremely ungallant. And quite incorrect. I told you yesterday that my husband invested in, uh…'

He raised a brow when she faltered.

'Never mind,' she muttered, flushing. 'It isn't important.'

Another smile curved his mouth. 'You don't like to talk about him, do you?'

Amy hesitated, then shook her head. 'He wasn't a very nice person.'

'Good. We needn't scruple to speak ill of the dear departed.'

She giggled again, a delightful gurgle of sound that had Marc feeling ridiculously pleased with himself.

Captivated by a playfulness he suspected was new and very fragile, he was about to continue along the same lines when the library door slammed open.

He glanced up, frowned at the exquisitely fashionable damsel storming across the threshold, and with some difficulty recognised his niece.

'Good God, Lucinda. Is that you?'

The visitor didn't waste time on this unflattering greeting. She caught up the full skirts of a powder-blue riding habit that was braided and frogged wherever braiding and frogging could be placed, marched straight up to her uncle and fixed him with a steely gaze. The effect was ruined somewhat by the sweeping black plume adorning her cap *à la hussar* that fell over her eyes, practically obscuring her vision.

'Hawkridge, you have to help me get married.'

Amy felt her face go blank again with shock. Hawkridge remained singularly unimpressed.

'Hawkridge?' he repeated, eyeing his niece up and down. 'What the devil happened to Uncle Marc?'

Lucinda dropped her skirts, elevated her small nose and swept the plume aside. It promptly bounced back into place. 'You may have noticed that I'm quite grown up now.' She extended a powder-blue gloved hand. 'How do you do, Hawkridge? It seems an age since I've seen you.'

Hawkridge contemplated the hand poised under his nose, studied the bobbing plume and burst out laughing. 'No wonder Bevan cursed that Bath academy,' he observed. 'Come down off your high horse, brat.'

His niece narrowed her striking blue eyes to glittering slits. 'The name,' she said through set teeth, 'is Lucinda.' Snatching her hand back, she yanked the feather aside with enough force to snap its delicate quill. The plume subsided sadly on to her shoulder. 'No wonder Mama despairs of you ever finding a wife. No woman in her right mind would have you.'

'Very likely not,' he agreed. 'But before we delve further into such a fascinating subject, I expect your newfound manners to extend to Mrs Chantry.'

Lucinda flushed, but tossed her ebony curls. 'Amy and I are friends. We don't need to stand upon ceremony. Besides, she's only—'

Hawkridge took a threatening step forward. Lucinda stopped in mid-protest and swallowed visibly.

'I was only going to say she's not much older than me,' she muttered after a moment. 'Hello, Amy.'

'Miss Nettlebed,' Amy acknowledged and, responding to

the visitor's imperious air, instinctively dropped a curtsy. Or started to.

Hawkridge wheeled and strode over to the desk, bending close as he passed her. 'Curtsy to that little minx, Mrs Chantry, and you won't sit down for a week.'

Amy halted in mid-curtsy. When her knees threatened to wobble, she straightened and glared at him over her shoulder.

He returned her scowl with a bland smile and propped himself against the desk.

'Now, *Lucinda*, what's all this idiocy about getting married at the age of sixteen?'

'I've turned seventeen, which you'd know if you ever stayed in Devon for longer than a minute. And it isn't idiocy, Uncle Marc, it's—' She stopped, and thrust out her lower lip. 'Oh, now look what you've done! You've spoilt it.'

'You mean your nonsensical pose of maturity slipped,' he corrected drily. 'I didn't think it'd last long.'

'Ohh!' Lucinda stamped her foot. 'You're as bad as Mama and Papa. Not to mention that horrid little toad, Crispin.'

'Dear me,' Amy murmured, finally gathering enough wit to remove herself from the battlefield. She began edging towards the door. 'Where has the morning gone? I'd better go and enquire after—'

'No, Amy, don't go.' Lucinda halted her progress by grabbing her arm. Short of tearing the sleeve out of her peach cambric gown, and being obliged to sew it in again, Amy was caught.

'You know all about Jeremy. Besides, it's thanks to you that he's attending our party tonight.'

'Indeed?' enquired Hawkridge, his tone suddenly so glacial that Lucinda released her captive in surprise.

Amy returned to the desk, ostensibly to pick up her coffee cup. 'Would you rather Lucinda met Mr Chatsworth clandestinely, sir?' she enquired in the same undertone he'd used to her.

'I'll reserve judgement until I meet him myself,' he replied, scowling. Then replaced the expression with a pleased smile. 'Why, I do believe your good influence is working on me already, Mrs Chantry.'

'If you have something to say about my affairs, Hawkridge, you may address yourself to me,' Lucinda interposed, advancing on her uncle before Amy could reply to this patently untrue statement.

'I wouldn't come too close to this desk, if I were you, Lucinda,' Hawkridge countered. 'There's a spider in the vicinity. A very large, black, hairy spider.'

Amy had forgotten the spider. Snatching up her skirts, she scanned the floor around her feet—mercifully spiderless—and backed off in a hurry. So did Lucinda.

'A spider?' she squeaked. 'How on earth did a spider get inside your library?'

'I was showing Mrs Chantry the secret passage.' He glanced at Amy, a devil in his eyes. 'She was struck speechless with amazement.'

'I should think so,' Lucinda declared indignantly. 'Really, Uncle Marc, aren't you a little *old* to be scaring people with spiders? I'd expect that sort of thing from that horrid toad, Crispin.'

Hawkridge raised his eyes heavenwards.

'But never mind that,' Lucinda continued, returning to the subject at hand with the tenacity of the young and self-absorbed. 'What are you going to do to help me?'

'Nothing.'

Her eyes narrowed again.

'For one thing, you're too young to be married, and for another, if Jeremy is the bounder Augusta mentioned in her letter, he hasn't even asked your father's permission to address you.'

'N...o...o,' Lucinda admitted reluctantly. 'But how can he when Papa won't grant him an interview?' Apparently feeling she'd stonewalled Hawkridge with this rhetorical question, she turned to Amy in appeal. 'You know how it is, Amy? After all, you must have been about my age when you were married.'

'A little older,' Amy demurred, conscious of Hawkridge's suddenly intent gaze. She waved a hand in studied carelessness. 'But, you know, I always wondered what a London Season would have been like. The balls, the parties, driving in the Park, all those young gentlemen vying for one's attention. Such fun. You must be looking forward to it.'

Lucinda looked a little startled. 'Well, yes, but…I'll still be able to have a Season. Dearest Jeremy and I will settle in Town. We'll be the most fashionable couple you've—'

'Dearest Jeremy is flush with funds, I take it?' Hawkridge put in silkily. 'He'll need to be to pay the dressmaker's bills, if that ridiculous get-up you're wearing is any example.'

'*Ridiculous?*' Lucinda's voice and colour rose alarmingly.

Amy hurried into the breach. 'I'm sure it's a very pretty habit, Miss Nettlebed. I'd like to wear that shade, myself, but it wouldn't appear to advantage on me.'

Lucinda subsided. 'Thank you, Amy.' She sent a disdainful glance in her uncle's direction. 'For your information, Hawkridge, Jeremy thinks I'd look delightful in sackcloth.'

'Sounds as if he's preparing you for a lifetime in the stuff.'

His niece ground her teeth audibly. 'Just because Jeremy doesn't have a title or a vault of money like you do is no reason to be sarcastic. I'll have plenty for the two of us from that estate old Aunt Cordelia left in trust for me.'

'And no doubt Jeremy is aware of that interesting fact.'

'No, he isn't,' Lucinda informed him, nose in the air. 'He told me he wouldn't have had the courage to approach me, if he thought I was wealthy.' A besotted smile spread over her face. 'Isn't that noble? Isn't that gallant? He's so charming, so—'

Hawkridge cast another long-suffering glance at the ceiling. 'Of course he is, you goose. It's his stock-in-trade.'

Lucinda stopped rhapsodising and glared at him. 'You don't know anything about it,' she cried. 'And, what's more, you don't know anything about gallantry or charm either. In fact, you're *worse* than that horrid little toad, Crispin.'

This was obviously an insult of the highest order. Hiding a smile, Amy glanced at Hawkridge to see how he was taking his niece's reversion to childhood. He wasn't bothering to hide his amusement.

'It seems to be the fate of younger brothers to always be referred to as horrid little toads,' he observed thoughtfully.

Lucinda stuck out her lower lip. 'What would you know about it?'

'I am a younger brother. And that reminds me. According to your mother, Crispin is about to totter straight into the grave. What's wrong with him? Apart from his toad-like qualities, that is.'

'Nothing.' Lucinda continued to pout. 'Just because he used to have those wheezing fits for days on end when he was a little boy, Mama fusses and worries until there's no bearing it. She wouldn't let Papa send Crispin to school—which would at least have stopped him tormenting me. I mean, what is the use of having a brother in the house if he won't help me?'

Amy gaped at this evidence of self-interest, but Hawkridge nodded approval.

'Crispin must have more sense than anyone's giving him credit for.'

'Ohh!' The floor received another stamp.

'Never mind the tantrum, Lucinda. I take it your brother isn't at death's door.'

'Of course he isn't. He only reclines on couches and looks pale so Mama will fetch and carry for him. No one cares about *my* suffering.'

'Now, that's not quite true. Your Papa mentioned yesterday

that you haven't had the chicken-pox, and I've just remembered that the house is rife with it. You'd better be off. Maids are dropping right and left.'

'*What!* You're talking about *chicken-pox* when my whole life might be *blighted*? Ohh!' Lucinda stamped one foot then the other, clenched her fists and began to pace. 'This is the most heartless family I've ever encountered,' she wailed. She kicked a foot-rest out of her path, causing Amy to step hastily aside. 'I came here to ask for your help, and what do I get?'

'A spanking if you're not careful,' Hawkridge threatened, amusement vanishing as he came upright in one swift movement. 'Behave yourself or leave.'

Lucinda blinked at him in shock, then tossed her head and retrieved her pose of offended dignity. Unfortunately, all the pacing, stamping and tossing had her plume abandoning dignity. It slid lower.

'I will certainly take my leave,' Lucinda replied with great hauteur. 'And don't bother looking for me any time in the near future. I don't intend to cross this threshold again until you learn some manners.'

Hawkridge grinned and promptly swept her an elegant bow. 'Miss Nettlebed, thank you so much for deigning to grace us with your presence this morning. Our delight at the brevity of your visit is exceeded only by our relief.'

'*Aaagh!*' After one shriek of frustration, Lucinda stormed towards the door. It was all too much for the plume. It slipped its moorings and floated to the floor, barely escaping decapitation by the violently slammed door.

'One can only hope,' Hawkridge murmured as a second muffled slam indicated that the front door had been subjected to the same treatment, 'that the doors in this house will withstand the recent violence visited upon them.'

Amy heard herself giggle for the third time that morning with a kind of stunned amazement. She'd never giggled before in her entire life. Now she seemed to be doing it every five minutes. The pained look Hawkridge gave her nearly set her off again.

'Oh, dear,' she managed, trying for a suitably sympathetic expression. 'I'm so sorry, my lord. Are you quite deafened?'

'Not quite,' he said, scowling. 'What the devil happened to Lucinda? She was always a brat, but a likeable one. A year or two ago she'd have been in that secret passage regardless of what might be lurking there, and probably dragging Crispin along with her. In fact, I'm sure the little wretches hid there one day in the hope of scaring the wits out of Pickles.'

'I'm afraid certain Young Ladies Academies pride themselves on turning out very *proper* young ladies, sir. But don't worry. I believe the effect is only temporary.'

He cocked a brow. 'How do you know?'

'I had a position in a school before my marriage,' she replied composedly. 'For a very brief time. Now, I really should go and make sure the maids are *not* dropping right and left, so if you'll excuse me—'

'No, don't go,' Hawkridge said quickly, putting out a detaining hand as she turned away.

Amy jerked back, more in surprise than real alarm, and he withdrew his hand at once. 'I mean,' he said, resuming his seat against the edge of the desk, 'you don't have to run away because we're alone. I have no intention of attacking you.'

She eyed his hands, clenched hard around the solid mahogany of the desk. 'That's very reassuring, my lord, but—'

'Tell me about this Chatsworth character. What's he like?'

Amy hesitated, conscious of a need for caution, but strangely reluctant to leave. 'I don't know. I haven't met him.'

He studied her wary expression, his smile wry. 'I'm not going to criticise your advice to Augusta, Mrs Chantry. I know it's preferable for Lucinda to meet Chatsworth under her parents' roof rather than clandestinely.'

'Oh. Well…I'm glad you approve, sir. Now, I really do have things…' She faltered again, flustered by a faintly amused regard that yet held something deeper, and utterly steady.

Then Hawkridge turned aside, indicating the nearest shelves and releasing her from the intensity in his grey eyes. 'Cataloguing the library,' he murmured. 'Grandmama told me you volunteered for the task. Since we seem to have exhausted the current topic of conversation, it is I, therefore, who should leave you in peace to continue.'

But he made no move to go.

Amy glanced towards the door, not quite sure whether she ought to agree or demur. After all, it *was* his library. Then as he looked back at her, a thought occurred that had her smiling.

'On the contrary, my lord. A task awaits you here that takes precedence over anything I may need to do.'

She crossed the room, opened the door, and glanced back. And this time her smile was alight with mischief. 'You have a very large, very black, very hairy spider to dispatch.'

Chapter Six

How was he supposed to concentrate on catching a spider after that smile?

Marc gave up the task after a fruitless five minutes, during which time he concluded that the spider had gone to ground. He couldn't keep his mind on the job anyway. Thoughts of Amy kept distracting him.

Little details. Like the fine arch of her brows; the delicacy of her hands. The shy mischief in her eyes and the tiny dimples that had appeared at the corners of her mouth when she'd smiled at him from the doorway.

She'd been lucky the entire length of the library had separated them, he thought, wryly amused at himself, because he'd been on the verge of doing something that wouldn't have helped his cause in the least. This hunt needed skill and patience. He'd mended a few fences this morning, but Amy was still wary, still controlled. Even to letting herself laugh.

His eyes narrowed as he thought about that. She wasn't intimidated, he decided after a moment, just…conscious of her behaviour. He could hardly blame her after their initial encounter.

Damn it, he'd never been so wrong about anyone—and the clues had been there, if he'd stopped being annoyed at his own response long enough to see them. The innocence in her clear gaze, the courage inherent in the tilt of that determined little chin. Even her scent was all wrong. The widow he'd imagined would have worn something cloying, far too sweet. The sweetness was there, but, like Amy herself, it was fragile, elusive, reminding him of lavender buds, tiny petals defensively closed until kissed by the warmth of the sun.

He had the feeling there'd been little sunshine in Amy's life.

Marc frowned again. If he hadn't been blinded by prejudice yesterday he would have seen immediately beneath Amy's guilty defiance without having to resort to force to get his answers.

On the other hand, he couldn't regret kissing her. Not when the conflict between suspicion and his instinctive male response to her had, for a few fleeting seconds, flushed from hiding the real woman behind her ladylike façade.

He intended to do it again. And in the process find out whatever it was she was hiding. That it was something to do with her husband he had no doubt, but he also didn't doubt for a minute that he'd be able to coax, persuade or otherwise prise the information out of her.

The sound of a carriage bowling up the drive interrupted his thoughts and drew him to the window. He grinned at the sight of his grandmother sitting in solitary splendour as her barouche swept up to the front door. He must remember to thank her for making herself scarce this morning—a decision he suspected had been deliberate. His beloved grandparent might be maddening on occasion, but she was no fool.

Somehow she'd known before he had. And approved.

With such an ally in his camp, Amy's fate was sealed.

The light-hearted mood that swept Amy out of the library that morning had vanished by mid-afternoon. She couldn't have said precisely when the clouds began to gather on her horizon but, as she walked back to the Manor after a trip to the village draper, they began to assume ominous proportions.

For some reason Lucinda's visit kept turning over and over in her mind. Several facts that she'd either been unaware of before, or unworried by—such as Jeremy Chatsworth sharing the same initials as her husband—suddenly assumed a significance that had apprehension sprinting around her stomach.

Instead of immediately sitting down to fashion a three-quarter overdress of silvery-grey gauze for her rose silk evening gown, she hunted up the *Morning Post* for a closer perusal of the report on the robberies at Bristol.

Nothing she read allayed her uneasiness in the slightest. The clouds slunk over the horizon and crept closer.

By the time she studied her reflection in her dressing-table mirror that evening, preparatory to setting out for Nettlebed Place, impending doom hovered about her like a persistent fog. She was not in the mood for a party.

Unfortunately, she had no choice but to attend. It was better to confront her suspicions immediately; to see Mr Chatsworth for herself—preferably before he clapped eyes on her—and to hope he had nothing to do with her past.

If he did, she could always feign illness and return home. It wouldn't take a great deal of effort.

Her plan was not destined to run smoothly.

Half an hour after the family dinner that preceded the Nettlebeds' party, Amy had discovered a very peculiar thing about such gatherings. It was impossible to search for one particular person while making sure she wasn't first seen by that person herself.

Of course, if Hawkridge would only behave himself, she'd be able to take cover behind one of the potted ferns with which Lady Nettlebed had adorned her drawing-room, and search to her heart's content. But every time she showed signs of retreating thereto, Hawkridge loomed at her side, cutting off retreat and introducing her to yet another guest.

Amy didn't know whether to feel guilty for being where she was, or annoyed at his high-handed tactics. What was worse, every time she gathered her wits, intending to deliver a protest, the sight of him, tall and darkly handsome in elegant black evening clothes, sent her thoughts off on several highly unsuitable tangents.

It was extremely unfair of him.

'I say, Mrs Chantry, you look bang up to the nines, but why are you wearing a cap?'

The demand had her turning to see Crispin, a dark-haired, willowy youth still some weeks short of his sixteenth birthday, come bounding up to her. He skidded to a halt, a pleased smile on his face, rather in the manner of an over-eager puppy waiting for a pat.

Amy's heart sank. She was torn between relief at the interruption, which enabled her to take a discreet step away from the immediate circle of guests, and dismay at the expression of canine devotion on Crispin's face.

'I'm a widow, Mr Nettlebed,' she explained, trying for a repressive tone that wouldn't entirely crush her youthful admirer.

'Yes, I know, but you don't look like one. In fact—'

Amy ceased to listen. Out of the corner of her eye she saw Hawkridge disengage from his conversation with one of his neighbours and turn a narrow-eyed stare of speculation on his nephew.

'—didn't have a chance to tell you at dinner,' Crispin concluded.

She had no idea what he'd been talking about. 'Yes, well, dinner was rather, er...'

'Rendered hideous by Lucinda's sulks,' Hawkridge finished for her.

'Told her Chatsworth wouldn't be there,' Crispin confided,

his attention diverted from Amy. His eager expression didn't falter, lending credence to the dowager's assertion that Crispin considered Hawkridge an out-and-outer. Narrow-eyed stares were clearly to be expected.

'Why should Papa invite him to a family dinner?' he continued. 'Fellow isn't a member of the family. I say, Uncle Marc, were you serious about teaching me to sail?'

'Yes. But there are conditions.'

The caveat didn't appear to bother Crispin. He launched into an enthusiastic description of an old sail-boat he'd discovered in an unused barn.

Amy glanced quickly at Hawkridge. The dinner table had been rendered hideous by Lucinda's displeasure that her darling Jeremy had been excluded from the intimate gathering; a distinct pall had also been cast over the meal when Hawkridge had demanded that his nephew render an account of the sports and pastimes he enjoyed.

The list had been disastrously short. Reclining on a couch while listening to his mama play soothing music had been at the top, followed closely by having her bathe his brow with lavender water. Only the sarcastic tone in which this information had been delivered had saved Crispin from instant annihilation. That had been reserved for Lord and Lady Nettlebed.

As the ensuing battle had raged about her ears, Amy would have been happy to call an end to the evening then and there. Her presence when she was almost as much a stranger to the family as Mr Chatsworth was bad enough. The fact that everyone—except Lady Hawkridge, who blithely provided a Greek chorus totally unrelated to the prevailing subject—felt free to rage and argue in front of her was singularly unnerving.

As Crispin's conversation began to include such mysterious terms as luffs, gaffs and booms, she cast a longing glance at the row of ferns placed artistically behind the sofa where her employer was holding court. *That* was her proper place. Not here beside Hawkridge, where she was being forced to wonder whether her assumption that morning that he was thinking of offering her a *carte blanche* was somewhat wide of the mark.

After all, a man didn't present his potential mistress to his family and friends when the female concerned didn't move in those circles in the first place.

At least, she didn't think so. But if he hadn't meant to insult her, if he hadn't been amusing himself, why had he kissed her?

Amy started to worry again—which worried her even more, because if her reactions to the possibility of a *carte blanche* were those of a proper lady, there wouldn't be any need to worry in the first place. Especially when she already had Mr Chatsworth to worry about.

Hmm.

She eyed the glass of champagne in her hand and wondered if the single sip she'd taken had gone straight to her head. Her thoughts seemed to be spinning in circles.

When she caught a glimpse of Lucinda, the centre of an animated group of young people, nervousness danced an accompanying reel in her stomach. Without conscious thought, Amy started edging towards the ferns again.

Propriety wasn't the only reason propelling her thence. If she could just catch a glimpse of Mr Chatsworth, just convince herself that he had nothing to do with her, that Lucinda's situation was sadly commonplace, that she *knew* he couldn't be—

'Hah! So you're the new companion, are you? Well, you're a demmed sight prettier than the last one.'

Amy froze several steps short of the ferns. She turned her head to find herself being examined by two pairs of critical blue eyes, one belonging to an elderly, silver-haired gentleman who was leaning heavily on a cane, the other to a younger man enough like his companion for her to make a reasonably accurate guess as to their identities.

It was all of a piece, she decided, turning fully. Nothing was going as planned tonight.

Before she could reply to the older gentleman's somewhat unconventional greeting, Lady Hawkridge rose from her sofa and flitted up to them, an innocently enquiring smile on her face.

'Good heavens, Bartholomew! Are you finally having Colborough Court redecorated? It's the only reason I can think of that would account for your separation from that armchair in front of the fire.'

'Very amusing, Clarissa.' Colborough's bushy grey brows drew together over a decidedly hawk-like nose. 'You can blame Eversleigh, here, for my presence. Young idiot's got no sense. See how many parties he'll feel like attending when he's over seventy and plagued by a gouty foot.'

'Your foot is no more gouty than mine is,' retorted her ladyship. 'You just use it as an excuse to grumble and grouch.'

'Much you know,' grumbled Colborough. 'Where's that mannerless grandson of yours? I've got a thing or two to say to him.'

Her ladyship rolled her eyes. 'Amy, as you've no doubt guessed, this is Lord Colborough and Viscount Eversleigh.' She patted the Viscount's arm. 'Marc's friend since boyhood, you know.'

Eversleigh bowed, a twinkle in his eyes. 'How do you do, Mrs Chantry? I'm glad to see that Marc managed to restrain himself.'

Amy's knees wobbled in the middle of a curtsy. Apparently Hawkridge's methods of dismissing his grandmother's companions were known far and wide.

Worse was to come.

As she straightened, Colborough subjected her to another close stare. 'Mrs Chantry, is it? Don't know the name. Recognise those eyes, though. So, you're a connection of the Daltons.'

'Uh…'

'A remote one, possibly,' murmured Hawkridge from directly behind her.

Amy jumped. Awareness rippled up and down her spine on a wave of tingling heat. He was so close the merest intake of air would bring her into contact with him.

Before she could do anything so perilous, a very small, still-rational part of her brain ordered her take a careful step to the left.

Hawkridge moved at the same time. In the same direction.

'Going somewhere, Mrs Chantry?' he enquired in a low growl.

She didn't have breath to answer. Bracing herself, she took a careful step to the right. With the same result.

Eversleigh grinned at them. 'You know, if you two wish to dance, they're making up sets in the upper room.'

Hawkridge curved his hands firmly around her shoulders to hold her in place and moved to stand beside her.

'Stow it, Pel,' he advised, and in the most fleeting of caresses, unnoticed by anyone but herself, let his hands slide an inch or two down her arms, pressed gently and released her.

'Colborough,' he acknowledged coolly, as if he hadn't managed to addle her wits all over again by what she could have sworn was reassurance. 'I'm surprised to see you here.'

'Not as surprised as I am,' growled his lordship. 'About time you came down to check on things, Hawkridge. Clarissa's been pestering me to hold a Public Day; she can pester you instead. And there's a man-milliner by the name of Tweedy hanging around her. You may oblige me by getting rid of him.'

'Oh, I never interfere in Grandmama's life,' Hawkridge stated, with a blithe disregard for the truth that had Eversleigh choking on a mouthful of champagne.

Lady Hawkridge, completely unperturbed by this reaction, slipped a hand into the crook of Colborough's arm. 'Why don't we take up Pelham's suggestion, Tolly, and join the country dance they're getting up.'

His lordship gaped at the dowager as if she'd suggested they fly through the window on his walking cane. 'Have you finally lost the few wits you possessed, Clarissa?'

'Of course not. But if you want Marc to hold a Public Day, we'll have to leave him to arrange it with Pel. We'll take a little walk instead.' Smiling sunnily, she whisked the cane out of Colborough's hand and tossed it over her shoulder. 'You won't need that.'

Colborough's face turned an alarming shade of red as his cane crashed into the ferns. 'By God, Clarissa, I ought to—'

'I refuse to promenade about the room with a man hobbling along on a cane.'

'*Promenade—*' The Earl made noises suggestive of an impending seizure. 'Where the devil do you think we are? The Steyne at Brighton?'

'Good heavens! Brighton! I haven't been there in years. Such fun as we used to have. Visiting Prinny's little cottage and…'

Still burbling on about the delights of Brighton, her ladyship led Colborough away.

Eversleigh regarded their departing backs and shook his head. 'You know, Marc, I'm as fond of your grandmother as if she was my own, but one of these days someone's going to wring her neck. She didn't even check her aim.'

'No need,' observed Hawkridge, slanting a sardonic look down at Amy. 'Who'd be lurking behind the ferns?'

'Well, there is that,' agreed Eversleigh. 'I suppose I'd better retrieve the dashed cane. When the old boy remembers to hobble, he'll probably use it on me if I don't get to it first.'

Amy came to life with a start. Taking a leaf from the dowager's book, she smiled brightly up at his lordship. 'Allow me, my lord.' She started to sidle towards the ferns. 'I'm sure Lord

Colborough won't use his cane on *me*, and you have a Public Day to plan with Lord Hawkridge.'

'Oh, nothing in that,' Eversleigh assured her, brows lifting as she continued to sidle. 'Hold 'em every summer. Enjoyable day, actually. Marc's people and mine hold a cricket match, and there's a picnic, and games for the children. You know the sort of thing.'

Amy didn't, but that didn't deter her from smiling more sunnily than before. The look that flashed into Hawkridge's eyes had her sidling faster, but the Fates finally decided to do a little smiling themselves. Lady Ingham swept up to them, greeting the gentlemen with her usual enthusiasm.

Amy felt a fern frond brush her shoulder and whisked herself out of sight while Hawkridge's attention was diverted.

Not that she couldn't easily be found, but at least she had a perfectly good excuse for lurking behind the ferns.

And Hawkridge looked as if he was going to be engaged for several minutes. Three or four other ladies had drifted across the room in Lady Ingham's wake, seemingly drawn to him like filings to a magnet. As Amy watched, he bowed to the latest arrival, a faint smile curving his mouth.

He'd been right about one thing, she reflected somewhat darkly. He could be perfectly civil. So civil that every lady in the room seemed completely unaware of the warrior concealed beneath his polite façade. Perhaps because the dangerous glitter in his grey eyes had been cloaked by a cool amusement that dared rather than daunted.

Another mask. Fascinating to watch.

Amy shook her head and wrenched her gaze away. She was not here to be fascinated by Hawkridge. She had someone else to study. Someone, she realised abruptly, pushing a fern frond aside, whose appearance was unknown to her. An instant later she told herself it didn't matter. The whole point of the exercise was *not* to see anyone she recognised.

She located Lucinda almost immediately. Several young

couples were engaged in an impromptu dance in the upper half of the drawing-room, but Lucinda had dropped out, and appeared to be arguing with someone who was moving swiftly towards the doorway leading to the hall.

The crowd shifted, re-formed; a kaleidoscope of black and white, interspersed with brilliant colours. She could only see the back of the man's head and shoulders, but when Lucinda placed a hand on his arm, gazing up with pleading eyes and indicating the room as though urging him to stay, Amy was convinced of the gentleman's identity.

Tall. Quite broad across the shoulders. Brown hair.

Her husband had been slim—*oh, thank God!*—and very fair.

She sagged against the nearest window frame as tension leached from her body. She hardly dared believe it. She was safe. Safe! Mr Chatsworth was totally unknown to her.

Her eyelids closed in relief, then, suddenly realising that someone might notice her propped against the wall as if she was about to collapse, she snapped them open again and straightened.

There was no need to collapse. Everything was all right. She was safe. And now that she wasn't worried sick, she could see that all those small similarities between her husband and Mr Chatsworth were really quite logical. Given the number of wealthy, well-born girls attending Young Ladies Academies, there was sure to be more than one gentleman who made a living by preying on such innocents. And sure to be more than one gentleman with the same initials as her husband.

She'd worried herself into a frenzy over nothing.

Relief rendered her positively euphoric. At that moment the entire world looked rosy; she was even prepared to believe that Mr Chatsworth was genuinely in love with Lucinda.

Remembering the glass of champagne in her hand, Amy lifted it to her lips and drained it with several healthy swallows. Then had to fan her suddenly warm face with her other hand.

'Mrs Chantry, will you stop doing that?'

Amy's hand paused in mid-flutter. Some of her rosy glow faded. Danger of an entirely different sort had arrived. She looked up at Hawkridge's exasperated countenance and promptly plastered a look of innocent enquiry on her face. 'Fanning myself, sir?'

'And don't give me that fluff-brained stare. You know very well what I'm talking about.'

She exchanged the fluff-brained stare for a disapproving frown. 'Well, if you would refrain from introducing me to all and sundry as though I was a friend of the family, I wouldn't need to hide behind ferns. Which, I might add, is my proper place.' She paused, and thought about that. 'No, not ferns precisely, but not in the middle of the dinner table. I mean, the middle of a party.'

Hawkridge eyed her empty glass and thoughtfully removed it from her hand.

Warming to her lecture, Amy swept on. 'And see what has come of it. Lord Colborough thinks I'm a member of the Dalton family, whoever they may be.'

'You probably are,' he murmured. 'Your father might have been destined for a humble curacy, Mrs Chantry, but I wouldn't be surprised to learn that your mother sprang from a minor branch of a noble family. In this case, the Daltons.'

She stared at him. 'Good heavens. What makes you say so?'

'Because you have more than surface elegance and manners. You have breeding.'

Her eyes went round.

'In fact, it didn't occur to me until Colborough mentioned it, probably because your hair is much lighter, but your eyes and lashes are exactly like Nick's.'

'Nick?'

'The Earl of Ravensdene. A friend of mine.'

'Oh. Another earl. There seem to be a lot of you. Earls, that is. Although there's a lot of you, as well.' She looked him up and down, and frowned. 'I don't think I meant to say that.'

Hawkridge's lips twitched. 'Tell me something, Mrs Chantry. Have you ever had champagne before tonight?'

'No,' Amy confessed. Drawing closer, she added confidingly, 'It wasn't on the menu at the poorhouse.'

His brows went up.

Amy didn't notice. She was too busy wondering why she'd said that, too. She caught sight of the glass in Hawkridge's hand and a dismaying explanation occurred to her. 'Oh, my goodness! I'm inebriated!'

This time the smile reached his eyes. 'Not at all, Mrs Chantry. Merely a little hazy. Probably because you hardly ate a morsel at dinner. Some fresh air should do the trick.' Depositing her glass on the edge of a fern-pot, he offered his arm. 'We'll go outside.'

'We certainly will not,' Amy contradicted, deciding to ignore his strictures on her eating habits. Owing to the faint spinning sensation in her head, she could only concentrate on one of his iniquities at a time. 'It would be most improper.'

Hawkridge fixed her with a look of heavy meaning. 'Trust me, it isn't as improper as the two of us continuing to lurk behind the ferns in this furtive fashion.'

'But *I* have a reason to lurk.' She frowned.

'Don't bother trying to recall it,' he said, correctly divining the cause of her expression. 'Besides, you may have noticed that the schoolroom brigade have adjourned to the terrace. Augusta ordered me to make sure their antics don't get out of hand since, according to her, I'm overly concerned about the well-being of her offspring. I came in search of you to request your assistance.'

'Ah. Now, that,' she pronounced, nodding incautiously, 'is exactly what a companion should do.' She placed her hand on his arm—mainly for balance, since nodding had caused the room to tilt in a very strange manner—and smiled sunnily up at him. 'Where is the terrace, my lord?'

Marc took a deep breath, resisted the temptation to take advantage of his quarry's delightfully hazy state, not to mention the cover afforded by his sister's over-enthusiasm for ferns, and began to steer Amy towards the nearest french windows. He felt extremely noble. The last thing he wanted was the company of the noisy crowd on the terrace. On the other hand, there wasn't a lot he could do at a party.

Although an interrogation on the subject of poorhouses wouldn't be a bad idea.

This piece of inspiration vanished as soon as they crossed the threshold. So did his feelings of nobility.

The softest of early-summer breezes enfolded them, carrying a heady combination of scents from the garden. It mingled with Amy's unique feminine essence, and, drifting upward on the warmth of her skin, rose to tease and tantalise.

Marc tensed as desire roared to life within him. The crowd on the terrace vanished. Every precept of civilised behaviour threatened to do the same. He wanted to sweep Amy into his arms and carry her into the dark recesses of the garden, to lie her down, cover her with his body; to sink into the warmth and scent of her until he was sated. Every instinct he possessed strained towards her, wanting…wanting…

Aching, he jolted to a stop a mere foot beyond the window, anchored only by the touch of her hand on his arm. A touch so light he barely felt it, and yet that alone held him back, even while his entire body hardened.

Shaken, Marc clenched his free hand and thanked Providence that the light spilling from the drawing-room was behind them.

And that the object of his fantasy had problems of her own.

She tripped when he halted so abruptly, and frowned down at the flagstones beneath her feet. 'I think the paving needs attention, my lord.'

'Take a deep breath,' he grated. And did the same. It didn't help. He focused on the crowd at the other end of the terrace and tried to remember why they were there.

'Is that a lot of people over there, or do I need to take some more deep breaths?'

A smile tugged at his lips despite himself. 'It's a lot of people,' he confirmed. 'Noisy people. We can supervise them from here. Would you like to sit down, Mrs Chantry?'

'I don't think so,' she said, subjecting the question to lengthy consideration.

'Then let us take a short stroll to those steps while we discuss—'

'Earls!'

The interruption was as abrupt as the sudden tension in the little hand resting on his arm. Marc looked down, brows raised. He got the distinct impression that Amy was avoiding his gaze.

'I don't have anything to do with them,' she said, flushing.

His eyes narrowed. She was recovering fast if she could come up with an apt red herring at short notice. On the other hand, red herrings could sometimes be just as informative as the truth. He decided to follow the bait.

'I hesitate to contradict you, Mrs Chantry, but you're talking to an earl right this minute.'

Amy waved that aside. 'I mean, I'm not a close connection of any earls.' She shook her head, apparently quite worried by the possibility. 'My mother would have told me.'

'I didn't say you were a close connection of the Daltons,' he corrected gently. 'However, we'll know for certain when I discover the name of your maternal grandfather.'

'What! But…' She stared up at him in dismay. 'I don't want you to discover any such thing. Why should you wish to do so? He's probably dead and—'

'Probably? I thought you said he was dead.'

Her colour deepened. 'It seemed a logical assumption, sir.

You must know that I can't be sure, however. Besides—' she lifted her chin '—he's dead as far as I'm concerned.'

'An understandable sentiment, Mrs Chantry, especially if you did indeed spend time in a—'

'So there you are, Hawkridge.' Lucinda stormed up to them, a vision in white sarcenet decorated with pink and white rose-buds. The same flowers were placed artfully among her curls. Unfortunately, the sweetly feminine costume did not match her expression. 'Now that you've forced poor Jeremy to leave, I hope you're satisfied.'

Marc resigned himself to postponing questions about Amy's acquaintanceship with the poorhouse. 'Spare us the histrionics, Lucinda. How did I cause Chatsworth to leave?'

'He said he was intimidated.'

Marc snorted. 'Since I exchanged no more than half a dozen words with him, I suggest he was intimidated by his surround-ings. You should be grateful to be spared future embarrass-ment. If he feels out of place here, how's he going to cope in London?'

A good question, Amy mused. She found herself harbouring a sneaky fellow feeling for Mr Chatsworth. Since he wasn't her husband come inconveniently to life, she could afford it— even if it was highly unlikely that anyone was going to fall in love with her and carry her off to the terrors of the metropolis.

The thought had a surprisingly lowering effect.

She pushed it aside in time to hear Hawkridge advise his niece to take herself off.

'I shall be happy to oblige you,' Lucinda retorted. 'Fortu-nately, there are others who show more sympathy for the ag-ony endured by—'

'Lucinda, please.' Lady Nettlebed, an attractive dark-haired matron, fashionably attired in midnight-blue silk, stepped on to the terrace. She had a shawl draped over one arm. 'You can be heard in the drawing-room. And you shouldn't have come straight from a warm room without a shawl.'

'Wrap it around Uncle Marc,' Lucinda recommended, stomping back to her friends. 'Preferably around his neck.'

Lady Nettlebed gazed after her daughter with acute dismay before turning a look of displeasure on Hawkridge. Since she was several years older than her brother, and was blessed with the same cool grey eyes and patrician features, the look might have been effective had it been turned on anyone else.

'As if encouraging Crispin to defy me isn't bad enough, you're now upsetting Lucinda. I hope you're satisfied, Marc.'

'I wish people would stop hoping that,' he muttered. 'It's not an imminent possibility.'

At the growled comment Amy felt a craven desire to melt into the shadows. Unfortunately, her hand was still resting on Hawkridge's arm; though the flagstones had ceased their sudden tendency to move, she wasn't as confident about the steadiness of her head. She made a mental note never to touch champagne again. It obviously had a very detrimental effect on her senses.

Rather like Hawkridge, actually.

As if to prove the point, the muscles beneath her hand tensed. The thrill that rippled through her at the awareness of leashed power was quite shocking. It was also totally unwarranted, because Hawkridge was clearly taking a grip on nothing more than his patience.

'If you'd calm down, Gussie, you'd see the wisdom of—'

'Calm down?' Lady Nettlebed's voice rose. 'When you wilfully intend to lead my only son into *danger*? No wonder Lucinda is so stubborn. I know who she gets it from.'

Amy cleared her throat discreetly. Since she couldn't melt into the shadows, her second impulse was to help.

'Ah…if Lucinda is stubborn, ma'am, perhaps it's no bad thing. She's unlikely to be led astray, or—or cozened into a hurried marriage.'

Lady Nettlebed glanced at her as though surprised to see her there, then shook her head. 'Oh, dear, how very rude of me. I'm so sorry, Amy. What with Lucinda giving me no peace, and Crispin not speaking to me at all, I scarcely know if I'm on my head or my heels. And all Grandmama can say is that Marc knows what he's doing.' She whisked a scrap of lace out of the dainty reticule hanging from her wrist and dabbed at her suddenly brimming eyes. 'Nobody understands.'

Hawkridge's mouth curved wryly. 'Gus, you know I won't let anything happen to your precious cub. I'll come over to-morrow and we'll talk about it. In the meantime, I can see Colborough getting redder in the face, so you'd better go back inside before Grandmama succeeds in driving him insane.'

'She's probably telling him about that awful Mr Tweedy inviting her to the Assembly Rooms at Teignmouth.' Lady Nettlebed sniffed and dabbed harder. 'You see what happens when you're in London, Marc? But *I* don't interfere. *I* don't tell you what you should do, or that you should visit more often, because I know why you stay away.'

With a final muffled sob, her ladyship whisked about and fled into the drawing-room.

'Well, well,' Hawkridge murmured, brows raised. He glanced down at Amy and smiled faintly. 'I'd apologise, Mrs Chantry, but you might as well know the worst.'

'Worst?' Amy eyed him suspiciously. 'What worst?'

'Families,' he said cryptically. 'I suspect you've never ex-perienced the dubious delights of domesticity at its most basic. Brace yourself. The next few weeks should prove enlighten-ing. Now, I think we've spent enough time as chaperons. We shall adjourn to the supper table, where you will eat more than you did at dinner, if I have to feed you myself.'

This rather high-handed decree sailed right over Amy's head. She was far too busy contemplating the dubious delight welling up inside her at the knowledge that Hawkridge wasn't planning an early departure.

She wasn't sure which emotion was uppermost, dubiety or

delight; both shimmered through her in equal proportions. The unsettling mix threatened to make her head spin all over again.

She tried to tell herself that she had no business feeling delight. After all, it was Hawkridge's portrait that had enthralled her, not the man. She told herself that dubiety wasn't necessary, because he would be kept too busy with a Public Day, teaching his nephew to sail, preventing his niece from eloping, and getting rid of Mr Tweedy, to enthrall her any further.

The result was not what she'd hoped for. Anticipation continued to swirl inside her until she felt as though she stood poised on the brink of a precipice. The sensation was somewhat alarming. Especially for one who had never coped very well with heights.

Under the circumstances, teetering on the brink of a precipice was not a good idea.

It was not a good idea at all.

Chapter Seven

It would have been too much to state that squirrels wearing very heavy boots had taken up residence inside Amy's head the following morning, but she felt a trifle frayed when she descended the stairs at an hour considerably later than her usual time of arising.

She couldn't entirely attribute her fragile state to the glass of champagne she'd imbibed the night before. Not when she'd spent several sleepless hours worrying about her indiscreet utterances at Lady Nettlebed's party. Not after the inordinate amount of time she'd spent remembering the gentle understanding in Hawkridge's voice when he'd tried to reassure his sister about Crispin.

Not when she'd passed the long hours before dawn contemplating the lowering suspicion that, like Lady Nettlebed, she knew why Hawkridge didn't spend a great deal of time in Devon. After all, constant encounters with the lady he'd wished to make his wife, only to see her married to another, could be nothing but painful.

Brooding over that explanation had caused another hour or two of unrest. All in all she had definitely lost the euphoric glow occasioned by her glimpse of Mr Chatsworth.

The sight that greeted her when she reached the hall did not augur well for its return any time in the near future. Mr Tweedy was standing in the library doorway, contemplating the hall as though assessing the value of its contents.

Amy regarded his portly form with displeasure. A scarlet waistcoat was stretched over his girth, making him look like a particularly well-fed robin. When he turned his head in her direction, beady eyes, a short beaky nose and ruddy cheeks adorned with side whiskers added to the illusion. His pursed lips curled upwards in a smile that set her teeth on edge.

'Ah, Mrs Chantry.' Tweedy minced forward, beaming and rubbing his hands together. 'And how are we this morning, after our little party last night? Not too overcome by the honour?'

Amy raised her brows. '*I* enjoyed a most convivial evening, sir.'

Tweedy's smile lost some of its brilliance. 'How fortunate. I believe one of the other guests—a Certain Young Gentleman, shall we say—left rather early. I thought you may have felt the same, er, discomfort. On the other hand, one must grasp one's opportunities to study the ways of polite company, mustn't one?'

The stony stare she sent him in response to this question bounced off Tweedy's armour of determined geniality without so much as inflicting a dent. Amy set her lips.

'Were you expecting to see Lady Hawkridge, sir? She has not yet come downstairs.'

'Oh, no, dear lady, I wouldn't dream of disturbing her ladyship. I merely stopped by to pay my respects on my way back from the village. Hawkridge's groom—Mawson, I believe—offered me a lift up the hill. I was happy to accept. The climb sometimes proves rather too much for one of my, er, mature years.'

Amy inclined her head. Since Tweedy's rented house was half a mile beyond the Manor and he usually made the trip to Ottersmead in his gig, she suspected he'd deliberately set out on foot, hoping for an 'accidental' meeting with Lady Hawkridge.

'Not that you young people will enter into my feelings on the matter,' he continued. 'I was saying so only a little while ago as I was chatting to Mr Chatsworth.' Tweedy tittered at his mild play on words. 'He was standing outside the Receiving Office, you know, when Mawson and I were both collecting mail.'

'Indeed, sir.'

'Always delightful to receive communications from one's friends, isn't it? However, the walk back to my cottage is rather long. When Hawkridge's groom gave me a lift, I offered to deposit your mail here in the library by way of thanks. I have seen your butler do so, and knew precisely where to put it.'

'I see.' Amy glanced quickly past Mr Tweedy into the library. The pile of letters on her desk—or rather, Hawkridge's desk—proved the veracity of Tweedy's excuse. She resigned herself to being polite. 'Thank you, sir.'

'Don't mention it, my dear. I'm always happy to be of service. Every little attention must be observed, mustn't it. I'm sure you understand. After all, your own position depends upon such careful observances, does it not?'

'I try to make myself useful to Lady Hawkridge,' Amy replied with as much patience as growing irritation allowed. She'd sensed Tweedy's dislike of her at their previous encounters, but the dowager's presence had prevented him from firing such openly barbed darts.

His smile slipped a little further. 'Indeed, Mrs Chantry, indeed. However, your usefulness has its limits. Ladies of a Certain Age need a man about the place to take care of those little matters of business that tend to puzzle the female mind.'

'This female mind is a little less easily puzzled than you might suppose,' Amy said drily. 'Besides, you may have noticed that Lord Hawkridge is in residence?' An ironic smile curved her mouth. 'He is quite enough man about the place.'

Tweedy permitted himself another titter. 'No doubt you find him rather intimidating,' he agreed archly. 'But he won't be here forever. I've heard he never stays longer than a week at the outside. Perhaps you, too, should start planning your departure, Mrs Chantry.'

Amy's brows rose. 'At your suggestion, sir? I hardly think so.'

'I merely suggest that you consider the future, my dear. Circumstances are forever changing, are they not? One should never dismiss advice out of hand. You could return to Bath and consider, er, employment with a gentleman. One with reasonable means, of course.'

'That advice, sir, is as unnecessary as it is unwarranted,' Amy informed him roundly. 'I have no intention of leaving Lady Hawkridge's employment. Nor do I anticipate any change in her ladyship's circumstances that would cause my employment to be terminated. Now, if you will excuse me...'

Tweedy's pursed lips puffed out in a small pout. 'Of course, Mrs Chantry, of course. Far be it from me to keep you from your duties. Perform them well, my dear, but keep in mind that informing Lady Hawkridge of this conversation is not one of them.'

'I wouldn't dream of repeating a conversation of such little significance, sir.'

'Yes, you are very confident, Mrs Chantry.' The pout became a spiteful sneer. 'No doubt you have become quite the favourite. I suspected as much. However—' with another glance about the hall '—there appears to be enough for two.' Tweedy stepped away from the library doorway to retrieve the beaver hat he'd placed on the hall table, and sent her a malicious smile. 'Perhaps Mr Chatsworth will be more amenable to advice from one who is older and wiser. Ottersmead is quite a large place, but I doubt it can accommodate all three of us.'

Already halfway to the front door to see off her unwelcome guest, Amy wheeled about and stared at him. 'What on earth do you mean by that, sir?'

'Think about it, my dear.' Tweedy minced past her to the door, opened it and started down the front steps. His parting words fell into the sunny morning like cold little pellets of rain. 'When one person in our walk of life is unmasked, people tend to ask questions about other newcomers to the district.'

Amy stared after him, frowning. Unease stirred faintly at the back of her mind. Though Tweedy clearly considered her a rival for the dowager's patronage, he'd always been perfectly civil to her, if not downright unctuous. He'd never given her any indication that he considered her anything other than a lady forced to find employment due to straitened circumstances.

What had made him suspect she was something else?

She closed the front door and walked slowly towards the library, pausing in front of the enormous gilt-framed mirror hanging above the hall table to examine her reflection. This morning, in deference to the faint ache behind her eyes, she'd tied her hair back with a simple band of Wellington green silk, leaving it free at the back to fall in artless ringlets to her shoulders. One or two tendrils had defied the ribbon to curl at her brow and temples, rendering the style rather informal for a companion. But not, she decided, studying her cream muslin gown adorned, today, with a green sash to match the ribbon, unsuitable for a morning at home.

What had Tweedy seen that apparently put her on a par with him and Mr Chatsworth?

What, for that matter, did Tweedy know of Mr Chatsworth? Did he suspect him of dishonesty merely because he himself lived by his wits, or did he have some definite knowledge that would discredit Lucinda's suitor? If he did, should she warn someone? Hawkridge? Lord Nettlebed? What could she say?

More uneasy than ever, Amy wandered into the library, her

gaze going straight to the pile of mail. Her frown deepened as she remembered that Pickles hadn't been in the hall. No doubt Tweedy had entered the house without ringing the bell; she had no trouble imagining him doing so. But most people on an errand of courtesy would have left the handful of letters in the hall, not made themselves further at home by strolling into the library as if they owned the place.

Simple presumption?

Or, she thought, focusing abruptly on the top of the pile where a folded and sealed square of paper bore her name and direction, had Tweedy originally intended to express his sentiments in writing?

Amy contemplated the missive for a moment, then picked it up and broke the seal. The sheet was devoid of message or signature, but as she smoothed out the folds another smaller piece of paper fluttered out. It appeared to be a cutting from a newspaper. She opened it.

And felt the blood drain from her face with a speed that had her grabbing for the edge of the desk for support. Shock coated her entire body in a sheet of ice. She couldn't move, couldn't think. Could only hold the report of the robbery at Bristol clenched in a hand that wanted to fling the paper aside and could not.

Dear God. Who would send her such a thing?

A violent tremor shuddered through her, breaking her frozen paralysis. Shaking with reaction, hardly able to look at the cutting without feeling sick, she hurried over to the fireplace. Paper and kindling were always laid, although since the advent of warmer weather a fire hadn't been necessary. She crouched, reaching for the tinder-box, then halted abruptly as rational thought reasserted itself.

How could she explain why she'd lit a fire on such a warm, sunny morning?

Amy eased her grip around the paper, took a deep breath, and forced herself to think.

No ghost had sent her that cutting; she'd established that Mr Chatsworth wasn't her husband—the only other person to whom the article would mean something. It had to be Tweedy; trying to frighten her away, but unable to resist baiting her verbally when he'd seen her.

No wonder he'd deposited the mail in the library where she would probably be the first to see it.

But why the cutting? Why would he assume it meant anything to her? She'd never encountered him before she'd come to live at Hawkridge Manor. Had he known her husband? Seen her with James from a distance? It was possible. Those who lived by their wits on the fringes of Society must sometimes encounter others of their ilk.

The more intelligent denizens of the criminal world were even more tightly knit.

But if Tweedy knew about her past, why hadn't he threatened her with outright exposure just now, instead of merely rendering advice?

Amy shook her head. There were too many unanswerable questions for the puzzle to be easily solved, but one thing seemed clear. Tweedy couldn't know everything or he would have used his knowledge to discredit her.

Amy set her lips in a determined line and stuffed the cutting into the pocket of her gown. If Tweedy thought he could intimidate her into leaving, he was in for a sad disappointment. Without proof, he could do nothing.

Feeling more defiant than brave, despite the logic of her reasoning, she put her hand on the woodbox to push herself upright. One of the logs shifted slightly. Before she could blink, something large, black and hairy scuttled into her line of vision. It stopped less than an inch from her fingers and stared at her with tiny malevolent eyes.

Amy forgot all about Mr Tweedy.

Marc strode into the hall, and was halfway up the stairs when an ear-splitting scream, reverberating with feminine fear and outrage, threatened to bring the house down.

Wheeling, he put his hand on the bannister, vaulted it and landed in the hall running.

When he burst through the library doorway a pounding heartbeat later, the sight that met his eyes pulled him up short.

Amy was standing on top of his desk, one hand clutching her throat, the other holding her skirts at a level that was not quite shocking and more than a little tantalising.

He allowed himself one quick glance at elegantly turned ankles and slender calves clad in white cotton stockings that for some odd reason sent a jolt of pure lust through him before lifting his gaze to her face.

'*You didn't get rid of that spider!*' she shrieked, still at the top of her lungs.

Marc closed the door, leaned back against it and decided it wouldn't improve matters to inform Amy that she'd just scared the wits out of him. 'I did try,' he said, with great self-restraint. The remark didn't appear to soothe her in the least.

'Well, you'll have to try again, my lord! And this time you'd better succeed!'

He took a deep breath, determinedly kept his gaze on her face—mainly for his own sanity—and relaxed the battle-ready tension in his muscles. 'Certainly, Mrs Chantry. If you'd give me the spider's precise location, I shall be happy to oblige you.'

'There.' Amy pointed a shaking hand at the woodbox. 'It climbed on to that log and…and stared at me.'

Marc quirked a brow. 'Stared at you.'

'Yes! As if I was its next meal!'

A muscle quivered in his cheek.

'Don't you dare laugh at me, sir.'

'I wouldn't dream of it, Mrs Chantry. Over here, you say?' He strode over to the fireplace and hunkered down to examine the log. A long thin leg protruded from beneath it. No doubt about it. The spider had taken refuge, its nerves shattered by the scream at close quarters. It would be an act of mercy to put the creature out of its misery.

Marc picked up the log and smacked it smartly down on the one beneath it, spider undermost.

Amy let out another shriek and clapped her hands over her ears.

Sternly suppressing a grin, Marc shook the corpse into the fireplace and straightened, brushing his hands. 'There. Nothing like rescuing a fair maiden from a spider to start the day.'

The fair maiden uncovered her ears and glared at him. 'Well, I'm very grateful for the rescue, my lord, but did you have to kill the poor creature?'

'Poor creature? A minute ago it was a carnivorous monster.'

Amy blushed and bit her lip.

Releasing the grin tugging at his lips, Marc strolled towards her. 'To tell you the truth, Mrs Chantry, I considered a speedy dispatch to be more merciful than chasing the spider all over the room, prior to showing it the door.'

'Oh.' She shuddered at the very thought. 'I see what you mean, sir. I dare say even a spider would be terrified by such an ordeal.'

'I meant it was more merciful for you,' he corrected drily. He stopped beside the desk and held out his hand. 'As it is, you may descend from your perch in perfect safety.'

Amy glanced briefly at his hand. He was apparently under the impression that descending from the desk was going to be easy.

When she didn't immediately avail herself of his assistance, he raised a brow. 'I assure you, Mrs Chantry, your assailant is quite dead.'

'Yes, I know that, sir. Thank you.'

'Well?'

Amy felt herself blushing again. 'Um—perhaps if you were to leave the room…'

Both brows went up. 'I beg your pardon?'

'I mean, what if the servants heard me scream? It would be very worrying for them, and—'

'This house is very old, Mrs Chantry. Its walls are thick. I doubt if anyone heard you from the servants' quarters. However, in case I'm mistaken, you'd better come down from there before someone feels moved to investigate.'

Amy sighed and gave up the task of trying to get rid of her rescuer so she could sit down on the desk and slither off. 'This is no doubt going to sound absurd, my lord, but…I have a small problem with heights.'

'Heights?' The quizzical gleam in his eyes turned incredulous. She watched in resignation as he measured the distance to the floor.

'Mrs Chantry,' he began in a reasonable tone that made her seriously consider screaming again, 'the road to the village is situated at a ''height''. You didn't appear to have any trouble with that. What is the problem here?'

'The problem, sir, is that this desk is not the road to the village. The road to the village, you might have noticed, is set at some distance from the edge of the cliff, causing one to look out over the sea. In fact, in several places there are trees blocking one's view of the descent. However, if I was to stand at the edge of the cliff and look straight down, I would probably *fall* down. That is not a desirable outcome, my lord.'

There was a suspicious hint of movement about his mouth. 'A most *un*desirable outcome, Mrs Chantry. However, take a look at your feet in relation to the floor. You are not standing on the edge of a cliff. The top of that desk is about three feet high. That is hardly what one would call a great height.'

Amy began to feel slightly desperate. 'From your point of view that may be true, sir, but my eyes are not in my feet. They're in my head—which is more than another five feet higher. That is over eight feet, my lord. Eight feet! And when I look directly down it seems a lot worse.'

'Then don't look down,' he suggested, the curve of his mouth suddenly, inexplicably, tender. 'Just step over the edge.'

When she stared at him, aghast at this reckless suggestion, he added softly, 'I'll catch you.'

Amy's breath caught instead. She had the strangest feeling he was talking about something far removed from stepping off a desk. Before she could decide precisely what, however, Hawkridge lowered his hand and tilted his head consideringly.

'Of course if you consider that too risky an option, I can always lift you down.'

It was the gently musing tone that did it. Amy straightened her spine and glared at him. 'Kindly give me your hand, sir.' She took a determined step forward. 'And if you say one word about this to—'

The door crashed open as Lady Hawkridge burst into the library in her usual whirlwind fashion.

Already teetering on the brink, Amy jerked her head up, wobbled for several unnerving seconds, then pitched forward.

'Good morning, Grandmama,' Hawkridge said calmly as she tumbled into his arms.

'Good morning, Marc dearest. How kind of you to help Amy off the desk.'

Amy made a strangled sound of shock and virtually leapt from Hawkridge's arms. The thought flashed through her mind that he'd let her go only because of his grandmother's presence, but there was no time to contemplate the hard tension in his body. The crumpled piece of paper in her pocket, shoved too hurriedly out of sight while she'd been in a crouched position, chose that moment to fall out.

Everyone watched its progress to the floor. When Hawkridge moved to retrieve it, Amy pounced. Snatching it out from under his fingers, she stuffed the paper back in her pocket.

'A…a recipe for Denmark Lotion,' she stammered wildly,

straightening like a marionette whose strings had been violently tugged.

Hawkridge studied her flushed face, his eyes so intent she wondered they didn't bore straight through to her scrambling wits. She turned to the dowager, knowing she should leave well alone but unable to stop babbling.

'I hope you don't mind me cutting it out of the paper, ma'am. It's very good for freckles, you know.'

'No, of course not, dear. But—' Lady Hawkridge tilted her head '—you don't have any freckles.'

'Well, no, but one never knows when a freckle may appear, does one? And since I take quite frequent walks to the village, I thought...'

She caught a glimpse of Hawkridge's politely raised brows and knew he didn't believe a word she was saying.

'Oh, dear, and I was about to ask if you'd take a basket of clothes to Lavender Cottage,' the dowager murmured, earning Amy's undying gratitude. 'But you may go in the barouche if you don't wish to walk, Amy.'

'Not at all, ma'am.' Her voice still sounded as if someone was shaking her back and forth. Amy took a steadying breath, and carefully avoided Hawkridge's gaze. 'I enjoy my walks to the village, especially when the objective is a visit at the Cottage.'

Her ladyship beamed. 'I know you take a great interest in our little project, dear. And the children love to see you.'

'Yes, well...' She started towards the door with what she hoped was a firm step. 'Let me fetch my bonnet and pelisse and—'

'Be back here in five minutes, Mrs Chantry. I'll drive you to the village.'

Amy's firm step faltered rather badly. There wasn't a single hint of suggestion in Hawkridge's tone. It was an order. She looked back over her shoulder.

He smiled—like a cat who had just put out a very large paw

and pinned down a mouse intent on escape. 'After all, we wouldn't want to expose your complexion to the elements any longer than is necessary, would we? And my greys are overdue for some exercise.'

She was in a great deal of trouble. Hawkridge seemed to have developed the habit of setting neat little traps for her without any warning. She could have refused a favour on her own account, but there was no gracious way to do so if he was going out anyway.

'Thank you, my lord,' she managed to say with creditable calm. 'I won't keep you above a moment.'

The curve of his mouth still held far too much satisfaction for her peace of mind. Amy tilted her chin. She might have been outwitted, but she was far from pinned down. She left the room as if driving into Ottersmead with Hawkridge was all her own idea.

'Are you quite comfortable, Mrs Chantry?'

As comfortable as one could be when expecting an interrogation to start at any moment.

'Yes, thank you, my lord. Your phaeton is exceptionally well sprung.'

Hawkridge cast an amused glance down at her as they bowled through the gates and turned on to the main road to Ottersmead. 'So that's why you have a death grip on the hood. You're afraid you'll bounce off at the first bump.'

Amy flushed and removed her hand, folding it over its clenched twin in her lap. 'I trust the road is not that perilous,' she returned somewhat drily.

'I trust so, too,' Hawkridge murmured. 'Especially as I thought this route might be less harrowing for you than the cliff road.'

She blinked at him, wondering if she'd heard correctly. The road they were on wound inland past woods and fields for a mile or two before dividing into two branches; the right lead-

ing to the main post road, the left curving back towards Ottersmead. The route lacked spectacular views and was longer.
She'd thought Hawkridge had chosen it so he'd have plenty
of time for interrogation.

Instead, he was taking her foolish fear of heights seriously.

No, she thought immediately. Impossible. He must be teasing her. After all, anyone who had trouble descending from a
desk had to expect a little raillery on the subject.

'Thank you, my lord. But as long as I see *terra firma* around
my feet in every direction, or I have something to hold on to,
I do not have a problem.'

His smile was wry. 'Does that mean I put the hood up to
no purpose? I thought you might feel more secure in a high
carriage if you couldn't look down.'

This time she gaped at him. Her brain seemed to be having
a great deal of trouble catching up with the conversation. Such
a small thing: raising the hood because she was perched several feet above the ground. She wouldn't have thought of it
herself until it was too late.

She shook her head in bemusement. 'I don't know what to
say, my lord. Thank you.'

He cast her a searching glance. 'You sound positively astonished, Mrs Chantry. Do you think me so incapable of care or
consideration?'

'No…no…of course not. I…' She floundered; caught in a
morass of surprise and conjecture. 'I mean, I know you care
about your family, but—'

When he raised a brow she sank deeper. 'Well, you only
have to look at the way you tell them how to run their—'

'Yes, Mrs Chantry?'

Amy took a firm grip on her wits. 'What I mean, sir, is that
you show great consideration for the welfare of your family.'

'To the point of telling them how to run their lives.'

The gleam in his eyes had her winning free of the verbal
quagmire tugging at her feet. 'If you must know, sir, it seemed

that way at last night's dinner. However, I quite understand
that you don't wish to see your young relatives fall into trouble
because of over-protection by one parent and a disinclination
to bestir—'

She finally managed to put a halt on her runaway tongue.

'A disinclination to bestir himself on the part of the other,'
Hawkridge finished for her. 'A telling summation, Mrs Chantry.'

He sounded more thoughtful than annoyed, but Amy
flushed. 'And one I had no right to make,' she said immediately. 'Please forgive me, sir, I—'

'Stop that,' he said very quietly.

She stopped. So did her breathing.

'You may say anything you wish to me, Mrs Chantry.' His
gaze was very direct. 'Anything. On any subject.'

Anything? On any subject?

'Uh, my lord…the road? It is starting to curve towards Ottersmead, and unless your horses know the way…'

He returned his gaze to the road, but not before she caught
the quick flash of laughter in his eyes. 'That wasn't the subject
I had in mind,' he murmured. His mouth curved in a faintly
crooked smile. 'I want you to trust me, Amy.'

'I…I do trust you, sir.'

'One wouldn't have thought so the other night when, after
I'd assured you I no longer suspected you of ulterior motives,
I was attempting to discover something of your background.'

When silence greeted that remark, he continued as if they
were discussing nothing more innocuous than the weather.

'But tell me where you received such an accurate insight
into my family. Was your own mother over-protective or
weak? Either would account for a marriage entered into when
you were scarcely past childhood.'

'I was seventeen!' Amy exclaimed indignantly. And obviously no more sensible now. He had just managed to slip
under her guard again by saying her name in that spine-

tingling, velvety dark tone. It was a tone he'd never used before.

She didn't want to think about why he was using it now. Or why he'd used her name. Or why he wanted her to trust him. He was going somewhere with this, but she was too bemused by the entire conversation to pay much attention to its point.

'And my mother was neither over-protective nor weak. In fact, she had very little to do with my marriage.'

'You managed the business yourself?'

'I had no choice, sir. Mama was ill for a long time before her death. I had to manage for both of us.'

'You're used to that, aren't you?' he said, glancing down. 'It's not a matter of trust, although you don't trust easily. It's a matter of independence.'

'You should be able to understand that, my lord. You, too, had to take charge at a young age. I dare say that's why everyone has become accustomed to leaning on you.'

'Never mind my family for the moment, Mrs Chantry. It's your reticence on the subject of your past that interests me. Although a predilection for fighting your own battles goes a long way towards explaining it.'

'I'm glad something's been made clear,' she muttered.

'The point I'm trying to make,' he said, sounding as if his patience was beginning to wear thin, 'is that you no longer need to be so independent.'

'Why not?'

'Because you're living under my protection, damn it. That means if you're in any kind of—'

'I don't see why I should stop fighting my own battles just because I'm living in your house. You don't lean on anyone.'

'That's different,' he bit out. 'I'm a man.'

'All the more reason to keep my independence,' Amy retorted, starting to feel rather annoyed herself. 'When a man is in charge, disaster usually results.'

'Is that why you lied about that scrap of paper this morning? To avoid disaster?'

She slammed back in her seat as if he'd whipped the horses into a headlong gallop.

Although why she should be so stunned was a mystery. He was merely running true to form.

'Perhaps I should have explained in greater detail, Mrs Chantry, the consequences of your continuing to fiddle with the truth.'

The very faintest thread of warning wound through the velvet of his tone. Outrage rescued Amy from her stunned paralysis. She actually felt her breasts swell as she drew in enough air to rend him limb from limb.

Metaphorically speaking.

'Let me tell you, sir, that a request for my trust is not of much use when it's immediately followed by threats! Yes, I did lie about that wretched piece of paper, and you would have done exactly the same in my place. In fact, you do do it. All the time!'

That switched his attention away from her iniquities.

He hauled on the reins so abruptly Amy had to grab for the hood to prevent herself being catapulted into the air. The horses plunged to a stop, snorting and squealing their indignation at their unaccustomed treatment.

Their owner added a few muttered curses to the din before they settled down. Tying the reins around the brake, he turned to her with a distinctly menacing glitter in his eyes. 'Would you care to explain that statement, Mrs Chantry?'

Amy swallowed, and decided she didn't particularly care to explain that statement in the least. She could hardly tell a prominent member of polite society that, despite his façade of civility, she had no trouble picturing him prowling through tracts of icy wilderness, hunting woolly mammoths and other such prehistoric creatures.

'You take me up much too fast, sir,' she muttered. 'All I

meant was that you use the same social...*lies*, if you will, that we all use to spare people's feelings.'

To her relief, the hard line of Hawkridge's mouth softened. An instant later he started to grin. 'Several members of polite society might argue with you on that score, Mrs Chantry.' Then, more soberly, 'Very well, I agree with you to a point. Most of us try to behave with some semblance of civility, but—'

'Indeed, we do, my lord. Just think what a shambles we'd be in without polite platitudes and—'

'I said I agree *to a point*. What I wish to know is whose feelings were you trying to spare this morning? And why?'

She clamped her lips together and lifted her chin.

'You don't want to look at me like that, Mrs Chantry. The result might be more than you'd expect.'

'More threats, sir?'

'Damn it, Amy, you were worried about something—and I'm not talking about that blasted spider. I understand you sparing my grandmother's feelings; mine are a damn sight less easily overset. Kindly forget your distrust of the male sex for a moment and tell me what the devil was on that paper?'

Amy sighed. Hawkridge was quite capable of sitting here in the middle of the road until he got an answer. She might as well give him one. If he asked to see the paper, she could always say she'd destroyed it.

Uncomfortably aware that lies seemed to be piling up on top of each other, she resolved to stick as closely to the truth as possible.

'If you must know, sir, I received a message from Mr Tweedy, warning me not to interfere in his pursuit of Lady Hawkridge.'

'What!' Hawkridge's eyes narrowed. 'You deduced all that from a newspaper cutting?'

'It was particularly applicable to my situation, sir.' *That* was certainly the truth. 'I thought such a thing would only upset her ladyship. Now, may we continue to Ottersmead before—'

'Particularly applicable— In what way?'

'It referred to the behaviour of servants. You know, if another carriage were to come around that bend—'

'Good God! Do you think that's going to be the end of the matter? For one thing, Mrs Chantry, you are not a servant. And for another, you will hand over any more warning letters to me. Is that clear?'

'It was *my* warning letter,' she retorted, wincing at the idiocy of the statement.

Hawkridge made a snarling sound in his throat and reached for the reins. Amy received the distinct impression he wanted to reach for her throat.

'This is no time for your stubborn independence,' he grated. 'Especially when your reasoning seems to lack any semblance of logic. Did you stop to consider for one moment that a modicum of distress on Grandmama's part *now*, might be preferable to the greater distress caused the longer Tweedy is allowed to run his course?'

'Lady Hawkridge would be no more distressed to see the back of Mr Tweedy than you would, sir. She is, however, kind-hearted enough to be upset on *my* account. *That* is what I wished to avoid.'

He whipped his head around to study her for a moment, then shortened the reins and gave his horses the office to start. 'Did Tweedy threaten you?'

'Not in so many words. He seemed to be labouring under a similar misapprehension about my past as your own.' Still smarting under the lash of his words, she elevated her nose. 'I would like to know what it is about me that immediately causes *some* people to assume the worst.'

Hawkridge winced. Amy was incensed enough to derive considerable pleasure from his reaction. It was small consolation for that remark about her lack of logic.

'In Tweedy's case, Mrs Chantry, he would probably assume the worst about anyone in your position. It isn't personal.'

'Hmph.'

'As for myself, I did admit I was wrong about you.'

'Hmmph!'

'And in all fairness, you must admit that Grandmama's previous lack of judgement, not to mention the lack of information about your background, greatly influenced my opinion.'

'*Hmmph!*'

'However, I'm happy to inform you that, even if I wasn't already convinced of your innocence in respect to your past, your present behaviour would do the trick.'

'I *beg* your pardon, sir?'

'That mutinous little chin is just begging to be captured so its owner can be thoroughly kissed.'

'*Wha—?*'

'Fortunately for you, the village is upon us.'

They swept into the main street of Ottersmead before Amy could get her mouth closed again.

Chapter Eight

'By the way,' Hawkridge said, as if he hadn't just sent her thoughts whirling off on several shockingly unsuitable tangents. 'Who are the clothes for?' He cast a glance at the basket reposing at her feet. 'Obviously not naked sculptors.'

Amy choked and regained her powers of speech. 'Really, my lord!'

He grinned. 'Yes, Mrs Chantry?'

Despite grappling with a nerve-tingling memory of the last time he'd kissed her, Amy giggled. It was useless trying to think of a quelling response in the face of that wicked grin. Besides, wickedness was rather reassuring. His remark about kissing her could be put down to the same diabolical tendency.

She sternly quelled a niggling feeling of disappointment.

'The clothes are intended for the children at Lavender Cottage,' she informed him with as much dignity as she could muster.

'Yes, I deduced that there were children at Lavender Cottage. Where is the place? I don't recall a house of that name in Ottersmead.'

'I believe it used to be known as the old Smitton residence. Lady Hawkridge rented it last month on behalf of the orphaned children and…and unmarried mothers of the parish.'

She felt the sharp glance he sent her like a flash of heat against her cheek and resolutely kept her eyes to the front. 'I'm surprised Lady Hawkridge hasn't mentioned the project to you.'

'I'm not,' he returned somewhat drily. 'The last tenant tried to rob her. Although how she could equate Bartle with orphans is beyond me. However, the Smitton place is on a steepish street. We'll leave my phaeton at the Green Man and walk.'

Amy took a moment or two to digest this information. She'd been rigidly braced for criticism or comment, even an implication, about the influence she must have asserted on behalf of the local orphans and unwed mothers; by the time she realised nothing of the sort was forthcoming, Hawkridge was turning his horses into the cobbled space in front of the inn.

She was instantly diverted by a noise from the Esplanade opposite that sounded like the squawking of several seagulls.

'I was under the impression the Society for the Beautification of our Village had already met this week,' Hawkridge remarked, frowning at the small crowd of ladies responsible for the racket. He drew his horses to a halt.

'They have, sir.'

'Then why is a good proportion of the membership waving to us from across the road?'

'I have no idea, my lord.' She waved back to the crowd of chattering ladies, hoping the excitement on every face wasn't caused by the fact that she was out driving with Hawkridge. 'Perhaps Lord Nettlebed can enlighten you. I believe the horse tethered a few yards away to your left is the chestnut he usually rides.'

Hawkridge followed her gaze as he tied off the reins. 'Hmm. And a bay gelding keeping it company.' He descended from the phaeton and strode around to her side. 'I wonder if it's too much to hope that Bevan is partaking of some exercise in company with his son.'

Before she could venture an opinion on the subject, another

phaeton, driven by Viscount Eversleigh, clattered into the yard and pulled up next to them. Lord Colborough's gruff tones smote her ears.

'Morning, Mrs Chantry. Hawkridge. Where the devil is Jennings? Hey! Jennings! Jennings, I say!'

'No need to yell, sir,' Eversleigh said, wincing. 'Good morning, Mrs Chantry. You're looking in tune with the season. That shade of green becomes you.'

Amy smiled at him. 'Thank you, my lord.'

Hawkridge scowled, seized her about the waist and whisked her out of the carriage before she could blink.

'Mrs Chantry is a widow,' he informed Eversleigh, setting her on her feet with a distinct thump. 'Widows wear dark colours.'

Amy snatched her hands away from his shoulders—where they'd shown a distressing tendency to linger—and glared at him, torn between umbrage at his lack of gallantry and relief that her exit from the phaeton had been accomplished so easily.

When she saw Eversleigh grinning, she all but dived back into the carriage in search of her basket.

'Going on a picnic?' he enquired innocently when she emerged with her property.

'We're dancing attendance on my grandmother's latest project,' said Hawkridge, sounding as if he was speaking through clenched teeth.

'Where is Clarissa?' growled Colborough in much the same tone. 'Off somewhere with that Tweedy fellow, I suppose.'

Hawkridge turned, an evil smile curling his lips. 'I have no idea,' he purred. 'But since Grandmama decreed this morning that our Public Day will be held in three days' time, you may be sure he'll take every opportunity on that occasion to push his suit.'

'Might as well hold it here and now,' Eversleigh remarked, forestalling the explosion gathering on his grandparent's countenance. 'Half the village seems to have gathered across the way, and here comes Nettlebed with Lucinda and the Inghams.'

'Hah!' barked Colborough, momentarily distracted. He watched the others stroll towards them for a moment before turning back to Hawkridge. 'You had a lucky escape there, Hawkridge, even though you might not have thought so at the time. Know Ashcroft had his doubts about letting his daughter marry you, and he was right. Sweet gal, Kitty Ingham, but not up to your weight. Would have bolted in fright at the first fence.' He chuckled.

Amy suddenly decided that she really ought to be on her way to Lavender Cottage. 'Uh…my lord—'

'I say, sir,' Eversleigh expostulated at the same moment. 'There's a lady present.'

'What's that got to do with anything?' demanded his grandparent. 'Mrs Chantry was married, wasn't she? She isn't going to swoon at a few blunt words. Stands to reason,' he added, as one throwing in a clincher. 'Hardy lot, the Daltons.'

'Good morning, everyone,' Lady Ingham called, before anyone could comment on this pronouncement. 'Isn't it a lovely day?' She caught sight of Amy as she rounded Eversleigh's phaeton, and promptly cut off her retreat. 'Oh, Mrs Chantry, did I hear Lord Colborough say you're a connection of the Daltons? Sarah is one of my dearest friends, you know. I saw her in London during the Season, but she and Ravensdene had to cut their stay short since she was expecting to be confined. Have you heard how she goes on? And the dear little baby?'

'Nick wrote to me a few weeks ago,' Hawkridge answered while Amy was still frantically sorting through a variety of responses. 'From the tone of his letter, I deduced that Sarah was in the pink of health and they're both besotted with the heir. And by the way, Kitty—' he sent Lady Ingham a very straight look '—Mrs Chantry's connection with the Daltons, if any, is very distant. She's never met them.'

'I understand,' Lady Ingham said immediately. She turned a warm smile on Amy. 'Don't worry, Mrs Chantry. I won't say anything. There's nothing more awkward than people assuming something about one that may not be true. But I'm sure Marc will find out the facts for you if you wish it. He's very good at that sort of thing.'

The remark was obviously meant as reassurance. Amy returned her ladyship's smile with a weak one of her own and wondered what that exchange of looks between Hawkridge and Kitty Ingham was all about. She already knew Hawkridge was a stickler for the truth on matters of importance. But she wasn't sure if Lady Ingham meant that the proper connections were also important to him.

Either alternative was disturbing as far as she was concerned.

She shook off the thought and took a firmer grip on her basket.

'My lord, if you don't mind, I'll…'

'Amy! There you are!' Lucinda appeared at her other side, clad in a scarlet riding-habit adorned with gold braid and epaulettes. The sight was so startling, it took Amy a moment to hear what Lucinda was saying. 'I'm so sorry you didn't meet Jeremy last night,' she rattled on. 'He particularly wished to speak to you because I told him you wanted to help us.'

'I beg your—'

'After all, you know what it's like to be in love.'

'Well—'

'But Jeremy is looking forward to meeting you at the Public Day.'

'Excellent,' said Hawkridge, drawing his niece's attention. 'Perhaps you'll remind me, Mrs Chantry, to recruit Chatsworth for the cricket team.' He raised a brow at Lucinda. 'I presume he did learn the game at school.'

Lucinda scowled and stuck out her lower lip.

'He did go to school, didn't he?'

'I think you'd better leave it right there,' Nettlebed advised as his daughter's countenance took on a dangerously angry hue. 'Are you ready to go, Lucinda? Your mama will be wondering what's become of us.'

'Yes, indeed, and so will little Anthony,' put in Lady Ingham. She tucked her hand in the crook of her husband's arm, neatly distracting him from his conversation with Colborough and Eversleigh.

Amy watched as he smiled down at his wife. He was some years older than Hawkridge, unremarkable in countenance, unassuming in manner, clearly happy to indulge his much younger wife.

'Ready to go, my dear?' He patted her hand, the glance he swept over the assembled company, resting for a moment on Amy. 'Mrs Chantry, I do hope you'll come and visit one day soon. Anthony is always talking about the pretty lady who helped him pick flowers a couple of weeks ago. Of course, he and his nurse were trespassing,' he added drolly to Hawkridge. 'The little scamp caught sight of your grandmother's roses when he was out for a walk, and was bound and determined to bring some home to his mama.'

'As if we don't have enough of our own,' Lady Ingham said, laughing. 'But do come, Mrs Chantry. Please don't feel you must wait on Lady Hawkridge. We're much of an age, you know, and I would so like us to be friends.'

Amy promptly sank beneath a tidal wave of guilt. The deluge came out of nowhere, swamping the faint ripples she'd felt before, and sending her hurtling into a maelstrom of regret, worry and recrimination.

By the time she surfaced the Inghams had departed and Nettlebed was assisting his daughter into the saddle.

As he reached for his own reins, he caught her eye and gave her a wry smile. 'I think you'd better come and visit us, too, Mrs Chantry. We could do with some sensible advice.'

Another wave of guilt threatened to roll over her. Amy

braced herself, determined not to lose her footing. When had the trickle she'd been living with become a flood? she wondered. Even last night hadn't been this bad. Until then, the only person she'd deceived was Lady Hawkridge, and she'd tried to make up for it by anticipating her ladyship's every whim; had even told herself that she might eventually confide in her benefactress.

Since Hawkridge had arrived, the list of people she was deceiving was growing to nightmarish proportions. She'd thought she would be living retired with an elderly widow, not becoming the recipient of all this kindly attention.

She didn't like it. She didn't want any attention. Unless it was Hawkridge paying—

No! She didn't mean that. She was becoming overwrought. Was it any wonder?

'What's Crispin doing this morning?' Hawkridge demanded, jolting her back to her surroundings.

'Who cares about him?' Lucinda retorted. 'Papa asked him to come riding with us, but he preferred to go off to some mouldy old barn.'

'Painting that yacht in the old boathouse,' Nettlebed explained. 'You'd better talk to Augusta, Marc. She's not happy. Not happy at all.'

'Later,' Hawkridge said briefly.

Amy suddenly realised he was watching her closely. She instantly plastered a smile to her face and looked up at Eversleigh, who had just emerged from the inn.

'God knows where Jennings is,' he remarked. 'Can't find him anywhere.'

'Does the fellow expect us to sit here all day?' barked Colborough. 'Although I can't say I blame him for making himself scarce with that screeching going on across the road. *Stop that infernal din!*' he roared suddenly, raising his voice to a pitch that could have been heard over cannon-shot. 'A man can't hear himself think!'

The ladies stopped chattering as if hands had been clapped over their mouths. They stared across the road, shock and horror on every countenance. Then, as Colborough half rose from his seat, they turned as one and fled down the street like a flock of panicked grey partridges.

Eversleigh groaned. 'Oh, very nicely done, sir. That should add to your reputation as a gentleman.'

Colborough glared at his grandson. 'It worked, didn't it?'

Hawkridge started to grin.

The Viscount raised his eyes heavenward. 'I don't see Jennings reappearing,' he pointed out. Then, with a swift glance at Hawkridge, he looked at Amy and winked. 'Do you want to try flushing him from cover, Mrs Chantry? Old Jennings always has an eye for a fetching female. You might have more success.'

The grin was wiped from Hawkridge's face in a flash. 'That,' he stated in nothing less than a snarl, 'was not amusing, Pel. Find him yourself. And you can tell him that if he wants to continue running the Green—'

He stopped dead as he caught sight of the sign hanging over the door.

Everyone except Nettlebed followed his gaze.

'Frog?' they chorused, in accents ranging from outrage to disbelief.

The painted image of a very fat, self-important green frog smirked back at them.

'Meant to warn you,' Nettlebed said gloomily. 'That's why the Society are so dashed excited. They thought a Green Frog made more sense than a Green Man. Poor old Jennings didn't stand a chance. Found him putting up the new sign not half an hour ago. Probably drowning his sorrows in the cellar.'

'Good God!' muttered Hawkridge. He seized Amy by the wrist. 'Pel, we have an errand to run. Track down Jennings and make him take down that ridiculous sign. I don't care what the Society thinks. This time they've gone too far.'

'I'm not telling them that,' Eversleigh began. 'They've probably gone to bring up Mrs ffollifoot and that Tredgett woman as reinforcements.'

'Then tell them Jennings will lose business if he changes the name of the inn. Tell them the damn sign fell down. Tell them anything you please. Just do it!'

He yanked the basket out of Amy's hand. 'As for you, Mrs Chantry, if you've quite finished receiving compliments and invitations from every male in the place, we'll depart before the Society has stone ducks waddling about the yard.'

'Stone doesn't waddle,' Amy informed him in stony accents. 'And I was not—'

She was hauled out of the yard with startling velocity.

'For heaven's sake, my lord!'

It was a testament to her outrage that she still had breath to protest. But Amy eyed the steep hill in front of her and decided to postpone the rest of her lecture until they arrived at Lavender Cottage. It wouldn't take long. She was being towed upwards with relentless despatch.

'You do realise, I suppose, that Lords Colborough and Nettlebed are staring after us with their mouths hanging open, and that Lord Eversleigh is doubled over with laughter,' she began when they halted at their destination.

Marc looked back over his shoulder. Since the cottage was situated less than a minute's walk from the inn and commanded an excellent view of its yard, the most cursory glance was all he needed to see that Amy was right.

He scowled, shoved the wicket gate open, and towed Amy up the path. 'I'm glad Pel finds the situation so amusing,' he growled, thumping a peremptory fist against the front door. 'He might not laugh so hard when I inform him that he has an odd notion of compliments.'

'He was only being kind, my lord. There was no need for you to stand there wielding a club.'

'Wielding a *club*?'

'Um…' She wasn't going to explain *that*.

'Never mind,' he said grimly. 'I've grasped the general picture.' He glared at the door. 'Doesn't Grandmama have a superintendent or someone running this place?'

'The matron is probably busy, sir. Charitable institutions are not like private residences where people are forever visiting.'

'And that reminds me. What the devil was Ingham about, issuing invitations for you to call? You only met him last night.'

'Lord Ingham is a gentleman, sir.' Her pointed stare told him he could have taken lessons in gentlemanly behaviour. 'He, too, was merely being kind.'

'Well, he can keep his gentlemanly kindness for Kitty. It's why she married him.'

The door opened just as he raised his fist again. The stout, motherly-looking woman in the doorway fell back a pace or two with a startled squawk.

Marc lowered his hand and turned his scowl into a smile. He noticed that Amy manufactured a similar expression. It rivalled the yellow front door for brilliance.

Obviously she felt even less like smiling than he did, but he didn't have time to contemplate the matter. The lady in the doorway was looking at him with bright-eyed expectation. He cast his mind back a couple of decades and came up with a name.

'Good morning, Mrs Fidler. How are you?'

'Well, if it isn't your lordship! Fancy you remembering me. I swear you weren't no more than a schoolboy when I left my place with Lady Hawkridge to marry Mr Fidler. I'm very well, sir, and enjoying my position here. It keeps me busy, Mr Fidler having been gathered to his reward two years ago.' She smiled and nodded, apparently not heart-broken by Mr Fidler's departure. 'And Mrs Chantry's brought you to see her ladyship's good work, which is only right and proper, I'm sure. Good morning, ma'am.'

'Good morning, Mrs Fidler. May we come in?'

'Lawks! Whatever is the matter with me, chattering here on the step? Of course, ma'am, of course. No doubt you'll want to see the children. Cora's taken them into the garden for their lessons.'

'What a lovely idea. Yes, I would like to see them. Perhaps you could show Lord Hawkridge about while I step outside.'

'Aye, that I will, ma'am. Are those the clothes Lady Hawkridge promised to send? Just pop them down right there, m'lord, and come this way.'

The fervent light of the charitably inclined gleamed in Mrs Fidler's eyes. As Amy took advantage of the situation to vanish down a short passage leading to another door, Marc resigned himself to a thorough tour of the premises. Fortunately the house was small. He saw and heard everything he needed to see and hear in twenty minutes. It was enough to inform him that, thanks to Amy's influence, Lavender Cottage was unlike every other almshouse in the entire country.

Escaping at last with the excuse that his horses would be growing restless, he made his way to the garden.

It, too, was small, but charmingly laid out with a winding path that followed the slope of the hillside in a series of descending steps as it meandered through a maze of flower beds. Wild roses ran amok among more formal arrangements, jasmine draped itself over the surrounding hedge, and everywhere he looked lavender nodded gently in the breeze, adding its perfume to the mix and making his head spin.

It must have been something like that, he thought, because the minute he saw Amy he felt as if he'd been kicked in the chest. All the air vanished from his lungs, the bright colours at the edges of his vision dimmed, as if the garden had disappeared in a mist, leaving only Amy framed in an incandescent circle of light.

He stopped, eyes narrowed against the brightness; the circle widened, and he saw that she was sitting on a child-sized chair in front of a group of half a dozen very small children, reading from a book open on her lap. Every little face upturned to her wore the same expression. Rapt attention.

He knew exactly how they felt, Marc thought suddenly. He could have sat there himself, endlessly, absorbing the play of expressions chasing each other across her face, listening to the soft lilt of her voice, filling himself with her essence every time he drew in a breath.

It wasn't desire, the strange longing that shook him then, although desire raked across his flesh with increasingly fiery claws whenever he saw her.

This was something else; something deeper, something so much a part of him that, if it was ever torn away, the loss would threaten his very soul.

He loved her.

The knowledge hit him with such finality he didn't even question it. As if he'd known the instant he'd learned she could match him, but had called it desire, protectiveness, anything, to prevent himself from again becoming a hostage to fate.

His entire body shuddered as a sense of unbearable vulnerability swept over him. For an infinitesimal second he was twenty again, waiting, helpless, for the news that two of the people he'd loved most in the world had been taken from him.

Then his hands fisted at his sides and he reminded himself that this time he wasn't helpless, this time he *could* protect. And this time, by God, if the same malevolent twist of fate stopped him protecting Amy, then he'd go with her into whatever lay beyond.

He clenched his teeth as a primal roar of human defiance rose in his throat, and as if Amy felt the storm of emotion raging within him, she looked up, her clear green eyes wide, her lips slightly parted.

He fought down instincts that were as violent as they were

primitive, steeled himself against agonising need, and strolled forward.

'My lord! Are you ready to go?' She leapt to her feet, causing the children to blink and transfer their attention to him. Their expressions went from rapt to severely disapproving.

Marc couldn't help smiling, albeit wryly. 'Something tells me I'm not going to be very popular if I take you away before you finish your story, Mrs Chantry, but I don't want to keep my horses standing any longer than is necessary.'

'It's all right, my lord. I'd just started another rhyme. Cora will be happy to finish it when she returns from putting her baby down for his nap.' She glanced down at the circle of faces. 'Stand up and say good morning to his lordship, children.'

There was a general scramble as the group got to their feet. 'Good morning, his lordship.'

Marc grinned. 'I'm afraid I must take Mrs Chantry home now,' he told them. 'But she will visit you again very soon, and you may see her at our Public Day if you wish.'

One urchin removed his thumb from his mouth. 'Will we see your horses, too?' he demanded.

'Yes, as long as you do precisely what my grooms instruct you to do while you're in the stables.'

Everyone nodded solemnly.

'Well, then,' said Amy, bestowing a smile on her charges that had his eyes narrowing thoughtfully. 'You may go and watch the kittens until Cora comes back, but no touching them, mind. Not until they're bigger.'

'I 'member,' lisped one little girl. ''Cos the mama cat will smell us on them and leave, and then they'll be orphans like us.'

'Yes, but you have Mrs Fidler to look after you now, Emmy. She isn't going to leave you.'

The child gave a shy smile, nodded and ran off. The rest streamed after her without wasting time on social niceties.

'You have a way with children, Mrs Chantry,' Marc observed, taking her arm to lead her out of the garden.

She eluded him the instant his fingers made contact, her smile winking out like a snuffed candle. 'Thank you, my lord. You would appear to possess a similar way, if you truly meant they may visit your stables.'

'I meant it. Mawson will see that neither they nor my horses come to any harm.'

'That's very kind of you. Now, if you don't mind waiting a second or two, I'll take my leave of Mrs Fidler and—'

'I've already taken the liberty of doing so on your behalf. If we go along this path, it will take us back to the street without having to go through the house. Mrs Fidler is an excellent woman, but she does tend to chatter.'

'Oh. Well…'

'Of course, chatter can sometimes be useful. I believe there are two other girls living here.'

'Uh…yes. Jane and Ellen.' Amy tried to pull herself together with the stern reminder that engaging Hawkridge's interest in the dowager's project was of more importance than the confused state of her emotions.

Unfortunately, it was difficult to ignore the fact that since they'd arrived at the cottage, she felt as if she'd been caught in a whirlpool.

First there'd been the strange cloud of depression that had descended on her when Hawkridge had made that comment about the reason for Kitty Ingham's choice of husband. If anything had been needed to confirm her assumption about his reasons for staying away from Devon, it had been those words.

Her reaction had given her quite a jolt. Her throat had felt tight; there'd been an odd ache in her chest. The last thing she'd felt like doing was smiling and chatting to Mrs Fidler as if there was nothing wrong.

She'd managed to throw off the sensation—after all, there *was* nothing wrong—but it had taken a surprising amount of effort. And then Hawkridge had managed to overturn her senses again when she'd glanced up to find him watching her with that piercing intensity in his grey eyes. It was the look she'd glimpsed in the library, only more so.

Utterly implacable. Fiercely determined. Almost…brutally relentless.

No, she thought at once, Hawkridge would never be brutal, but that look had been enough to cause her heart to leap quite violently into her throat and lodge there for several seconds.

And now he was being so polite, she was beginning to wonder if her disordered mind had been playing tricks on her.

'Jane and Ellen?' he prompted.

Amy jumped. 'Oh, yes.' Really! This wouldn't do. She'd presented a happy face to the children, she could manage a composed visage for Hawkridge. 'They've found positions as housemaids, sir. However, most such positions require people without dependents, which is why the children are housed at Lavender Cottage until they're older. The girls contribute a little towards their food and Cora is teaching them their letters.'

There, that was better. All she had to do was keep her mind on what was important, and forget what was not.

'And Cora's story?' he asked, holding the gate open for her.

'An all-too-common one, I'm afraid. She was seduced, abandoned by the man who had promised to marry her, and then lost her place when her mistress discovered her situation. Parish relief was her only recourse—respectable recourse, that is—but I can assure you, such relief is grudging and insufficient at best.'

He sent her a swift glance as they started down the hill. 'A sadly commonplace tale, indeed. Very similar to your mother's, except that her destitution was caused by your father's death.'

Amy felt her breath catch, even though she'd been expecting something of the sort since Hawkridge had discovered the purpose of Lavender Cottage.

'In case you're wondering, sir, Lady Hawkridge knows nothing of my mother, or of my own circumstances except that I'm—except that I was married. I admit I interceded when poor Cora was caught trying to milk one of your cows, but—'

'I wasn't criticising you, Mrs Chantry.' He smiled down at her, a smile so gently reassuring she felt her heart hesitate and flutter before it resumed its usual rhythm. 'I would expect nothing less of you than that you'd help a girl in Cora's situation. As for Grandmama, I'm only too happy for her to be involved in such a project. Her patronage of poets and artists and the like only seems to land her in trouble,' he finished drily.

Fortunately for her beleaguered mind, they reached the inn at that moment, saving her from the necessity of a reply. As Jennings bustled out, full of thanks and excuses, Amy leaned against a handy carriage wheel and tried to gather her wits.

She hoped the task wouldn't take long. She still had the conversational shoals of the drive home to negotiate.

Chapter Nine

They took the cliff road. Amy didn't know whether Hawkridge chose the route by force of habit or because he'd accepted her earlier assurances, and didn't have time to enquire. They had barely passed the vicarage when he returned to the subject of her past.

'Tell me about your mother, Mrs Chantry.' He glanced down at her. 'If I was correct in assuming her situation to be similar to Cora's, she must have been an exceptionally courageous young woman to rear you as she did.'

Amy debated for a moment, then decided that after visiting Lavender Cottage, his interest sprang from genuine concern.

'My mother's situation was somewhat worse, sir. At least Cora hasn't had to go into the poorhouse. You see, parish officials are loathe to support able-bodied adults. One must work. Which is all very well, but work isn't easy to find when one has a babe in arms, or even a young child clinging to one's skirts. Whenever Mama found a position, no matter how lowly, there were always…compromises to be made.'

'Involving the men in the situation?'

She made a small, assenting gesture. 'I was too young to know anything about it, of course, but I remember how she would sink into despair sometimes, that she often looked afraid. Eventually the poorhouse, or workhouse as they're coming to be known, must have seemed safer for both of us.'

'And harder to get out of than the Fleet, I imagine.'

'No one wants to lose free labour,' she said drily. 'You can't leave unless you can prove you won't be a charge on the parish, but how can one search for employment when one is forever kept busy and confined? It's a circle of hopelessness, especially for the simple, the old and sick, or children who, like myself, lack formal education.'

'You have more than formal education, Mrs Chantry. Thanks to your mother, I presume.'

Amy nodded. 'Most workhouses have classes for the younger children, but I was considered too old by the time we entered one. So, at night, Mama taught me everything she could remember from her own schooling.'

'Even how a lady should behave,' he murmured.

'She was a lady, sir! Not only by birth, but in all the ways that matter.'

He smiled faintly. 'Having met you, Mrs Chantry, I have no doubt on that score.'

Slightly mollified, Amy subsided. 'Eventually I was taken into the superintendent's house to be trained as a maid...'

'But?' he prompted.

'I grew older, sir. Old enough to draw the attention of the son of the house and...his friends.'

'Hmm. I think I hear ''doltish'' friends in there somewhere.'

The comment drew a smile from her. 'I began to look for another position,' she continued, more at ease. 'Whenever I was sent out on some errand or another. Eventually I found a place at the Misses Appleton's Academy for Young Gentlewomen. I...'

She glanced down, then lifted her chin. In this instance, at least, she would give him the truth. And hope it would pacify her conscience for a while.

'I lied, sir, to gain a position as a junior schoolmistress. I even had Mama write a reference purporting to be from a school in Yorkshire. It wasn't difficult to play the role. A junior mistress is more of a maid than anything else. She's expected to wait at table, supervise the laundering, serve tea to the senior teachers, that sort of thing. Any teaching is done by rote from *Miss Mangnell's Historical and Miscellaneous Questions,* and is restricted to the very youngest girls. And the Misses Appleton ran only a modest establishment. They didn't cater to the Upper Ten Thousand, as Mama put it.' Her confident façade wavered a little. 'I know I'm sadly lacking in the sort of accomplishments that might be expected of a companion, indeed of a lady, but—'

'Amy.'

The gentle tone, his steady gaze, had the rest of her speech vanishing into the ether.

'You are a lady,' he said quietly. 'A lady waiting for the right setting.'

He held her gaze an instant longer, then returned his attention to the road.

'Yorkshire?' he queried after a moment.

Amy tried to answer and discovered she'd just lost the thread of the conversation. 'Um… It was the first remote place I could think of, sir.'

He smiled at that. 'I expect the superintendent at the workhouse wasn't too pleased about your advancement in the world.'

'I told him only that I'd found another maid's position,' she confessed, still feeling strangely disoriented. 'Even that enraged him, although heaven knows he had plenty of other girls to choose from. He called me every name he could think of and threatened to throw Mama into the street.'

Marc's eyes narrowed. 'What stopped him?'

'She was ill by then, mainly because of the conditions in the place, and he was answerable to higher authorities. Not that I knew that at the time, but I told him I'd go to the local magistrate unless he allowed Mama to stay until I could find another place for her. Fortunately, it didn't take long. I paid for a small room off the kitchen of an inn, and Mama helped out with the work whenever she could in return for her food. We were lucky; they were good people.'

He nodded. 'She was there when you met your husband?'

'Yes.' Amy fixed her gaze on her hands. 'Actually, she met him first. He was staying there, and she became quite attached to him. He was…kind to her.'

Marc watched the myriad expressions cross her piquant little face and wondered at the last. Sadness and regret he understood, but there'd been…hesitation. Uncertainty. As if she might have said more, but had retreated into the safety of silence.

He stamped down on a surge of impatience to know the entire story. He *needed* to know. She'd been desperate to get her mother out of the poorhouse. Her dying mother. Desperate to get herself away from its superintendent—probably sensing, with the instincts of the small and vulnerable, that the man had another purpose in taking her into his house. But how desperate? She'd lied—he was glad of it; his blood ran cold when he thought of how close she'd come to having her innocence brutally stripped from her—but to what other straits had she gone?

He needed to know to protect her from any consequences.

'You were very close to your mother, weren't you?' he said, making his voice as soft and unthreatening as possible. 'You took care of each other.'

Her gaze flicked upwards, then away. She nodded. 'There were only the two of us, you see. All my life. When she died…'

There was silence for a moment, filled only with the sounds of birdsong, and the steady clip-clop of the horses' hooves. They topped the rise overlooking the sea, and he reined in, transferring the ribbons to one hand.

'I know,' he said, very low. He reached out and took one tightly clenched little fist in his free hand. 'I know.' And raising her hand to his mouth, he turned it and pressed his lips to the delicate tracery of veins at her wrist.

The pulse beneath her skin leapt and quivered. Probably because he'd startled her rather than in response to the caress, but even as he felt an answering tension invade his own muscles, she was drawing her hand away.

Faint colour tinted her cheeks. 'You…always manage to surprise me, my lord. I don't know why.'

His mouth curved in a somewhat crooked smile. 'Don't you?' he asked wryly. 'Given your opinion of my, er, tendency to wield a club, I find that hard to believe.'

Amy felt herself blushing again. The heat seemed to emanate directly from the faintly throbbing place where his lips had touched. It even threatened to cloud her mind, because, despite knowing that Hawkridge would find the rest of her story even harder to believe, she was rocked by an unexpected urge to tell it.

As if she hadn't already said enough! No wonder she was feeling rattled; as though someone had picked her up and shaken her to see what fell out.

The trouble was, she'd never trusted anyone enough to confide in them; the sense of vulnerability was nerve-racking. Although Hawkridge had prompted her with nothing more than the briefest of questions, spoken in the gentlest of tones.

And just now, his quiet acknowledgement of her loss—a loss he'd known himself—had aroused a sense…almost of kinship with him. A closeness she'd never expected to share with a man.

For some reason, that made her feel more vulnerable than ever, as if she'd just skated out on to very thin ice.

She resisted the urge to rub the still-tingling spot on her wrist, and scrambled back to safer ground.

'Goodness me, my lord! The view from here *is* quite spectacular, isn't it? I can see why Lady Hawkridge was so eager to show the spot to Mr Tweed—'

She stopped dead as another patch of thin ice threatened to crack beneath her feet. The heart-shaking smile on Hawkridge's face was abruptly replaced by narrow-eyed purpose.

'I think I'll have a word with this Tweedy fellow,' he growled. 'He's been a little too busy for my liking.'

'I can assure you, sir, that Lady Hawkridge is in no danger of being taken in.'

He scowled at her. 'Then what the devil does she think she's doing, running about the countryside, looking at views with Tweedy?'

Amy had a sudden vision of Lord Colborough's irascible countenance when discussing the same subject. 'You could always wait and see,' she suggested, wondering if her startling suspicion was correct.

The expression in Hawkridge's eyes seemed rather to imply that she'd taken leave of her senses. 'Wait around for the situation to deteriorate?' he demanded. He took up the reins and flicked them against the horses' rumps. 'No, thank you, Mrs Chantry. I know better.'

Somewhat incensed at having her suggestion summarily dismissed, she sat back and folded her arms. 'I'm sure you do, sir.'

'What does that mean? That you think you know more about the situation than I do?'

'Not at all, my lord.'

'Oh, yes, it does.' His scowl darkened. 'I know what's going on in that independent little mind. You think Grandmama should enjoy limitless freedom to get herself into trouble.'

'She might get herself out of it, too.'

'The way you were going to get yourself off that desk?' he asked silkily.

Amy stuck her nose in the air. 'I was going to sit down upon the desk and slide off it,' she informed him.

Marc had a sudden vision of her dress sliding upwards as she did so. The image nearly caused him to rip a layer of paint off his phaeton as he turned in at the gates.

The narrow escape didn't improve his mood. Not only was Amy sitting there beside him with a distinctly disapproving look on her face, he had just been struck by the several disagreeable facts.

He grimaced inwardly as he remembered his half-amused, supremely confident assertion that she belonged to him. As if possessing her physically was all; as if making her his wife, while needing skill and patience, was inevitable.

After what he'd learned this morning, marrying Amy might not be as easy as he'd supposed.

And his own position was to blame. The social gulf between them was wide. Though the circumstances of her birth were unknown, everyone was aware, at the very least, that she was a penniless widow without connections.

Not that he gave a damn about that, but Amy would. If he showed his hand too plainly in public, it would give rise to the sort of gossip that would shred her vulnerable little soul to pieces. Some well-meaning, but misguided, fool might even try to warn her against responding to him.

On the other hand, given her mother's situation and her general distrust of the male sex—rather justified, he had to admit—he suspected too overt a pursuit in private would send her fleeing again.

And then there was her damnable independence.

Marc scowled again. The entire business threatened to be a long, painstaking process. He didn't want painstaking. He wanted *her*. Now! Immediately! If not sooner.

He wanted the right to protect her, to ravish, to love. He wanted to make her laugh again. He wanted—

'Excuse me, my lord, but are you still exercising your horses? Or have you forgotten the way to the stables?'

Marc jerked his attention back to his driving to discover

he'd just overshot the turn to the stableyard. His horses, being the polite, well-bred animals they were, hadn't argued his apparent decision to circle the house.

He thought fast.

'It just occurred to me, Mrs Chantry, that if you don't ride, you probably don't drive.'

'Well, no, but—'

'Then this would be an excellent opportunity for me to teach you.'

'Oh.' For a second or two, she looked adorably confused. 'Thank you, my lord, but...I do have a considerable pile of mail waiting on my...I mean, waiting on your desk.'

They turned a corner. The gravel strip between terrace and lawn narrowed considerably. He didn't want to think about the damage his off-side wheels were doing to the grass.

'Some other time, perhaps,' he said smoothly. 'Tyrant though I am, I do believe that ladies should be able to drive themselves if the need arises.'

She frowned. 'I didn't say you were a tyrant, sir. Merely...extremely conscious of your responsibilities.' Her frown vanished. She looked inordinately pleased with the pronouncement.

Marc winced. 'It's a good thing I'm not inclined to be puffed up with my own importance,' he said drily. 'You would soon burst that particular bubble, Mrs Chantry.'

'Oh, dear.' She looked up at him in apparent concern, but he didn't miss the quick flash of mischief in her gaze. 'I'm sorry if I offended you, my lord. You did grant me leave to say anything I pleased to you. On any subject.'

'Something tells me I may have been a bit too liberal with that permission,' he muttered. 'Since you're exercising the license, however, tell me what I should have done on the previous occasions when Grandmama got herself into strife? Allowed her to be pestered by unwanted attentions or robbed blind? Waved Bartle off with the pearls, perhaps, or— Damn it! Now look what's happened!'

The horses trotted dutifully past the stable turn-off again. Amy glanced around as they swept by, and had to resist an insane urge to pat Hawkridge soothingly on the hand.

'I can certainly understand why you chased after Mr Bartle,' she said placatingly. 'But before that, have you ever waited for an outcome other than a continuance of trouble?'

To her surprise, every trace of wry humour vanished from his face. He flicked the reins against the horses' rumps with a white-knuckled restraint that sent her an abrupt reminder of the warrior beneath the gentleman. If he hadn't been confined in a carriage, Amy knew he'd be pacing.

'Once,' he said flatly. 'Once I waited for my parents to return from an afternoon's sailing. I waited too long to save them.'

Her lips formed a silent 'oh' of comprehension. Compassion welled inside her, wrenching at her heart. This time it was imperative she touch him, if not physically, as he'd touched her, then emotionally; that she let him know he wasn't alone in feeling loss and grief. Or guilt.

'Was it a storm?' she asked softly.

He was silent for the few seconds it took them to round the corner of the house and bowl along the carriageway to the front door. There he stopped the horses and tied off the reins, but he made no move to descend from the phaeton. Merely leaned forward slightly, resting his forearms on his thighs, his hands clasped loosely between them as he stared straight ahead.

Her heart ached when she thought of what he must be seeing in his mind's eye. 'I'm sorry,' she murmured. 'You don't have to—'

'No,' he said, and half-turned his head towards her, briefly. 'Time heals, Amy. I want you to know.' He paused for a second, as though remembering. 'There was a calm that afternoon, and fog. Not bad when the wind came up again, but still dangerous in patches. And though Pelham's father and mine had probably been rowing during the calm, they'd been too far out to sea to reach the cove and safety before dark. They were run down by a revenue cutter in pursuit of another craft. Smugglers, using the fog as cover.'

'I'm so sorry,' she whispered. 'That sort of waiting must have been terrible.'

He glanced down at his hands. 'It didn't get bad until nightfall. There was no reason to worry, we thought. Both my father and Pel's were experienced sailors, had often run under lights, in all weathers. But eventually my grandfather and I, with Pel and Colborough, went out looking for them. We found the cutter. They'd gone back, searching for survivors, but their speed had been such at the moment of impact that, by the time they came about, patched up the damage to their own boat, and tacked back to the spot, there was nothing.'

Nothing but wreckage, floating on the surface of the sea.

'Their bodies eventually washed ashore along the coast. Dr Twinhoe said it was very likely they'd all been killed on impact. Or injured so badly that even a minute's delay in rescue would have been too long once they were in the water. But I'll never be certain. If we'd gone out earlier...sailed back with them...the cutter might have seen two boats.'

'You weren't to know that such a thing would happen,' Amy said gently.

'No.' He turned his head at that, smiled faintly. 'Hindsight is a wonderful thing, isn't it? The revenue officer in charge probably regretted his decision to run without lights, in hindsight. He was hauled over the coals for it, of course, but he'd been chasing smugglers. No one was going to reprimand him too strongly for that. It was put down as an accident. Unfortunate, but unforeseen.'

'I'm glad you told me,' she murmured. 'Now I can better

understand Lady Nettlebed's distress at the thought of Crispin sailing.'

'She'll soon become reconciled. It's in his blood. We all learnt to sail practically before we could walk. Even Augusta. In fact, I think poor old Bevan paid his addresses to her out on the water more often than not.'

Amy tilted her head, instinctively finding the way to lead him back to the present. 'You allowed your sister to sail, my lord?' She widened her eyes at him. 'How very liberal of you.'

He grinned. 'Minx. I had nothing to do with it. At the time, I was still at the horrid little toad stage.' Then, more soberly, 'I hope you also better understand my own, er—'

She smiled at him. 'The word you're searching for is protectiveness, sir. It does you credit.'

His brows went up. 'A rather surprising remark, considering our earlier conversation.'

'Not at all,' she replied composedly. 'A woman appreciates a man who can be relied upon, no matter how independent she may be. So long as he respects her own abilities.'

'Oh, I respect your abilities, Amy. Believe me.'

The softly voiced assurance had her composure threatening to beat a hasty retreat into caution. 'Yes, well, according to Mrs Tredgett, protectiveness runs in your family, so—'

The rest was swallowed on a startled gulp as she realised what she'd said. It was useless hoping that Hawkridge hadn't been similarly struck.

'Aha!' He pinned her to her seat with a fiendishly anticipatory gleam. 'Gossiping with the Society, I see.'

Amy blushed as if she'd been found out in a heinous crime. 'Um…'

'Denial is useless, Mrs Chantry. You may as well tell me what else was said. I don't want you going about with any erroneous impressions.'

The words 'poor helpless orphan' jangled loudly in her

head. 'Helpless' now made more sense, but she didn't think Hawkridge would appreciate hearing it.

'Good heavens, my lord! Just look where the sun is. I really must be—'

She sprang up, remembered where she was, and sat down again.

Hawkridge smiled his cat-with-the-captured-mouse smile. 'Let me save you the trouble of sparing my sensibilities, Mrs Chantry. Knowing Mrs Tredgett and company, you were probably treated to an inaccurate description of my broken engagement to Kitty Ingham. God knows, they've all been speculating about it for the past five years.'

Amy's embarrassment vanished. She stopped worrying about how she was going to escape when she couldn't even manage the simple task of descending from a phaeton. She was suddenly, intensely interested in broken engagements. 'Inaccurate, sir? I mean, Miss Twinhoe did happen to mention...'

'Yes, I'm sure she did. She mentions it to everyone. To hear Miss Twinhoe tell it, I was jilted at the altar. The simple truth was that I'd proposed to Kitty in the mistaken belief that, because we'd known each other since childhood, she'd make me an excellent wife.'

'That seems a most, ah, logical decision, my lord.'

'A little too logical. The only reason I made it was that everyone was in a frenzy about the succession because I'd been held up on the road to Newmarket a few weeks earlier. And at that point I hadn't met anyone else who— Well, never mind.'

'Oh, dear. I'm so sorry, sir. I didn't mean to cause you to recall more painful memories.'

'The only painful part was getting myself winged by a highwayman before I managed to disarm him,' he said, grinning. 'There's no need to picture me as a heartbroken suitor. For one thing, my heart wasn't involved in the first place, and, for another, I began to suspect that Kitty, too, had a few misgivings. When I asked her about it, she was very grateful to be given the opportunity to cry off. Unfortunately, she felt so guilty about accepting in the first place, she's been trying to find a replacement ever since.'

'Good heavens. That was five *years* ago?'

'Yes.'

'And in all that time she hasn't found a lady to put up wi—I…I mean—'

He grinned again. 'Kitty hasn't. A couple of years ago, I thought I had, but I discovered—fortunately before any formal notices were sent out—that the lady concerned was acting under instructions from her very ambitious parents. When she was given a taste of one of her, er, duties, her acting skills proved unequal to the task.'

Amy was quite certain her eyes were going to pop right out of her head with astonishment. 'Oh, my,' she uttered, and was only prevented from adding 'how foolish of her' by the opening of the front door.

She almost slid off her seat in relief when she saw Lady Hawkridge.

'Yoo hoo! Amy. Marc.' The dowager waved from the top step. 'I think you'd better come in now. Amy will be getting freckles. And Marc, dearest, there seem to be some very peculiar ruts in the south lawn. Perhaps you'd have a word with Thorpe about them.'

Her ladyship disappeared.

'Pel was right,' Hawkridge muttered as the front door shut again. 'One of these days someone is going to wring Grandmama's neck.'

Amy didn't hear him. She was too busy trying to suppress a blush that wouldn't have left room for the smallest freckle. As Hawkridge sprang down from the phaeton and strode around to her side, she jumped to her feet, this time determined to leap to the ground and flee.

She had grievously underestimated the size of the carriage step and the distance of the leap.

Before she could make a fool of herself, Hawkridge was there.

'It's all right,' he said. 'I'll lift you down.'

Amy forgot about blushing and glared at him. 'This,' she declared, 'is ridiculous. I am not going through life being lifted down from desks and carriages.' She grabbed hold of the hood. 'Kindly stand aside, sir. I'm going to do this even if my head spins so fast it whirls right off my shoulders.'

He started to smile. 'Amy, *every* lady needs assistance descending from a high-perch phaeton. That's why they invented the things. We'll compromise. I'll hold your other hand while you step down.'

That sounded reasonable. Amy put out her hand and had it enveloped in a hold that felt rock steady. She could have been clinging to the iron railing adorning the Inghams' access to the beach.

Two steps and she was on the ground.

A delighted smile spread across her face. 'I did it!'

'No,' he contradicted very softly. '*We* did it. Think about that, Mrs Chantry.'

'Ah…yes. Well…' All she could think about was the hard grip of his fingers and the compelling purpose in his eyes. 'Thank you, my lord.'

His fingers tightened for an instant before he released her.

Amy stepped back. She had the distinct impression that she should keep stepping back, that she shouldn't stop stepping back until she was safely in the house. But something else, something quite alien to her naturally wary nature, was driving her.

She put out her hand, touched his arm—the merest butterfly touch, but the awareness of leashed power beneath her fingers was even stronger than it had been last night. She hoped her voice wouldn't betray that for some strange reason she was trembling inside. 'I do understand why you dislike waiting,' she said softly. 'But, this time...there can be no harm in it. Please.'

His eyes went light, and brilliantly intense.

Amy didn't wait to see with what expression. Wondering what on earth had possessed her, she snatched her hand away, turned, and fled into the house.

Marc wheeled and clamped both hands hard around the nearest object. The rim of the front off-side wheel dug into his palms. He didn't dare let it go, didn't dare watch Amy race into the house.

God, one little touch and his entire body was hard and throbbing. One little plea and he was shaking with the need to go after her, toss her over his shoulder and carry her upstairs to his bed, where he could demand the rest of the story—and a whole lot more.

He wondered if she'd understand *that*. Or the fact that the soft, sweetly serious expression in her eyes had threatened to tear apart the bars keeping his instincts caged.

Wait? He'd never felt less like waiting. Only one thing reconciled him to that course of non-action.

The promise he made to himself in that moment that, once he knew the whole story, he really was going to toss Amy over his shoulder and carry her off to his bed. And there she would stay until she agreed to marry him, even if he had to keep her tied up and helpless.

The thought had a certain appeal. But there was a catch.

He wanted Amy to love him in return, and that couldn't be forced.

Chapter Ten

The next few days were not spent in the peace and quiet that Amy had anticipated when she'd come to live at Hawkridge Manor.

Nor did she have a lot of time to wonder if she'd done the right thing in asking Hawkridge to wait, instead of interfering in any schemes hatched by his grandmother. When she'd dashed into the house after their excursion to Lavender Cottage, Pickles had been waiting to inform her that since a Public Day was to be held in three days' time, Things Would Have To Be Done.

Amy had gone in search of her employer, only to find that the dowager had departed to enjoy a picnic with Mr Tweedy on the beach below Colborough Court. Even though there was a perfectly good beach at Hawkridge.

This provocative behaviour confirmed Amy's opinion of her ladyship's intentions—in fact, she wondered with some amusement how long Lady Hawkridge had been trying to bring Colborough to heel, only to have her grandson put un-witting spokes in her wheel.

Less amusing was the realisation that her plan to join the dowager in her quest for jollification, and thus avoid danger, was rapidly coming to nought. In fact, she'd forgotten all about it.

Her lapse in memory had been bad enough although, in view of Hawkridge's apology after he'd kissed her the other night, quite understandable. What threatened to suspend her wits over a precipice was the added realisation that the scheme had lost its appeal.

Amy seized gratefully on the distraction of a Public Day. The Manor became a veritable hive of activity. Dust covers were removed from the state rooms; a section of the south lawn was rolled for a cricket pitch, causing several footmen to go about practising their bowling action; and, to the accompaniment of Mrs Pickles's instructions and exhortations, a seemingly endless army of macaroons marched out of the ovens.

At first, Hawkridge prudently removed himself from the fray by spending several hours at Nettlebed Place, helping Crispin prepare his boat to a state of seaworthiness that would satisfy that young man's mother.

Amy was glad of his absence. Truly she was. She decided it was a great deal easier to keep him out of her mind when he wasn't always underfoot. Unfortunately for this happy exercise in logic, there appeared to be no predictable pattern to his comings and goings. Instead of departing for Nettlebed Place in the morning and staying there until evening, he developed the knack of appearing just when she was returning a pile of books to a shelf an inch or two above her head, or lifting large vases of flowers.

There was nothing in his manner to give cause for alarm, but Amy began to feel…small. Delicate. Even fragile. Which was rather alarming in itself.

She began peering around corners whenever she had to carry anything heavy.

Then there were the disturbingly persistent thoughts that wafted through her head at odd moments during the day—

whether Hawkridge was there or not. The warmth that enfolded her when she remembered the touch of his mouth against her inner wrist; the tingling little arrows of heat that darted about inside her when she recalled the sudden intensity in his eyes before she'd fled into the house.

She made valiant efforts to put the tantalising memories out of her mind. Truly she did. She studied the portrait diligently, for instance, willing fascination with an inanimate object to return.

Hawkridge overturned the scheme by striding into the library in search of a boat-hook he'd mysteriously left there. And when she glared accusingly from him to the painting, he had the temerity to explain that it *had* been done fourteen years ago. The grin he wore when he left the room nearly caused her to heave the nearest available object at his head.

She brooded on his narrow escape for some time.

Finally, on the general principle that doubling her duties would leave her no time to think at all, Amy offered her assistance to the housekeeper.

It worked. Until Hawkridge managed to outwit her by cantering past the drawing-room windows at the precise moment she was dusting an extremely expensive jade statue. She managed not to drop the statue, but it was a near thing.

There were no two ways about it. The man appeared to great advantage on horseback.

Amy found herself entertaining a rather wistful longing to ride with him. Until her uncharacteristic lapse into the realms of fantasy was interrupted by a very junior housemaid, who had been instructed to inform her that his lordship refused to allow his grandmother to turn the state drawing-room, which housed innumerable priceless *objets d'art*, into a skittles alley in case the weather turned inclement.

At that point she decided that Hawkridge had formed a fiendish plot to overturn her wits, for diabolical reasons of his own, and sallied forth to try her own skills at distraction on the dowager.

Fortunately for the *objets d'art,* the weather was inclined to clemency. Everyone awoke on the appointed day to a soft misty haze that transformed itself into cloudless blue skies and brilliant sunshine by the time the gates were opened at nine o'clock.

Marc descended the stairs shortly beforehand, anticipating the pleasures of pursuit while he had an excellent excuse to spend an entire day with his quarry. Not that the past few days had been fruitless. Amy had started blushing, then frowning disapprovingly, whenever she saw him. It was a very encouraging sign.

A considerable setback, however, awaited him at the breakfast table. Crispin was sitting in Amy's place, under the doting eye of his great-grandmother, devouring food as if he hadn't seen any in a week.

'Thought I'd come over early to fetch that jib you have stored in your boathouse, Uncle Marc,' he said by way of greeting. 'Why are you dressed like that? You are going to help me clean it up, aren't you?'

'Good God, Crispin, you're as single-minded as your sister. Did you happen to notice the booths and tents set up on either side of the carriageway? We're holding a Public Day today. Good morning, Grandmama.' He bent to kiss her ladyship's cheek. 'You're looking delightful as usual. That's a very frivolous cap.'

'Thank you, dear.' The dowager twinkled up at him. 'I believe Pelham is bringing Bartholomew over. One must look one's best for such a momentous occasion.'

Marc eyed his grandparent's guileless countenance with suspicion. 'And since everyone for miles around attends these things, Mr Tweedy is sure to make an appearance. What are you up to, Grandmama?'

'Oh, just tying up a few loose ends, dearest. Have you seen Amy this morning? I wish she wouldn't work so hard, but the dear girl insisted on writing replies to those letters I gave her yesterday.'

'Don't worry. I'll see that she has the rest of the day free.'

Her ladyship beamed. 'Thank you, Marc. I thought you would.'

'What about my boat?' Crispin objected, as Marc walked over to the sideboard to help himself to a liberal portion of ham.

He turned to appraise his nephew's willowy build. 'Today you can play cricket. We need an extra man.'

Crispin looked taken aback for a moment. Then a broad smile spread across his face. 'Thank you, Uncle Marc. I haven't played cricket all that often, you know—dare say I'll be bowled out at the first ball—but it's capital sport.'

'Almost as much fun as sailing,' Marc murmured with an answering grin. 'You'd better go home, Crispin, and change out of those disreputable clothes. Put on something comfortable, it's going to be hot.'

'Right. See you later, Grandmama.' With a violent shove of his chair, Crispin was off. Pounding footsteps sounded in the hall; a second later the front door slammed.

'That boy is crying out for some male pursuits,' Marc observed as he carried his plate back to the table. 'Can't you have a word with Augusta, Grandmama?'

'I think you've already given her enough food for thought, dearest. She doesn't really wish to see Crispin become spoilt, you know, but old habits are hard to break. And he was very sickly as a small boy. To watch him struggle for air was quite terrifying.'

'Yes, I know. But Bevan should have taken a stand when Crispin grew older and got him out on the water. God knows, he used to sail as much as any of us, and it probably would've done the boy the world of good.'

'Of course, dear. I've always thought so, but you must remember that, in this particular matter, Nettlebed's feelings for your sister constrain him. It isn't only Crispin's health that concerns her. Her fear of sailing is very real. Indeed, you, too, still feel the effects of your parents' deaths.' Lady Hawkridge rose and patted his cheek on her way to the door. 'I'm so glad you've found a reason to stay at Hawkridge, Marc.'

Marc watched the door close gently behind his grandmother and gave a wry smile. His sister wasn't the only member of his family gifted with perception on that particular subject. Not that sailing held any fears for him, although he'd severely curtailed the activity out of consideration for the dowager. His reaction had gone much deeper.

He'd spent as little time as possible at Hawkridge.

He pushed his plate aside and rose to stroll over to the windows overlooking the small ornamental lake.

Mine, he thought, with a rush of possessiveness he hadn't allowed himself to feel for a very long time. Every field, every tree, every simple cotter's dwelling: his. He loved the place, had always loved riding over the land, keeping a watchful eye on the crops, discussing the latest methods of cattle-breeding with knowledgeable farmers. But those days had lost their magic when his father and grandfather had no longer been there to ride with him.

With the links to his immediate familial past abruptly severed, his future yet to unfold, emotionless duty had taken the place of the soul-deep sense of belonging that was his birthright.

But it hadn't entirely left him, he realised now. He'd been waiting; without knowing. Waiting for a reason to return home to stay. To live, to love, to reclaim his future.

With Amy.

Seized by a sudden sense of urgency, Marc wheeled, strode over to the door and flung it open. He crossed the hall in several long strides, subjected the library door to the same cavalier treatment, and opened his mouth to issue a comprehensive edict on the writing of letters when the sun was shining.

The effort was wasted. No widow possessed of a tantalising mixture of maddening reserve and mischievous charm was there to receive it.

His quarry had flown.

Amy was busily congratulating herself on finishing the dowager's letters before the crowd gathering on the lawn outside the library became too noisy. After sealing the last missive, she had exited through the french windows just as the occupants of Lavender Cottage, accompanied by Mrs Fidler and Cora, rounded the corner from the carriageway.

Shrill cries of delight greeted her appearance. Beneath the din she thought she heard a door slam somewhere, but she found herself being swept away on a tide of small children before she could glance back.

Eventually, leaving Mrs Fidler chatting with several acquaintances, the tide veered towards the stables, where her escort was rendered speechless with excitement at the offer of a ride on one of the farm horses.

'They'll talk about nothing else for a week,' Cora remarked, as the children lined up for the treat. She bounced the rosy-cheeked baby on her hip, and clucked at him.

Amy smiled and nodded, struck, not for the first time, by Cora's quiet manner of speech. She was a tall girl, too thin for her inches, but with her guinea-gold hair and blue eyes, already regaining her looks after a fortnight at Lavender Cottage. She was also a talented seamstress.

Amy was determined to see Cora set up her own dressmaker's establishment, where she'd be able to keep her child with her and earn enough to do more than survive.

'How is the little man?' she cooed, as the baby grinned at

her with toothless charm. 'May I hold him a moment, Cora? He's so adorable.'

'He's likely to dribble on your pretty gown, ma'am.'

'As if that matters,' Amy said, taking the baby. 'Are you cutting a tooth, then, little fellow?' She planted a kiss on one flushed cheek and nuzzled his neck, breathing in the sweet baby scent. He gurgled happily in response and batted her with a playful fist. Taking the hint, Amy lifted him into the air.

That was how Marc found her as he strode into the stable-yard. The sun shone on the tawny curls peeping from beneath the most ridiculous little cap he'd ever seen, her muslin gown shifted lovingly over her curves, and she was laughing, swooping a baby into the air and making the child laugh, too.

The kick of desire caught him so hard it almost knocked him backwards. He stopped short, braced against a raging torrent of lust, until he thought he had himself under control. At this point it wouldn't help his cause to throw Amy into the nearest stall and take her on a pile of straw until she was helpless and clinging to him.

But that was precisely what he wanted to do. And seeing her with the baby made it worse. He wanted it to be *his* baby she was holding. He wanted her to belong to him in the most primitive way possible. To plant his seed in her body and watch her grow big with his child. He wanted it with a fierce longing that startled even him.

He had a sudden premonition that it was going to be like this for the rest of his life. Every time he came upon Amy unexpectedly. Baby or no baby.

The thought didn't bother him particularly—given his nature he could expect nothing less—but if he didn't put them both into a position where he could do something about it in the immediate future, he simply wouldn't be answerable for the consequences.

To hell with discretion in public, he decided in that moment.

He'd just have to see that no one got near enough to Amy to meddle before he'd declared himself in private.

Setting his jaw, he strode forward.

The baby took one look at his face and burst into tears.

Chaos and mayhem erupted.

Dogs started barking wildly, leaping about, overturning pails and sending what had been an orderly line of children shrieking in all directions. His horses, unaccustomed to ear-splitting wails and loud clanging disturbing the peace of their existence, set up an accompanying chorus of protest and threatened to kick their stalls to pieces.

Amy and a girl he assumed was the baby's mother both started cooing like agitated pigeons in an attempt to stem the flood.

Everyone else turned to see what had caused the commotion. His grooms, who had all been standing around with vacuous smiles on their faces as they watched Amy play with the infant, indulged in one second of shock at his presence, then leapt into action. One scurried around gathering up children, another tried to quiet the dogs, the rest vanished into the stables to calm their precious charges.

Marc smiled grimly after them, then tried to soften the expression when he reached Amy.

The baby cried harder.

'Oh, dear, I can't imagine what is the matter with him,' Amy was saying, frantically trying to soothe her burden. 'Perhaps his tooth came through.'

'Here, give him to me, ma'am. He might have a bit of wind.'

'If I could make a suggestion,' Marc began.

Amy squeaked and jumped. 'Good heavens, my lord! Must you creep up on me like that? I almost dropped the baby.'

Marc eyed the bundle sobbing pitifully on its mother's shoulder and winced. 'I think I might have startled him,' he confessed.

'Well, if you insist on sneaking up on people like that, I'm not surprised. Go away at once.'

'For heaven's sake, ma'am...'

'It's all right...Cora, isn't it?' He smiled at the girl. 'Mrs Chantry is correct, as usual. We shall depart forthwith.'

'We?' Amy blinked at him. 'I didn't say—'

He cut her off by the simple expedient of taking her hand and tucking it into the crook of his arm. Then covered it with his other hand to prevent any escape. 'I really must insist that you accompany me, Mrs Chantry. Who knows how many susceptible infants may be scattered about the place? I'll need you to steer me clear of them.'

'But—' She glanced distractedly about the yard. The dogs were sulking at having their fun cut short, pails had been righted, the children were back in their places. 'The children haven't finished their rides.'

'All the more reason for us to leave while they're occupied.'

'But—'

With a conspiratory smile for Cora, which left her open-mouthed, he led Amy away. 'Amy, my love, I applaud your motives in starting Lavender Cottage. I will be more than happy for you to expand on the project if you wish, but I don't intend to be accompanied by a tribe of small children for the rest of the day.'

Amy's head threatened to spin as she tried to sort all that out. Several things rang ominous warning bells. The trouble was, she didn't know which bell was ringing loudest. The warm weight of Hawkridge's hand over hers didn't help in the decision.

'Um...I don't think it's proper for you to address me so informally, sir.' She might as well start at the top of the list.

'Why not?' he asked, refusing to co-operate.

She frowned. 'It supposes a closer relationship than, er...'

'Don't tell me you're a servant, Amy, because you're not.'

'Well, not precisely, but—'

'You can call me Marc, if it will make you feel better.'

She almost tasted his name on the tip of her tongue. Fortunately she stopped herself in time. 'That would be most improper, my lord. A companion does not put herself forward.'

'Just as well,' he murmured with a startling about-face. He came to a halt where the path from the stables met the carriageway. On their left lay the shrubbery. To the right the windows of the Manor gleamed benignly down on the crowds scattered over the lawn. 'I won't have to worry about you throwing yourself into the front line before hostilities commence.'

'What!' Her brain reeled anew. 'What *are* you talking about now, sir?'

'Colborough has arrived, armed with cane. And if I'm not mistaken, the smugly smiling butterball mincing along with Grandmama on his arm is Tweedy. Remind me to have a word with him when Colborough's finished. If there's anything left.'

'Oh, my goodness!' She stared in dismay from one party to the other. Colborough had clearly sighted prey and, brows beetling, head thrust forward, was bent on a collision course. 'Do something, my lord! We can't have bloodshed on the south lawn!'

'Why not? Tweedy deserves to lose a pint or two. For threatening you, if nothing else.'

'But...' She made a grab for her wits as they whirled past on the carousel that was her mind. 'He didn't threaten me. At least, not precisely. And I told you the other day he means nothing to Lady—'

'You told me not to interfere,' he interrupted ruthlessly. 'You also implied that Grandmama knows what she's doing.' He studied Colborough's rapidly reddening countenance. 'I hope you're right.'

'Oh, heavens!' Amy would have wrung her hands, but she was too busy trying to push Hawkridge towards the rapidly closing space between the combatants. It was like trying to push a wall. He didn't resist; he simply didn't move.

'This is no time for levity, my lord. Speak to Lord Colborough! Fetch Lord Eversleigh! *Do something!*'

He grinned. 'You may cease panicking, Mrs Chantry. Grandmama is veering off into the shrubbery in a manoeuvre that would turn Wellington green with envy. What are the odds that by the time Colborough reaches the spot, she and Tweedy will have vanished?'

'I am not interested in betting, my lord. Oh, my goodness, what am I saying? This won't be the end of it. You'll still have to—'

'Good God, you're right.' Turning on his heel in a move as rapidly executed as the dowager's, Hawkridge started towards the other side of the house. Amy had the choice of being whisked off her feet, or accompanying him. She chose the more dignified option.

'What are you doing, sir? It is no use leaving. Lord Colborough will only confront Mr Tweedy another time.'

'Grandmama can fight her own battles.' He slanted a challenging glance down at her. 'Isn't that what you prefer to do, Mrs Chantry? Which, I might add, is an attitude directly opposed to your attempt just now to shove me into the breach.'

She flushed. 'I didn't think you'd noticed.'

'I notice everything.'

'Indeed?' She glared at him. 'Then why didn't you go where I was trying to put you?'

'Because I didn't feel like being mowed down by Colborough. Nothing short of knocking him down would have prevented that unhappy outcome. Of course, if you have any other suggestions as to the disposal of my person, I'd be happy to hear them.'

'Don't tempt me, sir.'

He started to grin. 'You must admit the day promises to be interesting.' They turned the far corner of the house as he spoke and he paused to cast a comprehensive glance over the colourful throng on the lawn. 'In fact,' he added rather thoughtfully, 'very interesting.'

Amy followed his gaze. Several people seemed to be eyeing their sudden appearance with smiles of approval and satisfaction. She realised her hand was still tucked snugly in Hawkridge's arm and snatched it free.

'You appear to be very popular, my lord. No doubt everyone is happy to see you in residence.'

'If it comforts you to think so, Mrs Chantry.' He met her suspicious stare with a bland smile. 'Since we've arrived at the area set aside for civilised pastimes, would you like to try something? Archery, perhaps?'

Amy was not in the mood for civilised pastimes. 'Only if you're the target,' she retorted. Then closed her eyes in horror. 'Oh, no. Tell me I didn't say that.'

His shout of laughter had her cautiously slitting one eyelid open.

'You said it.' Wicked grey eyes glinted down at her. 'But on second thoughts, we'll try something else. Your aim, Mrs Chantry, is already far too accurate.'

Amy decided not to ask for clarification on anything Hawkridge might say that day. It was all too nerve-racking.

Deliciously nerve-racking.

She promptly read herself a lecture on the dangers of deliciously tingling nerves.

Despite the lecture, her nerves continued to tingle at odd moments during the morning. Hawkridge was entirely to blame for the phenomenon. Whenever he was stopped by a visitor, or drawn into conversation with one of his tenants, Amy very properly continued on her way, only to find him back at her side when she walked around a booth or paused to watch a game of horse-shoes.

She was wondering whether she should issue a protest in

the interests of propriety—and whether he'd take any notice
of it—when she caught a glimpse of the dowager through a
gap in the crowd and was promptly distracted.

'Look there, sir! Lady Hawkridge has exchanged Mr
Tweedy for Lord Colborough.'

Hawkridge turned his head, his height giving him a considerable advantage in locating his grandparent. 'So she has. I
wonder how she managed the task, or if she had some assistance from Colborough?'

'Oh, dear. How can you say that with such unconcern?
What do you think has become of Mr Tweedy?'

'I neither know nor care.' He cast a curious glance down at
her. 'I wouldn't have thought you cared a fig for Tweedy's
fate, either.'

'I don't wish to see the man come to any harm. After all,
he didn't actually threaten me in person.'

'Good God,' he muttered. 'A babe in the woods. You
should be locked up for your own good.'

Amy glared at him. 'I'm not quite the fragile little flower
you seem to think me, sir. What's more, Mr Tweedy doesn't
frighten me. And I must say it would serve you right if his
lifeless body was to be discovered by some innocent visitor.'

His frown vanished in a burst of laughter. 'God, you're a
delight. You know, Amy, when you cease being a companion,
you might try your hand at writing Gothic tales.'

Amy's eyes widened. She stopped walking so abruptly her
hand slipped from his arm. A quite hideous tremor of uncertainty caused the bright morning to dim suddenly, as if a cloud
had passed over the sun. 'Why should I cease being a companion, sir?'

'For no reason that should alarm you,' he said immediately,
sounding contrite. When she didn't respond, he touched a finger to her chin, tilting her face up to his. 'Don't worry,' he
said softly. 'I phrased that rather badly. I certainly don't wish
to see you depart.'

Just try it and see what happens, he added silently.

'Oh, well…' Amy lowered her lashes and looked away, flustered by the sudden fierceness in his grey eyes. Fortunately, Lady Hawkridge hove into view again, flitting from group to group like an animated butterfly towing a large cocoon in its wake. She noticed that Colborough had abandoned his cane in the interests of keeping up with the dowager's erratic progress.

It suddenly occurred to her that though her ladyship's progress appeared erratic, she was forging a similar path through the crowd to the one she and Hawkridge were taking, rather in the manner of an advance guard.

The notion struck her forcibly enough to have her digging in her heels when Hawkridge started off again.

'What's the matter?' he demanded. 'We can't stand here. Mrs Tredgett's seen us.'

'What? Oh…'

'Good morning, Mrs Chantry. My lord.' Mrs Tredgett's voice boomed out over the crowd, rendering escape impossible.

'Good morning, ma'am,' they chorused like a pair of obedient children. Amy met his eyes and had to smother a giggle.

Mrs Tredgett marched up to them. 'Perfect day,' she barked. 'See your roses are well advanced.' Having disposed of the niceties, she looked at Amy and waved her stick in the direction of her head. 'What's that you've got on your head, child?'

Amy blinked. 'A cap, ma'am.'

'Ridiculous piece of nonsense. No, don't start blathering on about being a widow. I've been a widow for forty years, but no one ever saw me wearing such fripperies. Might as well put a brand on a girl when she's still got her life ahead of her. Take it off. You're young enough to get away with it.'

Amy managed to close her mouth on yet another repetition that she was a widow. Thank goodness she hadn't needed to utter it; for a minute there she'd thought Mrs Tredgett had wanted to save her the trouble because she wouldn't have believed the statement.

She realised her fingers were gripping Hawkridge's arm, and relaxed her hold.

'I couldn't agree more, ma'am,' he said, watching her narrowly under the guise of examining her offending headwear. 'But such fripperies have their uses, you know.'

Mrs Tredgett chortled wheezily. 'And I'd wager you know 'em all,' she said, punching him playfully on the arm.

Hawkridge stood up manfully under the blow. 'A gentleman never contradicts a lady,' he murmured.

Amy nearly choked as Mrs Tredgett rocked about with laughter. Fortunately a seizure was prevented by Miss Pucklenett's breathless arrival.

'Good heavens, Maude, are you all right? You've gone quite purple in the face. How do you do, my lord? How do you do, Mrs Chantry? I've just been on a tour of the state rooms. Such elegance. Such exquisitely rendered ceiling murals. We were even permitted a tiny peep into the muniment room and the winter parlour, although they weren't strictly included in the tour.'

Mrs Tredgett recovered her voice and snorted. 'Anyone would think you'd never seen it all before, Clara. Pack of busybodies, if you ask me. Surprised you didn't march right through his lordship's bedchamber.'

'Heavens, Maude!' Miss Pucklenett's face turned bright red. 'What a thing to say. I assure you, sir…'

'It's all right, Miss Pucklenett. I gave strict instructions that my bedchamber was to be locked.'

Miss Pucklenett eyed him as one would an incendiary firecracker.

'And how are the Society's ducks coming along?' he asked with a fiendish smile. 'They *are* still ducks, I presume, and haven't been transformed into frogs?'

Miss Pucklenett promptly fell into a morass of half-sentences, flustered explanations and stammered excuses. She was eventually stopped by Mrs Tredgett who took her arm in a firm hold. 'Told you so, Clara. Silliest idea I ever heard, changing the name of the inn. Don't wonder his lordship put his foot down. But come along. We've taken up enough of everyone's time. Plenty more people waiting to meet Mrs Chantry, you know.'

She led Miss Pucklenett, whose mouth was still mutely opening and closing, towards the refreshment stall.

Amy gazed after them in consternation.

'No wonder Mrs Tredgett's been a widow for forty years,' Hawkridge observed. 'Mr Tredgett obviously departed for safer surroundings.'

'Um...'

'Her presence also explains why we haven't seen Pel all morning.'

'Yes, I dare say. My lord, what did Mrs Tredgett mean about people wanting to meet me?'

'Nothing in particular,' he said, resisting the urge to bend down and kiss the frown from her brow. 'Merely the natural interest everyone has in the happenings on the estates round-about.'

'Oh.' That was a reasonable explanation, Amy supposed.

They started off again and she caught another glimpse of the dowager, still moving ahead of them. Perhaps there was a set pattern to these things. After all, what did she know about Public Days?

She proceeded to learn. She learned that she'd been right in saying that Hawkridge was popular and that everyone was happy to see him—but the level of happiness seemed beyond what was usual, as if he'd never attended a Public Day before.

She learned that everyone wanted a chance to greet the lord of the manor—but that their greetings were so enthusiastic they struck her as more in the manner of a welcome; as if he'd returned after an absence of years, instead of paying regular, if brief, visits to his home.

She learned that nobody thought it odd that her hand remained tucked snugly into the crook of Hawkridge's arm, and decided, tentatively, that anyone who lived under his aegis was automatically accepted.

But it was all very odd. And there was something else about the beaming smiles on everyone's face that puzzled her. A kind of pleased satisfaction.

She would have been happy to join in the general air of approval, but she had the distinct feeling that she formed an unenlightened minority of one.

After a while, however, she forgot to worry about it. Once she and Hawkridge had traversed the lawn a couple of times, he declared his duty to be done and that it was time to enjoy themselves.

And Amy learned something else, something utterly irresistible. That, with Hawkridge, she could have fun.

Suddenly it was incredibly easy to converse with him, to laugh at the antics of a pair of puppets; to scold when they encountered Miss Twinhoe and he promptly threw that lady into confusion by expressing the hope that her heart-rending tale had lost nothing in the telling; to tease and coax him into letting her try her skill with a bow and arrow after all.

She learned how very safe she felt half-encircled in his arms as he showed her how to aim and release the bowstring; and how ridiculously thrilled she could be when she actually hit the target.

She learned that magic existed.

Somewhere, far, far back in her mind, a little voice warned that the sunny hours would disappear, taking the magic with them, but as morning flowed into afternoon it was easy to ignore the voice of caution. By the time a crowd gathered to watch the traditional cricket match, and she found herself ensconced on a rug beneath an ancient oak in company with the dowager and Lady Nettlebed, it had been silenced completely.

She settled back happily while Eversleigh's team accumulated an impressive number of runs, laughing with the rest whenever Nettlebed, who was the referee, had his decisions hotly debated.

'I don't know why Bevan puts himself through this year after year,' observed Augusta, idly waving a fan to move the warm, still air beneath the trees.

'Yes you do, dear.' The dowager patted her hand. 'Nettlebed would far rather argue than run up and down a cricket pitch.'

'Well, at least he can keep an eye on Crispin while he's out there. You don't think he's looking a little over-heated, do you, Grandmama?'

'Nettlebed, definitely. Crispin looks perfectly stout.'

Lady Nettlebed sighed. 'Oh, dear. I am *trying* not to be a fuss-budget.'

'Yes, I know, dear.'

'Do the boy good to run about a little,' Colborough put in gruffly.

He was ensconced in a rather magisterial fashion on a chair next to Lady Hawkridge, keeping up a running commentary on the players' skill, or lack of it. Amy cast a glance from him to the dowager, and was suddenly struck by something in their expressions. There was nothing blatantly obvious in their manner, but her ladyship's usual bright smile seemed to have a touch of smugness about it, while Colborough wore a resigned, but definitely proprietary air whenever he glanced at her.

She found herself wondering, not for the first time, about Tweedy's fate.

'Good God!' Colborough exploded, making her jump and switch her attention to the match. 'Told Pelham he should've given the lads a few pointers, but no. Said they'd played before. Where, might I ask? Look at that fool up at bat. Doesn't know a thing about the game. There! What did I tell you? Caught out!'

'Never mind, Tolly. That was the last of your batsmen. We can have tea.'

They had tea under the oaks; Pickles leading a procession of servants, bearing drinks and delicacies, out from the house. Everyone else who had stayed to watch the match converged on the stalls set up to dispense lemonade and ices.

And Amy forgot all about Colborough, Tweedy and the dowager. She took the teacup a maid handed her without taking her eyes off Hawkridge as he strode across the lawn towards her.

He'd stripped off his coat and cravat at the start of the match, but now his sleeves were rolled up to the elbows and he'd loosened the neck of his shirt. With his muscled forearms exposed, his face and throat sheened with sweat, and his black hair hanging over his brow, he looked more like one of his own grooms than a peer of the realm. Until one saw the authority stamped on his face.

He also looked thoroughly disreputable, heart-stoppingly handsome and more than a little dangerous.

Amy found herself fanning her face with a leafy twig, although she couldn't have said why she suddenly felt so flushed. It didn't help her soaring temperature that he came directly to her side and hunkered down on his heels, his eyes glittering, appearing lighter than ever in his tanned face.

'Enjoying yourself?' he asked, smiling at her with that warm light she'd noticed several times that day.

Quite ridiculously thrown by the question, she nodded and took cover behind her tea.

'Here you are, Marc.' Lady Nettlebed handed her brother a tall glass of chilled tea. 'I thought you might prefer this to a cup.'

'You thought correctly,' he said, and standing, tipped his head back and drained the glass with several long swallows.

Amy's gaze widened as she watched the process. One stray drop of tea escaped, trickled over his chin, and travelled downwards, slowly. Down over tanned, gleaming flesh, down over the rippling muscles of his throat, down into the opening of his shirt. Down.

She followed it. In her imagination. Down through the thicket of hair glimpsed through the fine lawn of his shirt, all the way down to his waist.

That's where she stopped, because suddenly she was looking at his face again where his waist had been a second ago.

She blinked, and went absolutely still, staring straight into eyes that had gone from warm to scorching in seconds.

He wanted her. There was no mistaking it. She'd never seen such savage, searing desire in a man's eyes, but every feminine instinct she possessed recognised it—and responded. She felt a shuddering urge to lie down, a need to *surrender*. The sense of acceptance, of awareness, that struck her in that moment was absolute, and utterly terrifying.

To her everlasting relief, Lady Nettlebed returned with another drink, and broke the spell.

'I hope you noticed that I haven't run, clucking, to Crispin's side,' she said archly as Hawkridge stood up. 'Although I'd rather he played cricket than sail.'

Hawkridge took the glass, demolished its contents—Amy didn't dare watch this time—and thrust it back into his sister's hand. 'I noticed.'

Lady Nettlebed's brows rose.

'Listen, Gus,' he said, in the same curt tone. 'If Crispin is boat-mad, the best thing I can do is teach him the proper way of going about things. And you might have a word to Bevan to that effect. God knows, the damn boat used to be his.'

'I already have,' Lady Nettlebed admitted. Then gave a

rather resigned sigh. 'If nothing else, the situation has brought Crispin closer to his father. Thank you for that, Marc.'

A faint smile touched his mouth. 'I'll repeat what I've already told you, Gussie. We won't sail out of the cove until Crispin knows what he's doing, he's promised he won't sail alone, and he'll wear a life-belt whenever we're out on the water. All right?'

His sister returned his smile with a wry one of her own, gave him a swift hug and returned to her husband's side.

Hawkridge watched her for a second, half-turned as though he would speak to Amy, then wheeled and strode back out to the pitch, his hands fisted at his sides.

Amy discovered she'd been holding her breath throughout the entire exchange. She gasped in some badly needed air. Good heavens, the heat must have melted her brain. She must have lost her senses. Surely Hawkridge hadn't looked at her as if…as if…

But he had.

And that wasn't all. She had the dreadful feeling that if he'd made one move towards her, just one, she would have lain back on the grass and let him…

Oh, heavens. She didn't know what, didn't dare think about it.

No wonder Kitty Ingham had broken her engagement, she thought suddenly as her restless, darting gaze halted on that lady.

Lord Colborough's remarks flashed through her mind; comprehension exploded with blinding clarity. No wonder Lord Ashcroft had entertained doubts about the entire business. Hawkridge might be able to conceal his true nature from society in general, but not from men who'd known him all his life. What father would want his innocent, gently bred daughter to face that blistering intensity on her wedding night?

The knowledge that she'd not only faced it when Hawkridge

had kissed her, but thrilled to it, sent streamers of heat flowing through her.

But he'd done nothing since.

Amy clutched her tea-cup as if the delicate china could somehow anchor her while she sorted out her wildly spinning thoughts. Hawkridge hadn't made any advances. At least, not the sort of advances a woman in her position could expect.

Of course, until she'd stared at him in that very improper manner, she hadn't given him any reason to suppose she would be amenable to improper advances. The thought that he might do something about it, *now*, made her tremble.

The realisation that immediately followed, that he would not, had her lips parting on a silent gasp of discovery.

Her gaze flew to where he was standing, tall and powerful, as he waited for Pelham to send down the first ball; the hard line of his mouth and the determined set of his jaw indicative of the fierce will that drove him. He possessed all the natural arrogance of a man used to commanding what he wanted, but it was also the dominance of a man whose first instinct was to protect, whose strength of will was built on a foundation of unshakeable honour.

He would no more dishonour her than he would himself.

Amy put her tea-cup carefully on the grass and contemplated the discovery that somehow, at some point in the past few days, she'd come to trust him. It made her feel incredibly safe. At the same time, the faintest whisper of sadness stirred at the back of her mind.

No, not sadness precisely. Wistfulness, perhaps.

She pushed the notion aside. She should be grateful for the sense of security that wrapped her around. She *was* grateful. No one knew the dangers to a woman of clandestine relationships better than she.

But as the match resumed, the dangers of improper liaisons faded slowly into oblivion. The vision of Hawkridge wielding a devastatingly effective bat drove every thought out of her head—except a deliciously improper, purely feminine appreciation of sheer masculine power.

The sight was riveting.

The return to earth, when it came, was shattering.

There was no warning. Nothing. She heard Lucinda call her name, looked up—

And looked straight into the face of disaster; into the face of the one man she had hoped never to see again.

Into the face of her husband.

Chapter Eleven

Amy froze. There was nothing else she could do. She went absolutely still while ice-cold fear trickled down her spine and her hands dampened. Lucinda's lips were moving, but she couldn't hear what the girl was saying. The world she'd created was shattering at her feet in vicious, razor-edged shards, waiting for her to take the first mis-step that would tear her to pieces.

Then, as a sharp crack from the direction of the lawn heralded another six, the world snapped back into place. A different world, perhaps, but one worth fighting for. Her mind went as cold and clear as the sheen of ice on her skin. As cold and clear as the mocking smile in the eyes of the man Lucinda was introducing as Jeremy Chatsworth.

He bowed. 'How do you do, Mrs Chantry?'

Oh, yes, she remembered those smooth tones, the polished bow. He held out his hand, quite confident she would respond.

And she did. She had no choice. Not here. Not now. She extended her hand; her fingers were enveloped, and pressed around the folded square of paper he slid into her palm.

'Mr Chatsworth,' she acknowledged coolly, and knew she hadn't betrayed herself. And *he* wouldn't expose her; to do so would be to expose his own lies. He would want a meeting before he did anything. He'd been very good at arranging meetings.

She laid her hand on her lap and waited. She was even able to summon a faint smile for Lucinda as the girl sat beside her.

'Is he not charming?' she whispered to Amy, as Chatsworth began talking to the dowager under the cold gaze of Lady Nettlebed. 'Is he not the most elegant gentleman you've ever seen?'

'Actually,' Amy returned coolly, 'I consider your uncle to be more elegant.'

'What! Uncle Marc!' Lucinda gaped across the lawn. 'Well, all I can say, Amy, is that you have a very odd notion of elegance. And, what's more, Jeremy is a great deal more amusing than Hawkridge.'

'I'm sure you think so.'

Lucinda's brows met for an instant. 'You sound rather strange. Are you feeling quite the thing?'

'No, as a matter of fact. I think it's the heat.' An avenue of escape opened.

'But you're quite pale.' Lucinda peered closer. 'Very pale, actually. You're not going to faint, are you? Jeremy particularly wishes to become acquainted with you.'

'I'm afraid our acquaintance will have to wait,' Amy said, rising to her feet. She managed the task of staying upright by the simple expedient of imagining the furore that would ensue if she didn't. Fortunately, her movement caught Lady Hawkridge's attention, making it unnecessary for her to intrude on the conversation.

'If you don't mind, ma'am,' she began before anyone else could comment on her lack of colour. 'I'll return to the house for a while. I have a slight headache.'

'Oh, dear. Are you sure, Amy? You'll miss the rest of the match.'

'Yes, I know. I'm sorry. I think it's the heat.' She wondered how often she'd be required to repeat the excuse before she could get away.

But the dowager nodded. 'I don't wonder at it. Lie down with a cool cloth over your brow, and you'll be better in a trice. Lucinda, go with her.'

'*No!* Please,' Amy added in a milder tone as several heads turned. 'I just need to be somewhere cooler for a while.'

'Of course, dear. Off you go.'

'Perhaps I could escort you, Mrs Chantry.' Jeremy Chatsworth leapt to his feet with what he no doubt considered to be the epitome of masculine grace.

She'd once thought so, too, Amy remembered.

She swept him an uninterested gaze, determined to have a moment alone before she had to confront him. 'No, thank you, sir.'

Turning, she walked away towards the house, conscious of a vague sense of astonishment that she could move at all when every joint and muscle felt frozen. Even when she emerged from the trees into full sunlight, there was no difference. The heat bounced off her as if she was encased in stone.

But her mind moved swiftly; thinking, thinking.

She wondered if Hawkridge had seen her leave.

That caused her to falter. She stopped, looked back. Everyone appeared very small and far away, she thought vaguely. Almost…faded. As if she'd stepped out of a misty painting.

But she could see Hawkridge clearly.

Something tore at her heart. A swift burning slash.

Perhaps it was the last tiny thread of magic being ripped away. It was silly, really, but she couldn't stop the sudden pang of wistful longing for what might have been. If the magic of the day had been real.

If it had been Hawkridge she'd met two years ago.

If he'd been of her station.

If.

Amy shook her head, set wistfulness firmly to one side, and, realising in that second that she was completely unobserved, took the few sideways steps necessary to take her into the shrubbery and out of sight.

The note had told her to meet him on the beach in ten minutes.

Well, he would just have to wait, Amy thought as she trod resolutely down the steps outside the Inghams' gates. She wasn't tackling the stony path leading to the beach below Hawkridge Manor for anyone. The stairs at least had a railing to hold on to. And the time spent walking back towards the Manor was necessary to prepare herself.

She stepped on to the pebbled beach, keeping her eyes on the uneven surface as she made her way around outcroppings of rock and small sunlit pools, until the pebbles became more scattered and she was walking on the strip of sand that formed a narrow crescent-shaped beach at the foot of the cliffs at Hawkridge. The sea whispered a few yards away, its secrets hidden beneath the sparkling blue surface.

She'd been here once before, with the dowager, and had been enchanted by the wild solitude of the place, the rugged cliffs, the crenellated formations of rocks that gave the beach the appearance of another world.

Now the almost-empty landscape looked strangely forbidding, even in the mellow golden light of late afternoon. A few people were still about, but they were some distance away and strolling in the same direction as herself, making their way back to the path and the Manor.

Not that she wanted anyone to witness her meeting with Chatsworth. So far she'd been lucky. Most of the people whom she'd met that morning were at the cricket match, and other visitors had been leaving in large enough quantities for her exit through the side gate to go unremarked.

Chatsworth had chosen his time well.

She wondered if Lucinda knew of the meeting. If the girl

had been told a clandestine meeting with Amy was necessary if she was to help them. She wished she'd thought to mention it to Lucinda, herself. She might not want witnesses, but the thought that no one knew where she was, or who she was with, was suddenly very disquieting.

But it was too late. She glanced up to find the man she'd known as James Chantry leaning against a large rock a few paces away and staring out to sea.

The cynical thought that the pose allowed her to admire his profile had a surprisingly calming effect on her nerves.

Amy took a deep breath and walked forward.

He turned his head as she approached. 'You took your time,' he said without preamble.

She gave a short inward laugh. A good thing she hadn't expected a concerned query about how she'd survived the past year. 'I didn't think you'd leave Lucinda so soon, James,' she answered mildly. 'Especially when you appear to have just arrived.'

He shrugged that off. 'Have to keep her eager for my company.' His lips twisted contemptuously. 'And the rest were only too happy to see me go.'

'Yes, well, you can hardly blame them for that.' She studied him, seeing few changes since their last meeting, when the scales had well and truly fallen from her eyes. 'Is that your real name?' she asked abruptly. 'James Chantry? Or is it Jeremy Chatsworth?'

'The first,' he said. And studied her thoughtfully. 'Don't worry, Amy. We're definitely married. I've been standing here wondering if that's an advantage or not.'

'Feel free to procure a divorce at any time,' she retorted.

He gave a short laugh. 'Still an innocent. Divorce requires several expensive steps, dear wife, resulting in an Act of Parliament. People of our station don't trot into the House of Lords every day and demand one. And an annulment,' he added smoothly, 'would prove most embarrassing for you. After all, I was perfectly capable of performing my husbandly duties. It was you who always found an excuse to avoid your obligations.'

Her chin lifted. 'I deserved more than a hurried tumble on your mistress's bed, James.'

'You didn't know Nan was my mistress at the time.'

'Maybe I sensed she was more than a friend when I discovered you were living with her! But that doesn't matter. We've had this argument before. You found me employment where the maids had to live in and were supposed to be unmarried. Did you expect me to open the back door and smuggle you into the house at night?'

'Why not?' he asked carelessly. 'You made sure I knew about the broken latch on the dining-room window so I could rob the place.'

She gasped and flinched back as if he'd struck her. 'That was unintentional. You *questioned* me, before I knew—'

She broke off as accusations and explanations tumbled through her mind with a speed that left her utterly sure of the conclusions. But she still had to ask. She still had to *hear* it.

Perhaps it was a perverse sense of her own guilt that had her wanting the final confirmation. Like probing a continually aching wound.

'Are you responsible for those robberies at Bristol? Did you set your friend up as a maid in one of those houses, like you did me, so she could let you in and pretend to be tied up with the rest?'

His smile mocked the memories evident in her shaking voice. 'You weren't as co-operative, if you recall, Amy. Bloody ungrateful, in fact, considering all the trouble I went to for you. Yes, the Bristol robberies were my work. I needed money after I met Lucinda.'

'But the last robbery was less than a week ago.'

'God, Amy, you ought to know that money doesn't stretch

far when you're living in this sort of style.' He ran his gaze over her. 'You must have spent a bit yourself.'

She ignored that. 'So…it was you who sent me that cutting. It wasn't Tweedy.'

'Tweedy? What made you think it was him?'

'He brought the mail into the house that morning. The paper with my name on it was on top. Do you mean he had nothing to do with it? You don't know him?'

'Never met the man until a fortnight ago. He was merely a distraction for Hawkridge's groom. It was easy to slip the note into the pile of mail on the seat of Mawson's gig while Tweedy was begging a lift. I didn't expect him to actually deliver it, but I'm not surprised he couldn't resist nosing through the stack.'

So Tweedy was of no importance to her. His words that day had been pure spite, motivated by his ambitions towards the dowager. And, she thought suddenly, she wouldn't be surprised if they never saw him again. Colborough appeared to have routed him completely.

She realised Chatsworth was still speaking. Somehow it was easier to call him that in her mind. To give herself some badly needed distance from the threat he posed.

'I thought the cutting would give you a little warning before I turned up out of the blue,' he was saying. 'Which is more than the bloody nasty start you gave me when I saw you at Nettlebed Place the other night.'

He rapped it out as if she should have had more consideration. Amy inwardly shook her head. 'I saw you, too, but I thought…' She gestured slightly. 'The dyed hair is obvious, but…'

He shrugged. 'A little padding in the shoulders of my coat, a higher heel on the shoes. It's amazing how one's appearance can be changed with a little ingenuity and effort.'

'Costly effort, I imagine. You look finer than when I met you.'

'All in a worthy cause. But you can relax, Amy. The third robbery was the last. Nan's gone back to London. You can't have the same maid hiring on and disappearing too many times in the one town, and she was starting to nag me to tell her what else I'm getting up to. Still, it netted me enough to last until—'

'Until what? Until you seduce Lucinda? You won't find her so easy, James. She's headstrong, but she knows her own worth.'

'Then she won't refuse marriage. And headstrong suits my purposes very well.'

Amy stared at him, horrified. 'But you *can't* marry her! It would be bigamy!'

He laughed aloud at that, but a second later his eyes narrowed, almost with hatred. 'You know, you're a dangerous woman, Amy. That innocent, fragile look pulls a man in, makes him want to look after you. Until he discovers the truth.'

'And that is?'

'You're strong-minded. Too bloody strong-minded. It's not a trait men want in a woman. Especially when added to stubbornness, independence, and a damned inconvenient set of morals. If you want to get on in this world, let our situation be a lesson to you. You quickly lose your appeal and become a nuisance.'

'Thank you,' she said drily. 'I'm glad you explained that to me. For several weeks I actually blamed myself for driving you into another woman's arms, because I wouldn't join you in London until Mama…'

'You *were* to blame,' he interjected nastily when she faltered. 'But never mind that. Just make sure your morals don't get in my way this time.'

'I don't know why you expect me to put a spoke in your wheel, James. Lord Nettlebed is no fool. If you offer for his daughter, he'll immediately make enquiries into your background and that will be the end of it.'

'Not quite. When Nettlebed discovers that Jeremy Chatsworth has no background, he'll pay handsomely through the nose to be rid of me. Especially when he knows his darling, headstrong daughter is capable of eloping.'

'And if Lucinda refuses to elope?'

'I've already thought of that,' he said, in such a dismissive tone that she hoped, fervently, that Lucinda's heart wasn't truly engaged. 'Seeing you with the old lady the other night gave me the idea. If nothing else works out, you're perfectly placed to help me toss the Manor. Some of the stuff in there must be worth a bloody fortune.'

'Are you *mad*?' She stared at him in amazement. 'If I wouldn't help you before, what makes you think I'll help you now?'

'Because if you don't,' he said very softly, 'if you even breathe a word to anyone about anything I've told you, I'll be forced to reveal the details of the Tinsley job to the proper authorities. Anonymously.'

Fear clamped an ice-cold vise around her heart. Her stomach churned. 'I didn't know what you intended! I—'

A snap of his fingers cut her off. 'Do you think they'll care a fig for that? Oh, no, Amy. Not when you took your share of the proceeds and ran.'

He was right. Dear God, he was right, and the knowledge haunted her every waking moment. And most of her sleeping ones as well.

'It was that or sell myself. Or go back...'

'To the poorhouse,' he finished for her. 'Well, whenever you feel like refusing to co-operate, remember that life in the Hulks or on a convict ship is worse than the poorhouse.'

She didn't answer. Let him think her frightened, cowed by the threat of transportation or worse. He was looking so satisfied, so smugly confident that his threat would keep her under control.

And why not? She'd never defied him before. Never flatly refused to fall in with his plans. She'd been horrified, disillusioned, frightened by the glimpse of violent temper he'd shown her. She'd argued. She'd pleaded. But she hadn't defied him.

She'd fled.

'We'd better go back,' she said quietly, and turned away to retrace her steps. 'It's getting late.'

He gave a satisfied grunt and straightened away from the rock. 'Where the hell are you going? The path's over here.'

'I prefer to use the stairs beyond that outcrop of rocks.'

'Don't be an idiot, Amy. The tide's coming in.'

She stared in dismay as she realised Chatsworth was right. They hadn't been on the beach all that long, but apparently time made no difference to the tide. Water was sweeping up to the rocks, cascading into the pools she'd picked her way around earlier, rushing into crevices and exploding in fountains of spray when it could go no further. Even from where she stood, the power of the waves was awesome. Apart from the inconvenience of getting wet to the knees—or higher by the time she reached the spot—if she lost her footing on that treacherous section of beach she'd be swept under before she knew it.

But the path didn't look any more inviting.

Amy glanced up at it and called herself every kind of fool for being where she was in the first place. The cliff at this point wasn't precisely vertical, but it was steep enough to make the ascent look like a daunting task. The thought that everyone at the Manor no doubt spent most of the summer months scampering up and down it made her shudder.

'What's the matter?' Chatsworth demanded, giving her an impatient scowl. Then his frown cleared and he grasped her arm with ungentle fingers.

'God, don't tell me you're still indulging that stupid fear of heights. Get moving, Amy, before there's no beach left for us to stand on.'

He jerked her towards the path as he spoke. Amy let the momentum carry her up the first few feet before she shook her arm free.

'It's all right, James. Your gallant assistance is no longer needed.' She grabbed hold of a protruding chunk of rock and used it for balance while she gathered her skirts in her other hand. They were going *up*, she told herself. She wouldn't have to look down.

'Then hurry,' he snapped behind her. 'There might be awkward questions asked if people see us together. We don't want any suspicions about you until your usefulness is finished.'

'So considerate,' she muttered.

'Yes, that's all very well, but we could have finished our business and walked back a few minutes apart if you hadn't felt obliged to question everything I said. But that's you all over, Amy. Nothing but trouble.'

Amy raised her eyes heavenward and started climbing. In truth, the path wasn't as daunting as it had appeared from the beach, in some places there was even a natural step or two, but with only one hand free and several loose stones underfoot, progress was slow.

Despite that, however, she was doing rather well. She was even beginning to congratulate herself on conquering her fear—as long as she didn't look down—until the path made a slight turn that took it on a parallel course across the cliffside for several feet, and from the corner of her eye she saw nothing but space.

'Oh, God.'

She ground to a halt, closing her eyes before her head started swimming.

But that only made it worse. Without sight, her other senses sharpened. The wind, which until then had been nothing more than a mild breeze, suddenly seemed to buffet her with the express intention of knocking her off her feet.

She opened her eyes again, keeping her gaze to the right. A stunted bush grew out of the cliff almost level with her face. She stared at it until her eyes watered, trying to pretend that bushes were all around her, but her limbs were so rigid, she couldn't even put out a hand to grab a branch in case the movement caused her to lose her balance.

'For God's sake, Amy. What's the matter now? We're nearly there.'

The sound of Chatsworth's impatient voice snapped open some of her mental shackles. She could breathe again.

'James, I'm sorry, but do you think you could go ahead and let me hold on to your hand? I don't think I can trust my balance.'

'Hold my *hand*? Are you out of your mind? How's that going to look when we get to the top? This path doesn't take us back to the road, you know; we're going to end up on the other side of Hawkridge's home wood. What if people are still wandering about?'

'I'm sure they'll only think—'

'God, anyone would think you hadn't been living here for a month. Get out of my way, Amy. I'm not your bloody nursemaid.'

He pushed roughly past her as he spoke, but not to her left as Amy half-expected. Stung by his scorn, she had just managed a tentative lean towards the cliff when he stormed by on the inside of the path, shoving her sideways and sending her stumbling into the top branches of another shrub that was growing up only a few inches below the path.

Amy gave a short gasping scream as she felt the shrub tear loose beneath her weight. As if at a signal, the entire edge of the path crumbled, seeming to gather momentum as the first stones she'd dislodged in her stumble began bouncing down the cliff. She didn't have time to turn, to grab hold of anything, to dig in her heels.

In the single sickening instant before she lost her footing and the world turned over, she caught a glimpse of Chatsworth's startled face. Then the ground dropped from beneath her feet.

Marc was not in a good mood. He didn't know how one small female could manage to disappear between one second and the next, and stay missing, but he was going to find out. And then he was going to put a stop to it.

Amy was supposed to be in the house. More specifically, in her bedchamber. Recovering from a headache.

She wasn't anywhere in the house. He knew because he'd just spent a fruitless thirty minutes searching the place. He also knew she wasn't in her bedchamber because he'd damned propriety and looked in there, too.

She had obviously taken herself and her headache elsewhere.

Perhaps she'd walked back to Lavender Cottage with its inhabitants.

He paced up and down the terrace while he considered the notion. It would have made sense, except that she wouldn't have gone for a long walk in the heat if she'd had a headache.

But if her head wasn't aching, why had she left? She'd seemed perfectly happy sitting under the trees watching him play cricket. The fact that her gaze had been on him whenever he'd glanced across the lawn had been very encouraging. Unfortunately, it had also been frustrating, because she'd looked so deliciously flushed and soft, he'd wanted to drag her behind the nearest tree and see how much more flushed and soft he could get her.

His frustration wasn't eased when he'd walked off the field at tea to find Amy looking up at him in a way that had caused him to resort to the recitation of complicated mathematical equations in order to stand up with some degree of comfort.

He'd managed to keep his mind on the task, but only because they'd had an audience.

Things had improved a fraction when play had resumed. There he'd been, systematically demolishing every ball Pelham sent down to him, with a single-minded ruthlessness that at least gave him an outlet for his physical frustration, and the next instant he'd looked across to the trees to discover that Amy had disappeared.

So had his concentration. The next ball had thudded into the stumps, sending bailes flying to the accompaniment of relieved cheers from the opposition.

Marc scowled at the memory. He'd been well on his way to a century, damn it. Mrs Amaris Chantry had a lot to answer for.

'Marc? What are you doing out here? Your grandmama wants to know if you wish to eat dinner, or have supper later.'

He wheeled about to see Kitty Ingham step through the French windows from the library.

'I don't know about you,' she continued, 'but I've been eating all day. Dinner is the last thing on my mind.'

'Hello, Kitty. I didn't know you and Ingham were still here.'

'Anthony's nurse took him home a couple of hours ago,' she said, reaching him and slipping a hand through his arm. 'But Lady Hawkridge invited us to stay if we wished. I was looking forward to a chat with Mrs Chantry, but I believe she's indisposed.'

'So she said, but she's not in her room.' He frowned, sweeping the outskirts of the home wood with an all-seeing gaze. Nothing moved in the shadows that had formed now that the sun had slipped below the horizon.

'Are you worried about her, Marc? She might have gone for a walk now that it's cooler.'

'I'm not particularly worried; there's still plenty of light and she wouldn't go near the cliff, but I didn't realise the dinner-hour had arrived. If she has gone for a walk, she should be back by now.' He glanced down and gave Kitty a quick smile. 'Tell Grandmama supper will be fine. I think I'll go for a walk, myself.'

'But your sister is here, too, and Pelham and Lord Colborough.'

'They'll survive without my presence.'

Her lips curved upward. 'I'm sure they will. Would you like some company on your walk?'

He grinned. 'No, I wouldn't.'

Kitty laughed. 'I didn't think so. Is Mrs Chantry the one, Marc? I do hope so. Augusta and I are running out of eligible cousins, friends and acquaintances. Not that any of the girls we've cast in your way for the past five years would have done anything except make you thoroughly miserable.'

'Thank you very much,' he said sardonically. 'Why did you keep trotting them out in that case?'

'I meant that none of them were capable of feeling as you do,' she said gently. 'I wasn't, myself.'

His ironic smile disappeared. 'Did I frighten you, Kitty? Is that the true reason you broke our engagement? I know you married Ingham because he's the gentle, unassuming sort, but—'

'No!' She shook her head vigorously. 'I wasn't afraid of *you*, only of disappointing you. I know I tried to explain it at the time, and couldn't. But I hadn't been married myself, then, so I didn't know about intimate relationships.'

'For God's sake, Kitty, what did you think I was going to do to you? I'm not a brute. I am capable of treating a wife with consideration.'

'Oh, dear, now I've made you cross. Marc, I didn't mean that at all. Of course you're capable of consideration. You're the best person I know. Apart from Ingham, that is,' she added with a smile. 'But some people feel more...*passionately* than others. I know I'm not one of them, and that suits me perfectly well, but you couldn't be happy in a marriage where polite consideration was the order of the day.' She raised herself on tiptoe to kiss his cheek. 'And I do want you to be happy, my best and dearest friend.'

'Apart from Ingham, that is.'

She giggled and gave him a little shove. 'Go and find Mrs Chantry. I think she may cast a few obstacles in your way, but something tells me you won't give her up as easily as you did me.'

'I won't give her up at all,' he said, and grinned.

She was alive. And the world had stopped spinning.

Amy clung to that knowledge and didn't let herself think about anything else until her heart stopped pounding. She wished it would hurry up and settle down, because she wanted to hear if rescue was on the way.

Then she realised she could hear other sounds. The wind; the rushing of the sea; the startled screech of a gull as it swooped past her. She even heard the quick flap of the bird's wings as it veered away.

But she couldn't hear anyone hurrying to the rescue.

'James?'

The name emerged from her throat in a tentative croak. Nothing stirred; no one answered.

She called again, louder.

Silence.

Of course he was gone. He probably hadn't even waited to see if she'd fallen all the way to the beach.

Perhaps she had.

She opened her eyes, cautiously.

And immediately choked on a strangled cry of terror. *Oh, God.* She was lying face down on some sort of ledge, so close to the brink she could see over it. The space she occupied was tiny, barely enough to take her full length. If her legs had been stretched out her feet would have dangled over the edge.

Below her the sea swirled and eddied as the tide continued to rush in. She almost felt the pull of it, dragging her over, dragging her down.

No!

The cry of denial tore from her throat and was whipped away by the wind. Her fingers dug into the stony ground so desperately her nails broke. She squeezed her eyes shut again on the realisation that in front of her and on both sides there was nothing but empty sky.

Something was whimpering. Several seconds passed before Amy realised it was herself making those terrified animal sounds. Had she fainted? Dear God, don't let her faint. She would fall over the edge for sure.

The edge. She had to get away from it. She couldn't stay here all night. Clearly, no one except James had witnessed her fall, and he would think first of himself. As far as he was concerned, she might be dead and he might be blamed if any-one saw him near the scene. He would be long gone. There was no one to raise the alarm; no one would realise she was missing. Why should they indeed? Everyone thought she was lying down in her room, not lying on a stony ledge suspended over nothing.

Don't think of it! Don't think of it!

Her hands were still clutching dirt and stones. Think about that, she ordered herself. She wouldn't fall while she still clung to the earth beneath her. It only felt like she was about to fall when she opened her eyes. So she wouldn't open her eyes and she wouldn't let go.

But if she didn't open her eyes, how was she going to crawl back from the edge? She didn't even know if there was enough room to crawl backwards.

Don't think about that either. There was room. There had to be.

She dug her fingers in harder, and concentrated on breathing. Only on breathing. James had said she was strong-minded. If ever there was a time to demonstrate strong-mindedness, this was it.

In. Out.

Dust tickled her nose. Grit shifted somewhere.

She shut out the distractions and concentrated. After a while breathing became easier. She started to imagine that the ledge was wider. Very carefully, she built up the picture in her mind. She could move. There wasn't a sheer drop right in front of her face. She could ease some of the tension in her fingers. She even imagined that the ledge sloped upward a little, making it safer, that there were bushes on either side, closing her in.

And that Hawkridge was waiting for her, his hand out-stretched, ready to steady her if she stumbled, to lead her to safety.

When his image was firm in her mind she moved one leg backwards, very slowly. There was room. At least a yard, maybe more. Taking a deep breath, keeping her eyes tightly shut, Amy shifted, one muscle at a time, until she was lying against the cliff.

The tiny sense of security afforded by the rock digging into her side had her muscles turning to water. Tears of relief welled in her eyes; she started to cry. Heaven knew what the combination of dust and dirt and tears was doing to her face, she thought, and started to laugh instead. The laugh ended in a hiccup, but at least it stopped her crying. She began to wonder if she was injured, and was vaguely astonished that the question hadn't occurred to her before.

Well, it had occurred now. She put the picture of a wide ledge surrounded by bushes to one side of her mind and concentrated on herself, beginning with her head. It was difficult to be sure with her eyes closed, but if she didn't count incipient hysteria, she seemed to be in one piece. She ached and throbbed in several places, her left thigh stung rather badly, but nothing appeared to be broken. Despite a hazy memory of landing with a jarring thud, it was clear she hadn't fallen all that far.

The knowledge didn't provide her with any great comfort. Given her terror of falling any further, it was useless trying to get back to the path. She didn't even know if there still was a path.

After reaching that conclusion, there was really nothing left for her to do except call out every few seconds, and wait to be rescued.

By the time dusk was more than a grey tinge in the sky, Marc had exchanged vague concern for real worry. He'd combed the shrubbery, the orchard, the home wood, and even the stables, without result, and had despatched a groom to Lavender Cottage, only to be informed on the man's return that no one had seen Amy since the middle of the afternoon.

Frowning, he watched the groom retreat to the servants' hall. Then, struck by the sudden notion that Amy might have run away for some obscure reason, he returned to her room and flung open the doors of her wardrobe.

Her clothes were still there, hanging in a neat row; her rose silk evening gown, the peach cambric, a warmer dress of biscuit-coloured wool, and her green pelisse. She'd been wearing her cream muslin.

Something stabbed at his heart at the sight of the tiny collection, but he didn't spare the time to think about that, or his relief that she hadn't run away. Worry congealed into a ball of fear that lay cold and heavy in his gut.

For some reason, his certainty that Amy wouldn't go near the cliff was no longer rock-solid. He didn't think she would go willingly, but when he considered the fact that she was hiding something, and that Tweedy hadn't been seen since the dowager had apparently abandoned him for Colborough, certainty tottered and threatened to crumble.

Wheeling, Marc strode out of Amy's room, took the stairs in several perilous bounds and left the house through the front door. He didn't stop to tell anyone of his suspicions—he'd already entered the drawing-room once, ascertained that Amy wasn't there, and stalked out under the astonished stares of its occupants. No need to give the crowd in there any more reason to speculate on his sanity.

But as he headed back towards the woods, he saw Crispin approaching from the direction of the lake.

'I say, Uncle Marc, that's a capital little row—' His nephew stopped, goggle-eyed, as he strode past him without pause.

An instant later, the boy was on his heels. 'What's up?' he asked breathlessly. 'Where are you going?'

'The beach.'

'The beach? But the tide's in. Probably up to the high-water mark by now.'

He didn't need Crispin to tell him that. Fear spread its ice-cold fingers wider.

The sensation wasn't pleasant. Anger, he decided, was a very good antidote. When he found Amy he was going to throttle her. And then he was going to tell her in no uncertain terms that she was never to go anywhere without him again. In time, if she behaved herself, he might let her go from room to room without an escort, but that was all she could expect.

The absurd thoughts didn't alleviate his fear one bit.

'Amy's missing,' he said curtly to his nephew. 'She might have gone to the beach, and she hasn't a notion of how fast the tide comes in.'

There was one thing to be said for the boy. He didn't need to have things spelled out.

'It's all right, Uncle Marc. If she couldn't get back to the path in time, she'd climb the rock where that dim-witted poet wanted Grandmama to sit for him.'

'Maybe. Heights upset her balance.'

'Better to feel giddy than to drown.'

Marc sent his nephew a quick, wryly amused glance. 'Right on the nail,' he said. 'Thanks, Crispin, I needed that.'

'You like Amy, don't you, Uncle Marc? So does Mama. She thinks bad things have happened to her. She says that sometimes when Amy doesn't know anyone's watching her, she looks frightened.'

'Your mama is a clever lady.'

'Well, sometimes. Look, there's the path. Good thing it's not really dark yet. Can you see anyone down there?'

Marc swore. 'Damn it, I should have taken the time to grab a lantern. Stay behind me, Crispin. Something's not quite—' He broke off before he'd descended more than a dozen steps, and swore again. Comprehensively.

The landscape looked terrifyingly different to the last time he'd seen it.

Crispin peered past his arm. 'Good Lord! Half the path's gone.'

The boy's voice rang out in the still air. A faint echo carried back to them. And then another voice.

'Crispin? Is that you?'

The cry had Marc's head coming up like a hunter scenting prey.

'Amy!' He started downwards again, moving as fast as possible with rubble shifting beneath his feet. 'Crispin, stay where you are! The path starts again further down, but this section appears to have fallen straight down the cliff.'

'No, wait, Uncle Marc!' Crispin yelled excitedly. 'I can see her.' He pointed a steady finger. 'Look! Through those bushes over there. There's some sort of ledge, and I can see a scrap of white.'

Marc turned his head in the direction Crispin was pointing, and felt his heart shudder to a stop. From where he stood, balanced on the cliff-side, the view was better than Crispin's.

The small huddled form his nephew had glimpsed was lying only feet from the edge of a sheer fifty-foot drop to the sea.

He swept the scene around her with swiftly assessing eyes. 'Christ! She must have gone over with the landslide. And the ledge broke her fall.'

'How are we going to get to her?'

'I'll get to her. Crispin, I want you to go back to the house as fast as you can without running yourself short of breath.'

'I'll be all right, Uncle Marc. What do you want me to do?'

'Fetch Pelham and half a dozen strong men. The strongest; they'll have to take both our weights. We'll need lanterns, plenty of thick rope—' he glanced in Amy's direction again, thinking of injuries '—and blankets. You'd better warn everyone else, but tell them not to panic. Amy's alive. That's all they have to worry about at present.'

Crispin followed his gaze. 'She hasn't called out again. Do you think she's all right?'

Marc refused to contemplate any alternative. 'She'd better bloody well be all right,' he grated, 'because when I get her out of this, I'm going to beat her to within an inch of her life!'

'Good Lord!' Even from where he stood, Marc saw his nephew's eyes widen. 'You're not really, are you, Uncle Marc?'

'Of course I'm not. But the fantasy is extraordinarily satisfying.'

Crispin flashed him a quick grin. 'We'll be back before you know it,' he said, and disappeared.

Chapter Twelve

She hadn't called out again because she was struggling to hold back the torrent of tears dammed up behind her eyelids.

He was here. The relief of it threatened to overwhelm her fragile reserves of strength.

'Amy!'

Marc. His voice came from somewhere above her, but closer than before.

'*Amy!* Answer me, damn it!'

She dragged in a breath. 'Yes.'

'All right.' His voice lowered. She counted two heartbeats before he spoke again.

'Can you cover your head with your arms? There's a slight overhang above you. I'm going to lower myself over it to reach your ledge, and I'll probably dislodge a few stones in the process.'

Her eyes flew open in alarm. She knew immediately that she'd made a ghastly mistake. Without daylight to dazzle her eyes after they'd been closed so long, she could see with hideous clarity. Her carefully constructed vision of a wide ledge shattered and vanished.

'You can't!' She clamped her eyes shut as the sky spun dizzily. Her fingers dug into rock. If she could have crawled inside the ledge beneath her, she would have. 'There isn't room!'

'Yes, there is. It's all right. Just lie very still.'

He didn't have to tell her to do that. She'd been still for so long, she didn't think she could move. Even to obey his instruction to cover her head. What did it matter, anyway? She was already covered in dust and rubble.

A hail of pebbles rained down on her as she contemplated that aspect of the situation. A light thud sounded a mere inch or two away, and she sensed a darker shadow come between herself and the early-night sky.

He must have landed like a cat.

The thought vanished when she felt his hands touch her hair.

'Marc.' It was a whisper of thankfulness.

'Yes,' he murmured. 'I'm here, love. Let me see if you're hurt.'

'No, I'm...' Her voice wobbled and she took another shuddering breath. She wanted to cry again. It was weak and foolish, but she couldn't help it.

'Shh.' His hands moved over her head and face, brushing away dust and dirt. Then, as if he was examining something incredibly fragile, he ran his hands over her arms, gently circled her ribs, carefully felt the length of her spine, stroked downwards.

And flipped her tangled skirts up to her thigh.

'My lord!' The urge to cry vanished.

'Yes?'

'What are you doing?'

'Seeing if anything's broken.'

'But...' She started to shiver inside. Her fingers dug in harder, but only because the warmth of his touch startled her so. She almost forgot her precarious position for a few heady moments. 'There's nothing broken,' she managed to say.

'I'm blocking out what little light there is, but I think you're right.'

'Of course I'm right. They're my bones. I ought to know if they're broken or not.'

'Hmm. If you're well enough for indignation, you can't be too badly hurt. Can you sit up? I'll check your other leg.'

Amy contemplated the question. Momentary forgetfulness was one thing; moving quite another. 'No.'

He was back at her head in a flash, cradling it in one large hand. She felt him bend closer.

'Is there something wrong with your back? Is that why you can't move? Are you in pain?'

His urgency had her feeling stupidly weepy again. She began to feel as if she was on a see-saw. 'It's not that,' she said wretchedly. 'I can't move, or I'll fall.'

He exhaled on a long breath. 'No. You won't fall, Amy. I won't let you.'

'You don't understand. I have to open my eyes to move, and I can't.' Her lower lip trembled. 'I *can't*.'

He touched his fingers to her face, brushed them over her lashes. 'Yes, you can, darling. I'm between you and the edge. Just open your eyes and look at me.'

His voice was so deeply tender, she simply did as he asked. As if she was impelled by something that would have bade her follow him—even over the edge if he'd suggested it.

Her lashes fluttered up. She blinked rapidly a couple of times, ready to retreat into darkness, then her gaze focused on the reassuring bulk that leaned over her in the gloom, and stayed.

'That's better. Now…' He covered her hands with his, gently easing the tension in her fingers. 'Slowly.'

The instant she felt Marc lift her into a sitting position, Amy grabbed hold of his arms and hung on. The muscles beneath her hands were like iron. She wanted to fling herself against him and burrow in.

'I thought of you, you know.' The shaky admission was out before she knew it.

'Did you?' He propped her against the cliff and, without making any attempt to pry her fingers loose from his arms, carefully probed the side she'd been lying on.

'Yes.' She shivered as his hand moved over her ribs. 'Whenever my pretend ledge wavered, I'd think of the way you held my hand when I stepped down from the carriage, and it would steady again.'

She felt the swift glance he sent her, but he continued checking downwards.

'I called out, too. Until my voice got too croaky. I didn't think anyone would come until morning.'

His hand stilled, tightened fractionally, then continued.

'Did Tweedy bring you here?'

'Tweedy?' She took a moment to bring the man's image to mind. 'No.'

'Then what in the world possessed—? No, never mind. We'll get you home first.'

That was good. But for some unaccountable reason she couldn't think why. Everything began to take on a strange, dream-like quality. As if it was happening to someone else. Even the touch of Marc's hand on her thigh evoked nothing more than a rather detached interest in her various wounds.

'Is anything broken?' she asked without any real concern.

'No, but I think this leg's been bleeding.'

'It was stinging,' she said vaguely, and tried to remember what she'd been doing before it all started. 'Did you win the cricket?' she asked suddenly.

'Yes.'

'That's nice.'

'Oh, God, Amy—'

'Yes, my lord?'

'Nothing. I—'

A shout from above interrupted him. He loosened the grip

she had on him and shackled her wrists in his hands. But that was all right, she thought. As long as he was holding on to her, she'd be safe. She heard him shout something back. The conversation seemed to go on for a long time; she recognised Eversleigh's voice, heard one or two others, then a rope came snaking down from somewhere and Marc reached out to pull it in.

She kept her gaze where it was. On his face. His eyes were washed of colour in the night, but, glittering faintly, utterly steady, they stayed on hers, commanding her trust.

'Amy, I'm going to tie the rope around myself. You can hold on to me while I do it.'

She nodded, and hung on when he transferred her hands to his shoulders.

'Good girl. Now I'm going to stand up with you. We won't fall because there's at least six men up there holding the rope, and I'll be holding you.'

Her heart lodged in her throat. Some of the dream-like quality faded, but before she could protest against standing on that precariously small ledge in the middle of nowhere, she was on her feet and locked in Marc's arms.

She flung her own arms around his neck, pressed her face to his shoulder. Reality crept terrifyingly closer. 'Don't let me go!'

'Never,' he vowed, his mouth very close to her ear. Then, looking upwards and raising his voice, 'All right, Pel. Keep the rope taut, even when we're back on the path.'

A confirming shout came back.

'What are we going to do?' she asked, trying to keep her voice from shaking.

'I'm going to carry you up to the top of the cliff,' he said as calmly as if they were going for a walk in the gardens.

'But—'

Her voice dried up completely when he swept her skirts upward again and lifted her against him.

'Put your legs around me,' he ordered.

The sharp command didn't give her any choice. Amy obeyed, simply because she sensed the alternative would be a great deal worse. Such as hanging over his shoulder with an excellent view of the drop below them.

To her dismay, the last comforting threads of detachment were whipped away by the cool wind gusting against her bare legs. She was abruptly, *excruciatingly*, aware that she was clinging to Hawkridge in the most intimate way possible, as if she was going to crawl right inside his clothes and cling to his bare flesh.

'Oh, my goodness!'

'Hold on tight,' he said, transferring one hand to the rope. 'You'll feel us drop a little when I step off the ledge, but we're perfectly safe.'

He hoped. Marc prayed his men had a good grip on the rope. This was the moment when they were most at risk—for the few seconds between swinging out from the ledge and making contact with the cliff again—when the sudden jolt on the men's arms as they took his and Amy's combined weights would test their strength, and the strength of their life-line.

The rope around his chest was also going to tighten rather painfully. It was for that reason he hadn't tied Amy to him. If he was safe, she would be, too, because he had no intention of letting her go. And judging by the way she was clinging to him, nothing short of an earthquake was going to wrench her loose.

Deciding not to give either of them any more time to think about it, he stepped over the edge.

Amy gave a short gasping scream and clung tighter. Then gasped again when his feet slammed into the cliff with a force that jolted every bone in his body.

'Are you all right?' he grated. He'd tried to protect her as much as possible, but there wasn't a lot he could do with only one arm to shield her from the impact.

'Yes.' Her voice was a squeak. 'Are we there?'

'Not quite. We're making for the path.' He forebore to tell her that he was virtually walking her across the treacherous face of the landslide, with their safety dependent on the men above them, until they reached the place where the path started again.

But she obviously had a good imagination. And it was running riot.

'Oh, my goodness!' She pressed her face harder into his shoulder. 'Are you sure those men know what they're doing?'

'I'm sure.'

'What if the path falls to pieces again when we get to it?'

'We've still got the rope.'

'What if the rope breaks?'

'It won't.'

'But what if—?'

'Amy, are you always this pessimistic?'

Her legs tightened, pressing her more intimately against him. He took a moment to reflect on the perversity of a body that could harden instantly in response even in the face of mortal danger.

'Only when I'm dangling over a cliff at the end of a rope in the dark,' she quavered.

He didn't feel like smiling at the breathless answer. 'Just keep quiet and hold on.'

Ten seconds later, she was off again.

'Have you done this a lot, my lord?'

He set his teeth. 'All the time when I was a boy.'

'You climbed this cliff with a rope when you were a boy?'

'It seemed like an interesting challenge at the time.'

'But—'

'Amy, I know you're terrified, but could you refrain from conversation until a more convenient time?'

'Terrified. Yes, you could say that.' She waited a breath. 'I was only going to say that one would have to assume you were lighter then.'

'*Amy*—'

His feet hit a patch of flat ground and he knew they'd reached the path. Easing his grip on the rope for a second, he prised Amy's arms from around his neck and hitched her over his shoulder before she had any warning. Her legs fell from around his waist and he used his free hand to return her skirts to a state of modesty before clamping his arm about them.

'I liked it better the other way,' she said in a very small voice.

Wonderful. She liked torturing him.

'I don't suppose… No. I dare say it must have been very uncomfortable for you, my lord.'

'Uncomf—' Gritting his teeth, he started upwards. 'Amy, when I get you out of this, I'm going to either kiss you witless or put you over my knee. I haven't decided yet. Unless you wish me to make the decision while your pretty little rear is so close to hand, I suggest you shut up.'

She shut up all the rest of the way to the top of the cliff.

She remained silent when they finally reached safety. But that was probably because several people began talking at once.

Eager hands reached to pull them over the top. He recognised his grandmother's anxious tones. Colborough was barking instructions. His sister and Nettlebed joined in. Crispin was yelling encouragement as he continued to haul in rope with an action that would have earned him line-honours at a regatta.

'What the devil—' Marc began, lowering Amy to the ground and releasing her. He yanked the rope from around his chest before he was hauled in with it, then, warned by the tiniest of sighs, whirled and snatched Amy back into his arms as she sank against him in a dead faint.

'Such a dreadful thing to happen, Dr Twinhoe. Why, we've all been up and down that path hundreds of times, with never a thought that it might collapse.'

The dowager wrung her hands, then scurried over to the bed where Amy was lying, an unwilling prisoner. She began plumping up pillows. 'There, that's better, isn't it, dear?' She didn't wait for an answer, but flitted across to the windows, where she drew the curtains against the bright morning sunlight.

'From what his lordship was telling me last night, dear lady, all the rain we've had recently must have softened the soil.' Dr Twinhoe closed up his bag and patted Amy's hand. 'When Mrs Chantry tripped and stumbled against a shrub on the side of the path, the roots tore loose, together with a great chunk of earth and stones, and started a small landslide.'

'Dreadful!'

'Yes, indeed. But, fortunately, Mrs Chantry's injuries are minor. A nasty bump on the head, a bad gash and various scratches and bruises. I won't remove the bandage on her leg this morning. Just dropped in to see how she was going on. Dare say you have a touch of the headache, my dear.'

Amy opened her mouth.

'Who could wonder at it?' exclaimed the dowager, pattering back to the bedside. 'So very kind of you to call in, Dr Twinhoe. What would we do without you?'

Amy closed her mouth again.

'I expect you would go on perfectly well,' he responded, twinkling. 'A day or two in bed and plenty of quiet is what's needed here. I'll leave a dose of laudanum with you, m'lady, now that we know the head injury isn't serious. Sleep is the best cure for a shock of such magnitude, but I expect Mrs Chantry to be able to drop off without any assistance.'

'Especially after very little sleep last night,' her ladyship agreed. 'Marc kept poking his head in every hour or so and telling us to wake her to see if she was still sensible. Quite absurd of him. Amy is always sensible, aren't you, dear?'

Amy's lips parted.

'Bit of a new-fangled thing that, waking the patient for a bump on the head.'

Her lips closed again.

Dr Twinhoe shook his own head. 'Hawkridge told me he'd seen it done in the Peninsula. Can't do any harm, I suppose. Now, before I go—' he raised his bushy brows at the dowager '—tell me who informed Mr Tweedy that chicken-pox is rife in the village?'

Her ladyship's eyes opened to their widest extent. 'Good heavens, I've no idea. What makes you ask?'

'Merely that Tweedy came knocking on my front door before I'd swallowed my breakfast this morning, and wanted my opinion about a spot on his nose. Man's an idiot. Told him he'd been out in the sun too long yesterday, but he insisted that chicken-pox was all over the place.'

'Well, fancy that. Of course, I did tell Lord Colborough that one of our maids had come down with it, but I can't imagine why he would pass the information on to dear Mr Tweedy. Why do you think, Amy?'

She took a breath.

'Mumbled something about a walking cane and being threatened with the ffollifoot girls.'

Amy exhaled and subsided into the bedclothes.

Dr Twinhoe frowned. 'The man must have been drinking, and at a disgracefully early hour, too.'

'Disgraceful,' agreed the dowager. 'I shall tell him so, if I see him again.'

'Don't think you will,' said Dr Twinhoe, picking up his bag and heading for the door. 'He was driving his gig, and there was a chest and a carpet-bag in the back. I'll call in again tomorrow, Mrs Chantry. In the meantime I don't want you to leave that bed. No reason to.'

'No, indeed, Amy, dear.' Her ladyship scurried around the bed and produced a small silver bell which she placed by

Amy's hand. 'I'm sure you must be perfectly exhausted, answering questions every few minutes. Now, you have a nice, long sleep before you worry about receiving all the visitors who are calling in to see how you go on. If you need even the smallest thing, just ring this little bell.' After straightening the already straight quilt and giving the pillows a final pat, Lady Hawkridge tip-toed out of the room after Dr Twinhoe.

Amy contemplated the closed door for several seconds. When she was quite sure that the dowager was being true to her promise to keep visitors away, she sat up. No dire consequences followed.

She could have told Dr Twinhoe, if he or anyone else had allowed her to speak, that such would prove to be the case. Lying about in bed, for whatever reason, had not been encouraged in the poorhouse.

And she had every reason to leave her bed. Her mind had been made up last night when she'd recovered her senses, when all the fuss and commotion had died down, when everyone had come to the conclusion that she'd gone down to the beach for some fresh air and had tripped on the path.

She had a vague recollection that it was Hawkridge who'd put the tale about, but, despite the aches and pains and confusion that had constituted the rest of her night, she hadn't been fooled into thinking he believed the story.

A quick frown creased her brow. There was something else he'd said. When they were on the ledge. Something she felt was important, but that had been lost in the confusion that followed.

After a moment she shook her head. It no longer mattered. She was going to tell him everything. No matter what the risk. It wasn't only for Lucinda's safety. She truly believed her intervention wouldn't be necessary; the girl was too closely guarded. She simply couldn't continue to lie to him.

Not any more. Not to him.

She would have to leave, of course. She didn't think Hawkridge would throw her to the wolves—remembering the way he'd cradled her all the way back to the house, she didn't think he could be so gentle and tender one moment, and behave with such heartlessness the next—but he would hardly want her to stay. She knew he disliked lies and pretence—she could hardly blame him—and she'd lied to him, to his grandmother, to everyone. And they'd all been so kind to her.

The weight of guilt threatened to drag her under the bed-clothes again, to hide until she could creep out of the house unobserved. But that was the coward's way, and she wouldn't be able to live with herself if she took it.

Moving gingerly, Amy climbed out of bed and proceeded to dress herself in her peach cambric gown. The cream muslin was but a memory; even Amy's thrifty soul conceded that no amount of scrubbing and mending could restore its tatters to anything resembling a dress.

Clothed, she examined her reflection in the mirror. It was the first time she'd seen herself since the accident. The sight made her wince. Her arms were decorated with darkening bruises intersected by scratches of varying lengths, and a wide bandage circled her head, holding a cold compress in place over one eyebrow. Thanks to its presence, her hair fell to her shoulders in wildly tousled ringlets, despite Lady Nettlebed's ministrations last night which had removed a collection of leaves and twigs.

There was another bandage around her thigh, but that, at least, was out of sight. The same couldn't be said for the graze along one collarbone. As for her hands...

Amy shuddered and set about rectifying the situation.

Ten minutes later she tip-toed to the door, opened it and peeped out. Given that the bell Lady Hawkridge had left with her wouldn't have been heard more than a few feet away, she half-expected to see a maid on duty outside her room.

The passage was empty.

On a sigh of relief, she slipped silently out of the room and, moving like a wary, slightly battered little ghost, set off in search of Hawkridge.

Pacing up and down the terrace—or anywhere else for that matter—was becoming something of a habit.

Marc brooded grimly on the fact that he was going to wear a path in the flagstones, or in any one of a number of carpets.

On the other hand, the exercise did serve to keep his tightly coiled body occupied, while he planned strategies in his mind.

Unfortunately, only one strategy had any appeal. As soon as Amy awoke from her nap, he was going to lay everything out for her in no uncertain terms.

Politely, of course. He wasn't going to yell. After all, she'd been through a harrowing ordeal. But he would be firm.

He paused at the far end of the terrace and considered the plan. A slight modification was necessary. He was going to lay *almost* everything out for her in no uncertain terms.

Enough to give him the right to look after her from now on. Enough to protect her. To cherish her. To win her heart.

Enough to make sure she didn't get herself into any more situations that threatened to shred his self-control into tiny, little pieces and toss them to the four winds.

He started pacing again.

She was going to marry him. He wasn't going to brook any defiance. She could forget her independence for five minutes and admit that she needed him. He'd saved her life, damn it. He'd proved that when a male took over, disaster didn't ensue. In fact, if anyone had caused a disaster, it was Amy for going to the beach in the first place.

He ground to another halt, eyes narrowed in thought, as he remembered that he still didn't know why she'd indulged in a pastime guaranteed to terrify her.

Something told him the answer to that little question would prove very enlightening.

'Uh…my lord? May I have a word with you?'

Several words. And then—

He stopped in mid-thought, whipping around when he realised the tentative little voice he'd heard wasn't in his head.

A giant fist slammed into his heart. Every strategy involving politeness, consideration and even a modicum of civilised behaviour fell at his feet and smashed on the flagstones. Amy stood a few feet away, looking as if someone had taken a club to her.

'What the devil are you doing out of bed?' he yelled. 'Damn it, Amy, do I have to climb in there with you to make sure you stay put?'

Amy blinked at the outraged question and resisted an insane urge to nod. She had the feeling that if she did, she'd be back in bed, with Hawkridge, before she could take another breath.

The thought caused such a pang of longing, she forgot why she'd left her bed in the first place.

'This is it!' he snarled, starting to pace with an abruptness that made her jump. 'This is the final straw!'

She blinked again, wondering what she'd missed.

'I waited.' He halted and transfixed her with an accusing glare. 'I did what you asked, and look what happened! You nearly got yourself killed!'

'But—'

'And why? Because I was *waiting*. For you to tell me what was going on. For you to trust me. And have you? No! You'd rather cling to your stubborn independence.'

'But—'

'Well, no more! You've had a free rein long enough. I'm pulling it in.'

She narrowed her eyes at him. 'I beg your pardon, my lord?'

'Look at you!' he demanded, running his gaze over her with glittering thoroughness. 'Just look at yourself.'

Before she could tell him that she already had, and didn't wish to repeat the experience, he closed the distance between them in three long strides. One sharp tug and he'd whisked away the shawl she'd draped about her arms. It went sailing on to the flagstones.

Amy gazed after it in bemusement. Then jumped when Hawkridge touched the scratches on her arms.

A visible tremor shuddered through him. His voice went hoarse. 'God, Amy. Look at you.'

She looked at him instead, her eyes widening at the sudden raw emotion in his face.

He studied her injuries for a moment, then still holding her wrists as if she was made of fragile glass, raised her hands to his mouth and pressed first one abraded little palm to his lips, then the other.

A river of sensation flowed all the way to Amy's toes and back again. She forgot about everything except the heart-shaking tenderness with which he touched her. He was warmth and strength and safety. Everything she needed in that moment.

'My lord...' She gazed up into the darkening grey of his eyes and couldn't remember what she'd been about to say.

'Hush,' he murmured, and releasing her hands, drew her into his arms. 'It's going to be all right, little Amy.'

Bending his head, he took her mouth with his.

It was the sweetest, gentlest, most intensely cherishing kiss Amy could have imagined. No, she thought hazily in the instant before her mind blanked and she softened against him. She could never have imagined a kiss like this.

His arms tightened about her with the utmost care, cradling her. He parted her lips, but so tenderly she yielded without a qualm. He stroked his tongue into her mouth with a deep, slow, possessive caress that had every muscle in her body melting to the consistency of warm honey.

She stopped thinking and let herself feel. Just for this moment. Just for this one kiss. Surely no one could begrudge her this, before she had to destroy everything she held—

No!

Awareness, barely acknowledged and almost instantly suppressed, dashed a wave of cold reality over her in the same moment that Hawkridge broke the kiss.

He continued to hold her, but she felt as if a yawning chasm had opened between them. Heat blazed in his eyes; it couldn't warm her. His body felt like coiled steel, but her senses had gone numb.

She didn't dare think what she'd just thought.

She didn't *dare*.

His brows drew together and he touched a hand to her face. 'Amy? What is it, love?'

She stiffened and drew herself out of his arms. 'I…have to talk to you.'

'Yes, I know. But not here.' His gaze swept over the windows opening onto the terrace. 'The place is swarming with concerned neighbours, who will very likely feel obliged to interrupt us if they catch sight of you. Can you walk as far as the shrubbery?'

She nodded. It was all she could manage. His sudden shift from outrage to tenderness already had her emotions teetering precariously on the brink. Her voice threatened to fail her completely when she thought of the kindness of the people she'd come to know.

The people she'd deceived, she reminded herself ruthlessly. She had no right to indulge in foolish tears and wistful yearnings. Even less right to be treated like a fragile lady who was going to shatter if handled too carelessly.

'We can go further afield, if you wish, my lord.' She deliberately made her voice cool and polite. 'I really am much better this morning. And I assure you, I have as little desire to be interrupted as yourself.'

He sent her a quick, frowning glance. 'Not for the same reason, I suspect. Don't worry, Amy. I've done this the wrong way around, but there's nothing to distress you.'

'I seem to be rather less distressed than yourself, my lord.

And…' her pose of remote politeness trembled on its shaky foundations '…I haven't thanked you yet for saving my life. Indeed, at risk to your own.'

'That's all right,' he said with a wicked grin. 'I'll savour my reward when you recover.'

'Well, you've already kissed me wit—'

His eyes flashed silver fire.

Amy swallowed and tried to recover lost ground with a touch of humour. It took an incredible effort. 'I mean…I trust you're not going to carry out your threat to beat me.'

'So you remember what I said last night.'

'Yes.' They turned into the shrubbery as she spoke. 'But since you were under a considerable strain at the time, I didn't place a lot of credence in it.'

Hawkridge jerked to a stop. Without warning, he was looming over her.

'Considering that kiss we shared not two minutes ago,' he grated menacingly, 'that was a big mistake. The only reason I'm not putting you over my knee, Mrs Chantry, is that it would be difficult to find a spot that isn't already black and blue.'

Amy stared into the blazing eyes so close to hers, and decided it would be better to stay silent until she had her thoughts in some sort of order. She seemed to be having a great deal of trouble keeping up with Hawkridge's changes of mood. He was bouncing from outrage to concern to a rather ominous edge of danger with a speed that left her already shaken wits reeling.

'Here,' he growled, straightening. 'Sit down before you fall down.'

She was steered over to one of the benches set at intervals along the enclosed walk, and released. Her legs gave way thankfully.

'Now—'

'Before you start, my lord—' *and before she lost her courage* '—I have something to say.'

'So do I,' he said. 'And I've already waited long enough to say it. In fact, more than long enough to confirm my opinion that waiting for certain people to come to their senses is extremely unrewarding.'

Her spine straightened. She lifted her chin. 'You consider waiting *three days* to be excessive, my lord?'

'More than excessive.'

'Well! All I can say is—' She stopped, suddenly realising she *didn't* know what to say. In fact, she was completely baffled.

'Why are we having this conversation?' she asked, her voice rising. 'Nothing has happened to Lady Hawkridge. What were you waiting for, anyway? Why should you care if I trusted you or not? Why—?'

'Because you're going to marry me, damn it! It would be gratifying if you trusted me, too.' He glared at her astonished face for a second, then turned aside and took several impatient strides along the path. *'Bloody hell!'*

Amy gazed after him, her brain reeling in shock. She couldn't think. She couldn't speak. She couldn't move.

Perhaps she hadn't heard correctly.

When Hawkridge wheeled about and strode back to her, she hadn't moved so much as an eyelash.

He sat down, laid his arm along the back of the bench and covered the small fists clenched in her lap with his other hand. His eyes blazed, demanding her compliance.

'Amy, I know you prefer to fight your own battles, but last night made it patently obvious that you can't fight every battle alone. I want the right to protect you. To…care for you. You're going to marry me.'

'But…' Something shuddered and threatened to break open deep inside her. She trembled.

'There's no need to be afraid,' he said at once. 'I know we've only known each other a week; that doesn't matter.'

The words aroused a faint sense of surprise. She felt as if she'd known him forever. As if she'd recognised him that very first day.

The terrifying awareness inside her shuddered again, harder.

He tightened his hold on her hands. 'Say yes.'

A flicker of indignation sprang to life. She hung on to it, almost as desperately as she'd clung to Hawkridge last night. 'How can I do that, my lord, when you haven't asked me a question?'

He half-smiled at that. 'And give you the chance to say no? Do I look like a fool?'

No, never. He looked like the man she loved.

Oh, God!

She squeezed her eyes shut, as if cutting out the sight of him would take the knowledge away. She couldn't breathe. Because if she took another breath, then time would move on and awareness would become knowledge and—

But sheer physical reflex, far beyond her fragile control, released the breath she was holding, and like the tide sweeping over the rocky beach below them, awareness, knowledge, acceptance, broke free and flooded every part of her being. Heart and mind and soul.

She loved him.

How had it happened? How had she not known it until this moment?

The questions meant nothing; they were gone as soon as she asked them. All she knew was that she'd been offered a piece of heaven—and had to stay in the hell of her own making.

'Amy?'

She opened her eyes, looked at him. At those stern, handsome features. At eyes that could glitter with fierce intensity or gleam with wicked laughter. At the hard mouth that had possessed hers with devastating gentleness. At the face that would haunt her for the rest of her life.

She was vaguely aware that Hawkridge was speaking again. Vaguely aware of his rueful laughter as he said, 'All right, Amy, if it's the question you want, you shall have it. Will you do me the very great honour of becoming my wife?'

'I...can't,' she said almost inaudibly. And almost doubled over with the pain of saying the words. Oh, how could she bear it? If she'd been alone she would have fallen to the ground in a tiny ball of agony and waited there for her heart to finish bleeding.

As it was, she had to draw back, to wrench one hand free, to press her fingers to her stomach. She was dying inside. And it was going to take forever; she could see by his expression that he wasn't going to accept her refusal.

'Why can't you?' he asked with a gentleness that tore at her soul. She wondered if knives could be as sharp, as brutally cutting. The pain stole her breath. She couldn't speak, couldn't answer him.

'You're not still entertaining the idiotic notion that you're a servant, are you, Amy? Because if you are—'

A quick shake of her head cut him off.

He waited for a moment, then his eyes narrowed, his voice went hard. 'Is it because you're illegitimate? I don't care about that; it isn't your fault, anyway.'

'No.' She uttered the word through dry lips. 'It isn't that. I—' She broke off, turned her face away. If she'd been able to, she would have turned away completely, shielding herself from the storm she sensed building within him.

'Then why, damn it? Do you think I'll tell you how to run your life? Is that it? I won't. I respect your independence. Your strength. It's one of the things I—'

'*Please,*' she whispered, almost choking on the lump in her throat. She had to stop this. She had to get away until she'd regained control of herself, until the pain eased. If it ever did. She owed him an explanation, she knew that. But not now.

'Please *what*?' he exploded, getting abruptly to his feet. He took a step or two away from the bench before whirling to face her. There was a white line about his mouth, but she was too distressed to worry about the reason for it.

'God, Amy, you can't leave it like that!'

She wondered vaguely why not. He'd accepted Kitty Ingham's refusal, hadn't he?

'Did Chantry mistreat you?' he demanded. 'Do you think I will? Tell me *why*.'

'All right!' she cried, breaking under his insistence. When he took a step towards her, she sprang to her feet, holding out a hand to ward him off. Her breath kept catching. She had to wait until she had enough air to say it quickly.

'I can't marry you…because my husband isn't dead.'

She saw the shock hit him, turn his face white. Then his eyes narrowed, and she knew he was thinking back, searching for anything that might have given her away.

Pain stabbed through her, relentless, brutal, crippling.

'I know…there's more…but…' Her voice became wholly suspended by tears. 'Later,' she whispered. 'When I can speak. When I can…'

It was impossible to continue. Turning blindly, Amy walked towards the shrubbery entrance. She didn't know how she managed it; even then she had to stop for an instant. She drew in a breath, wondered how she would get to the house; told herself she would crawl there before she gave in to the agony tearing her apart.

She knew Hawkridge was standing where she'd left him. She could feel the violent storm of emotion raging around him. But she couldn't look back, couldn't let him see…

'I'm sorry,' she uttered. 'I'm so sorry. I wish…'

Gathering her last ounce of resolve, she took an experimental step. And another. Then, knowing she was out of the shrubbery, and out of his sight, she broke into a stumbling run, gaining momentum, until she was fleeing towards the house as if every demon inhabiting her personal hell howled after her in savage, triumphant glee.

Chapter Thirteen

She made straight for the library. She didn't know why. Sheer instinct, perhaps. A hunted creature fleeing to the place where she'd found a measure of safety.

Or had she fled here in a last desperate bid to deny the pain, and the cause of it?

But there was no denial. No shield against pain. No hiding from the truth.

Amy stared up at the portrait, her arms held tight across her waist, and knew with an anguish that tore at her heart that, without noticing, without knowing, she'd taken the step from fascination with an image to love of the man.

How could she not? she thought, groping her way to a chair and sinking on to it. The portrait was of a boy, striking, commanding interest, but ultimately meaning little.

The reality was a man, strong, protective, honourable; commanding all, meaning everything.

Amy made a tiny sound of pain and began to rock back and forth. She couldn't think clearly. And yet, somewhere in her mind, she knew she'd have to go upstairs, pack, make sure she hadn't left her room untidy.

She'd have to speak to Lady Hawkridge. Tell her...

She stopped rocking, seizing on the thought. Yes. That she

could do. Before anything else, she'd end this deception, tell the dowager the truth, apologise.

As if that would make it better, she thought, getting stiffly to her feet. The cut on her leg ached; she scarcely felt it. What was a cut on the leg compared to the vicious claws embedded in her heart?

She deserved it, she thought suddenly in an agony of self-blame. Not only because she'd deceived people, but because she'd been so heedless, so foolish. What had she been thinking? What…?

But that was it. She'd been thinking only of Hawkridge, focusing so intently on him, on his actions, his words, that she'd ignored the love blossoming secretly in her heart.

Well, no more hiding from the truth, she told herself, moving towards the door. She could never put him out of her mind, she was his into eternity, but one day, maybe, the worst of the pain would ease, and if she set things right with the dowager, she would still have some pride.

The door opened on the thought, causing her to jump. Lady Hawkridge peeped into the room.

'Why, Amy, dear…what are you doing out of bed? I just looked in upstairs to see if you were sleeping and you weren't there.'

Amy took a moment to let her startled nerves settle. For a second there she'd thought…hoped…feared…

'You've been crying,' continued the dowager, coming into the room and closing the door. 'You know, Amy, I don't wish to scold, but you really shouldn't—'

Her ladyship broke off, her suddenly shrewd gaze studying Amy's face. She nodded. 'This isn't because of last night. It's not because you're in pain.'

'No, ma'am.' Amy glanced down at her arms, still clasped tightly across her waist. 'At least, not that sort of pain.'

'Well…' Lady Hawkridge crossed the room and sat down on the sofa set to one side of the fireplace. 'That explains why

Marc went charging off on that wicked black stallion of his not five minutes ago. Come and sit down, dear, and tell me all about it.' She patted the seat next to her.

Amy felt her lower lip tremble. She sank her teeth into it until it steadied, then complied, seating herself beside her employer and clasping her hands tightly together.

'I presume Marc made you an offer,' the dowager began, startling Amy into looking at her. 'And since I've never seen anyone looking so miserable after accepting one, I presume you refused.'

'Yes, ma'am. I— How did you know?'

Her ladyship smiled. 'Amy dear, I've known since I met you that you're perfect for Marc. He obviously didn't take much longer to come to the same conclusion.'

'Perfect?' She shook her head. 'Ma'am, even excluding the facts of which you're as yet unaware, I'm penniless. I have no family. At least, none that I know of. I—'

The dowager clucked her tongue. 'Good heavens! Marc must have expressed himself with an extraordinary lack of address if you think that sort of thing is important to him.'

'It isn't only my lack of connections,' she said very low. 'My parents weren't even married. Mama and I spent years in the poorhouse. I…I've lied to you consistently, ma'am. Mostly by omission, but also in pretending to be a widow. There was good reason for it. At least, I thought so at the time, and if you'll allow me to explain—'

'Amy, dearest, explanations will make no difference at all.'

Amy's eyes widened in dismay. Every drop of blood drained from her face. 'They won't?'

'Oh, you poor child.' Her ladyship moved closer and put a comforting arm about her shoulders. 'I seem to be as *maladroite* as Marc is today. It must be the disappointment. I was so sure everything was going along swimmingly. Of course, you may explain, Amy. But it won't make any difference to the way I feel about you.' Perhaps sensing from her companion's rigid posture that comfort would only shred her control further, Lady Hawkridge removed her arm from about Amy's shoulders and sat back. 'I still wish to welcome you into the family, and I fully intend to do so.'

'But...' Amy shook her head in bemusement. 'You don't seem to understand, ma'am. I'm illegitimate. My first proper post was as a kitchenmaid to the superintendent of the poorhouse, and after that I wasn't much more than a housemaid. I've been masquerading as a lady's companion. Indeed, as a lady. And—' She took a shaky breath. 'Far from being a widow, I have a husband who is very much alive.'

'Oh, dear,' said the dowager, pursing her lips in grave consideration. 'Yes, indeed. That is a problem. I wonder what we should do about him?'

Amy could only stare at her employer in mute confusion. Her mind, battered already by heartbreak, remorse and unbearable pain, was completely unable to cope with anything else. She simply waited. For judgement. Castigation. She knew not what.

Lady Hawkridge lapsed into silent contemplation for several minutes, then sat up with an air of decision. 'Have you told Marc about your husband, Amy?'

She nodded. 'And I just realised... I'm sorry. I should have thought of it before... But I was so distressed, and... I have to warn Lord Nettlebed.'

The dowager untangled this incoherent speech and seized on the point that was missing. 'Why?'

Amy took a ragged breath. 'Ma'am, my husband is Mr Chatsworth.'

'Good heavens!' Lady Hawkridge fell back against the sofa, a hand to her heart.

'Yes.' Amy braced herself for blame, recrimination, and revulsion.

'God bless my soul, what a dreadful shock to have one's husband return from the grave like that. Not that I wouldn't have wished to see Marc's grandpapa, because I was very much attached to him. But he was a good person, which it seems to me your husband is not.'

'Uh…'

'When did you find out?'

Amy's brain reeled anew. 'Yesterday. Oh, ma'am, you don't have any reason to believe me when I've lied to you, but I truly didn't know. You see, he left the party early the other night, and—'

'Well, of course, you didn't know, Amy. And you haven't actually lied to me, dear, except about being a widow, which I dare say is quite understandable now that I know Mr Chatsworth is your husband. What's more, I wager you've told Marc a great deal more about yourself *without* lying.'

'Yes.' She glanced down at her hands. 'I wanted to tell him everything, but…I didn't know why. *Then*.'

'Hmm.' Lady Hawkridge's mind was clearly on more pressing matters. 'What did Marc say about Mr Chatsworth?'

'I only told him my husband was alive, and Marc…that is, Lord Hawkridge didn't say *anything*. Not that I wondered about that. I could scarcely speak, myself.'

'No, indeed.' The dowager sat up again and patted her hand sympathetically. 'As for Marc's uncharacteristic silence, well, you must have given him quite a shock. You know, Amy, when a man has laid bare his heart, and been rejected, for whatever reason, he will not be thinking with any clarity of intellect.'

'He didn't mention his heart,' Amy pointed out in a very small voice.

Lady Hawkridge shook her head. 'Really, Amy, I can only imagine that your head must have received a harder bump than we first believed. Why else would Marc ask you to marry him if he wasn't in love with you?'

'Because he wants me, ma'am. Oh, dear, that sounds terrible. I mean, I think he does. That is, he looked at me as if he does. I think.'

The dowager frowned. 'It seems to me that you both require assistance in clarifying *what* you think. Let me make one thing clear. Marc would not offer marriage purely to satisfy his physical urges.'

'I know that, ma'am. If I'd expected any sort of offer at all, it would have been a *carte blanche*. But I've come to know him, you see. He's very protective, and honourable, and…'

'Yes, Marc is protective and honourable,' affirmed his fond grandparent, ignoring the sudden sheen of tears in Amy's eyes. 'But he's also an unattached, exceptionally healthy young man. He's taken mistresses before from what one would term the ranks of respectable widows. If that had been his intention in regard to you, the only circumstance that might have stopped him is the fact that you're my companion. And that could easily be overcome. I don't wish to cause you further distress, Amy, but, once you'd responded to his advances, he would simply have made you an offer that would ensure your future financial security and thus satisfy any male notions of honour.'

Amy felt a faint spark of interest. 'He's done that before, ma'am?'

A rather mischievous gleam lit her ladyship's eyes. 'One shouldn't confess to knowing about such things, but yes. When you're married, it will be different, of course. Knowing Marc as I do, I shouldn't think he'd even look at another woman.'

'But we're not going to be married.' Anguish, momentarily stifled in talking about Hawkridge, returned with devastating force. Amy dug her ragged nails into her palms to stop another onrush of tears. The sting of last night's grazes barely registered. 'Whatever his reason for proposing marriage…I've destroyed it. Even if I wasn't already married, I deceived him. Just like that other lady. He won't want to see me again.'

'Of course he will,' declared her ladyship stoutly. 'And when he does, you will have to tell him everything.'

'I intend to, ma'am. If he'll listen.' Imbued by her employer's determination, she stiffened her spine. 'If he won't, I'll write him a letter. Perhaps you'd give it to him when I'm gone.'

'I don't think you should make any plans to go anywhere, Amy. It sounds as if Marc already has enough to overset his temper. Chasing you all over the countryside isn't likely to improve his mood.'

'No, ma'am.'

'What we shall do is go upstairs so you can rest in bed while we decide what to tell Bevan.'

'Yes, ma'am.'

'A brief note to the effect that an acquaintance recognised Mr Chatsworth yesterday and warned us that he's a fortune-hunter of the worst kind should suffice. Until Marc is aware of the facts, the fewer people who know Chatsworth is your husband, the better.'

'Yes, ma'am.'

'And then, Amy, after you've told me the entire story, you are going have a nice, long sleep, even if I have to tip Dr Twinhoe's laudanum down your throat.'

'But, ma'am—'

'You don't wish to show Marc a haggard countenance, do you?'

'No, ma'am.'

'That's better.'

Surprisingly, she did sleep—for several hours—the vicissitudes of the past two days proving more effective than Dr Twinhoe's laudanum. The long rest enabled Amy to rise from her bed with nerves fluttering in her stomach, but decision firming her spine.

None of the decisions involved leaving Hawkridge Manor.

At least, not yet. She couldn't leave before finding out if the dowager was right in thinking that Hawkridge was in love with her.

And if he was...

Oh, if he was...

But Amy suppressed the pang of yearning immediately. She'd sealed pain away in a dark corner of her mind, but there it crouched, waiting to spring out and devour the tiny flicker of hope that burned, valiant but terrifyingly fragile, in the deepest recesses of her heart. She couldn't risk that vulnerable flame by thinking too far ahead. It would be enough if he still wanted her.

Besides, her ladyship hadn't known all the facts when she'd voiced that opinion. Hawkridge did know her background and, knowing it, would never have proposed an improper liaison.

Which meant that she would have to propose it.

Amy reached for her clothes and began dressing. It was a good thing she was accustomed to fighting her own battles, she mused, because she was going to need every ounce of determination she possessed. She couldn't afford to stumble. If she hesitated just once, if Hawkridge suspected for one instant that she was quaking inside, his highly developed protective instincts would strip her of all hope.

So she planned. And she waited. She waited so long that when the front door banged, hours after the dowager had looked in on her way to bed, she leapt out of her chair and almost stumbled from sitting curled up for so long.

Putting a hand to the mantel to steady herself, Amy stood poised, listening, hardly daring to breathe in case she missed the sound of his footsteps passing her door. Until she was sure it was him.

A faint echo of his voice came to her as he spoke to Pickles. He must have reached the top of the stairs. She slumped, only then acknowledging that she'd been worried about him. He'd been gone so long and—

His footsteps, muted by the carpet, stopped outside her door.

Amy froze, her gaze flying to the doorknob. A pulse pounded in her temples; her breath seized.

His footsteps moved on. A door closed further along the hall.

She gasped in air, dashed over to the door and flung it open.

The empty hall, lit by candelabra at regular intervals, stretched before her.

Amy pressed a hand to her breast to slow her breathing. Her heart thudded against her palm, her vision blurred. And in the misty haze that formed before her eyes she saw her mother, Cora and every unmarried woman she'd ever encountered in the poorhouse, their thin hands clasped, warning in their faces, despair stealing their youth.

Except her mother. The misty image smiled with a serenity never attainable in life, and, for the first time, Amy understood why her mother had left home and family, casting aside every semblance of security, for a love that was stronger than any fear of consequence. A love that was worth any risk. A love that needed to give, of everything she was.

Lifting her chin, she walked down the hall and knocked softly on Hawkridge's door.

It was opened before she'd lowered her hand. He loomed over her, big and powerful, just as she'd first seen him, his brows drawing together in a quick frown.

'Amy? What the devil—?'

He broke off, glanced swiftly towards the stairs, then grabbed her hand and yanked her into the room. 'What the devil are you doing here at this time of night?' he demanded in a wrathful undertone. 'Don't you know that Pickles is going about the house snuffing out candles?'

He thumped the door shut, making her start. Amy's eyes widened. She hadn't anticipated a flood of reproaches, but Hawkridge looked neither heartbroken nor filled with revulsion. His fingers were still gripping her hand, but the frown between his brows indicated annoyance more than anything else.

'I have to speak to you,' she said at last, and tried to stop the fingers of her other hand from shredding her skirts.

He studied her frowningly for an instant, then released her hand, raising his own to touch the faint bruise on her forehead. 'You've taken your bandage off,' he murmured.

And he'd removed his coat and cravat. But she registered the small details only because she didn't want to think about the remote calmness in his voice, the lightness of his touch.

Had she destroyed everything? Was it too late?

But even as the pain so carefully locked away threatened to break free, his gaze flashed back to hers and without warning his eyes turned molten, brilliant, searing. The blast of heat hit her like a wall of flame. She gasped, almost staggering back. He wheeled, strode across the room to the windows, and shoved his fists into his breeches pockets.

'All right. I'm listening.'

Amy swallowed. She was shaking all over after that coruscating look, but not with doubt. He still wanted her.

She clutched determination to her like a shield and launched into the speech she'd rehearsed for hours.

'My lord, you did me the very great honour, this morning, of asking me to be your wife, and though I had to refuse, I wasn't…specific enough in my refusal.'

He turned slowly to face her. She couldn't be sure in the shadows where he stood, but she thought his mouth quirked. 'Amy, I think "I can't marry you because my husband isn't dead", is rather specific.'

'As far as marriage goes, yes.' She swallowed again. 'But—I could be your mistress.' Despite her resolve, the last words were whispered.

But he heard them. He came forward, until only a few feet separated them. When she looked into his eyes, her heart started racing like the hooves of a runaway team.

'You're willing to be my mistress? To put yourself in such a vulnerable position?'

'Yes.'

'Why?'

'Because last night...we could have been killed, and I would never have known...' She shook her head sharply. 'I realised that being with you, belonging to you, is more important than safety or logic or all the sensible things that say I shouldn't do this. I know you won't abandon me if there should be a child, or leave me destitute if you tire of me. And—'

'Tire of you?' Marc stared at her, trying to clear the haze that seemed to be impeding his thought processes. He couldn't remember everything Amy had said. An explanation for her offer hammered somewhere in his brain, but all he could think about was the offer itself.

She was willing to give herself to him without any assurances as to her future, without the security of marriage, to take the risks her mother had taken.

She was willing to trust him.

'Why?' he said again.

Amy lifted her chin. She would give him this. She would give him everything. 'Because I love you.'

A shudder racked his powerful body. She could see it from where she stood. He whipped his hands out of his pockets, closed the distance between them in two long strides and caught her up in his arms.

'Oh, God, Amy! Amy! It's going to be all right. I promise. You don't have to worry. I—'

He broke off, pressing his mouth to her hair, her face, her throat. He was shaking, she realised in wonder. The strength in him was overwhelming—he could have crushed her without thinking about it—but he was shaking, shuddering like a blooded stallion straining at the bit.

She couldn't think beyond that. He'd seemed so invulnerable. Not to hurt, but to her. His was the position of power, his the control. She hadn't suspected she could affect him so. Just for an instant, she had a glimmer of understanding, that there was more here, in his fierce embrace, than simple desire, but he was speaking again, his voice so low she couldn't make out the words, and the feeling slipped away. All she knew was that urgent male hunger roughened his voice in a way that sent chills of excitement feathering over her flesh, that the coiled tension in his body made her press against him in a purely feminine instinct to assuage that hunger.

Then he lifted her, strode over to the bed and lowered her on to it, and she ceased thinking at all. He came down over her, pinning her to the bed before she'd taken another breath.

Amy trembled as she felt his weight for the first time, gasped as he pressed a knee between her thighs, parting them, bringing their bodies into such intimate contact that her senses swam. She'd known he was big, but lying beneath him like this, completely at the mercy of his much greater strength, was too much. Too soon. Too fast. Excitement set fire to every nerve-ending, but she hadn't expected him to claim her seconds after her offer to become his mistress.

She gripped his shoulders, not certain if she was going to cling or try to hold him off. 'My lord…'

'Marc,' he said, pressing urgent little kisses over her face. 'Say it.'

'Marc—'

The rest was smothered as his mouth came down on hers. His fingers speared through her hair, holding her head still; his tongue plundered, penetrating, retreating, over and over until she couldn't think beyond the demands he was making. Every muscle in her body trembled and went weak, preparing for surrender.

Every muscle in his shuddered and went rigid, ready to conquer. The arms about her were like iron; his shoulders tensed, seeming to curve over her, around her. He crushed her into the bedding, moving against her with a fierce urgency that rendered their clothing well nigh invisible.

She made a small frantic sound, the hard thrust of his body overwhelming her almost to the point of insensibility, and as abruptly as the storm had broken, it ceased. Marc wrenched his mouth from hers and stared down at her.

'Amy. God, what am I doing? I can't make love to you like this.'

She gazed back at him, shaking. Her eyes felt as if they were eclipsing her entire face. His were blazing. 'You can't?'

'No.' The word was a hoarse groan. His chest heaved as he struggled to control his breathing. 'I've never been so close to losing control. I could hurt you.' He moved again, this time with a slow yearning thrust that sent a wave of piercingly sweet pleasure through her. If his weight hadn't held her down, she would have arched.

He let his head fall forward until his brow rested on hers. His teeth clenched. 'And, apart from that, I can't make love to you here.'

'Why—?'

'Don't move.'

She blinked at him. 'I didn't move.'

'You're breathing, damn it.' He took a breath himself. 'Bloody hell!'

Flattening his hands on either side of her head, he pushed himself away from her with such force she felt as if part of her had gone with him. But even as the wrenching sense of loss took hold, he was scooping her up off the bed and carrying her across the room.

'Not a word,' he growled softly, and set her on her feet to one side of the door.

He opened it, glanced up and down the hall, then, drawing her out of the room, shut the door and led her back to her own chamber.

The instant he closed her door she was in his arms again and his mouth was on hers.

Just as well, Amy thought hazily. Her legs weren't going to hold her up another second. She was trembling like a leaf in a tempest, tossed this way and that, but even as she quivered in anticipation of another storm, she realised his embrace was different. He held her as if he'd never let her go, the rigid male flesh pressed to her was no less intimidating, but she sensed the urgency driving him was under an iron-fisted control.

And knowing it, she yielded, sinking into the warmth and strength enfolding her, lifting her mouth for his kiss, parting her lips for his possession, until a new and pulsing heat began throbbing deep inside her.

'God,' he muttered, lifting his head and staring down into her dazed eyes. 'I don't know what's worse. Not kissing you at all, or kissing you knowing that's all we're going to do for the moment.'

'It is?' she asked hazily. She looked about the room and finally caught up with him. 'Is that why you brought me back here?'

'No.' He bent to nip her lower lip in the gentlest of tiny bites, then put her firmly away from him. 'I brought you back here because we don't want the maids finding you in the wrong bed in the morning, or wondering why you're up and dressed before dawn. My appearance at that hour won't arouse any questions. I often ride early.'

'Oh.' That tiny bite had obviously unhinged her wits. She couldn't seem to think straight. Did that mean he was going to stay all night? But in that case, why was he pacing over to the window as if he wanted to put as much distance between them as possible?

'I thought you meant that because I was hurt, we weren't… But I really am much better now and—'

She forgot the rest when he swung about to face her. The

fierce desire in his eyes had the muscles in her lower body dissolving into liquid fire.

'Oh, yes,' he said, very softly, as if she'd asked a question. 'I'm more than capable of making love to you without adding to your bruises. I'm just trying to keep my distance long enough for us to talk.'

'Talk? Oh, heavens!' She made her shaky way to a chair and sank onto it. 'Yes, my lord. I think you *had* better stay over there. I just remembered that I have a great deal to say.'

Despite the barely contained intensity vibrating in the air around him, a wicked smile dawned. 'Say it fast.'

Amy swallowed. 'This will come as something of a shock.'

'After this morning, Amy, I'm immune to shocks.'

'I don't think so, sir. You see, my husband is Mr Chatsworth.'

'What?'

'Yes.' She clasped her hands. 'I didn't know until yesterday because I didn't see him at Nettlebed Place, but it's all right because Lady Hawkridge wrote a note to Lord Nettlebed warning him that James is a fortune-hunter who preys on innocent schoolgirls. That's one of the things he does. He knows the parents will pay him off rather than risk a scandal. Not that he actually elopes with them. He used to disappear, and now he's married to me, but nobody knows that except you and Lady Hawkridge.'

This breathless speech was destined to remain unacknowledged for several seconds. Not that Hawkridge appeared to be struck dumb with shock, Amy thought, studying him anxiously. He was watching her, but the frown in his eyes seemed more thoughtful than anything else.

'That isn't all,' she went on, determined to get everything out at once. 'He slipped me a note yesterday, telling me to meet him on the beach so he could blackmail me into helping him with Lucinda, and if she won't elope with him, he thinks I'll help him rob you and Lady Hawkridge. But I won't.' She leaned forward, her eyes pleading. 'I *won't*! I'd rather be transported than betray you so.'

His eyes narrowed with sudden attention. 'Why is transportation a threat?'

'I helped him before.' The memory washed the colour from her cheeks. Her fingers gripped, entwined, tangled. 'But I didn't mean to. I didn't *know*.'

'Amy.' He came forward and hunkered down before her, covering her restless hands with one of his. 'It's all right, sweetheart. I had to ask, to know what you'd done so I can protect you, but there's no need to be afraid. No one's going to hurt you. This is what you almost told me the other day, isn't it?'

'Yes. I wanted to tell you.' She clung to the steady reassurance in his eyes, the strength of his hand. 'You see, a few weeks after I met James, he asked me to marry him. I think…I think it was impulse. Perhaps he wanted me and knew I'd accept nothing less than marriage. He said he wanted to take care of me, although it was I who was employed. That was odd. He had money, but no apparent means of support. When I asked about it, he talked vaguely of investments. I believed him—what did I know of such things?'

He nodded. 'Go on.'

'After we married James wanted us to move to London where he had friends, but Mama was too ill. She couldn't travel and I wouldn't leave her, so he went alone, saying he'd find work and a place for us to live. I had to leave the school to nurse Mama and, at first, James did send money, but his letters became fewer, and angrier, and finally stopped altogether.'

Hawkridge stroked his thumb across her hands. 'And then?'

She glanced down briefly. 'After Mama died I followed James to London. He got quite a shock when I turned up. It was almost as if he'd forgotten my existence. I even had to spend that first night at a coffee-house because there was no room where he was living—or so he said. But the next day he found me a place as housemaid to Lord Tinsley.'

'An exceedingly wealthy Viscount,' Hawkridge put in drily. 'You don't need to tell me the rest, Amy. Several pieces have finally dropped into place. Such as your reaction to that report in the *Morning Post*.'

'You know what that cutting was about?' she asked, her eyes widening.

'I looked through my own copy of the paper. That article was the only one that seemed apt.' A wry smile curved his mouth. 'I know you asked me to wait until you confided in me, but, as *you* know, waiting is not my favourite pastime. I intended to find out what had upset you, one way or another.'

She blinked at him. 'Asked you to wait—? But…I was talking about your grandmother.'

His brows went up. 'Grandmama seems to be doing quite well on her own account, if the conversation I had earlier today with Colborough is any indication. But never mind that. Am I right in assuming that Chatsworth broke into Tinsley's house, tied you up along with the rest of the servants and robbed the place?'

'Yes.' She would have wrung her hands again if Hawkridge hadn't been holding them. 'I didn't mean to help him, but James asked questions about the family and their movements and so forth, and I answered. I felt so guilty about leaving him on his own for weeks and weeks, and then we still couldn't live together. The only way we could meet was when I was sent out to the market or given a half-hour off. I was so anxious to make up for my neglect, for my coldness, as he put it, that I didn't think twice when he questioned me. I thought he was making an effort to be nicer.' She shook her head. 'Stupid! *Stupid!*'

'No,' he said sharply. 'Innocent. Frightened. Alone.' His fingers tightened on each word, until, realising he might be hurting her, he released her and stood up.

'Do you think a judge will take that into account?' she asked shakily, watching him pace over to the window again. She wished she still had his warmth to cling to. 'You see, that isn't all. When I realised what I'd done, what James had done, we had the most dreadful argument. I'd been totally mistaken in him. He told me he'd struck up an acquaintance with Mama and I to find out if there were any wealthy pupils at the Misses Appleton's school, and since he'd given up the scheme for my sake, I had to help him in his other endeavours.

'The Tinsley robbery wasn't the first, nor did he intend it to be the last. I refused, of course. I threatened to inform against him, but he laughed. He pointed out that the money he'd given me previously, indeed, the money he forced on me then, would convict me along with him. After all, who would believe a girl from the poorhouse? So...I took the money and ran.'

He turned. 'To Bath?'

'No. Not then. I went to some little town... I can't even remember its name. I found work at an inn, but, after a while, the innkeeper... Well, I had to wedge a chair against my door every night. One night he started to smash his way in, and I climbed out of the window and ran away again. He hadn't paid me, of course. I'd been there less than the half-year, but I still had some of the money that James had given me. This time I managed to think—running from a drunken innkeeper wasn't as frightening as running from transportation or the gallows—so while I walked to the next town, I planned.

'I'd heard the Tinsleys' housekeeper talk about Bath, that it was full of elderly widows, so I bought a fashionable dress, travelled by various stages to Bath and took a room at a respectable inn. I thought if I posed as a widow, I might have a better chance of being employed by one.'

When no comment on that assumption was forthcoming, she made a little gesture. 'That's all.'

That probably wasn't even half of it, Marc thought savagely, pacing restlessly about the room. He couldn't be still. His entire body was coiled and tense with the need to lash out at something. If that drunken lout of an innkeeper had appeared before him, he would have smashed his fist into the man's face, and once started, he probably wouldn't be able to stop.

As for Amy's matter-of-fact account of walking about the countryside, alone, in the middle of the night, his blood ran cold at the thought of what might have happened to her.

Not frightened? She must have been terrified. Facing the world with nothing and no one; with the spectre of criminal charges hanging over her. And then to find safety, only to have the past rear its head.

'On the other hand,' he said aloud, wheeling abruptly to face her, 'that makes things easier.'

She looked confused. 'Posing as a widow?'

Yes, he thought grimly. That made things very much easier. But he wasn't going to inform Amy of that.

'The coincidence that caused Chatsworth to choose Lucinda and follow her home,' he said.

She shook her head. 'I should have realised that a place like Bath, with its Young Ladies' Academies and wealthy older people, would be a target for someone like James.'

'You could have stumbled across him at any time, Amy. That sort of criminal life requires regular changes of residence. But it doesn't matter now. The point is, he's here, where we can deal with him.'

Chaining the primitive savage prowling beneath the surface, he crossed the room, took her hands and drew her to her feet. 'But we'll talk about that later.'

'What are you going to do?' she whispered.

'Right now?' he asked very softly, and framed her face in his hands. 'I'm going to make love to you.'

He watched her eyes widen, felt the tremor that rippled through her, and had to clamp a firmer hold around the reins of control. She'd been hurt scarcely more than twenty-four hours ago. Tonight she needed gentleness.

If he kept telling himself that, he might be able to manage it.

He lowered his head to kiss her.

'Um…my lord?'

It was the tone of voice that warned him. He paused, looked into her eyes, and felt a reluctant smile tug at his lips. 'Yes?'

One little hand came up to rest against his chest. 'There's just one more thing.'

'This time I'm not making any predictions as to my immunity to shocks. What is it?'

'At first I wasn't going to tell you, but I promised myself I wouldn't lie to you again, even by omission.'

'You never lied to me about your true nature, Amy. That's all I cared about. Now, tell me.'

'You promise you'll still make love to me?'

'Yes, damn it. What—?'

'I haven't done this before.'

He thought his heart stopped. He knew his brain had. 'I beg your pardon?' he asked very politely.

'I never lived with James. The day we married I had to go right back to the school, and in London he was living with another woman, although I didn't know it at the time. We never—' She blushed, enchanting him. 'Made love.'

He took several deep breaths. It was a good thing he was already prepared to be gentle, he thought, because the knowledge that Amy was innocent, that she was his, *only* his, threatened to banish every instinct except the violently throbbing need to possess her.

'Did you love him?' he asked abruptly, and knew he hadn't asked before because he hadn't wanted to hear the answer.

'No.' She regarded him solemnly. 'I know that now. If I'd loved him, I would have made more of an effort to be a true wife. I liked him. He was very charming at first, but I didn't love him. Maybe I was afraid of being alone after Mama died.'

Her gaze dropped to her hand, still resting against his shirt, then lifted again. 'I'm not afraid of being alone any more. I was prepared to leave, when I thought you wouldn't want me because I'd lied to you. I know I can survive on my own. I've done it. That isn't why I went to your room tonight. I *choose* to be with you, to be your mistress, for as long as you want me.'

'Oh, God, Amy—'

He swooped, taking her mouth before the next words were clear in his mind. Forever, he thought hazily. He wanted her forever. As his mistress, his wife, the mother of his children.

He had to tell her that, had to reassure her that everything would be all right, but coherent thought was impossible with her lips softening and parting beneath his, with the sweet scent of her skin filling his senses, with her body trembling before he'd even touched her.

Later. He was going to need every ounce of control he possessed to take her gently. If the savage inside him had to wait, so could reassurance.

He broke the kiss long enough to pick her up and carry her over to the bed, the soft surrender in her eyes enough to bring his body to full aching arousal in seconds.

But she blinked it away when he stood her beside the bed, and he felt her tense.

'Don't be frightened,' he murmured. 'You took me by surprise before. I won't lose control this time. I won't hurt you.'

'It wasn't exactly frightening,' she said, so earnestly he had to smile. 'Just…faster than I expected.' She blushed, and met his gaze shyly. 'But it was exciting. I liked it.'

The smile reached his eyes. 'Let's see how you like slow,' he murmured and, holding her gaze with his, reached behind her to unfasten the buttons at the back of her dress.

Chapter Fourteen

Slow promised to dazzle her senses.

His arms encircled her; sweet captivity. His hands exerted the gentlest pressure to draw her closer as his fingers slipped buttons free of their fastenings. Her dress loosened, fell away to pool at her ankles.

Amy tipped her head back, wanting Marc to kiss her, to distract her from the nervousness quivering inside her. She wanted him, but she'd never stood before a man and let him undress her. When he loosened the ribbons of her chemise and swept the straps aside, the sudden shyness took her by surprise.

Then he lifted a finger to trace the long scratch across her collarbone, bent and repeated the caress with his mouth, and shyness vanished in the wave of emotion that swept over her.

She swayed and brought her hands up to his chest. The fine lawn of his shirt bunched in her fists, making her blink as she realised that she, too, wanted to touch, to see him without the trappings of civilisation.

'Yes,' he said huskily, straightening as her hands fluttered over his chest. 'Take my shirt off, sweetheart.'

Amy tilted her head, distracted by the practicalities of the task. He'd unfastened the garment earlier, but she'd have to tug it free of his breeches and lift it over his head. And her arms were restricted.

But the goal was too seductive. Without a second's thought, she shimmied free of the confining straps drooping down her arms and reached for his shirt. A quick flick of his fingers had the top button of his breeches undone to facilitate her task. Then she hit a snag.

Her chemise shifted minutely. She glanced down to see its lacy edge clinging precariously to the upper slopes of her breasts. She wasn't built to keep a chemise in place by gravity alone. It was one thing for Marc to remove her garments with gentle care; quite another for her to toss aside years of modesty while flinging shirts about.

She looked up at him. 'You're too tall for me.'

A pulse was beating rapidly in his throat, but he smiled. 'Stand on tip-toe and pull. I'll help.'

Amy took a deep breath, hoped it would improve the situation, and obeyed. The shirt came off, her chemise succumbed to gravity, and she overbalanced into his arms.

They came around her instantly, holding her crushed to his chest. Wild little sunbursts of heat exploded inside her as her nipples rasped against hair-roughened muscle. She forgot about modesty. The sensations winging through her were too enthralling to leave room for anything else. She would have cried out in wonder at the piercing intensity of the pleasure, but Marc's mouth was on hers, swallowing the sound and taking the soft little whimpers that followed.

She flung her arms around his waist, clinging to his strength; her own had deserted her. His mouth was hot, his arms hard, the smooth flesh of his back burning her hands as she pressed them to the long muscles bracketing his spine. She parted her lips, aching for the intimacy of having him inside her mouth, needing to be part of him and knowing only that way.

Marc shuddered heavily as Amy's tongue met his with shy

eagerness, as she joined him in a sensuous dance of demand
and retreat. Sliding, stroking, tasting, taking. Her wild response went to his head like potent brandy; the softness of her
breasts, their firm little peaks pressed to his chest, had his body
hardening to the point of agony.

He tore his mouth from hers before he gave in to the urge
to take her right there on the floor.

'Amy, sweetheart, we have to slow down.'

She blinked up at him, her eyes dazed with the beginnings
of arousal. 'I thought we were going slow.'

'In that case, we'd better try slower.'

'I don't think that's a good idea,' she said weakly. 'I'm
finding it very difficult to stand.'

He gritted his teeth against another wave of need, and
prayed he'd have the strength to keep his footing against the
undertow of aching desire. The sweet openness of her response
almost brought him to his knees; it also threatened to shred
his control.

'Then we'll lie down,' he said hoarsely, and lifted her on
to the bed, turning away immediately before he managed to
shock her right out of her dazed state. The single glance he
had of soft round breasts, their rosy little crowns begging
mutely for attention had the reins of control slipping and sliding through his fingers as though he'd never seen a naked
woman before. He didn't dare look at her until he'd retrieved
them.

Unfortunately, Amy wasn't co-operating. She slithered
down the bed and reached out to touch his thigh. The need to
turn, to move so that questing little hand could slide over the
front of his breeches, had his teeth clenching so hard his jaw
cracked.

'It's very odd, my lord, but when I touch you, it makes me
feel quite incredibly weak.'

'And you make me feel incredibly powerful,' he grated,
sitting down to yank off his boots. Too damn powerful. For

the first time he understood how his primitive ancestors had been capable of dragging the women of their choice into a cave and taking them whether they were willing or not. He, too, could have plundered, ravaged, devoured. And he would, he promised himself as the second boot hit the floor. But not this time.

She was already bruised.

He turned his head on the thought. Amy made a move as though she would cover her breasts, then went still, watching him. The love and trust in her eyes shook him to his soul, clearing the mists of desire long enough for him to see the pale blue mark that curved around her ribs. He already knew her arms looked like she'd been dragged through a row of hedges. God knew what he couldn't see.

Grimly determined to find out, Marc turned fully towards her and pushed her petticoats up to her knees. She'd put on her white stockings but no shoes. He drew her stockings off, taking note of each small wound as it was revealed. None were serious, but he glimpsed the bandage beneath the froth of her petticoats, remembered the sight of her blood on his hands when they'd returned to the house last night, and shook with the need to pull her up into his arms, to feel her against him, warm and safe and alive.

When he got his hands on her husband—

He shut off the thought instantly. Chantry, or Chatsworth or whatever he chose to call himself, had no place here.

Amy stirred and reached out to touch the hand he'd fisted beside her hip. 'See. I'm not really black and blue all over.'

Marc sent her a look that told her precisely what he thought of that assessment, but his touch was gentle as he lifted one little foot and brushed his lips across the scratch on her instep.

Amy felt her toes curl.

Her petticoat slid higher as he touched his mouth to the faint graze on her calf. Heat bloomed. He kissed the bruise on her knee; she sank deeper into the bed. He swirled his tongue gently around another on her thigh; every muscle quivered and went limp.

'Marc?'

'Hmmm.'

'Are you going to kiss every single bruise?'

'Every single one,' he murmured, and turned his attention to her other leg.

Amy thought of the various locations of her wounds. 'Oh, my goodness.'

His mouth curved against her inner thigh. The hot tingle of excitement that resulted distracted her so much she didn't realise her bunched-up petticoat and chemise were being removed until cool air brushed her skin.

She shivered, but not with cold. He curved his hand to her waist, brushed his thumb across the underside of her breast, stroked downward until the heel of his palm rested above the soft triangle shielding her femininity. And everywhere he touched, she burned.

'You're so tiny,' he whispered. 'So soft.'

'You're not,' she breathed, scarcely able to speak. She didn't have to touch him to know the truth of that statement; sudden tension defined his muscles in a way that had her softening inside in a response as primitive as the sheer physical power of his body. She wanted to move, to arch into his touch, but the shuddering stillness in him held her in a vise of almost unbearable anticipation.

'No,' he said, and her eyes widened at the guttural tone of his voice. 'I'm bigger than you. Harder. Stronger.' His gaze flashed to hers, silver fires burning, and she trembled with helpless excitement. 'Does that frighten you?'

Very slowly she moved her head from side to side.

'It should,' he said. And suddenly his hand was shaking against her flesh. 'It should, because it scares the hell out of me. Oh, God, Amy—'

He bent; his arms went around her, clasping her hips as he

pressed his face to the softness of her belly. She felt the sharp edge of his teeth, the hot sweep of his tongue. 'I could devour you,' he said hoarsely. 'Take you to places you haven't even dreamed of. Dark places, where all you'll know, all you'll want, all you'll feel, is me, inside you, taking you, until you scream with the pleasure of it. And I'll keep you there forever. Mine! Always!' His arms tightened. 'Now are you scared?'

For a moment she couldn't speak. Her lips parted, but she couldn't answer. Love flooded her entire being, love so powerful, so all-encompassing she wondered her heart didn't simply shatter with the pressure of it. And with it came a swift bright flash of awareness—that in the battle he waged between savage desire and equally fierce protectiveness, it was she who held the balance.

She lifted her hand, touched his head. 'I'll never be afraid with you, Marc. No matter where you take me. No matter how long you keep me there. I know you'll never hurt me.'

'No,' he vowed. 'Never. You never have to be afraid again.' He shuddered as a measure of control returned, wondering how she'd done it, how she'd drawn him back from the brink of savagery. And knew, when he straightened to look at her, that it was her fragility and trusting innocence that had given him the strength to harness his instincts. Not the easy control he'd used with other women.

A fragility that was all too apparent in the delicate body he could have lifted with one hand; an innocence that brought a blush to her cheeks even as she smiled.

'I'm not afraid now,' she said softly, and held out her hand. 'And I won't break.'

'I hope not,' he rasped as his fingers enveloped hers. 'Because I can't seem to concentrate on bruises when so many other sweet places are waiting to be kissed.'

She blushed again, but her gaze travelled over him as if she, too, wanted to savour. The tip of her tongue moistened her lips and, with a hoarse sound of need, Marc lowered himself over her.

Amy cried out softly as his weight came down on her. He was so big, so strong. The dark pelt on his chest brushed her breasts, excitingly male to her female. She stroked her hands through it, slid them upwards. Such hard muscle beneath warm supple skin. She felt both safe and deliciously wanton lying beneath him like this, the sense of vulnerability that had overwhelmed her before lessened with her legs locked between his.

'We're so different,' she murmured, stroking her hands downward again. Her fingers found two hard male nipples nestled in whorls of hair and she stroked curiously.

His breath hissed between his teeth.

'Oh, I'm sorry.' Her gaze flew to his. 'Did that hurt?'

A smile glittered through the blazing intensity in his eyes. 'You tell me,' he growled. And cupping one breast in his hand, he stroked his thumb across its ruched pink tip.

Amy gasped and jerked as a thrilling little *frisson* of pleasure darted through her.

'Did it hurt?' he murmured.

'N…no.'

'Good,' he said, and did it again, slower, firmer.

Fire streaked straight to the place where her legs were pressed together. He made a rough sound in his throat and stroked her again and again, until her nipple was a hard little bud of throbbing sensation, until she was whimpering, clinging, trying to anchor herself as her senses threatened to fly apart.

A protest, a plea, parted her lips, but even as she arched in frantic demand, Marc bent his head and closed his mouth hotly over the peak he'd tormented and her vision hazed. She fell back against the sheets, lost in the fierce pleasure of his mouth at her breast.

He didn't stop until she was quivering and writhing beneath

him, and then only so he could deliver the same sweet torment to her other breast.

'I knew you'd be like this,' he rasped. 'Sweet and hot and wanting.'

Amy moaned under the fresh onslaught, barely hearing the husky words. Wanting? She burned. She *craved*. Hot little sparks kept cascading through her. She was aching in places that hadn't even been bruised. She needed him to touch the throbbing place between her legs, needed to part them, to cradle his hard male flesh against her, to have him fill the aching emptiness within, but he kept his own legs clamped about hers.

The thought came to her that he was restraining her so he could hold on to his own control, and with a sound of frustration, she shifted, struggling to get her hands between them, to be rid of the one remaining barrier.

'No, Amy. Wait.' He lifted his mouth from her breast, his breath bathing the wet, rosy tip. 'You really are tiny, darling. I have to be sure you're ready for me.'

'I am ready,' she said with sudden fierceness. 'I want you.'

He gave a short, ragged laugh and kissed her, quick and hard. 'God, you don't even know what I'm talking about, do you? And right now, it doesn't seem to matter.'

He rolled away, shucked his breeches in one swift move, and was back beside her in seconds. It was time enough for Amy to see what he meant.

'Oh, my goodness.'

'Don't worry,' he growled as he gathered her into his arms. 'The seemingly impossible is not only attainable, but, as of this second, as inevitable as the tides.' His mouth came down on hers. He parted her legs with his hand and slid one long finger into her secret, most female flesh.

She gave a muffled cry, startled by the invasion and the intense wave of pleasure that broke over her. The wet, gliding sensation of his thumb on a place she'd never been aware of before was so shockingly, deliciously voluptuous, she forgot about the mind-numbing intimacy of his touch and simply responded; arching, moving in counterpoint to his caresses in a dance as old as time.

The pressure of his mouth turned almost brutally demanding, but his hand remained so gentle the combination made her senses swim. She felt her body melt beneath his fingers, felt her legs widen in wanton invitation, felt the waves building, higher and higher. Then he carefully lifted her bandaged leg over his hip and her eyes flew open at the first seeking touch of his body. Her breath seized. Her heart had raced past frantic long ago. She stared up at him, quivering with a primitive awareness of his size and power, of her vulnerability.

'Marc?'

He framed her face with his hands, holding her still for his gaze as he rocked against her, the gentle movements in stark contrast to the tension shuddering through his body. 'Hush,' he murmured. 'It will be all right, darling. Just be still. I'll try not to hurt you, but if I do…it will only be for a moment.'

His face was hard-edged with passion, his eyes narrowed, fiercely intent, but his voice was so darkly tender she felt it resonate deep inside her, relaxing her, easing his way.

'It doesn't matter,' she gasped, every particle of her being suddenly focused on the place where they joined. He was barely moving, entering her only an inch or two at a time before drawing back. The sensation was driving her wild. She wanted more of him, all of him.

With a small frantic sound she lifted herself, sheer female instinct guiding her to wrap her legs around him—and with an almost audible crack the chains of his control snapped open. A harsh groan tore from his throat. Clamping an arm around her hips to hold her still, he thrust hard, driving himself to the hilt.

A lightning flash of pain streaked through her, gone in seconds. Pleasure followed instantly, flooding her with sensations beyond belief. She trembled uncontrollably, aching for more.

There had to be more. She sensed it in the streamers of heat coiling tighter and tighter inside her, but Marc held rigidly still, his breathing harsh against her cheek.

'Are you all right?' he ground out.

'Yes.' Her voice was high and thin, almost soundless. Somewhere in her mind she knew he was waiting for her body to adjust to his, but all she could think of was the urgency building inside her, the incredible sense of joining. One. Inseparable. Hearts beating wildly in tandem, breaths mingling, limbs clinging. And the heavy throbbing of his flesh within hers, the soft secret pulses of her response that made him groan and shudder with the effort at control.

With heart-shattering care he withdrew a short way, then pressed deeper. She moaned and arched, her head falling back over his arm. Steel and heat locked around her. His lips seared her throat. 'Amy…I don't think I can go slow anymore.'

'I don't want you to,' she cried. 'Oh, Marc…Marc..'

'Yes!' he said hoarsely, and pressing his face to her hair, he began to move with a power that had her crying out in mingled shock and excitement. Her senses reeled, recovered, then revelled in his fierce possession. Tension wound, tighter, tighter; heat flooded her until she thought she couldn't take anymore. She would burn, like lightning exploding until there was nothing left.

She sobbed frantically, trying to fight free of the coiling heat, to catch up to her soaring senses, to *breathe*. He muttered something; words of reassurance, of demand, she couldn't tell. Then he slid one hand beneath her hips and lifted her into his thrusts, and the unbearable tension sprang open, flooding her with pleasure so intense she screamed, knowing nothing but the wild pulsing of her body; wanting nothing but the exquisite release washing over her; feeling only him, inside her, all around her, taking her. Blind and helpless with the ecstasy of it, she gave herself up to him.

And with her utter surrender Marc loosed the savage in him.

Clamping his mouth over Amy's to swallow her cries, he thrust again and again into the hot silken depths of her body, driving for his own release until the world vanished in a white-hot blaze of completion.

'You *are* going to marry me.'

The gravelly-voiced decree wafted down through the layers of oblivion in which she floated.

Amy stirred and tried to drift upwards. It wasn't the first time she'd surfaced. She vaguely remembered tender kisses following the storm; the comfort of a cool, damp cloth between her legs; the secure haven of strong arms. She'd drifted, feeling utterly replete. As if something she hadn't even known was missing was now, forever, part of her.

Marc.

She smiled and tried to snuggle closer. And discovered that Marc was lying half-over her. He was heavy. She contemplated a vague protest, then decided it was too much trouble. She couldn't move anyway. Every muscle and bone in her body had melted.

'Amy.'

The soft demand halted another descent into lassitude. Amy opened her eyes and blinked sleepily up at him. 'Hmmm?'

Amusement curved his mouth, but his eyes glittered with a lazy sensuality that caused an echo of pleasure to hum inside her.

She closed her eyes again to savour the sensation.

He put his lips to her ear. 'You know, there's a certain etiquette that must be observed in these situations, Mrs Chantry.'

'There is?'

'One does not go to sleep when one's partner is trying to conduct a conversation.'

'Oh.' Amy prised her eyelids open. Limp though she was,

she managed to curl an arm around his neck. 'Not asleep,' she sighed, and stretched languourously beneath him.

Her very limp form was abruptly crushed to the bedding. Marc came over her, thrust her legs apart with his and pressed himself against her in unmistakable demand.

Amy's eyes snapped fully open. She was suddenly feeling a vast deal more wide awake.

'That's better,' he growled, and moved back slightly.

She pouted in disappointment. She'd never pouted before in her entire life.

'Stop trying to distract me,' he ordered. But he bent to stroke his tongue across her lower lip. 'We need to talk.'

'We do?' That was going to be difficult, she mused, because he'd just succeeded in thoroughly distracting her.

'Yes. You're going to marry me.'

'What?' Her brain reeled.

'Amy, see if you can pay attention here. We're getting married.'

'But...' She tried to rally her startled wits. 'How? I mean...oh, Marc, I want to marry you more than anything in the world, but—'

The rest was smothered by a fierce kiss. When he finally let her up for air, her senses were whirling.

'Divorce,' he said succinctly, and smiled.

Amy blinked at the expression. Only a simpleton would have called it nice; the set of his mouth held far too much deadly purpose.

'Divorce? But...the Earl of Hawkridge can't marry a divorced woman. Think of the scandal.'

'Believe me, my little innocent, there'll be a great deal more scandal when people start suspecting you're my mistress. Which they will,' he added when she opened her mouth to argue, 'because, after tonight, I have no intention of staying out of your bed. The only scandal attached to a discreet divorce brought by a woman is when the husband contests the charges, causing some very nasty linen to be aired in public.'

She considered that. 'What makes you think James won't contest? Not because he wants me, but…' She looked up at him, sudden distress shaking her voice. 'I don't want you to give him money. To…to…*buy* me.'

'Amy.' He stroked her tousled curls, then cupped her face in his hands. 'My sweet, beautiful Amy. I'm not going to buy you. I'd never do that to you. Chatsworth won't contest a divorce.' His face went hard. 'If he tries it, he'll end up on the gallows.'

Her swift intake of air had him cloaking the murderous look he knew was in his eyes. 'So might I,' she whispered.

'No.' The answer was immediate, and absolute. 'We can get him on the Bristol robberies, which have nothing to do with you. As for what happened in London, if Chatsworth is stupid enough to mention your name, his rantings will be put down to revenge because you warned Lucinda's family about him.'

'But…Lord Tinsley…'

He lifted a quizzical brow. 'Darling, how often did the Tinsleys see you during the few weeks you spent dusting the furniture? Once? Twice? They'd never recognise you, especially now.'

'No. I suppose…' Her eyes widened when she realised she'd run out of· 'buts'. For the first time, hope shimmered on her horizon. She almost believed the tiny golden flame wouldn't wink out if she dared to seize it.

'I'll find out from Lucinda where Chatsworth is staying, and see him in the morning,' Marc was saying, as if that was all it would take. 'He's not at the Green Man, but he must be somewhere within reasonable distance.'

Amy's mind reeled at his unshakable confidence. If nothing else, she believed that James would try to turn the situation to his advantage. Or that he'd turn violent if his plans were thwarted.

She shivered slightly. 'You will be careful, won't you, Marc? James has a temper. I didn't see it until the robbery. One of Lord Tinsley's footmen tried to resist and James beat the man insensible, even though the first blow had subdued him. And the other day…I don't think he meant to hurt me, but if he hadn't shoved past me on that path, I probably wouldn't have fallen.'

'So that's how it happened.' Marc's eyes narrowed. 'Chatsworth can count himself lucky if he lives long enough to make it to the gallows.'

She lifted her hand to his cheek. 'Nothing terrible happened,' she said softly. 'I'm still here, thanks to you.'

'Your idea of terrible, and mine, are several hundred degrees apart,' he muttered. Then his voice lowered, went dark. 'But you're right. You're here, in my arms, and—' he gathered her closer until she could feel the throbbing urgency in his body '—if I don't have you again right now, I'll go out of my mind.'

Amy blinked up at him. She'd thought the tension rippling through his muscles for the past several minutes had been caused by anger at Chatsworth. Obviously, she had been grievously mistaken.

'Good heavens, my lord! Have you been in this state the entire time we've been discussing my divorce?'

The smile glinting in his eyes held both wickedness and rueful amusement. 'Thanks to you, Mrs Chantry, I've been in this state since I walked into this house last week. What do you intend to do about such a sorry situation?'

'Hmm,' she murmured, and made a little purring sound in her throat as she savoured the male power beneath her hands. Leashed, his strength enthralled her. Unleashed, it was a ravishment of her senses that she couldn't wait to feel again. 'I shall set my mind to thinking of a solution, sir.'

'Think fast,' he ordered, and pressed his fingers to the soft curls between her legs with an urgency that had a broken cry of pleasure rippling from her throat.

'Shh,' he whispered, easing the pressure to a touch that merely tantalised. His kiss smothered her immediate demand for more. When he lifted his mouth a fraction, the wildfire of excitement had subsided to a simmer. She had the distinct impression that he intended to make her simmer for a very long time.

'What?' she asked hazily.

'It's probably too late, but try to be quiet.'

'I thought you wanted to make me scream.' The mists cleared somewhat. 'You did make me scream.'

'Darling, when we're married you can scream to your heart's content—and mine. No one will hear you from my chambers. But until then we must be discreet.'

'Oh. Well, I'll do my best, sir.'

'Do more than that,' he growled. 'Grandmama's room is right across the hall.'

'Oh, dear.' She laughed up at him with her eyes, and, deciding she wasn't going to be the only one to simmer, slid her hand down his body. 'How very inconvenient for you.'

He clamped his fingers around her wrist and glared at her. 'I haven't made a practice of seducing my grandmother's companions, Mrs Chantry.'

Amy passed her predecessors under rapid review. 'I should hope not, sir.'

For a moment Marc stared in surprise, then his shoulders started shaking in silent laughter. Amy giggled. The little wriggle she gave as she tried to muffle the sound in his throat was too much. Amusement vanished.

'Never mind,' he muttered, loosing her wrist. 'I'll find a way to keep both of us quiet.'

He didn't have to. When simmer turned to incendiary heat, when the leashed power of his body exploded into desperate, driven need, sweeping her away on a tide of exquisite sensation, Amy found a way to keep quiet that proved very effective indeed. For the second time in as many days, she swooned clean out of her senses.

And this time, when she stirred in the warm safety of his arms, she surfaced to the sweetest discovery of all.

'I've been waiting to tell you,' he murmured, and touched his mouth to hers with heart-shaking tenderness. 'I love you, Amy.'

He loved her.

Amy walked along the cliff road towards Ottersmead, trying to suppress the urge to skip every few steps. She'd told everyone she needed a walk in the fresh air, but, of course, she was really hoping to meet Marc on his way back to Hawkridge.

With that goal in sight, she simply couldn't have stayed in the house another minute; she was too restless with anticipation. Happiness bubbled inside her as if she'd drank several glasses of champagne. The whole world looked radiant and fresh and new. The sea was bluer than ever, the sun beamed down with golden radiance, flowers bloomed by the roadside in riotous abandon.

And Marc loved her.

He loved her enough to risk the scandal of divorce so she would be free to marry him.

Her feet executed several skips before she could stop them. The resulting twinges in her thighs reminded her that she'd spent almost an entire night indulging in unaccustomed exercise.

Amy giggled, and skipped again in sheer defiance of twinging muscles. She would never forget such a night. Never. She had followed him, without hesitation, into those dark places where passion held sway, because love had lit the way. Nor had she felt anything less than Marc's true equal. Though the urgency of his desire had seduced her again and again, he'd gifted her with the sense of her own seductive power. He was so very male that, for the first time in her life, she'd gloried in being female.

Amy hugged herself as little thrills winged through her at the memories, tripped around a curve in the road and came face to face with her husband.

'Oh!' She jerked to a stop. The world lost some of its radiant brightness. She blinked and looked around. There was no one else in sight. 'James.'

'Well, well.' His lip curled. 'If it isn't my fortunate little wife, none the worse for her tumble. I was coming to call on you, Amy, but this is better. Saves me the trouble of finding a private place where we can talk.'

She took a step back. 'I don't think we have anything to say to each other.'

'You only need to listen,' he told her, cutting off her retreat by seizing her arm. 'Come on. Over here.'

He began to pull her across to a small grove of trees that stood between the cliff and the road at that point. She expected him to stop as soon as they were out of sight. When he didn't, she began to dig in her heels.

'This is far enough,' she warned as they broke free of the trees. The edge of the cliff lay a mere twenty feet beyond. She kept her gaze away from it. 'I mean it, James. We're out of sight, if that's what you want.'

'What I want?' he repeated, halting and jerking her around to face him. He released her, much to her relief. 'If I ever got what I wanted, Amy, you'd have broken your neck in that fall the other day.'

Her lashes flickered, the only sign that fear slid down her spine at his words. 'Did you push me deliberately?' she demanded.

'Of course not.' He shrugged in dismissal. 'It would've been a convenient accident, nothing more. But since you are still around, and since Lucinda has been packed off to stay with friends for several weeks, and no one will tell me where she is, I need to make some alternate plans.' He came closer, his eyes cold with suspicion. 'I don't suppose you had anything to do with Lucinda's departure, did you, Amy?'

'I know nothing about the Nettlebeds' plans,' she said with perfect honesty.

'Good. Because if I find out you did know something, I'll make sure you suffer another accident, one with more permanent results. I could do it right here and now. There's no one around.'

Amy didn't answer. She was reasonably sure James's threats were empty while she was still of some use to him. Her mind was racing down another track. Marc would have gone first to Nettlebed Place and, since James was annoyed rather than furious, it was clear no confrontation had taken place. With his quarry apparently flown, Marc would be on his way back to Hawkridge.

The thought had barely occurred when she heard hoofbeats, coming fast. Before James could stop her, Amy turned and dashed for the trees.

It was useless, of course—he'd only been a yard or two away—but her intention was to get closer to the road where a cry could be heard over the constant hushing of the sea. When James's fingers closed around her arm, she drew breath and screamed.

'Marc!'

'You bitch!' James jerked her to a halt and wheeled, dragging her back towards the cliff.

Amy didn't bother crying out again; all her strength was needed to slow James down, to give the rider time to catch them. She didn't know if it was Marc—screaming his name had been pure instinct—but she prayed that even a stranger wouldn't ignore a woman's scream coming from the trees.

She went limp with relief when she realised she was right.

The hoofbeats stopped abruptly, then came the sounds of a horse being ridden swiftly after them.

Brilliant sunshine struck her eyes a second later.

'Let me go, James,' she said quickly. 'You don't want to arouse any more suspicions.'

It was a desperate bid to gain her freedom, but she knew her scream had already destroyed his plan to use her, indeed had destroyed everything, for what explanation could he give, even to a stranger? She saw the knowledge in his eyes, saw rage explode into violent purpose. As a huge black horse crashed into the open, he dragged her closer to the cliff, shifted his grip to her wrist and flung her out at arm's length.

Amy staggered; she'd been expecting a blow. Then, as she regained her balance, she saw the rider and a sob of thankfulness rose in her throat.

Marc, eyes blazing, mouth set hard; avenging fury astride a wild-eyed, demonic monster. She wouldn't have been surprised to see flames shoot from the horse's flaring nostrils as it reared and pawed the air before Marc brought the animal back under control and turned it to face them head-on.

She glanced quickly at James. He had to release her. What choice did he have?

But his lips drew back in a snarl, and she knew. Revenge. Or distraction to give himself time to escape. He held her at an angle, his body part-way between her and the brink, but one hard swinging pull would be all that was needed to send her staggering. Sheer momentum would do the rest.

She couldn't fight him, couldn't even cling in a bid to take him with her. To do so she'd have to get closer, and his arm was locked, holding her in position.

'Back up!' he yelled. 'Back up or she goes over the cliff.'

Marc didn't hesitate. He didn't argue; he didn't try reason; he didn't ask what James could possibly hope to gain in killing her. In the split second before he moved, Amy saw murderous fury flash in his eyes. He slashed his reins across the horse's neck, drove his heels into the animal's flanks and charged straight at Chatsworth's outstretched arm.

Amy screamed, flinching away instinctively. She was released so abruptly she stumbled. A huge black shape flashed past her. She felt a blast of heat, heard the scream of an angry stallion, then she hit the ground and rolled.

The horse was still screaming. Or maybe it was her. Dazed, she tried to turn, to see...

Then Marc was there, snatching her up in his arms, his hand holding her cheek pressed tightly to his chest so she couldn't see, couldn't hear. When he eased the pressure seconds later, all was quiet again. The screaming had stopped.

'It was James, wasn't it?' she said shakily, clinging to him. 'He went over the edge.'

But Marc wasn't concerned with Chatsworth. 'Amy. Oh, God, sweetheart—' His hands ran over her, searching. 'Are you all right? When I saw you on the ground... Did Demon touch you?'

'No.' His urgency steadied her, strengthened her. She sorted through the blur of the last few minutes and drew back to look up at him. 'You used him...Demon...as a weapon.'

- 'Yes.' His eyes were still blazing, still violent. 'I would have used anything, anyway I could.'

'I would, too,' she whispered, and burrowed close again. 'Oh, Marc.'

His arms closed about her with fierce protectiveness, pressing her cheek to his heart. The violent pounding beneath her ear gradually slowed to a strong, steady beat. The sun felt warm again, birds resumed their morning chorus; leaves rustled, flowers nodded in the breeze. And she was filled with a passionate sense of gladness that she was alive, that both she and Marc were safe.

James had had choices. And in trying to destroy her, had destroyed himself.

'Do you think we should go down there?' she asked softly. 'Do something?'

'I will in a moment,' he said. 'But there's no possibility that Chatsworth will have survived that fall. There are no convenient ledges at this point; he'll have broken his neck on the rocks.'

Amy shuddered.

His mouth touched the top of her head, then he put her away from him, curving his hands around her arms as though holding her steady. 'Darling, what I have to do could take a couple of hours. You're going to have to be very strong. I want you to go home—Yes,' he emphasised gently when her lips parted on a protest. 'Go home and instruct Mawson to bring the gig to the top of the Inghams' steps. I'll ride back there, retrieve Chatsworth's body and bring it up that way.'

'But…' Amy tried to think. 'Won't you be seen?'

'All the better,' he said somewhat grimly. 'The only thing we wish to hide is your past involvement with Chatsworth and, thanks to his penchant for secluded meeting-places, we'll be able to manage it if I act fast. All you need to say is that while we were walking back to Hawkridge, we heard a cry and discovered that someone had fallen over the cliff. Only Grandmama is to know the truth. Can you do that, sweetheart?' His hands tightened. 'I know it's asking a lot to pretend that you haven't just been terrified for your life, or that Chatsworth was nothing more than a recent acquaintance when in reality—'

She stopped him with a finger against his lips, and a gaze that held all the gentle feminine strength in her nature. 'Marc, it's because of me that *you*'re involved. I can do whatever you ask of me.'

'Why did I even doubt it?' he murmured, and smiled in rueful acknowledgement. 'Go home, darling. I'll be there as soon as I can.'

Chapter Fifteen

'So you sent Mr Chatsworth over the cliff. Well, that will certainly save a lot of trouble.'

Lady Hawkridge nodded thoughtfully while she reviewed the story related to her by her grandson, then smiled benignly at the pair opposite.

From the shelter of Marc's arm, Amy gazed at her employer in astonishment. They were in the library, the dowager ensconsed on an armchair, while she and Marc occupied the sofa. No doubt her wits were still somewhat scattered; she was finding it very difficult to reconcile her ladyship's angelic appearance with her ruthless practicality.

Marc apparently had no such trouble. She glanced up to see a look of amusement cross his face.

'I didn't intend to kill him, Grandmama. There was only a second in which to act. Chatsworth might have been armed, he was certainly threatening to send Amy over the cliff, but most people, when charged by a horse, tend to forget everything in the interests of getting out of the way. When Demon's shoulder struck him he must have been closer to the edge than I thought.'

'Of course, dear. However, since you were saving Amy's life, no one will think anything of it.'

'Since no one else was about, they won't know that Amy's life was in danger,' Marc corrected. 'We don't want people wondering why Chatsworth would try to kill someone he'd only just met. Listen carefully. Chatsworth met with an unfortunate accident while out for a walk. In a distracted state of mind owing to the frustration of his ambitions towards Lucinda, he took the wrong path down to the beach, slipped and lost his footing.'

'Quite logical,' agreed the dowager. 'Why, poor little Amy had a fall on the *right* path not two days ago. Very dangerous places, cliffs. We must put up a warning sign.' She nodded decisively. 'Where did you take him, Marc? Not to Mr ffollifoot, I trust.'

'No. I don't want Amy reminded of him every time she goes past the churchyard. I returned him to his last place of abode, fortunately outside our parish boundary.'

'Thank you,' Amy said with real gratitude. 'But, Marc, with Lucinda gone, how did you discover where James was staying?'

'I saw Lucinda before she left, sweetheart. Thanks to Grandmama's note conveying a warning from a supposedly disinterested source, she was shaken enough to let drop that he was putting up at a tavern a few miles down the coast.' His lips curled. 'It isn't one of your more salubrious places. When Mawson and I turned up with Chatsworth's body, the tapkeeper promptly claimed his belongings in lieu of payment. I went through them to make sure there was nothing to incriminate you, and handed them over. There was money in Chatsworth's pockets. If the tap's feeling generous, he might part with enough to pay for a proper burial.'

'Oh, heavens.' Amy bit her lip, guiltily aware that she should be more shocked at this ruthless disinterest in the fate of her husband's remains.

Marc glanced down at her, his eyes hard. 'Don't expect me

to feel sympathy for the man, Amy. He would've killed you without compunction.'

'Yes, indeed.' Lady Hawkridge shuddered. 'What a dreadful time you must have had with him, Amy. In London, too. What will you do about his lodgings there, Marc? Search them?

'Only if Amy thinks there might be anything that could link her to him.'

He sent her a questioning look as he spoke, but Amy was already shaking her head. 'Only our marriage lines, and I have those. I didn't keep James's letters, nor write any myself.' She paused. 'He wouldn't have kept such things. He was very secretive, very careful to keep his plans to himself until he was ready to act.'

Marc's eyes narrowed thoughtfully. 'So his cohorts might not know that he was going by the name of Chatsworth while he was in this vicinity, or that he was in Devonshire at all.'

'Very likely not, judging by what he said yesterday. In any case, I don't think he told anyone he'd married me.' She frowned. 'Do you think his friends might enquire into his death?'

'They'll have to hear about it, first. Frankly, I doubt they'll even enquire into his protracted absence. Given Chatsworth's recent activities, their immediate assumption will be that he's been caught and imprisoned in Bristol to await transportation or hanging. Anyone else involved in the robberies will lie low to save their own skins.'

'The only sensible thing to do,' Lady Hawkridge concurred. She gathered up the stitching she'd been engaged with before Marc had returned to the house and prepared to rise. 'Well, that seems to take care of everything. So comforting to know that we don't have to worry about Amy's former husband popping up again.'

'Oh, ma'am, I'm so sorry to have brought all this trouble upon you. I only hope that poor Lucinda isn't dreadfully hurt after learning that Mr Chatsworth…I mean, James…was a for-tune-hunter.'

'Lucinda is young and resilient,' Marc informed her, rising to assist his grandmother. 'When I left her this morning, she was already vowing never to be taken in again. She plans to be an ice-maiden and is going to wear nothing but white, and possibly silver. I give the role three months.'

'Oh dear.'

'And besides, Amy, it wasn't you who caused any trouble,' Lady Hawkridge added. 'It was all Mr Chatsworth's doing. Now, I think you should go upstairs and lie down. The last two days and nights have been so fraught with shocks and surprises you've hardly had any sleep. And we don't want you looking peaky on your wedding day.'

'Uh…'

'Just leave everything to me.' The dowager beamed. 'There's nothing I enjoy more than planning a wedding. And, in this case, we have two nuptials to arrange. However, I think you and Amy should be married first, Marc. We don't want things happening out of their proper order. People can count, you know, and Amy will be very sensitive to such gossip.'

Ignoring the wildly conflicting emotions chasing one an-other across her companion's suddenly rosy countenance, the dowager tripped towards the door.

Marc crossed the room to open it for her, a wry smile curv-ing his mouth. 'Colborough isn't going to ask me for your hand, is he, Grandmama? Because if he does, I'd feel duty bound to inform him that you're a very dangerous female.'

'I'd rather you didn't, dearest. Acquiring a new wife at Bar-tholomew's age is quite enough for him. Besides, I'm perfectly capable of bestowing my hand without your permission.' Smiling serenely, her ladyship left the room.

'That puts me in my place,' Marc observed ruefully. 'I can see I'm going to have a great deal of trouble curbing the in-dependent tendencies of the females about the place.'

Amy rose somewhat shakily. Far from wishing to claim her independence, she felt more in need of support than the dowager. No doubt it was the result of all the shocks and surprises, but her legs seemed somewhat reluctant to hold her upright.

'Is it really all over?' she asked.

'It's over.' Marc turned. The glittering triumph in his eyes had her breath seizing. 'And we're just beginning. I stopped by the vicarage on my way home. We'll be married as soon as Mr ffollifoot has the licence ready. Probably in a day or two.'

'*A day or two?*' Her voice rose to a squeak, then all but vanished. 'Oh, my goodness.'

He started towards her. 'Is that an argument?'

'No, my lord.'

'You realise you won't be independent any more? You'll be *mine*.'

'Yes, well…'

'I'm over-protective. I'm possessive.'

'Yes, I do believe I've noticed that.'

'My instincts are downright primitive. In fact, when it comes to your safety—' he stopped a pace or two away, his eyes fierce '—it wouldn't be too much to state that I'm a savage.'

Amy took a deep breath. Her legs might be wobbly, but Marc was clearly the one in need of reassurance. Closing the distance between them, she touched her fingers to his cheek. 'I know,' she said softly. 'That must be why I'm not worried about becoming a nuisance to you when you discover I'm not really as helpless as I look.'

He frowned and captured her hand. 'What?'

'Just something someone once said to me. You know, Marc, when food or clothing was scarce in the poorhouse, I often had to protect Mama's share, and mine, with tooth and claw, so there's really no need to warn me about your instincts.' A dimple peeped at the corner of her mouth. 'Better to worry about what sort of instincts our children will inherit.'

His face went blank. 'Children?'

'Yes.' She tilted her head. 'I presume you do want children, my lord. You'll need an heir for one thing, and a little baby would be—'

'Baby?' he said in such a strange voice that she stopped. His eyes went violently intense. 'A baby?'

He swooped.

Amy found herself lifted, tossed over his shoulder and carried out of the library before she could utter more than a small startled shriek.

She contemplated the marble tiles passing rapidly before her eyes and tried to retrieve her wits. 'For heaven's sake, my lord! What are you doing?'

'Taking you to bed.'

'*To bed?* But it's the middle of the day! What will people think?'

'You're supposed to be resting. No one needs to know what else you'll be doing.'

'But…I didn't mean we had to get started on the project right this minute.'

'Mrs Chantry,' he murmured, in a voice that made her suddenly glad she wasn't ascending the stairs under her own steam. 'We're going to start on the project the minute I get you into my cave. I mean, bed.'

'Oh, my goodness.'

He carried her into his room and deposited her on the bed before she could think of anything else to say.

Head spinning, wits still whirling, Amy struggled up on her elbows, only to sink back down again when Marc strode across to the door, locked it, then turned and paced slowly towards her.

Holding her gaze with his, he removed his coat and tossed it aside. Then, ignoring the havoc his boots were going to wreak on the bedspread, he came down over her and gathered her into his arms.

'That's better,' he growled, and kissed her.

No, she thought hazily, he *sank* into her. And she melted into him. Passion flared, dark and searing, but beyond the meeting of lips, of tongues, of huskily whispered desires, she found a deep well of tenderness, a gentle cherishing, and a need that bade her lay her heart before him, to give him everything, her strength, her vulnerability and all that lay between.

How easy it was. To yield, completely. To take, utterly. His hands framed her face; he took her deeper, until she knew nothing but the total joining of all that they were. Minds touched, hearts merged, souls entwined. When he lifted his head, she was soft and pliant, his. He was hers, until death and beyond; she knew it absolutely.

'I love you,' he murmured against her mouth. 'Love you…love you. My sweet Amy.'

'I didn't believe this was possible,' she whispered back. 'Not really. Until now. Oh, Marc, I love you so. I know I have a lot to learn, that I'm not—'

He silenced her with a gentle finger across her lips. 'Do you want proof that you're a lady?' he asked. 'I know in you I've found the other half of myself. Nothing else matters. I don't care what brought you here, only that I found you. But if you like, if you give me your grandfather's name, I'll write to Ravensdene, have him search his family records to see if there's a link to your mother. Only if *you* wish it, Amy.'

'I think I would like that,' she said after a moment's reflection.

'Then I'll do it, but remember when I said you were a lady waiting for the right setting? Now you have it.'

She thought about that, and a joyous smile spread over her face. 'In your cave?'

He smiled back at her. 'That, too. But most of all—' he

bent to emphasise each point with a kiss '—in my home…in my life…in my heart.'

Amy's breath caught at the deep note of sincerity in his voice. She looked into her own heart and saw the tiny flame of hope, so fragile only hours ago, transformed into truth, burning bright and clear and steady.

And as Marc gathered her closer, she saw reflected in his brilliant grey eyes, their future.

The family she'd never had, times of care and laughter, and a love that would grow stronger and deeper through all the years ahead.

* * * * *

Sensual Romance™
4 brand new titles each month
...sassy, sexy
and seductive.
Available on subscription every month
from the Reader Service™
GEN/21/RS2

Historical Romance™
4 brand new titles each month
...rich, vivid
and passionate
Available on subscription every month
from the Reader Service™
GEN/04/RS2